Masterpieces

OF

Mystery

Masterpieces
OF
Mystery

The Prizewinners

Selected by ELLERY QUEEN

C O N T E N T S

INTRODUCTION *by Ellery Queen* 9

N O B E L   P R I Z E W I N N E R S

THE RETURN OF IMRAY *by Rudyard Kipling* 11

THE CURSE OF THE FIRES
  AND OF THE SHADOWS *by William Butler Yeats* 22

THE MIRACULOUS REVENGE *by Bernard Shaw* 28

THE WILLOW WALK *by Sinclair Lewis* 47

THE NEIGHBORS *by John Galsworthy* 77

RANSOM *by Pearl Buck* 83

AN ERROR IN CHEMISTRY *by William Faulkner* 106

THE CORSICAN ORDEAL OF
  MISS X *by Bertrand Russell* 123

THE MURDER *by John Steinbeck* 142

P U L I T Z E R   P R I Z E W I N N E R S

CORONER'S INQUEST *by Marc Connelly* 154

A JURY OF HER PEERS *by Susan Glaspell* 160

IT TAKES A THIEF *by Arthur Miller* 180

THE MURDER IN THE
  FISHING CAT *by Edna St. Vincent Millay* 188

TABLOID NEWS *by Louis Bromfield* 204

THE AMATEUR OF CRIME *by Stephen Vincent Benét* . . 218

A DAYLIGHT ADVENTURE *by T. S. Stribling* 236

GOODBYE, PICCADILLY *by John P. Marquand* 251

ONLY ON RAINY NIGHTS *by Mark Van Doren* 304

CLERICAL ERROR *by James Gould Cozzens* . . . 318

THE HUNTING OF
  HEMINGWAY *by MacKinlay Kantor* 322

THE BOTTLE MINE *by Kenneth L. Roberts* 343

INTRODUCTION

DEAR READER:

Volume Two of MASTERPIECES OF MYSTERY contains stories of crime, detection, mystery, and suspense written by nine Nobel Prizewinners and twelve Pulitzer Prizewinners. You didn't know that some of the most famous figures in literature wrote tales of crime and detection? You will be delightfully surprised.

The Nobel Prizes were established by the will of Alfred Bernhard Nobel (1833–1896), Swedish chemist and the inventor of dynamite, and have come to be accepted as the world's most prestigious honors. Each year five Nobel Prizes are awarded to those who "have conferred the greatest benefit on mankind in the field of physics, chemistry, physiology or medicine, literature, and peace." The prizes consist of a gold medal, a diploma with the citation of award, and a sum of money which varies according to the income of the Nobel Foundation. In 1974 the cash prize in each category was about $125,000. A sixth prize— in economics—was first given in 1969 by Sweden's national bank, Sveriges Riksbank, and dedicated to the memory of Mr. Nobel. The Prizewinners in literature—the field that concerns us in this anthology—are selected by the Swedish Academy.

The presentation ceremony is held every year on December 10—the anniversary of Alfred Nobel's death—in Stockholm, except for the peace prize which is awarded in Oslo. (We are indebted to THE OFFICIAL ASSOCIATED PRESS ALMANAC of 1975 for this information.)

The seventh Nobel Prize for literature was awarded in 1907 to Rudyard Kipling who is represented in this volume by a detective story.

The 55th Nobel Prize for literature was awarded in 1962 to John Steinbeck who is also represented in this anthology. His contribution is a story of crime.

9

In between you will find William Butler Yeats, Bernard Shaw, Sinclair Lewis, John Galsworthy, Pearl Buck, William Faulkner, and Bertrand Russell, all with stories of crime, detection, or mystery.

The Pulitzer Prizewinners in this anthology are equally distinguished. Pulitzer Prizes are also awarded annually, but they are restricted to achievements in the field of American journalism, letters, and music. The monetary prizes derive from the income of a fund left by Joseph Pulitzer, a renowned American newspaper publisher, to the trustees of Columbia University. Pulitzer awards began in 1917 and are made each May. The cash prizes in letters, of $500 each, are for fiction, drama, history, biography, and poetry. (We are indebted for these facts to THE COLUMBIA ENCYCLOPEDIA.)

We have chosen stories by twelve Pulitzer Prizewinners, including tales of crime, mystery, and detection by Marc Connelly, Susan Glaspell, Arthur Miller, Edna St. Vincent Millay, Louis Bromfield, Stephen Vincent Benét, T. S. Stribling, John P. Marquand, Mark Van Doren, James Gould Cozzens, MacKinlay Kantor, and Kenneth L. Roberts.

It is difficult—no, virtually impossible—to imagine a more illustrious roster of authors' names than you will find in this second volume of MASTERPIECES OF MYSTERY—two Blue Ribbon Panels offering you the *crème du crime*.

Happy reading!

ELLERY QUEEN

THE RETURN OF IMRAY

BY RUDYARD KIPLING

Rudyard Kipling was born of English parents in Bombay on December 30, 1865. His infancy was spent in the care of native *ayahs*, so that he learned Hindustani concurrently with English. He attended school in England and returned to India in 1883. There he learned journalism and began to write stories and verse. Between 1891 and 1897 he married, lived in London and Brattleboro, Vermont, and published *The Light That Failed, Barrack-Room Ballads, Jungle Books, Captains Courageous*, etc. After observing the Boer War as an editor in South Africa he wrote *Kim*.

IMRAY ACHIEVED THE IMPOSSIBLE. Without warning, for no conceivable motive, in his youth, at the threshold of his career he chose to disappear from the world—which is to say, the little Indian station where he lived.

Upon a day he was alive, well, happy, and in great evidence among the billiard tables at his Club. Upon a morning, he was not, and no manner of search could make sure where he might be. He had stepped out of his place; he had not appeared at his office at the proper time, and his dogcart was not upon the public roads. For these reasons, and because he was hampering, in a microscopical degree, the administration of the Indian Empire, that Empire paused for one microscopical moment to make inquiry into the fate of Imray. Ponds were dragged, wells were plumbed, telegrams were despatched down the lines of railways and to the nearest seaport town—1200 miles away; but Imray was not at the end of the dragropes nor the telegraph wires. He was gone, and his place knew him no more. Then the work of the great Indian Empire swept forward, because it could not be delayed, and Imray from being a man became a mystery—such a thing as men talk over at their tables in the Club for a month, and then forget utterly. His guns, horses, and carts were sold to the highest bidder. His superior officer wrote an altogether absurd letter to his mother, saying that Imray had unaccountably disappeared, and his bungalow stood empty.

After three or four months of the scorching hot weather had gone by, my friend Strickland, of the Police, saw fit to rent the bungalow from the native landlord. This was before he was engaged to Miss Youghal—an affair which has been described in another place—and while he was pursuing his investigations into native life. His own life was sufficiently peculiar, and men complained of his manners and customs. There was always food in his house, but there were no regular times for meals. He ate, standing up and walking about, whatever he might find at the sideboard, and this is not good for human beings. His domestic equipment was limited to six rifles, three shotguns, five saddles, and a collection of stiff-jointed mahseer rods, bigger and stronger than the largest salmon rods. These occupied one-half of his bungalow, and the other half was given up to Strickland and his dog Tietjens—an enormous Rampur slut who devoured daily the rations of two men. She spoke to Strickland in a language of her own; and whenever, walking abroad, she saw things calculated to destroy the peace of Her Majesty the Queen-Empress, she returned to her master and laid information. Strickland would take steps at once, and the end of his labors was trouble and fine and imprisonment for other people. The natives believed that Tietjens was a familiar spirit, and treated her with the great reverence that is born of hate and fear. One room in the bungalow was set apart for her special use. She owned a bedstead, a blanket, and a drinking trough, and if anyone came into Strickland's room at night her custom was to knock down the invader and give tongue till someone came with a light. Strickland owed his life to her, when he was on the Frontier, in search of a local murderer, who came in the gray dawn to send Strickland much farther than the Andaman Islands. Tietjens caught the man as he was crawling into Strickland's tent with a dagger between his teeth; and after his record of iniquity was established in the eyes of the law he was hanged. From that date Tietjens wore a collar of rough silver, and employed a monogram on her night blanket, and the blanket was of double woven Kashmir cloth, for she was a delicate dog.

Under no circumstances would she be separated from Strickland; and once, when he was ill with fever, made great trouble for the doctors, because she did not know how to help her master and would not allow another creature to attempt aid. Macarnaght, of the Indian Medical Service, beat her over her head with a gun-butt before she could understand that she must give room for those who could give quinine.

A short time after Strickland had taken Imray's bungalow, my business took me through that Station, and naturally, the Club quarters being full, I quartered myself upon Strickland. It was a desirable bungalow, eight-roomed and heavily thatched against any chance of leakage from rain. Under the pitch of the roof ran a ceiling-cloth which looked just as neat as a whitewashed ceiling. Unless you knew how Indian bungalows were built you would never have suspected that above the cloth lay the dark three-cornered cavern of the roof, where the beams and the underside of the thatch harbored all manner of rats, bats, ants, and foul things.

Tietjens met me in the verandah with a bay like the boom of the bell of St. Paul's, putting her paws on my shoulder to show she was glad to see me. Strickland had contrived to claw together a sort of meal which he called lunch, and immediately after it was finished went out about his business. I was left alone with Tietjens

13

and my own affairs. The heat of the summer had broken up and turned to the warm damp of the rains. There was no motion in the heated air, but the rain fell like ramrods on the earth, and flung up a blue mist when it splashed back. The bamboos, and the custard-apples, the poinsettias, and the mango trees in the garden stood still while the warm water lashed through them, and the frogs began to sing among the aloe hedges.

A little before the light failed, and when the rain was at its worst, I sat in the back verandah and heard the water roar from the eaves, and scratched myself because I was covered with the thing called prickly-heat. Tietjens came out with me and put her head in my lap and was very sorrowful; so I gave her biscuits when tea was ready, and I took tea in the back verandah on account of the little coolness found there. The rooms of the house were dark behind me. I could smell Strickland's saddlery and the oil on his guns, and I had no desire to sit among these things. My own servant came to me in the twilight, the muslin of his clothes clinging tightly to his drenched body, and told me that a gentleman had called and wished to see someone. Very much against my will, but only because of the darkness of the rooms, I went into the naked drawing-room, telling my man to bring the lights. There might or might not have been a caller waiting—it seemed to me that I saw a figure by one of the windows—but when the lights came there was nothing save the spikes of the rain without, and the smell of the drinking earth in my nostrils. I explained to my servant that he was no wiser than he ought to be, and went back to the verandah to talk to Tietjens. She had gone out into the wet, and I could hardly coax her back to me; even with biscuits with sugar tops. Strickland came home, dripping wet, just before dinner, and the first thing he said was,

"Has anyone called?"

I explained, with apologies, that my servant had summoned me into the drawing-room on a false alarm; or that some loafer had tried to call on Strickland, and thinking better of it had fled after giving his name. Strickland ordered dinner, without comment, and since it was a real dinner with a white tablecloth attached, we sat down.

At 9 o'clock Strickland wanted to go to bed, and I was tired too. Tietjens, who had been lying underneath the table, rose up, and swung into the least exposed verandah as soon as her master moved to his own room, which was next to the stately chamber set apart for Tietjens. If a mere wife had wished to sleep out of doors in that pelting rain it would not have mattered; but Tietjens was a dog, and therefore the better animal. I looked at Strickland,

14

expecting to see him flay her with a whip. He smiled queerly, as a man would smile after telling some unpleasant domestic tragedy. "She has done this ever since I moved in here," said he. "Let her go."

The dog was Strickland's dog, so I said nothing, but I felt all that Strickland felt in being thus made light of. Tietjens encamped outside my bedroom window, and storm after storm came up, thundered on the thatch, and died away. The lightning spattered the sky as a thrown egg spatters a barn door, but the light was pale blue, not yellow, and looking through my split bamboo blinds, I could see the great dog standing, not sleeping, in the verandah, the hackles alift on her back and her feet anchored as tensely as the drawn wire-rope of a suspension bridge. In the very short pauses of the thunder I tried to sleep, but it seemed that someone wanted me very urgently. He, whoever he was, was trying to call me by name, but his voice was no more than a husky whisper. The thunder ceased, and Tietjens went into the garden and howled at the low moon. Somebody tried to open my door, walked about and about through the house and stood breathing heavily in the verandahs, and just when I was falling asleep I fancied that I heard a wild hammering and clamoring above my head or on the door.

I ran into Strickland's room and asked him whether he was ill, and had been calling for me. He was lying on his bed half dressed, a pipe in his mouth. "I thought you'd come," he said. "Have I been walking round the house recently?"

I explained that he had been tramping in the dining-room and the smoking-room and two or three other places, and he laughed and told me to go back to bed. I went back to bed and slept till the morning, but through all my mixed dreams I was sure I was doing someone an injustice in not attending to his wants. What those wants were I could not tell; but a fluttering, whispering, bolt-fumbling, lurking, loitering Someone was reproaching me for my slackness, and, half awake, I heard the howling of Tietjens in the garden and the threshing of the rain.

I lived in that house for two days. Strickland went to his office daily, leaving me alone for eight or ten hours with Tietjens for my only companion. As long as the full light lasted I was comfortable, and so was Tietjens; but in the twilight she and I moved into the back verandah and cuddled each other for company. We were alone in the house, but none the less it was much too fully occupied by a tenant with whom I did not wish to interfere. I never saw him, but I could see the curtains between the rooms quivering where he had just passed through; I could hear the

15

chairs creaking as the bamboos sprung under a weight that had just quitted them; and I could feel when I went to get a book from the dining-room that somebody was waiting in the shadows of the front verandah till I should have gone away. Tietjens made the twilight more interesting by glaring into the darkened rooms with every hair erect, and following the motions of something that I could not see. She never entered the rooms, but her eyes moved interestedly: that was quite sufficient. Only when my servant came to trim the lamps and make all light and habitable she would come in with me and spend her time sitting on her haunches, watching an invisible extra man as he moved about behind my shoulder. Dogs are cheerful companions.

I explained to Strickland, gently as might be, that I would go over to the Club and find quarters there. I admired his hospitality, was pleased with his guns and rods, but I did not much care for his house and its atmosphere. He heard me out to the end, and then smiled very wearily, but without contempt, for he is a man who understands things. "Stay on," he said, "and see what this thing means. All you have talked about I have known since I took the bungalow. Stay on and wait. Tietjens has left me. Are you going too?"

I had seen him through one little affair, connected with a heathen idol, that had brought me to the doors of a lunatic asylum, and I had no desire to help him through further experiences. He was a man to whom unpleasantnesses arrived as do dinners to ordinary people.

Therefore I explained more clearly than ever that I liked him immensely, and would be happy to see him in the daytime; but that I did not care to sleep under his roof. This was after dinner, when Tietjens had gone out to lie in the verandah.

"'Pon my soul, I don't wonder," said Strickland, with his eyes on the ceiling-cloth. "Look at that!"

The tails of two brown snakes were hanging between the cloth and the cornice of the wall. They threw long shadows in the lamplight.

"If you are afraid of snakes of course—" said Strickland.

I hate and fear snakes, because if you look into the eyes of any snake you will see that it knows all and more of the mystery of man's fall, and that it feels all the contempt that the Devil felt when Adam was evicted from Eden. Besides which its bite is generally fatal, and it twists up trouser legs.

"You ought to get your thatch overhauled," I said. "Give me a mahseer rod, and we'll poke 'em down."

"They'll hide among the roof beams," said Strickland. "I can't stand snakes overhead. I'm going up into the roof. If I shake 'em down, stand by with a cleaning rod and break their backs."

I was not anxious to assist Strickland in his work, but I took the cleaning rod and waited in the dining-room, while Strickland brought a gardener's ladder from the verandah, and set it against the side of the room. The snake-tails drew themselves up and disappeared. We could hear the dry rushing scuttle of long bodies running over the baggy ceiling-cloth. Strickland took a lamp with him, while I tried to make clear to him the danger of hunting snakes between a ceiling-cloth and a thatch, apart from the deterioration of property caused by ripping out ceiling-cloths.

"Nonsense!" said Strickland. "They're sure to hide near the walls by the cloth. The bricks are too cold for 'em, and the heat of the room is just what they like." He put his hand to the corner of the stuff and ripped it from the cornice. It gave with a great sound of tearing, and Strickland put his head through the opening into the dark of the angle of the roof beams. I set my teeth and lifted the rod, for I had not the least knowledge of what might descend.

"H'm!" said Strickland, and his voice rolled and rumbled in the roof. "There's room for another set of rooms up here, and, by Jove, some one is occupying 'em!"

"Snakes?" I said from below.

"No. It's a buffalo. Hand me up the two last joints of a mahseer rod, and I'll prod it. It's lying on the main roof beam."

I handed up the rod.

"What a nest for owls and serpents! No wonder the snakes live here," said Strickland, climbing farther into the roof. I could see his elbow thrusting with the rod. "Come out of that, whoever you are! Heads below there! It's falling."

I saw the ceiling-cloth nearly in the center of the room bag with a shape that was pressing it downwards and downwards towards the lighted lamp on the table. I snatched the lamp out of danger and stood back. Then the cloth ripped out from the walls, tore, split, swayed, and shot down upon the table something that I dared not look at, till Strickland had slid down the ladder and was standing by my side.

He did not say much, being a man of few words; but he picked up the loose end of the tablecloth and threw it over the remnants on the table.

"It strikes me," said he, putting down the lamp, "our friend Imray has come back. Oh! you would, would you?"

There was a movement under the cloth, and a little snake wrig-

17

gled out, to be back-broken by the butt of the mahseer rod. I was sufficiently sick to make no remarks worth recording.

Strickland meditated, and helped himself to drinks. The arrangement under the cloth made no more signs of life.

"Is it Imray?" I said.

Strickland turned back the cloth for a moment, and looked.

"It is Imray," he said; "and his throat is cut from ear to ear."

Then we spoke, but together and to ourselves: "That's why he whispered about the house."

Tietjens, in the garden, began to bay furiously. A little later her great nose heaved open the dining-room door.

She sniffed and was still. The tattered ceiling-cloth hung down almost to the level of the table, and there was hardly room to move away from the discovery.

Tietjens came in and sat down; her teeth bared under her lip and her forepaws planted. She looked at Strickland.

"It's a bad business, old lady," said he. "Men don't climb up into the roofs of their bungalows to die, and they don't fasten up the ceiling cloth behind 'em. Let's think it out."

"Let's think it out somewhere else," I said.

"Excellent idea! Turn the lamps out. We'll get into my room."

I did not turn the lamps out. I went into Strickland's room first, and allowed him to make the darkness. Then he followed me, and we lit tobacco and thought. Strickland thought. I smoked furiously, because I was afraid.

"Imray is back," said Strickland. "The question is—who killed Imray? Don't talk, I've a notion of my own. When I took this bungalow I took over most of Imray's servants. Imray was guileless and inoffensive, wasn't he?"

I agreed; though the heap under the cloth had looked neither one thing nor the other.

"If I call in all the servants they will stand fast in a crowd and lie like Aryans. What do you suggest?"

"Call 'em in one by one," I said.

"They'll run away and give the news to all their fellows," said Strickland. "We must segregate 'em. Do you suppose your servant knows anything about it?"

"He may, for all I know; but I don't think it's likely. He has only been here two or three days," I answered. "What's your notion?"

"I can't quite tell. How the dickens did the man get the wrong side of the ceiling-cloth?"

There was a heavy coughing outside Strickland's bedroom door.

This showed that Bahadur Khan, his body-servant, had wakened from sleep and wished to put Strickland to bed.

"Come in," said Strickland. "It's a very warm night, isn't it?"

Bahadur Khan, a great, green-turbaned, six-foot Mohammedan, said that it was a very warm night; but that there was more rain pending, which, by his Honor's favor, would bring relief to the country.

"It will be so, if God pleases," said Strickland, tugging off his boots. "It is in my mind, Bahadur Khan, that I have worked thee remorselessly for many days—ever since that time when thou first camest into my service. What time was that?"

"Has the Heaven-born forgotten? It was when Imray Sahib went secretly to Europe without warning given; and I—even I—came into the honored service of the protector of the poor."

"And Imray Sahib went to Europe?"

"It is so said among those who were his servants."

"And thou wilt take service with him when he returns?"

"Assuredly, Sahib. He was a good master, and cherished his dependents."

"That is true. I am very tired, but I go buck shooting tomorrow. Give me the little sharp rifle that I use for black buck; it is in the case yonder."

The man stooped over the case, handed barrels, stock, and fore-end to Strickland, who fitted all together, yawning dolefully. Then he reached down to the gun case, took a solid-drawn cartridge, and slipped it into the breech of the .360 Express.

"And Imray Sahib has gone to Europe secretly! That is very strange, Bahadur Khan, is it not?"

"What do I know of the ways of the white man, Heaven-born?"

"Very little, truly. But thou shalt know more anon. It has reached me that Imray Sahib has returned from his so long journeyings, and that even now he lies in the next room."

"Sahib!"

The lamplight slid along the barrels of the rifle as they leveled themselves at Bahadur Khan's broad breast.

"Go and look!" said Strickland. "Take a lamp. Thy master is tired, and he waits thee. Go!"

The man picked up a lamp, and went into the dining-room, Strickland following, and almost pushing him with the muzzle of the rifle. He looked for a moment at the black depths behind the ceiling-cloth; at the writhing snake under foot; and last, a gray glaze settling on his face, at the thing under the cloth.

"Hast thou seen?" said Strickland.

19

"I have seen. I am clay in the white man's hands. What does the Presence do?"

"Hang thee within the month. What else?"

"For killing him? Nay, Sahib, consider. Walking among us, his servants, he cast his eyes upon my child, who was four years old. Him he bewitched, and in ten days he died of the fever—my child!"

"What said Imray Sahib?"

"He said he was a handsome child, and patted him on the head; wherefore my child died. Wherefore I killed Imray Sahib in the twilight, when he had come back from office, and was sleeping. Wherefore I dragged him up into the roof beams and made all fast behind him. The Heaven-born knows all things. I am the servant of the Heaven-born."

Strickland looked at me.

"Thou art witness to this saying? He has killed."

Bahadur Khan stood ashen gray in the light of the one lamp. The need for justification came upon him very swiftly. "I am trapped," he said, "but the offense was that man's. He cast an evil eye upon my child, and I killed and hid him. Only such as are served by devils," he glared at Tietjens, crouched stolidly before him, "only such could know what I did."

"It was clever. But thou shouldst have lashed him to the beam with a rope. Now, thou thyself wilt hang by a rope. Orderly!"

A drowsy policeman answered Strickland's call. He was followed by another. Tietjens sat wondrous still.

"Take him to the police station," said Strickland.

"Do I hang, then?" said Bahadur Khan, making no attempt to escape, and keeping his eyes on the ground.

"If the sun shines or the water runs—yes!" said Strickland.

Bahadur Khan stepped back one long pace, quivered, and stood still.

"Go!" said Strickland.

"Nay; but I go very swiftly," said Bahadur Khan. "Look! I am even now a dead man."

He lifted his foot, and to the little toe there clung the head of the half-killed snake, firm fixed in the agony of death.

"I come of land-holding stock," said Bahadur Khan, rocking where he stood. "It were a disgrace to me to go to the public scaffold: therefore I take this way. Be it remembered that the Sahib's shirts are correctly enumerated, and that there is an extra piece of soap in his washbasin. My child was bewitched, and I slew the wizard. Why should you seek to slay me with the rope? My honor is saved, and—and—I die."

At the end of an hour he died, as they die who are bitten by the little brown *karait*, and the policemen bore him and the thing under the cloth to their appointed places.

"This," said Strickland, very calmly, as he climbed into bed, "is called the Nineteenth Century. Did you hear what that man said?"

"I heard," I answered. "Imray made a mistake."

"Simply and solely through not knowing the nature of the Oriental, and the coincidence of a little seasonal fever. Bahadur Khan had been with him for four years."

I shuddered. My own servant had been with me for exactly that length of time. When I went over to my own room I found my man waiting, impassive as the copper head on a penny.

"What has befallen Bahadur Khan?" said I.

"He was bitten by a snake and died. The rest the Sahib knows."

"And how much of this matter hast thou known?"

"As much as might be gathered from One coming in the twilight to seek satisfaction. Gently, Sahib. Let me pull off those boots."

I had just settled to the sleep of exhaustion when I heard Strickland shouting from his side of the house—

"Tietjens has come back to her place!"

And so she had. The great deerhound was couched stately on her own bedstead on her own blanket, while, in the next room, the idle, empty ceiling-cloth waggled as it trailed on the table.

THE CURSE OF THE FIRES
AND OF THE SHADOWS

BY WILLIAM BUTLER YEATS

Dublin-born poet and dramatist William Butler Yeats spent most of his childhood in London and County Sligo, the childhood home of his Protestant parents. With Lady Gregory he founded the Abbey Theatre and the Irish Academy. He married in 1917 and from 1922 to 1928 was a member of the Irish Senate. When he died in 1939 at the age of 73, the *New Republic* wrote, "He died like Shelley at the height of his powers and with half his work unwritten."

THE CURSE OF THE FIRES
AND OF THE SHADOWS

ONE SUMMER NIGHT, when there was peace, a score of Puritan troopers under the pious Sir Frederick Hamilton, broke through the door of the Abbey of the White Friars at Sligo. As the door fell with a crash they saw a little knot of friars gathered about the altar, their white habits glimmering in the steady light of the holy candles. All the monks were kneeling except the abbot, who stood upon the altar steps with a great brass crucifix in his hand. "Shoot them!" cried Sir Frederick Hamilton, but nobody stirred, for all were new converts, and feared the candles and the crucifix. The white lights from the altar threw the shadows of the troopers up on to roof and wall. As the troopers moved about, the shadows began to dance among the corbels and the memorial tablets. For a little while all was silent, and then five troopers who were the bodyguard of Sir Frederick Hamilton lifted their muskets, and shot down five of the friars. The noise and the smoke drove away the mystery of the pale altar lights, and the other troopers took courage and began to strike. In a moment the friars lay about the altar steps, their white habits stained with blood. "Set fire to the house!" cried Sir Frederick Hamilton, and a trooper carried in a heap of dry straw, and piled it against the western wall, but did not light it, because he was still afraid of crucifix and of candles. Seeing this, the five troopers who were Sir Frederick Hamilton's bodyguard went up to the altar, and taking each a holy candle set the straw in a blaze. The red tongues of fire rushed up towards the roof, and crept along the floor, setting in a blaze the seats and benches. The dance of the shadows passed away, and the dance of the fires began. The troopers fell back towards the door in the southern wall, and watched those yellow dancers springing hither and thither.

For a time the altar stood safe and apart in the midst of its white light; the eyes of the troopers turned upon it. The abbot whom they had thought dead had risen to his feet and now stood before it with the crucifix lifted in both hands high above his head. Suddenly he cried with a loud voice, "Woe unto all who have struck down those who have lived in the Light of the Lord, for they shall wander among shadows, and among fires!" And having so cried he fell on his face dead, and the brass crucifix rolled down the steps of the altar. The smoke had now grown very thick, so that it drove the troopers out into the open air. Before them were burning houses.

Behind them shone the Abbey windows filled with saints and martyrs, awakened, as from a sacred trance, into an angry and animated life. The eyes of the troopers were dazzled, and for a while could see nothing but the flaming faces of saints and martyrs. Presently, however, they saw a man covered with dust who came running towards them. "Two messengers," he cried, "have been sent by the defeated Irish to raise against you the whole country about Manor Hamilton, and if you do not stop them you will be overpowered in the woods before you reach home again! They ride northeast between Ben Bulben and Cashel-na-Gael."

Sir Frederick Hamilton called to him the five troopers who had first fired upon the monks and said, "Mount quickly, and ride through the woods towards the mountain, and get before these men, and kill them."

In a moment the troopers were gone, and before many moments they had splashed across the river at what is now called Buckley's Ford, and plunged into the woods. They followed a beaten track that wound along the northern bank of the river. The boughs of the birch and quicken trees mingled above, and hid the cloudy moonlight, leaving the pathway in almost complete darkness. They rode at a rapid trot, now chatting together, now watching some stray weasel or rabbit scuttling away in the darkness. Gradually, as the gloom and silence of the woods oppressed them, they drew closer together, and began to talk rapidly; they were old comrades and knew each other's lives. One was married, and told how glad his wife would be to see him return safe from this harebrained expedition against the White Friars, and to hear how fortune had made amends for rashness. The oldest of the five, whose wife was dead, spoke of a flagon of wine which awaited him upon an upper shelf; while a third, who was the youngest, had a sweetheart watching for his return, and he rode a little way before the others, not talking at all. Suddenly the young man stopped, and they saw that his horse was trembling. "I saw something," he said, "and yet I do not know but it may have been one of the shadows. It looked like a great worm with a silver crown upon his head." One of the five put his hand up to his forehead as if about to cross himself, but remembering that he had changed his religion he put it down, and said, "I am certain it was but a shadow, for there are a great many about us, and of very strange kinds." Then they rode on in silence. It had been raining in the earlier part of the day, and the drops fell from the branches, wetting their hair and their shoulders. In a little they began to talk again. They had been in many battles against many a rebel together, and now told each other over again

24

the story of their wounds, and so awakened in their hearts the strongest of all fellowships, the fellowship of the sword, and half forgot the terrible solitude of the woods.

Suddenly the first two horses neighed, and then stood still, and would go no further. Before them was a glint of water, and they knew by the rushing sound that it was a river. They dismounted, and after much tugging and coaxing brought the horses to the riverside. In the midst of the water stood a tall old woman with grey hair flowing over a grey dress. She stood up to her knees in the water, and stooped from time to time as though washing. Presently they could see that she was washing something that half floated. The moon cast a flickering light upon it, and they saw that it was the dead body of a man, and, while they were looking at it, an eddy of the river turned the face towards them, and each of the five troopers recognised at the same moment his own face. While they stood dumb and motionless with horror, the woman began to speak, saying slowly and loudly, "Did you see my son? He has upon his head a crown of silver." Then the oldest of the troopers, he who had been most often wounded, drew his sword and said, "I have fought for the truth of my God, and need not fear the shadows of Satan," and with that rushed into the water. In a moment he returned. The woman had vanished, and though he had thrust his sword into air and water he had found nothing.

The five troopers remounted, and set their horses at the ford, but all to no purpose. They tried again and again, and went plunging hither and thither, the horses foaming and rearing. "Let us," said the old trooper, "ride back a little into the wood, and strike the river higher up." They rode in under the boughs, the ground-ivy crackling under the hoofs, and the branches striking against their steel caps. After about twenty minutes' riding they came out again upon the river, and after another ten minutes found a place where it was possible to cross without sinking below the stirrups. The wood upon the other side was very thin, and broke the moonlight into long streams. The wind had arisen, and had begun to drive the clouds rapidly across the face of the moon, so that thin streams of light were dancing among scattered bushes and small fir trees. The tops of the trees began also to moan, and the sound of it was like the voice of the dead in the wind; and the troopers remembered that the dead in purgatory are said to be spitted upon the points of the trees and upon the points of the rocks. They turned a little to the south, in the hope that they might strike the beaten path again, but they could find no trace of it.

Meanwhile, the moaning grew louder and louder, and the dancing of the moonlight seemed more and more rapid. Gradually they began to be aware of a sound of distant music. It was the sound of a bagpipe, and they rode towards it with great joy. It came from the bottom of a deep, cuplike hollow. In the midst of the hollow was an old man with a red cap and withered face. He sat beside a fire of sticks, and had a burning torch thrust into the earth at his feet, and played an old bagpipe furiously. His red hair dripped over his face like the iron rust upon a rock. "Did you see my wife?" he said, looking up a moment; "she was washing! she was washing!" "I am afraid of him," said the young trooper, "I fear he is not a right man." "No," said the old trooper, "he is a man like ourselves, for I can see the sun freckles upon his face. We will compel him to be our guide"; and at that he drew his sword, and the others did the same. They stood in a ring round the piper, and pointed their swords at him, and the old trooper then told him that they must kill two rebels, who had taken the road between Ben Bulben and the great mountain spur that is called Cashel-na-Gael, and that he must get up on the horse before one of them and be their guide, for they had lost their way. The piper pointed to a neighbouring tree, and they saw an old white horse ready bitted, bridled, and saddled. He slung the pipe across his back, and, taking the torch in his hand, got upon the horse, and started off before them, as hard as he could go.

The wood grew thinner now, and the ground began to slope up toward the mountain. The moon had already set, but the stars shone brightly between the clouds. The ground sloped more and more until at last they rode far above the woods upon the wide top of the mountain. The woods lay spread out mile after mile below, and away to the south shot up the red glare of the burning town. The guide drew rein suddenly, and pointing upwards with the hand that did not hold the torch, shrieked out, "Look; look at the holy candles!" and then plunged forward at a gallop, waving the torch hither and thither. "Do you hear the hoofs of the messengers?" cried the guide. "Quick, quick! or they will be gone out of your hands!" and he laughed as with delight of the chase. The troopers thought they could hear far off, and as if below them, rattle of hoofs; but now the ground began to slope more and more, and the speed grew more headlong moment by the moment. They tried to pull up, but they could not, for the horses seemed to have gone mad. The guide had thrown the reins onto the neck of the old white horse, and was waving his arms and singing in Gaelic. Suddenly they saw the thin gleam of a river, at an immense distance below, and knew that they were upon the brink of the abyss that is now called Lug-na-Gael, or in English the

26

Stranger's Leap. The six horses sprang forward, and five screams went up into the air, a moment later five men and horses fell with a dull crash upon the green slopes at the foot of the rocks.

THE MIRACULOUS REVENGE

BY BERNARD SHAW

Bernard Shaw was born in Dublin on July 26, 1856. His father was a ne'er-do-well and his mother an overprotective, talented musician. Shaw became a music critic in London and was one of the founders of the socialist Fabian Society. In 1898, while living only on greens, he collapsed, and was helped back to health by Charlotte Frances Payne-Townsend, whom he married. Among the most celebrated of his plays are *Arms and the Man, Caesar and Cleopatra, Man and Superman, Major Barbara, Androcles and the Lion, Pygmalion* and *St. Joan of Arc.*

I ARRIVED IN DUBLIN on the evening of the 5th of August, and drove to the residence of my uncle, the Cardinal Archbishop. He is, like most of my family, deficient in feeling, and consequently averse to me personally. He lives in a dingy house, with a sidelong view of the portico of his cathedral from the front windows, and of a monster national school from the back. My uncle maintains no retinue. The people believe that he is waited upon by angels. When I knocked at the door, an old woman, his only servant, opened it, and informed me that her master was then officiating in the cathedral, and that he had directed her to prepare dinner for me in his absence. An unpleasant smell of salt fish made me ask her what the dinner consisted of. She assured me that she had cooked all that could be permitted in His Holiness' house on a Friday. On my asking her further why on a Friday, she replied that Friday was a fast day. I bade her tell His Holiness that I had hoped to have the pleasure of calling on him shortly, and drove to a hotel in Sackville Street, where I engaged apartments and dined.

After dinner I resumed my eternal search—I know not for what: it drives me to and fro like another Cain. I sought in the streets without success. I went to the theatre. The music was execrable, the scenery poor. I had seen the play a month before in London, with the same beautiful artist in the chief part. Two years had passed since, seeing her for the first time, I had hoped that she, perhaps, might be the long-sought mystery. It had proved otherwise. On this night I looked at her and listened to her for the sake of that bygone hope, and applauded her generously when the curtain fell. But I went out lonely still. When I had supped at a restaurant, I returned to my hotel, and tried to read. In vain. The sound of feet in the corridors as the other occupants of the hotel went to bed distracted my attention from my book. Suddenly it occurred to me that I had never quite understood my uncle's character. He, father to a great flock of poor and ignorant Irish; an austere and saintly man, to whom livers of hopeless lives daily appealed for help heavenward; who was reputed never to have sent away a troubled peasant without relieving him of his burden by sharing it; whose knees were worn less by the altar steps than by the tears and embraces of the guilty and wretched: he had refused to humor my light extravagances, or to find time to talk with me of books, flowers, and music.

29

Had I not been mad to expect it? Now that I needed sympathy myself, I did him justice. I desired to be with a true-hearted man, and to mingle my tears with his.

I looked at my watch. It was nearly an hour past midnight. In the corridor the lights were out, except one jet at the end. I threw a cloak upon my shoulders, put on a Spanish hat, and left my apartment, listening to the echoes of my measured steps retreating through the deserted passages. A strange sight arrested me on the landing of the grand staircase. Through an open door I saw the moonlight shining through the windows of a saloon in which some entertainment had recently taken place. I looked at my watch again: It was but one o'clock; and yet the guests had departed. I entered the room, my boots ringing loudly on the waxed boards. On a chair lay a child's cloak and a broken toy. The entertainment had been a children's party. I stood for a time looking at the shadow of my cloaked figure upon the floor, and at the disordered decorations, ghostly in the white light. Then I saw that there was a grand piano, still open, in the middle of the room. My fingers throbbed as I sat down before it, and expressed all that I felt in a grand hymn which seemed to thrill the cold stillness of the shadows into a deep hum of approbation, and to people the radiance of the moon with angels. Soon there was a stir without too, as if the rapture were spreading abroad. I took up the chant triumphantly with my voice, and the empty saloon resounded as though to an orchestra.

"Hallo, sir!" "Confound you, sir—" "Do you suppose that this—"

I turned; and silence followed. Six men, partially dressed, and with disheveled hair, stood regarding me angrily. They all carried candles. One of them had a bootjack, which he held like a truncheon. Another, the foremost, had a pistol. The night porter was behind trembling.

"Sir," said the man with the revolver, coarsely, "may I ask whether you are mad, that you disturb people at this hour with such a noise?"

"Is it possible that you dislike it?" I replied, courteously.

"Dislike it!" said he, stamping with rage. "Do you suppose we enjoy it?"

"Take care: he's mad," whispered the man with the bootjack.

I began to laugh. Evidently they did think me mad. Unaccustomed to my habits, and ignorant of music as they probably were, the mistake, however absurd, was not unnatural. I rose. They came closer to one another; and the night porter ran away.

"Gentlemen," I said, "I am sorry for you. Had you lain still and listened, we should all have been the better and happier. But what

30

you have done, you cannot undo. Kindly inform the night porter that I am gone to visit my uncle, the Cardinal Archbishop. Adieu!"

I strode past them, and left them whispering among themselves. Some minutes later I knocked at the door of the Cardinal's house. Presently a window on the first floor was opened; and the moonbeams fell on a gray head, with a black cap that seemed ashy pale against the unfathomable gloom of the shadow beneath the stone sill.

"Who are you?"

"I am Zeno Legge."

"What do you want at this hour?"

The question wounded me. "My dear uncle," I exclaimed, "I know you do not intend it, but you make me feel unwelcome. Come down and let me in, I beg."

"Go to your hotel," he said sternly. "I will see you in the morning. Good night." He closed the window.

I felt that if I let this rebuff pass, I should not feel kindly towards my uncle in the morning, nor, indeed, at any future time. I therefore plied the knocker with my right hand, and kept the bell ringing with my left until I heard the door-chain rattle within. The Cardinal's expression was grave as he confronted me on the threshold.

"Uncle," I cried, grasping his hand, "do not reproach me. Your door is never shut against the wretched. I am wretched. Let us sit up all night and talk."

"You may thank my position and not my charity for your admission, Zeno," he said. "For the sake of the neighbors, I had rather you played the fool in my study than upon my doorstep at this hour. Walk upstairs quietly, if you please. My housekeeper is a hard-working woman: the little sleep she allows herself must not be disturbed."

"You have a noble heart, uncle. I shall creep like a mouse."

"This is my study," he said, as we entered an ill-furnished den on the second floor. "The only refreshment I can offer you, if you desire any, is a bunch of raisins. The doctors have forbidden you to touch stimulants."

"By heaven!" He raised his finger. "Pardon me: I was wrong to swear. But I had totally forgotten the doctors. At dinner I had a bottle of *Grave*."

"Humph! You have no business to be traveling alone. Your mother promised me that Bushy should come over here with you."

"Pshaw! Bushy is not a man of feeling. Besides, he is a

31

coward. He refused to come with me because I purchased a revolver."

"He should have taken the revolver from you, and kept to his post."

"Why will you persist in treating me like a child, uncle? I am very impressionable, I grant you; but I have gone round the world alone, and do not need to be dry-nursed through a tour in Ireland."

"What do you intend to do here?"

I had no plans; and instead of answering I shrugged my shoulders and looked round the apartment. There was a statuette of the Virgin upon my uncle's desk. I looked at its face, as he was wont to look in the midst of his labors. I saw there eternal peace. The air became luminous with an infinite network of the Jeweled rings of Paradise descending in roseate clouds upon us.

"Uncle," I said, bursting into the sweetest tears I had ever shed, "my wanderings are over. I will enter the Church, if you will help me. Let us read together the third part of *Faust,* for I understand it at last."

"Hush, man," he said, half rising with an expression of alarm.

"Do not let my tears mislead you. I am calm and strong. Quick, let us have Goethe—"

"Come, come. Dry your eyes and be quiet. I have no library here."

"But I have—in my portmanteau at the hotel," I said, rising. "Let me go for it. I will return in fifteen minutes."

"The devil is in you, I believe. Cannot—"

I interrupted him with a shout of laughter. "Cardinal," I said noisily, "you have become profane; and a profane priest is always the best of good fellows. Let us have some wine; and I will sing you a beer song."

"Heaven forgive me if I do you wrong," he said; "but I believe God had laid the expiation of some sin on your unhappy head. Will you favor me with your attention for a while? I have something to say to you, and I have also to get some sleep before my hour for rising at half-past five."

"My usual hour for retiring—when I retire at all. But proceed. My fault is not inattention, but oversusceptibility."

"Well, then, I want you to go to Wicklow. My reasons—"

"No matter what they may be," said I, rising again. "It is enough that you desire me to go."

"Zeno! Will you sit down and listen to me?"

I sank upon my chair reluctantly. "Ardor is a crime in your eyes, even when it is shown in your service," I said. "May I turn down the light?"

"Why?"

"To bring on my sombre mood, in which I am able to listen with tireless patience."

"I will turn it down myself."

I thanked him, and composed myself to listen in the shadow. My eyes, I felt, glittered. I was like Poe's raven.

"Now for my reasons for sending you to Wicklow. First for your own sake. If you stay in town, or in any place where excitement can be obtained by any means, you will be in Swift's Hospital in a week. You must live in the country, under the eye of one on whom I can depend. And you must have something to do to keep you out of mischief, and away from your music and painting and poetry, which, Sir John Richards writes to me, are dangerous for you in your present morbid state. Second, because I can entrust you with a task which, in the hands of a sensible man, might bring discredit on the Church. In short, I want you to investigate a miracle."

He looked attentively at me. I sat like a statue.

"You understand me?" he said.

"Nevermore," I replied, hoarsely. "Pardon me," I added, amused at the trick my imagination had played me, "I understand you perfectly."

"I hope you do. Well, four miles distant from the town of Wicklow is a village called Four Mile Water. The resident priest is Father Hickey. You have heard of the miracles at Knock?"

I winked.

"I did not ask you what you think of them, but whether you have heard of them. I see you have. I need not tell you that even a miracle may do more harm than good to the Church in this country, unless it can be proved so thoroughly that her powerful and jealous enemies are silenced by the testimony of followers of their heresy. Therefore, when I saw in a Wexford newspaper last week a description of a strange manifestation of the Divine Power which was said to have taken place at Four Mile Water, I was troubled in my mind about it. So I wrote to Father Hickey, bidding him give me an account of the matter if it were true, and, if not, to denounce from the altar the author of the report, and to contradict it in the paper at once. This is his reply. He says—well, the first part is about Church matters: I need not trouble you with it. He goes on to say—"

"One moment. Is that his own handwriting? It does not look like a man's."

33

"He suffers from rheumatism in the fingers of his right hand; and his niece, who is an orphan, and lives with him, acts as his amanuensis."

"Stay. What is her name?"

"Her name? Kate Hickey."

"How old is she?"

"Tush, man, she is only a little girl. If she were old enough to concern you, I should not send you into her way. Have you any more questions to ask about her?"

"None. I can fancy her in a white veil at the rite of confirmation, a type of faith and innocence. Enough of her. What says the Reverend Hickey of the apparitions?"

"They are not apparitions. I will read you what he says. Ahem! 'In reply to your inquiries concerning the late miraculous event in this parish, I have to inform you that I can vouch for its truth, and that I can be confirmed not only by the inhabitants of the place, but by every person acquainted with the former situation of the graveyard referred to, including the Protestant Archdeacon of Baltinglas, who spends six weeks annually in the neighborhood. The newspaper account is incomplete and inaccurate. The following are the facts: About four years ago, a man named Wolfe Tone Fitzgerald settled in this village as a farrier. His antecedents did not become known, and he had no family. He lived by himself, was very careless of his person, and when in his cups, as he often was, regarded the honor neither of God nor man in his conversation. Indeed, if it were not speaking ill of the dead, one might say that he was a dirty, drunken, blasphemous blackguard. Worse again, he was, I fear, an atheist; for he never attended Mass, and gave His Holiness worse language even than he gave the Queen. I should have mentioned that he was a bitter rebel, and boasted that his grandfather had been out in '98, and his father with Smith O'Brien. In the end, he went by the name of Brimstone Billy, and was held up in the village as the type of all wickedness.

"'You are aware that our graveyard, situated on the north side of the water, is famous throughout the country as the burial place of the nuns of St. Ursula, the hermit of Four Mile Water, and many other holy people. No Protestant has ever ventured to enforce his legal right of interment there, though two have died in the parish within my own recollection. Three weeks ago, this Fitzgerald died in a fit brought on by drink, and a great hullabaloo was raised in the village when it became known that he would be buried in the graveyard. The body had to be watched to prevent its being stolen and buried at the crossroads. My people were greatly

34

disappointed when they were told I could do nothing to stop the burial, particularly as I of course refused to read any service on the occasion. However, I bade them not interfere, and the interment was effected on the 14th of July, late in the evening, and long after the legal hour. There was no disturbance. Next morning, the *entire* graveyard was found moved to the south side of the water, with only one newly-filled grave left behind on the north side; and thus they both remain. The departed saints would not lie with the reprobate. I can testify to it on the oath of a Christian priest; and if this will not satisfy those outside the Church, everyone, as I said before, who remembers where the graveyard was two months ago, can confirm me.

" 'I respectfully suggest that a thorough investigation into the truth of this miracle be proposed to a committee of Protestant gentlemen. They shall not be asked to accept a single fact on hearsay from my people. The ordinance maps show where the graveyard was, and anyone can see for himself where it is. I need not tell your Eminence what a rebuke this would be to those enemies of the Holy Church that have sought to put a stain on her by discrediting the late wonderful manifestations at Knock Chapel. If they come to Four Mile Water, they need cross-examine no one. They will be asked to believe nothing but their own senses.

" 'Awaiting your Eminence's counsel to guide me further in the matter, I am, etc.'

"Well, Zeno," said my uncle, "what do you think of Father Hickey now?"

"Uncle, do not ask me. Beneath this roof I desire to believe everything. The Reverend Hickey has appealed strongly to my love of legend. Let us admire the poetry of his narrative, and ignore the balance of probability between a tale told by a Christian priest and a whole graveyard swimming across a river in the middle of the night and forgetting to return."

"Tom Hickey is telling no lie, sir. But he may be mistaken."

"Such a mistake amounts to insanity. It is true that I myself, awaking suddenly in the depth of night, have found myself convinced that the position of my bed had been reversed. But on opening my eyes the illusion ceased. I fear Mr. Hickey is mad. Your best course is this: send down to Four Mile Water a perfectly sane investigator; an acute observer; one whose perceptive faculties, at once healthy and subtle, are absolutely unclouded by religious prejudice. In a word, send me. I will report to you the true state of affairs in a few days, and you can then make arrangements for transferring Hickey to the asylum."

"Yes, I had intended to send you. You are wonderfully sharp; and you would make a capital detective if you could only keep your mind to one point. But your chief qualification for this business is that you are too crazy to excite the suspicion of those whom you may have to watch. For the affair may be a trick. If so, I hope and believe that Hickey has no hand in it. Still, it is my duty to take every precaution."

"Cardinal, may I ask whether traces of insanity have ever appeared in our family?"

"Except in you and in my grandmother, no; and you resemble her personally. Why do you ask?"

"Because it has often occurred to me that you are, perhaps, a little cracked. Excuse my candor; but a man who has devoted his life to the pursuit of a red hat; who accuses everyone else besides himself of being mad; and who is disposed to listen seriously to a tale of a peripatetic graveyard, can hardly be quite sane. Depend upon it, uncle, you want rest and change. The blood of your grandmother is in your veins."

"I hope I may not be committing a sin in sending a ribald on the Church's affairs," he replied, fervently. "However, we must use the instruments put into our hands. Is it agreed that you go?"

"Had you not delayed me with this story, which I might as well have learned on the spot, I should have been there already."

"There is no occasion for impatience, Zeno. I must first send to Hickey to find a place for you. I shall tell him that you are going to recover your health, as, in fact, you are. And, Zeno, in Heaven's name be discreet. Try to act like a man of sense. Do not dispute with Hickey on matters of religion. Since you are my nephew, you had better not disgrace me."

"I shall do you infinite credit."

"I wish you would, although you would hardly be an acquisition to the Church. And now I must turn you out. It is nearly three o'clock, and I need some sleep. Do you know your way back to your hotel?"

"I need not stir. I can sleep in this chair. Go to bed, and never mind me."

"I shall not close my eyes until you are safely out of the house. Come, rouse yourself, and say good night."

The following is a copy of my first report to the Cardinal:
My Dear Uncle,

The miracle is genuine. I have affected perfect credulity in order to throw the Hickeys and the countryfolk off their guard with me. I have listened to their method of convincing sceptical strangers. I

36

have examined the ordinance maps, and cross-examined the neighboring Protestant gentlefolk. I have spent a day upon the ground on each side of the water, and have visited it at midnight. I have considered the upheaval theories, subsidence theories, volcanic theories, and tidal wave theories which the provincial *savants* have suggested. They are all untenable. There is only one scoffer in the district, an Orangeman; and he admits the removal of the cemetery, but says it was dug up and transplanted in the night by a body of men under the command of Father Tom. This also is out of the question. The interment of Brimstone Billy was the first which had taken place in four years, and his is the only grave which bears a trace of recent digging. It is alone on the north bank, and the inhabitants shun it after nightfall. As each passerby during the day throws a stone upon it, it will soon be marked by a large cairn. The original graveyard, with a ruined stone chapel still standing in its midst, is now all on the south side—except the single grave of Brimstone Billy. You may send down a committee to investigate the matter as soon as you please. There can be no doubt as to the miracle having actually taken place, as recorded by Hickey. As for me, I have grown so accustomed to it that if the county Wicklow were to waltz off with me to Middlesex, I should be quite impatient of any expressions of surprise from my friends in London.

Is not the above a business-like statement? Away, then, with this stale miracle. If you would see for yourself a miracle which can never pall, a vision of youth and health to be crowned with garlands forever, come down and see Kate Hickey, whom you suppose to be a little girl. Illusion, my lord cardinal, illusion! She is seventeen, with a bloom and a brogue that would lay your asceticism in ashes at a flash. To her I am an object of wonder, a strange man bred in wicked cities. She is courted by six feet of farming material, chopped off a spare length of coarse humanity by the Almighty, and flung into Wicklow to plow the fields. His name is Phil Langan; and he hates me. I have to consort with him for the sake of Father Tom, whom I entertain vastly by stories of your wild oats sown at Salamanca. I exhausted all my authentic anecdotes the first day, and now I invent gallant escapades with Spanish donnas, in which you figure as a youth of unstable morals. This delights Father Tom infinitely. I feel that I have done you a service by thus casting on the cold sacerdotal abstraction which formerly represented you in Katie's imagination a ray of vivifying passion.

What a country this is! A Hesperidean garden: such skies! Adieu uncle, adieu.

Zeno Legge

Behold me, then, at Four Mile Water, in love. I have been in love frequently, but not oftener than once a year had I encountered a woman who affected me as seriously as Katie Hickey. She was so shrewd, and yet so flippant! When I spoke of art she yawned. When I deplored the sordidness of the world she laughed and called me "poor fellow!" When I told her what a treasure of beauty and freshness she had she ridiculed me. When I reproached her with her brutality she became angry, and sneered at me for being what she called a fine gentleman. One sunny afternoon we were standing at the gate of her uncle's house, she looking down the dusty road for the detestable Langan, when she said:

"How soon are you going back to London?"

"I am not going back to London, Miss Hickey. I am not yet tired of Four Mile Water."

"I'm sure Four Mile Water ought to be proud of your approbation."

"You disapprove of my liking it, then? Or is it that you grudge me the happiness I have found here? I think Irish ladies grudge a man a moment's peace."

"I wonder you have ever prevailed on yourself to associate with Irish ladies, since they are so far beneath you."

"Did I say they were beneath me, Miss Hickey? I feel that I have made a deep impression on you."

"Indeed! Yes, you're quite right. I assure you I can't sleep at night for thinkin' of you, Mr. Legge. It's the best a Christian can do, seein' you think so mighty little of yourself."

"You are triply wrong, Miss Hickey: wrong to be sarcastic with me, wrong to pretend that there is anything unreasonable in my belief that you think of me sometimes, and wrong to discourage the candor with which I always avow that I think constantly of myself."

"Then you had better not speak to me, since you say I have no manners."

"Again! Did I say you had no manners? The warmest expressions of regard from my mouth seem to reach your ears transformed into insults. Were I to repeat the Litany of the Blessed Virgin, you would retort as though I had been reproaching you. This is because you hate me. You never misunderstand Langan, whom you love."

"I don't know what London manners are, Mr. Legge, but in Ireland gentlemen are expected to mind their own business. How dare you say I love Mr. Langan?"

"Then you do not love him?"

"It is nothing to you whether I love him or not."

"Nothing to me that you hate me and love another?"

"I didn't say I hated you. You're not so very clever yourself at understandin' what people say, though you make such a fuss because they don't understand you." Here, as she glanced down the road again, she suddenly looked glad.

"Aha!" I said.

"What do you mean by 'Aha!' "

"No matter, I will now show you what a man's sympathy is. As you perceived just then, Langan—who is too tall for his age, by the way—is coming to pay you a visit. Well, instead of staying with you, as a jealous woman would, I will withdraw."

"I don't care whether you go or stay, I'm sure. I wonder what you would give to be as fine a man as Mr. Langan."

"All I possess: I swear it! But solely because you admire tall men more than broad views. Mr. Langan may be defined geometrically as length without breadth; altitude without position; a line on the landscape, not a point in it."

"How very clever you are!"

"You do not understand me, I see. Here comes your lover, stepping over the wall like a camel. And here go I, out through the gate like a Christian. Good afternoon, Mr. Langan. I am going because Miss Hickey has something to say to you about me which she would rather not say in my presence. You will excuse me?"

"Oh, I'll excuse you," said he boorishly. I smiled, and went out. Before I was quite out of hearing, Kate whispered vehemently to him, "I *hate* that fellow."

I smiled again, but I had scarcely done so when my spirits fell. I walked hastily away with a coarse threatening sound in my ears like that of the clarinets whose sustained low notes darken the woodland in *Der Freischütz*. I found myself presently at the graveyard, now on the south side of the water. It was a barren place, enclosed by a mud wall with a gate to admit funerals, and numerous gaps to admit the peasantry, who made short cuts across it as they went to and fro between Four Mile Water and the market town. The graves were mounds overgrown with grass: there was no keeper; nor were there flowers, railings, or any of the conventionalities that make an English graveyard repulsive. A great thornbush, near what was called the Grave of the Holy Sisters, was covered with scraps of cloth and flannel, attached by peasant women who had prayed before it. There were three kneeling there as I entered, for the reputation of the place had been revived of late by the miracle; and a ferry had been established close by, to conduct visitors over the route taken by the graveyard. From where I stood I could see on

39

the opposite bank the heap of stones, perceptibly increased since my last visit, marking the deserted grave of Brimstone Billy. I strained my eyes broodingly at it for some minutes, and then descended the river bank and entered the boat.

"Good evenin' t'your honor," said the ferryman, and set to work to draw the boat hand over hand by a rope stretched across the water.

"Good evening. Is your business beginning to fall off yet?"

"Faith, it never was as good as it mightabeen. The people that comes from the south side can see Billy's grave—Lord have mercy on him!—across the wather; and they think bad of payin' a penny to put a stone over him. It's them that lives towrst Dublin that makes the journey. Your honor is the third I've brought from south to north this blessed day."

"When do most people come? In the afternoon, I suppose?"

"All hours, sur, except afther dusk. There isn't a sowl in the counthry ud come within sight of that grave wanst the sun goes down."

"And you, do you stay here all night by yourself?"

"The holy heavens forbid! Is it me stay here all night? No, your honor: I tether the boat at siven o'clyock, and lave Brimstone Billy—God forgimme!—to take care of it t'll mornin'."

"It will be stolen some night, I'm afraid."

"Arra, who'd dare come next or near it, let alone stale it? Faith, I'd think twice before lookin' at it meself in the dark. God bless your honor, and gran'che long life."

I had given him sixpence. I went to the reprobate's grave and stood at the foot of it, looking at the sky, gorgeous with the descent of the sun. To my English eyes, accustomed to giant trees, broad lawns, and stately mansions, the landscape was wild and inhospitable. The ferryman was already tugging at the rope on his way back (I had told him I did not intend to return that way), and presently I saw him make the painter fast to the south bank, put on his coat, and trudge homeward. I turned towards the grave at my feet. Those who had interred Brimstone Billy, working hastily at an unlawful hour and in fear of molestation by the people, had hardly dug a grave. They had scooped out earth enough to hide their burden, and no more. A stray goat had kicked away a corner of the mound and exposed the coffin. It occurred to me, as I took some of the stones from the cairn and heaped them so as to repair the breach, that had the miracle been the work of a body of men, they would have moved the one grave instead of the many. Even from a supernatural point of view, it seemed strange that the sinner should have banished the elect, when, by their superior numbers, they might so much more easily have banished him.

It was almost dark when I left the spot. After a walk of half a mile, I recrossed the water by a bridge, and returned to the farmhouse in which I lodged. Here, finding that I had had enough of solitude, I only stayed to take a cup of tea. Then I went to Father Hickey's cottage.

Kate was alone when I entered. She looked up quickly as I opened the door, and turned away disappointed when she recognized me.

"Be generous for once," I said. "I have walked about aimlessly for hours in order to avoid spoiling the beautiful afternoon for you by my presence. When the sun was up I withdrew my shadow from your path. Now that darkness has fallen, shed some light on mine. May I stay half an hour?"

"You may stay as long as you like, of course. My uncle will soon be home. He is clever enough to talk to you."

"What! More sarcasms! Come, Miss Hickey, help me to spend a pleasant evening. It will only cost you a smile. I am somewhat cast down. Four Mile Water is a paradise, but without you it would be a little lonely."

"It must be very lonely for you. I wonder why you came here."

"Because I heard that the women here were all Zerlinas, like you, and the men Masettos, like Mr. Phil—where are you going to?"

"Let me pass, Mr. Legge. I had intended never speaking to you again after the way you went on about Mr. Langan today; and I wouldn't either, only my uncle made me promise not to take any notice of you, because you were—no matter. But I won't listen to you any more on the subject."

"Do not go. I swear never to mention his name again. I beg your pardon for what I said: you shall have no further cause for complaint."

She sat down, evidently disappointed by my submission. I took a chair, and placed myself near her. She tapped the floor impatiently with her foot. I saw that there was not a movement I could make, not a look, which did not irritate her.

"You were remarking," I said, "that your uncle desired you to take no notice of me because—"

She did not answer.

"I fear I have offended you again by my curiosity. But, indeed, I had no idea that he had forbidden you to tell me the reason."

41

"He did not forbid me. Since you are so determined to find out—"

"No, excuse me. I do not wish to know, I am sorry I asked."

"Indeed! Perhaps you would be sorrier still to be told. I only made a secret of it out of consideration for you."

"Then your uncle has spoken ill of me behind my back. If that be so, there is no such thing as a true man in Ireland. I would not have believed it on the word of any woman alive save yourself."

"I never said my uncle was a backbiter. Just to show you what he thinks of you, I will tell you, whether you want to know it or not, that he bid me not mind you because you were only a poor mad creature, sent down here to be out of harm's way."

"Oh, Miss Hickey!"

"There now, you have got it out of me!—and I wish I had bit my tongue out first. I sometimes think that you have a bad angel in you."

"I am glad you told me this," I said gently. "Do not reproach yourself for having done so, I beg. Your uncle has been misled by what he has heard of my family, who are all more or less insane. Far from being mad, I am actually the only rational man named Legge in the three kingdoms. I will prove this to you, and at the same time keep your indiscretion in countenance by telling you something I ought not to tell you. It is this. I am not here as an invalid or a chance tourist. The Cardinal, a shrewd if somewhat erratic man, selected mine from all the long heads at his disposal to come down here and find out the truth of Father Hickey's story. Would he have entrusted such a task to a madman, think you?"

"The truth of—who dared to doubt my uncle's word? And so you are a spy, a dirty informer!"

I started. The adjective she had used, though probably the commonest expression of contempt in Ireland, is revolting to an Englishman.

"Miss Hickey," I said, "there is in me, as you have said, a bad angel. Do not shock my good angel—who is a person of taste— quite away from my heart, lest the other be left undisputed monarch of it. Hark! The chapel bell is ringing the angelus. Can you, with that sound softening the darkness of the village night, cherish a feeling of spite against one who admires you?"

"You come between me and my prayers," she said hysterically, and began to sob. She had scarcely done so when I heard voices without. Then Langan and the priest entered.

"Oh, Phil," she cried running to him, "take me away from him! I

42

can't bear—" I turned towards him, and showed him my dog-tooth in a false smile. He felled me at one stroke.

"Murder!" exclaimed the priest.

"He's an informer," sobbed Kate. "He came down here to spy on you, uncle, and to try and show that the blessed miracle was a make-up. I knew it long before he told me, by his insulting ways. He wanted to make love to me."

I rose with difficulty from beneath the table, where I had lain motionless for a moment.

"Sir," I said, "I am somewhat dazed by the recent action of Mr. Langan, whom I beg, the next time he converts himself into a fulling-mill to do so at the expense of a man more nearly his equal in strength than I. What your niece has told you is partly true. I am indeed the Cardinal's spy, and I have already reported to him that the miracle is a genuine one. A committee of gentlemen will wait on you tomorrow to verify it, at my suggestion. I have thought that the proof might be regarded by them as more complete if you were taken by surprise. Miss Hickey: that I admire all that is admirable in you is but to say that I have a sense of the beautiful. To say that I love you would be mere profanity. Mr. Langan: I have in my pocket a loaded pistol, which I carry from a silly English prejudice against your countrymen. Had I been the Hercules of the plowtail and you in my place, I should have been a dead man now. Do not redden: you are safe as far as I am concerned."

"Let me tell you before you leave my house for good," said Father Hickey, who seemed to have become unreasonably angry, "that you should never have crossed my threshold if I had known you were a spy—no, not if·your uncle were the Pope himself."

Here a frightful thing happened to me. I felt giddy, and put my hand to my head. Three warm drops trickled over it. Instantly I became murderous. My mouth filled with blood; my eyes were blinded with it; I seemed to drown in it. My hand went involuntarily to the pistol. It is my habit to obey my impulses instantaneously. Fortunately, the impulse to kill vanished before a sudden perception of how I might miraculously humble the mad vanity in which these foolish people had turned upon me.

"And let *me* tell you," Langan was saying, "that if you think yourself handier with cold lead than you are with your fists, I'll exchange shots with you, and welcome, whenever you please. Father Tom's credit is the same to me as my own; and if you say a word against it, you lie."

"His credit is in my hands," I said. "I am the Cardinal's witness."

"There is the door," said the priest, holding it open before me.

43

"Until you can undo the visible work of God's hand your testimony can do no harm to me."

I bowed to Kate and walked out. It was so dark that I could not at first see the garden gate. Before I found it, I heard through the window Father Hickey's voice saying, "I wouldn't for ten pounds that this had happened, Phil. He's as mad as a march hare. The Cardinal told me so."

I returned to my lodging and took a cold bath to cleanse the blood from my neck and shoulder. The effect of the blow I had received was so severe that even after the bath and a light meal I felt giddy and languid. There was an alarm clock on the mantelpiece: I wound it, set the alarm for half-past twelve, muffled it so that it should not disturb the people in the adjoining room, and went to bed, where I slept soundly for an hour and a quarter. Then the alarm roused me, and I sprang up before I was thoroughly awake. Had I hesitated, the desire to relapse into perfect sleep would have overpowered me. Although the muscles of my neck were painfully stiff, and my hands unsteady from my nervous disturbance, produced by the interruption of my first slumber, I dressed myself resolutely, and, after taking a draught of cold water, stole out of the house. It was exceedingly dark; and I had some difficulty in finding the cowhouse, whence I borrowed a spade, and a truck with wheels, ordinarily used for moving sacks of potatoes. These I carried in my hands until I was beyond earshot of the house, where I put the spade on the truck and wheeled it along the road to the cemetery. When I approached the water, knowing that no one would dare to come thereabout at such an hour, I made greater haste, no longer concerning myself about the rattling of the wheels. Looking across to the opposite bank, I could see a phosphorescent glow, marking the lonely grave of Brimstone Billy. This helped me to find the ferry station, where, after wandering a little and stumbling often, I found the boat, and embarked with my implements. Guided by the rope, I crossed the water without difficulty, landed, made fast the boat, dragged the truck up the bank, and sat down to rest on Billy's grave.

For nearly a quarter of an hour I sat watching the patches of jack-o'-lantern fire, and collecting my strength for the work before me. Then the distant bell of the chapel clock tolled one. I rose, took the spade, and in about ten minutes uncovered the coffin, which smelt horribly. Keeping to windward of it, and using spade as a lever, I contrived with great labor to place it on the truck. I wheeled it without accident to the landing place, where, by placing the shafts of the truck upon the stern of the boat and lifting the foot by main

44

strength, I succeeded in embarking my load after twenty minutes' toil, during which I got covered with clay and perspiration, and several times all but upset the boat. At the southern bank I had less difficulty in getting truck and coffin ashore, and dragging them up to the graveyard.

It was now past two o'clock, and the dawn had begun—so that I had no further trouble from want of light. I wheeled the coffin to a patch of loamy soil which I had noticed in the afternoon near the Grave of the Holy Sisters. I had warmed to my work; my neck no longer pained me; and I began to dig vigorously, soon making a shallow trench, deep enough to hide the coffin with the addition of a mound. The chill pearl-colored morning had by this time quite dissipated the darkness. I could see, and was myself visible, for miles around. This alarmed me, and made me impatient to finish my task. Nevertheless, I was forced to rest for a moment before placing the coffin in the trench. I wiped my brow and wrists and again looked about me. The tomb of the holy women, a massive slab supported on four stone spheres, was gray and wet with dew. Near it was the thornbush covered with rags, the newest of which were growing gaudy in the radiance which was stretching up from the coast on the east. It was time to finish my work. I seized the truck, laid it alongside the grave, and gradually prized the coffin off with the spade until it rolled over into the trench with a hollow sound like a drunken remonstrance from the sleeper within. I shoveled the earth round and over it, working as fast as possible. In less than a quarter of an hour it was buried. Ten minutes more sufficed to make the mound symmetrical, and to clear the traces of my work from the adjacent sward. Then I flung down the spade and sighed with relief.

But I recoiled as I saw that I was standing on a barren common, covered with furze. No product of man's handiwork was near me except my truck and spade and the grave of Brimstone Billy, now as lonely as before. I turned toward the water. *On the opposite bank was the cemetery*—with the tomb of the holy women, the thornbush with its rags stirring in the morning breeze, and the broken mud wall. The ruined chapel was there too, not a stone shaken from its crumbling walls, not a sign to show that it and its precinct were less rooted in their place than the eternal hills around!

I looked down at the grave with a pang of compassion for the unfortunate Wolf Tone Fitzgerald, with whom the blessed would not rest. I was even astonished, though I had worked expressly to this end. But the birds were astir, and the cocks crowing. My landlord was an early riser. I put the spade on the truck again and hastened back to the farm, where I replaced them in the cowhouse. Then I stole into the house, and took a clean pair of boots, an overcoat, and a silk hat. These, with a change of linen, were sufficient to make my appearance respectable. I went out again, bathed in the Four Mile Water, took a last look at the cemetery back in its original site, and walked to Wicklow, whence I traveled by the first train to Dublin.

Some months later, at Cairo, I received a packet of Irish newspapers, and a leading article, cut from *The Times*, on the subject of the miracle. Father Hickey had suffered the meed of his inhospitable conduct. The committee, arriving at Four Mile Water the day after I left, had found the graveyard exactly where it had formerly stood. Father Hickey, taken by surprise, had attempted to defend himself by a confused statement, which led the committee to declare finally that the miracle was a gross imposture. *The Times*, commenting on this after adducing a number of examples of priestly craft, remarked, "We are glad to learn that the Rev. Mr. Hickey has been permanently relieved of his duties as the parish priest of Four Mile Water by his ecclesiastical superior. It is less gratifying to have to record that it has been found possible to obtain two hundred signatures to a memorial embodying the absurd defense offered to the committee, and expressing unabated confidence in the integrity of Mr. Hickey."

THE WILLOW WALK

BY SINCLAIR LEWIS

Sinclair Lewis was the son of a Minnesota doctor. He started college at Oberlin and transferred to Yale. He published his first novel, *Hike and the Aeroplane*, a story for boys, in 1912. After publishing *Main Street* (1920) and *Babbitt* (1922) he won the Pulitzer Prize for *Arrowsmith* (1925), which he refused on the grounds that the prize was awarded for the best presentation of "the wholesome atmosphere of American life," not literary merit. He was the first American to win the Nobel Prize for Literature.

FROM THE DRAWER OF HIS TABLE Jasper Holt took a pane of window glass. He laid a sheet of paper on the glass and wrote, "Now is the time for all good men to come to the aid of their party."

He studied his round business-college script and rewrote the sentence in a small finicky hand, that of a studious old man. Ten times he copied the words in that false pinched writing. He tore up the paper, burned the fragments in his large ashtray, and washed the delicate ashes down his stationary washbowl. He replaced the pane of glass in the drawer, tapping it with satisfaction. A glass underlay does not retain an impression.

Jasper Holt was as nearly respectable as his room, which, with its frilled chairs and pansy-painted pincushion, was the best in the aristocratic boarding house of Mrs. Lyons. He was a wiry, slightly bald, black-haired man of thirty-eight, wearing an easy gray flannel suit and a white carnation. His hands were peculiarly compact and nimble. He gave the appearance of being a youngish lawyer or bond salesman. Actually he was senior paying teller in the Lumber National Bank in the city of Vernon.

He looked at a thin expensive gold watch. It was six thirty, on Wednesday—toward dusk of a tranquil spring day. He picked up his hooked walking stick and his gray silk gloves and trudged downstairs. He met his landlady in the lower hall and inclined his head. She effusively commented on the weather.

"I shall not be here for dinner," he said amiably.

"Very well, Mr. Holt. My, but aren't you always going out with your swell friends though! I read in the *Herald* that you were going to be a star in another of those society plays in the Community Theater. I guess you'd be an actor if you wasn't a banker, Mr. Holt."

"No, I'm afraid I haven't much temperament." His voice was cordial, but his smile was a mere mechanical sidewise twist of the lip muscles. "You're the one that's got the stage presence. Bet you'd be a regular Ethel Barrymore if you didn't have to take care of us."

"My, but you're such a flatterer!"

He bowed his way out and walked sedately down the street to a public garage. Nodding to the night attendant, but saying nothing, he started his roadster and drove out of the garage, away from the center of Vernon, toward the suburb of Rosebank.

He did not go directly to Rosebank. He went seven blocks out of his way and halted on Fandall Avenue—one of those petty main thoroughfares which, with their motion picture palaces, their groceries, laundries, undertakers' establishments and lunchrooms, serve as local centers for districts of mean residences.

He got out of the car and pretended to look at the tires, kicking them to see how much air they had. While he did so he covertly looked up and down the street. He saw no one whom he knew. He went into the Parthenon Confectionery Store.

The Parthenon Store makes a specialty of those ingenious candy boxes that resemble bound books. The back of the box is of imitation leather, with a stamping simulating the title of a novel. The edges are apparently the edges of a number of pages. But these pages are hollowed out, and the inside is to be filled with candy. Jasper gazed at the collection of book boxes and chose the two whose titles had the nearest approach to dignity—*Sweets to the Sweet* and *The Ladies' Delight*. He asked the clerk to fill these with the less expensive grade of mixed chocolates, and to wrap them.

From the candy shop he went to the drug store that carried an assortment of reprinted novels, and from these picked out two of the same sentimental type as the titles on the booklike boxes. These also he had wrapped.

He strolled out of the drug store, slipped into a lunchroom, got a lettuce sandwich, doughnuts, and a cup of coffee at the greasy marble counter, took them to a chair with a table arm in the dim rear of the lunchroom and hastily devoured them. As he came out and returned to his car he again glanced along the street.

He fancied that he knew a man who was approaching. He could not be sure. From the breast up, the man seemed familiar, as did the customers of the bank whom he viewed through the wicket of the teller's window. When he saw them in the street he could never be sure of them. It seemed extraordinary to find that these persons, who to him were nothing but faces with attached arms that held out checks and received money, could walk about, had legs and a gait and a manner of their own.

He walked to the curb and stared up at the cornice of one of the stores, puckering his lips, giving an impersonation of a man inspecting a building. With the corner of an eye he followed the approaching man. The man ducked his head as he neared, and greeted him, "Hello, Brother Teller." Jasper seemed startled, gave the "Oh! Oh, how are you!" of sudden recognition, and mumbled, "Looking after a little bank property."

The man passed on.

Jasper got into his car and drove back to the street that would take him out to the suburb of Rosebank. As he left Fandall Avenue he peered at his watch. It was five minutes to seven.

At a quarter past seven he passed through the main street of Rosebank and turned into a lane that was but little changed since the time when it had been a country road. A few jerry-built villas of freckled paint did shoulder on it, but for the most part it ran through swamps spotted with willow groves, the spongy ground covered with scatterings of dry leaves and bark. Opening on this lane was a dim-rutted grassy private road which disappeared into one of the willow groves.

Jasper sharply swung his car between the crumbly gateposts and along the bumpy private road. He made an abrupt turn, came in sight of an unpainted shed, and shot the car into it without cutting down his speed, so that he almost hit the back of the shed with his front fenders.

He shut off the engine, climbed out quickly and ran back toward the gate. From the shield of the bank of alder bushes he peered out. Two clattering women were going down the public road. They stared in through the gate and half halted.

"That's where that hermit lives," said one of them.

"Oh, you mean the one that's writing a religious book and never comes out till evening? Some kind of a preacher?"

"Yes, that's the one. John Holt, I think his name is. I guess he's kind of crazy. He lives in the old Beaudette house. But you can't see it from here—it's clear through the block, on the next street."

"I heard he was crazy. But I just saw an automobile go in here."

"Oh, that's his cousin or brother or something—lives in the city. They say he's rich, and such a nice fellow."

The two women ambled on, their clatter blurring with distance. Standing behind the alders Jasper rubbed the palm of one hand with the fingers of the other. The palm was dry with nervousness. But he grinned.

He returned to the shed and entered a brick-paved walk almost a block long, walled and sheltered by overhanging willows. Once it had been a pleasant path; carved wooden benches were placed along it, and it widened to a court with a rock garden, a fountain, and a stone bench.

The rock garden had degenerated into a riot of creepers sprawling over the sharp stones; the paint had peeled from the fountain, leaving its iron cupids and naiads eaten with rust. The bricks of the wall were smeared with lichens and moss and were untidy with windrows of dry leaves and caked earth. Many of the bricks were

50

broken; the walk was hilly in its unevenness. From willows and bricks and scuffled earth rose a damp chill.

But Jasper did not seem to note the dampness. He hastened along the walk to the house—a structure of heavy stone which, for this newish Midwestern land, was very ancient. It had been built by a French fur trader in 1839. The Chippewas had scalped a man in its dooryard. The heavy back door was guarded by an unexpected expensive modern lock.

Jasper opened it with a flat key and closed it behind him. It locked on a spring. He was in a crude kitchen, the shades of which were drawn. He passed through the kitchen and dining room into the living room. Dodging chairs and tables in the darkness as though he was used to them he went to each of the three windows of the living room and made sure that all the shades were down before he lighted the student lamp on the gate-legged table. As the glow crept over the drab walls Jasper bobbed his head with satisfaction. Nothing had been touched since his last visit.

The room was musty with the smell of old green rep upholstery and leather books. It had not been dusted for months. Dust sheeted the stiff red velvet chairs, the uncomfortable settee, the chill white marble fireplace, the immense glass-fronted bookcase that filled one side of the room.

The atmosphere was unnatural to this capable business man, this Jasper Holt. But Jasper did not seem oppressed. He briskly removed the wrappers from the genuine books and from the candy-box imitations of books. One of the two wrappers he laid on the table and smoothed out. Upon this he poured the candy from the two boxes. The other wrapper and the strings he stuffed into the fireplace and immediately burned.

Crossing to the bookcase he unlocked one section on the bottom shelf. There was a row of rather cheap-looking novels on this shelf, and of these at least six were actually such candy boxes as he had purchased that evening.

Only one shelf of the bookcase was given over to anything so frivolous as novels. The others were filled with black-covered, speckle-leaved, dismal books of history, theology, biography—the shabby-genteel sort of books you find on the fifteen-cent table at a secondhand bookshop. Over these Jasper pored for a moment as though he was memorizing their titles.

He took down *The Life of the Rev. Jeremiah Bodfish* and read aloud: "In those intimate discourses with his family that followed evening prayers I once heard Brother Bodfish observe that Philo Judaeus—whose scholarly career always calls to my mind the ad-

51

umbrations of Melanchthon upon the essence of rationalism—
were a mere sophist—"

Jasper slammed the book shut, remarking contentedly, "That'll
do. Philo Judaeus—good name to spring."

He relocked the bookcase and went upstairs. In a small bedroom
at the right of the upper hall an electric light was burning. Presumably the house had been deserted till Jasper's entrance, but a
prowler in the yard might have judged from this ever-burning light
that someone was in the residence.

The bedroom was Spartan—an iron bed, one straight chair, a
washstand, a heavy oak bureau. Jasper scrambled to unlock the
bottom drawer of the bureau, yank it open, take out a wrinkled
shiny suit of black, a pair of black shoes, a small black bow tie, a
Gladstone collar, a white shirt with starched bosom, a speckly
brown felt hat and a wig—an expensive and excellent wig with
artfully unkempt hair of a faded brown.

He stripped off his attractive flannel suit, wing collar, blue tie,
custom-made silk shirt, and cordovan shoes, and speedily put on
the wig and those gloomy garments. As he donned them the
corners of his mouth began to droop. Leaving the light on and his
own clothes flung on the bed he descended the stairs. He was
obviously not the same Jasper, but less healthy, less practical, less
agreeable, and decidedly more aware of the sorrow and long
thoughts of the dreamer.

Indeed it must be understood that now he was not Jasper Holt,
but Jasper's twin brother, John Holt, hermit and religious fanatic.

John Holt, twin brother of Jasper Holt the bank teller, rubbed
his eyes as though he had for hours been absorbed in study, and
crawled through the living room, through the tiny hall, to the front
door. He opened it, picked up a couple of circulars that the post-
man had dropped through the letter slot in the door, went out and
locked the door behind him. He was facing a narrow front yard,
neater than the willow walk at the back, on a suburban street more
populous than the straggly back lane.

A street arc illuminated the yard and showed that a card was
tacked on the door. John touched the card, snapped it with a nail of
his finger to make sure it was securely tacked. In that light he could
not read it, but he knew that it was inscribed in a small finicky hand:
*Agents kindly do not disturb, bell will not be answered, occupant of the house
engaged in literary work.*

John stood on the doorstep until he made out his neighbor on
the right—a large stolid commuter who was walking before his

house smoking an after-dinner cigar. John poked to the fence and sniffed at a spray of lilac blossoms till the neighbor called over, "Nice evening."

"Yes, it seems to be pleasant."

John's voice was like Jasper's but it was more guttural, and his speech had less assurance.

"How's the story going?"

"It is—it is very difficult. So hard to comprehend all the inner meanings of the prophecies. Well, I must be hastening to Soul Hope Hall. I trust we shall see you there some Wednesday or Sunday evening. I bid you good night, sir."

John wavered down the street to the drug store. He purchased a bottle of ink. In a grocery that kept open evenings he got two pounds of cornmeal, two pounds of flour, pound of bacon, a half pound of butter, six eggs, and a can of condensed milk.

"Shall we deliver them?" asked the clerk.

John looked at him sharply. He realized that this was a new man, who did not know his customs. He said rebukingly, "No, I always carry my parcels. I am writing a book. I am never to be disturbed."

He paid for the provisions out of a postal money order for thirty-five dollars and received the change. The cashier of the store was accustomed to cashing these money orders, which were always sent to John from South Vernon, by one R. J. Smith. John took the bundle of food and walked out of the store.

"That fellow's kind of a nut, isn't he?" asked the new clerk.

The cashier explained: "Yep. Doesn't even take fresh milk—uses condensed for everything! What do you think of that! And they say he burns up all his garbage—never has anything in the ashcan except ashes. If you knock at his door he never answers it, fellow told me. All the time writing this book of his. Religious crank, I guess. Has a little income though—guess his folks were pretty well fixed. Comes out once in a while in the evening and pokes round town. We used to laugh about him, but we've kind of got used to him. Been here about a year, I guess it is."

John was serenely passing down the main street of Rosebank. At the dingier end of it he turned in at a hallway marked by a lighted sign announcing in crude housepainter's letters: SOUL HOPE FRATERNITY HALL. EXPERIENCE MEETING. ALL WELCOME.

It was eight o'clock. The members of the Soul Hope cult had gathered in their hall above a bakery. Theirs was a tiny, tight-minded sect. They asserted that they alone obeyed the scriptural tenets, that they alone were certain to be saved, that all other denominations were damned by unapostolic luxury, that it was

53

wicked to have organs or ministers or any meeting places save plain halls.

The members themselves conducted the meetings, one after another rising to give an interpretation of the scriptures or to rejoice in gathering with the faithful, while the others commenced with "Hallelujah!" and "Amen, brother, amen!" They were plainly dressed, not overfed, somewhat elderly, and a rather happy congregation. The most honored was John Holt.

John had come to Rosebank only eleven months before. He had bought the Beaudette house with the library of the recent occupant, a retired clergyman, and had paid for them in new one-hundred-dollar bills. Already he had great credit in the Soul Hope cult. It appeared that he spent almost all his time at home, praying and reading and writing a book.

The Soul Hope Fraternity were excited about the book. They had begged him to read it to them. So far he had only read a few pages, consisting mostly of quotations from ancient treatises on the Prophecies. Nearly every Sunday and Wednesday evening he appeared at the meeting and in a halting and scholarly way lectured on the world and the flesh.

Tonight he spoke polysyllabically of the fact that one Philo Judaeus had been a mere sophist. The cult were none too clear as to what either a Philo Judaeus or a sophist might be, but with heads all nodding in a row they murmured, "You're right, brother! Hallelujah!"

John glided into a sad earnest discourse on his worldly brother Jasper, and informed them of his struggles with Jasper's itch for money. By his request the fraternity prayed for Jasper.

The meeting was over at nine. John shook hands all round with the elders of the congregation, sighing, "Fine meeting tonight, wasn't it? Such a free outpouring of the Spirit!" He welcomed a new member, a servant girl just come from Seattle. Carrying his groceries and the bottle of ink he poked down the stairs from the hall at seven minutes after nine.

At sixteen minutes after nine John was stripping off his brown wig and the funereal clothes in his bedroom. At twenty-eight after, John Holt had become Jasper Holt, the capable teller of the Lumber National Bank.

Jasper Holt left the light burning in his brother's bedroom. He rushed downstairs, tried the fastening of the front door, bolted it, made sure that all the windows were fastened, picked up the bundle of groceries and the pile of candies that he had removed from the booklike candy boxes, blew out the light in the living room

54

and ran down the willow walk to his car. He threw the groceries and candy into it, backed the car out as though he was accustomed to backing in this bough-scattered yard, and drove along the lonely road at the rear.

When he was passing a swamp he reached down, picked up the bundle of candies, and steering with one hand removed the wrapping paper with the other hand and hurled out the candies. They showered among the weeds beside the road. The paper which had contained the candies, and upon which was printed the name of the Parthenon Confectionery Store, Jasper tucked into his pocket. He took the groceries item by item from the labeled bag containing them, thrust that bag also into his pocket, and laid the groceries on the seat beside him.

On the way from Rosebank to the center of the city of Vernon he again turned off the main avenue and halted at a goat-infested shack occupied by a crippled Norwegian. He sounded the horn. The Norwegian's grandson ran out.

"Here's a little more grub for you," bawled Jasper.

"God bless you, sir. I don't know what we'd do if it wasn't for you!" cried the old Norwegian from the door.

But Jasper did not wait for gratitude. He merely shouted, "Bring you some more in a couple of days," as he started away.

At a quarter past ten he drove up to the hall that housed the latest interest in Vernon society—The Community Theater. The Boulevard Set, the "best people in town," belonged to the Community Theater Association, and the leader of it was the daughter of the general manager of the railroad. As a wellbred bachelor Jasper Holt was welcome among them, despite the fact that no one knew much about him except that he was a good bank teller and had been born in England.

But as an actor he was not merely welcome: he was the best amateur actor in Vernon. His placid face could narrow with tragic emotion or puff out with comedy, his placid manner concealed a dynamo of emotion. Unlike most amateur actors he did not try to act—he became the thing itself. He forgot Jasper Holt and turned into a vagrant or a judge, a Bernard Shaw thought, a Lord Dunsany symbol, a Noel Coward man-about-town.

The other one-act plays of the next program of the Community Theater had already been rehearsed. The cast of the play in which Jasper was to star were all waiting for him. So were the ladies responsible for the staging. They wanted his advice about the blue curtain for the stage window, about the baby-spot that was out of order, about the higher interpretation of the role of the page in the piece—a role consisting of only two lines, but to be played by one of the most popular girls in the younger set.

After the discussions, and a most violent quarrel between two members of the play-reading committee, the rehearsal was called. Jasper Holt still wore his flannel suit and a wilting carnation; but he was not Jasper; he was the Duc de San Saba, a cynical, gracious, gorgeous old man, easy of gesture, tranquil of voice, shudderingly evil of desire.

"If I could get a few more actors like you!" cried the professional coach.

The rehearsal was over at half-past eleven. Jasper drove his car to the public garage in which he kept it and walked home. There he tore up and burned the wrapping paper bearing the name of the Parthenon Confectionery Store and the labeled bag that had contained the groceries.

The Community Theater plays were given on the following Wednesday. Jasper Holt was highly applauded, and at the party at the Lakeside Country Club, after the play, he danced with the prettiest girls in town. He hadn't much to say to them, but he danced fervently, and about him was a halo of artistic success.

That night his brother John did not appear at the meeting of the Soul Hope Fraternity out in Rosebank.

On Monday, five days later, while he was in conference with the president and the cashier of the Lumber National Bank, Jasper complained of a headache. The next day he telephoned to the president that he would not come down to work—he would stay home and rest his eyes, sleep and get rid of the persistent headache. That was unfortunate, for that very day his twin brother John made one of his frequent trips into Vernon and called at the bank.

The president had seen John only once before, and by a coincidence it had happened on this occasion also that Jasper had been absent—had been out of town. The president invited John into his private office.

"Your brother is at home—poor fellow has a bad headache. Hope he gets over it. We think a great deal of him here. Will you have a smoke?"

As he spoke the president looked John over. Once or twice when Jasper and the president had been out at lunch, Jasper had spoken of the remarkable resemblance between himself and his twin brother. But the president told himself that he didn't really see much resemblance. The features of the two were alike, but John's expression of chronic spiritual indigestion, his unfriendly manner, and his hair—unkempt and lifeless brown, where Jasper's was

56

sleekly black about a shiny bald spot—made the president dislike John as much as he liked Jasper.

And now John was replying, "No, I do not smoke. I can't understand how a man can soil the temple with drugs. I suppose I ought to be glad to hear you praise poor Jasper, but I am more concerned with his lack of respect for the things of the spirit. He sometimes comes to see me at Rosebank and I argue with him, but somehow I can't make him see his errors. And his flippant ways—!"

"We don't think he's flippant. We think he's a pretty steady worker."

"But he's play-acting! And reading love stories! Well, I try to keep in mind the injunction, 'Judge not, that ye be not judged.' But I am pained to find my own brother giving up immortal promises for mortal amusements. Well, I'll go and call on him. I trust that some day we shall see you at Soul Hope Hall in Rosebank. Good day, sir."

Turning back to his work, the president grumbled, "I am going to tell Jasper that the best compliment I can hand him is that he is not like his brother."

And on the following day, another Wednesday, when Jasper reappeared at the bank, the president did make this jesting comparison, and Jasper sighed, "Oh, John is really a good fellow, but he's always gone in for metaphysics and Oriental mysticism and Lord knows what, till he's kind of lost in the fog. But he's a lot better than I am. When I murder my landlady—or say, when I rob the bank, Chief—you go get John, and I bet you the best lunch in town that he'll do his best to bring me to justice. That's how square he is!"

"Square, yes—corners just sticking out! Well, when you do rob us, Jasper, I'll look up John. But try to keep from robbing us as long as you can. I'd hate to have to associate with a religious detective in a boiled shirt!"

Both men laughed, and Jasper went back to his cage. His head continued to hurt, he admitted. The president advised him to lay off for a week. He didn't want to, he said. With the new munition industries due to the war in Europe there was much increase in factory pay rolls, and Jasper took charge of them.

"Better take a week off than get ill," argued the president late that afternoon.

Jasper did let himself be persuaded to go away for at least a week-end. He would run up north to Wakamin Lake the coming Friday, he said; he would get in some black-bass fishing, and be back on Monday or Tuesday.

Before he went he would make up the pay rolls for the Saturday payments and turn them over to the other teller. The president thanked him for his faithfulness, and as was his not infrequent custom, invited Jasper to his house for the evening of the next day—Thursday.

That Wednesday evening Jasper's brother John appeared at the Soul Hope meeting in Rosebank. When he had gone home and magically turned back into Jasper, this Jasper did not return the wig and garments of John to the bureau but packed them in a suitcase, took the suitcase to his room in Vernon and locked it in his wardrobe.

Jasper was amiable at dinner at the president's house on Thursday, but he was rather silent, and as his head still throbbed he left the house early—at nine thirty. Sedately carrying his gray silk gloves in one hand and pompously swinging his stick with the other, he walked from the president's house on the fashionable boulevard back to the center of Vernon. He entered the public garage in which he stored his car. He commented to the night attendant, "Head aches. Guess I'll take the 'bus out and get some fresh air."

He drove away at not more than twenty-five miles an hour, heading south. When he had reached the outskirts of the city he speeded up to a consistent thirty-five miles an hour. He settled down in his seat with the unmoving steadiness of the long-distance driver, his body quiet except for the tiny subtle movements of his foot on the accelerator, of his hand on the steering wheel—his right hand across the wheel, holding it at the top, his left elbow resting easily on the cushioned edge of his seat and his left hand merely touching the wheel.

He drove down in that southern direction for fifteen miles—almost to the town of Wanagoochie. Then by a rather poor side road he turned sharply to the north and west, and making a huge circle about the city drove toward the town of St. Clair. The suburb of Rosebank, in which his brother John lived, is also north of Vernon. These directions were of some importance to him; Wanagoochie eighteen miles south of the mother city of Vernon; Rosebank, on the other hand, eight miles north of Vernon, and St. Clair twenty miles north—about as far north of Vernon as Wanagoochie is south.

On his way to St. Clair, at a point that was only two miles from Rosebank, Jasper ran the car off the main road into a grove of oaks and maples and stopped it on a long-unused woodland road. He stiffly got out and walked through the woods up a rise of ground to a cliff overlooking a swampy lake. The gravelly farther bank of the cliff rose perpendicularly from the edge of the water.

In that wan light distilled by stars and the earth he made out the reedy expanse of the lake. It was so muddy, so tangled with sedge grass that it was never used for swimming, and as its inhabitants were only slimy bullheads, few people ever tried to fish there. Jasper stood reflective. He was remembering the story of the farmer's team which had run away, dashed over this cliff, and sunk out of sight in the mud bottom of the lake.

Swishing his stick he outlined an imaginary road from the top of the cliff back to the sheltered place where his car was standing. Once he hacked away with a large pocketknife a mass of knotted hazel bushes which blocked that projected road. When he had traced the road to his car he smiled.

He walked to the edge of the woods and looked up and down the main highway. A car was approaching. He waited till it had passed, ran back to his own car, backed it out on the highway, and went on his northward course toward St. Clair, driving about thirty-five miles an hour.

On the edge of St. Clair he halted, took out his kit of tools, unscrewed a spark plug, and sharply tapping the plug on the engine block, deliberately cracked the porcelain jacket. He screwed the plug in again and started the car. It bucked and spit, missing on one cylinder, with the short-circuited plug.

"I guess there must be something wrong with the ignition," he said cheerfully.

He managed to run the car into a garage in St. Clair. There was no one in the garage save the night washer who was busy over a limousine with sponge and hose.

"Got a night repair man here?" asked Jasper.

"No, sir; guess you'll have to leave it till morning."

"Hang it! Something gone wrong with the carburetor or the ignition. Well, I'll have to leave it then. Tell him—say, will you be here in the morning when the repair man comes on?"

"Yes, sir."

"Well, tell him I must have the car by tomorrow noon. No, say by tomorrow at nine. Now, don't forget. This will help your memory."

He gave a quarter to the man who grinned and as he tied a storage tag on the car inquired, "Name?"

"Uh—my name? Oh, Hanson. Remember now, ready about nine tomorrow."

Jasper walked to the railroad station. It was ten minutes of one. Jasper did not ask about the next train into Vernon. Apparently he

59

knew that there was a train stopping here at St. Clair at 1:37. He did not sit in the waiting room but in the darkness outside, on a truck behind the baggage room.

When the train came in he slipped into the last seat of the last car, and with his soft hat over his eyes either slept or appeared to sleep. When he reached Vernon he got off and came to the garage in which he regularly kept his car. He stepped inside. The night attendant was drowsing in a large wooden chair tilted back against the wall in the narrow runway which formed the entrance to the garage.

Jasper jovially shouted to the attendant, "Certainly ran into some hard luck. Ignition went wrong—I guess it was the ignition. Had to leave the car down at Wanagoochie."

"Yuh, hard luck, all right," assented the attendant.

"Yump. So I left it at Wanagoochie," Jasper emphasized as he passed on.

He had been inexact in this statement. It was not at Wanagoochie, which is south, but at St. Clair, which is north, that he had left his car.

He returned to his boarding house, slept beautifully, hummed in his morning shower bath. Yet at breakfast he complained of his continuous headache and announced that he was going up north to Wakamin to get in some bass fishing and rest his eyes. His landlady urged him to go.

"Anything I can do to help you get away!" she queried.

"No, thanks. I'm just taking a couple of suitcases, with some old clothes and some fishing tackle. Fact, I have 'em all packed already. I'll probably take the noon train north if I can get away from the bank. Pretty busy now, with these pay rolls for the factories that have war contracts for the Allies. What's it say in the paper this morning?"

Jasper arrived at the bank, carrying the two suitcases and a neat, polite, rolled silk umbrella, the silver top of which was engraved with his name. The doorman, who was also the bank guard, helped him to carry the suitcases inside.

"Careful of that bag. Got my fishing tackle in it," said Jasper to the doorman, apropos of one of the suitcases which was heavy but apparently not packed full. "Well, I think I'll run up to Wakamin today and catch a few bass."

"Wish I could go along, sir. How is the head this morning? Does it still ache?" asked the doorman.

"Rather better, but my eyes still feel pretty rocky. Guess I've been using them too much. Say, Connors, I'll try to catch the train north at eleven-seven. Better have a taxicab here for me at eleven. Or no; I'll let you know a little before eleven. Try to catch the eleven-seven north, for Wakamin."

"Very well, sir."

The president, the cashier, the chief clerk—all asked Jasper how he felt; and to all of them he repeated the statements that he had been using his eyes too much and that he would catch a few bass at Wakamin.

The other paying teller, from his cage next to that of Jasper, called heartily through the steel netting, "Pretty soft for some people! You wait, I'm going to have hay fever this summer and I'll go fishing for a month!" .

Jasper placed the two suitcases and the umbrella in his cage, and leaving the other teller to pay out current money he himself made up the pay rolls for the next day—Saturday. He casually went into the vault—a narrow, unimpressive, unaired cell with a hard linoleum floor, one unshaded electric bulb, and a back wall composed entirely of steel doors of safes, all painted a sickly blue, very unimpressive, but guarding several millions of dollars in cash and securities. The upper doors, hung on large steel arms and each provided with two dials, could be opened only by two officers of the bank, each knowing one of the two combinations. Below these were smaller doors, one of which Jasper could open, as teller. It was the door of an insignificant steel box, which contained $117,000 in bills and $4000 in gold and silver.

Jasper passed back and forth, carrying bundles of currency. In his cage he was working less than three feet from the other teller. Mechanically, unobtrusively, Jasper counted out bills to amounts agreeing with the items on a typed schedule of the pay rolls. Apparently his eyes never lifted from his counting and from the typed schedule which lay before him. The bundles of bills he made into packages, fastening each with a paper band. Each bundle he seemed to drop into a small black leather bag which he held beside him. But he did not actually drop the money into these pay-roll bags.

Both the suitcases at his feet were closed and presumably fastened, but one was not fastened. And though it was heavy it contained nothing but a lump of pig iron. From time to time Jasper's hand, holding a bundle of bills, dropped to his side. With a slight movement of his foot he opened that suitcase and the bills slipped from his hand down into it.

The bottom part of the cage was a solid sheet of stamped steel and from the front of the bank no one could see this suspicious

61

gesture. The other teller could have seen it, but Jasper dropped the bills only when the other teller was busy talking to a customer or when his back was turned. In order to delay for such a favorable moment Jasper frequently counted packages of bills twice, rubbing his eyes as though they hurt him.

After each of these secret disposals of packages of bills Jasper made much of dropping into the pay-roll bags the rolls of coin for which the schedule called. It was while he was tossing these blue-wrapped cylinders of coin into the bags that he would chat with the other teller. Then he would lock up the bags and gravely place them at one side.

Jasper was so slow in making up the pay rolls that it was five minutes to eleven before he finished. He called the doorman to the cage and suggested, "Better call my taxi now."

He still had one bag to fill. He could plainly be seen dropping packages of money into it, while he instructed the assistant teller, "I'll stick all the bags in my safe and you can transfer them to yours. Be sure to lock my safe. Lord, I better hurry or I'll miss my train! Be back Tuesday morning, at latest. So long; take care of yourself."

He hastened to pile the pay-roll bags into his safe in the vault. The safe was almost filled with them. And except for the last one not one of the bags contained anything except a few rolls of coin. Though he had told the other teller to lock his safe, he himself twirled the combination—which was thoughtless of him, as the assistant teller would now have to wait and get the president to unlock it.

He picked up his umbrella and two suitcases, bending over one of the cases for not more than ten seconds. Waving goodbye to the cashier at his desk down front and hurrying so fast that the door-man did not have a chance to help him carry the suitcases, he rushed through the bank, through the door, into the waiting taxicab, and loudly enough for the doorman to hear he cried to the driver, "M. & D. Station."

At the M. &. R.R. Station, refusing offers of redcaps to carry his bags, he bought a ticket for Wakamin, which is a lake resort town one hundred and forty miles northwest of Vernon, hence one hundred and twenty beyond St. Clair. He had just time to get aboard the eleven-seven train. He did not take a Pullman chair, but sat in a day coach near the rear door. He unscrewed the silver top of his umbrella, on which was engraved his name, and dropped it into his pocket.

When the train reached St. Clair, Jasper strolled out to the vestibule, carrying the suitcases but leaving the topless umbrella behind. His face was blank, uninterested. As the train started he dropped down on the station platform and gravely walked away. For a second the light of adventure crossed his face, and vanished.

At the garage at which he had left his car the evening before he asked, "Did you get my car fixed—Mercury roadster, ignition on the bum?"

"Nope! Couple of jobs ahead of it. Haven't had time to touch it yet. Ought to get at it early this afternoon."

Jasper curled his tongue round his lips in startled vexation. He dropped his suitcases on the floor of the garage and stood thinking, his bent forefinger against his lower lip.

Then: "Well, I guess I can get her to go—sorry—can't wait—got to make the next town," he grumbled.

"Lot of you traveling salesmen making our territory by motor now, Mr. Hanson," said the foreman civilly, glancing at the storage check on Jasper's car.

"Yep. I can make a good many more than I could by train."

He paid for overnight storage without complaining, though since his car had not been repaired this charge was unjust. In fact, he was altogether prosaic and inconspicuous. He thrust the suitcases into the car and drove away, the motor spitting. At another garage he bought another spark plug and screwed it in. When he went on, the motor had ceased spitting.

He drove out of St. Clair, back in the direction of Vernon—and of Rosebank where his "brother" lived. He ran the car into that thick grove of oaks and maples only two miles from Rosebank, where he had paced off an imaginary road to the cliff overhanging the reedy lake.

He parked his car in a grassy space beside the abandoned woodland road. He laid a light robe over the suitcases. From beneath the seat he took a can of deviled chicken, a box of biscuits, a canister of tea, a folding cooking kit and a spirit lamp. These he spread on the grass—a picnic lunch.

He sat beside that lunch from seven minutes past one in the afternoon till dark. Once in a while he made a pretense of eating. He fetched water from the brook, made tea, opened the box of biscuits and the can of chicken. But mostly he sat still and smoked cigarette after cigarette.

At dusk Jasper finished a cigarette down to the tip, crushed out the light, and made the cryptic remark: "That's probably Jasper Holt's last smoke. I don't suppose you can smoke, John—damn you!"

He hid the two suitcases in the bushes, piled the remains of the

63

lunch into the car, took down the top of the car, and crept down to the main road. No one was in sight. He returned. He snatched a hammer and a chisel from his tool kit and with a few savage cracks so defaced the number of the car stamped on the engine block that it could not be made out.

He removed the license plates and placed them beside the suitcases. Then, when there was just enough light to see the bushes as cloudy masses, he started the car, drove through the woods and up the incline to the top of the cliff, and halted, leaving the engine running.

Between the car and the edge of the cliff which overhung the lake there was a space of about one hundred and thirty feet, fairly level and covered with straggly red clover. Jasper paced off this distance, returned to the car, took his seat in a nervous, tentative way, and put her into gear, starting on second speed and slamming her into third.

The car bolted toward the edge of the cliff. He instantly swung out on the running board. Standing there, headed directly toward the sharp drop over the cliff, steering with his left hand on the wheel, he shoved the hand throttle up—up—up with his right. He safely leaped down from the running board.

Of itself, the car rushed forward, roaring. It shot over the edge of the cliff. It soared twenty feet out into the air. It turned over and over, with a sickening drop toward the lake. The water splashed up in a tremendous noisy circle. Then silence.

In the twilight the surface of the lake shone like milk. There was no sign of the car on the surface. The concentric rings died away. The lake was secret and sinister and still. "Lord!" ejaculated Jasper, standing on the cliff; then: "Well, they won't find that for a couple of years anyway."

He turned to the suitcases. Squatting beside them he took from one the wig and black garments of John Holt. He stripped, put on the clothes of John, and packed those of Jasper in the bag. With the cases and the license plates he walked toward Rosebank, keeping in various groves of maples and willows till he was within half a mile of the town.

He reached the stone house at the end of the willow walk and sneaked in the back way. He burned Jasper Holt's clothes in the grate, melted down the license plates in the stove, and between two rocks he smashed Jasper's watch and fountain pen into an unpleasant mass of junk, which he dropped into the cistern for rain water. The silver head of the umbrella he scratched with a chisel till the engraved name was indistinguishable.

He unlocked a section of the bookcase and taking a number of packages of bills in denominations of one, five, ten, and twenty dollars from one of the suitcases he packed them into those empty candy boxes which, on the shelves, looked so much like books. As he stored them he counted the bills. They came to $97,535.

The two suitcases were new. There were no distinguishing marks on them. But taking them out to the kitchen he kicked them, rubbed them with lumps of blacking, raveled their edges, and cut their sides, till they gave the appearance of having been long and badly used in traveling. He took them upstairs and tossed them up into the low attic.

In his bedroom he undressed calmly. Once he laughed: "I despise those pretentious fools—bank officers and cops. I'm beyond their fool law. No one can catch me—it would take me myself to do that!"

He got into bed. With a vexed "Hang it!" he mused, "I suppose John would pray, no matter how chilly the floor was."

He got out of bed and from the inscrutable Lord of the Universe he sought forgiveness—not for Jasper Holt, but for the denominations that lacked the true faith of Soul Hope Fraternity.

He returned to bed and slept till the middle of the morning, lying with his arms behind his head, a smile on his face.

Thus did Jasper Holt, without the mysterious pangs of death, yet cease to exist, and thus did John Holt come into being not merely as an apparition glimpsed on Sunday and Wednesday evenings but as a being living twenty-four hours a day, seven days a week.

The inhabitants of Rosebank were familiar with the occasional appearances of John Holt, the eccentric recluse, and they merely snickered about him when on the Saturday evening following the Friday that has been chronicled he was seen to come out of his gate and trudge down to a news and stationery shop on Main Street.

He purchased an evening paper and said to the clerk, "You can have the *Morning Herald* delivered at my house every morning—27 Humbert Avenue."

"Yuh, I know where it is. Thought you had kind of a grouch on newspapers," said the clerk pertly.

"Ah, did you indeed? The *Herald*, every morning, please. I will pay a month in advance," John Holt replied.

John attended the meeting of the Soul Hope Fraternity the next evening—Sunday—but he was not seen on the streets again for two and a half days.

There was no news of the disappearance of Jasper Holt till the following Wednesday when the whole affair came out in a violent, small-city, front-page story, most excitingly headlined:

PAYING TELLER
SOCIAL FAVORITE—MAKES GETAWAY

The paper stated that Jasper Holt had been missing for four days and that the officers of the bank, after first denying that there was anything wrong with his accounts, had admitted that he was short $100,000, said one report. He had purchased a ticket for Wakamin, this state, on Friday and a trainman, a customer of the bank, had noticed him on the train, but he had apparently never arrived at Wakamin.

A woman asserted that on Friday afternoon she had seen Holt driving an automobile between Vernon and St. Clair. This appearance near St. Clair was supposed to be merely a blind, however. In fact, our able Chief of Police had proof that Holt was not headed north, in the direction of St. Clair, but south, beyond Wanagoochie—probably for Des Moines or St. Louis.

It was definitely known that on the previous day Holt had left his car at Wanagoochie, and with their customary thoroughness and promptness the police were making search at Wanagoochie. The Chief had already communicated with the police in cities to the south and the capture of the man could confidently be expected at any moment. As long as the Chief appointed by our popular Mayor was in power, it went ill with those who gave even the appearance of wrong-doing.

When asked his opinion of the theory that the alleged fugitive had gone north, the Chief declared that of course Holt had started in that direction, with the vain hope of throwing pursuers off the scent, but that he had immediately turned south and picked up his car. Though he would not say so definitely, the Chief let it be known that he was ready to put his hands on the fellow who had hidden Holt's car at Wanagoochie.

When asked if he thought Holt was crazy, the Chief laughed and said, "Yes, he's crazy two hundred thousand dollars' worth. I'm not making any slams, but there's a lot of fellows among our political opponents who would go a whole lot crazier for a whole lot less!"

The president of the bank, however, was greatly distressed and strongly declared his belief that Holt, who was a favorite in the most sumptuous residences on the Boulevard, besides being well known in local dramatic circles, and who bore the best of reputations in the bank, was temporarily out of his mind, as he had been suffering

66

from pains in the head for some time past. Meantime, the bonding company, which had fully covered the employees of the bank by a joint bond of $200,000 had its detectives working with the police on the case.

As soon as he had read the paper John took a trolley into Vernon and called on the president of the bank. John's face drooped with the sorrow of the disgrace. The president received him. John staggered into the room, groaning, "I have just learned in the newspaper of the terrible news about my brother. I have come—"

"We hope it's just a case of aphazia. We're sure he'll turn up all right," insisted the president.

"I wish I could believe it. But as I have told you, Jasper is not a good man. He drinks and smokes and play-acts and makes a god of stylish clothes—"

"Good Lord, that's no reason for jumping to the conclusion that he's an embezzler!"

"I pray you may be right. But meanwhile I wish to give you any assistance I can. I shall make it my sole duty to see that my brother is brought to justice if it proves that he is guilty."

"Good of you," mumbled the president.

Despite this example of John's rigid honor he could not get himself to like the man. John was standing beside him, thrusting his stupid face into his.

The president pushed his chair a foot farther away and said disagreeably, "As a matter of fact, we were thinking of searching your house. If I remember, you live in Rosebank?"

"Yes. And of course I shall be glad to have you search every inch of it. Or anything else I can do. I feel that I share fully with my twin brother in this unspeakable sin. I'll turn over the key of my house to you at once. There is also a shed at the back where Jasper used to keep his automobile when he came to see me." He produced a large, rusty, old-fashioned door key and held it out, adding, "The address is 27 Humbert Avenue, Rosebank."

"Oh, it won't be necessary, I guess," said the president, somewhat shamed, irritably waving off the key.

"But I *want* to help somehow! What can I do? Who is the detective on the case? I'll give him any help—"

"Tell you what you do: go see Mr. Scandling of the Mercantile Trust and Bonding Company and tell him all you know."

"I shall. I take my brother's crime on my shoulders—otherwise I'd be committing the sin of Cain. You are giving me a chance to try to expiate our joint sin, and, as Brother Jeremiah Bodfish was wont to say, it is a blessing to have an opportunity to expiate a sin, no

67

matter how painful the punishment may seem to the mere physical being. As I may have told you I am an accepted member of the Soul Hope Fraternity, and though we are free from cant and dogma it is our firm belief—"

Then for ten dreary minutes John Holt sermonized: quoted forgotten books and quaint, ungenerous elders; twisted bitter pride and clumsy mysticism into a fanatical spider web. The president was a churchgoer, an ardent supporter of missionary funds, for forty years a pew-holder at St. Simeon's Church, but he was alternately bored to a chill shiver and roused to wrath against this self-righteous zealot.

When he had rather rudely got rid of John Holt he complained to himself, "Curse it, I oughtn't to, but I must say I prefer Jasper the sinner to John the saint. Uff! What a smell of damp cellars the fellow has! He must spend all his time picking potatoes. Say! By thunder, I remember that Jasper had the infernal nerve to tell me once that if he ever robbed the bank I was to call John in. I know why now! John is the kind of egotistical fool that would muddle up any kind of a systematic search. Well, Jasper, sorry, but I'm not going to have anything more to do with John than I can help!"

John had gone to the Mercantile Trust and Bonding Company, had called on Mr. Scandling, and was now wearying him by a detailed and useless account of Jasper's early years and recent vices. He was turned over to the detective employed by the bonding company to find Jasper.

The detective was a hard, noisy man, who found John even more tedious. John insisted on his coming out to examine the house in Rosebank and the detective did so—but sketchily, trying to escape. John spent at least five minutes in showing him the shed where Jasper had sometimes kept his car.

He also attempted to interest the detective in his precious but spotty books. He unlocked one section of the case, dragged down a four-volume set of sermons, and started to read them aloud.

The detective interrupted, "Yes, that's great stuff, but I guess we aren't going to find your brother hiding behind those books!"

The detective got away as soon as possible, after explaining to John that if they could use his assistance they would let him know.

"If I can only expiate—"

"Sure, that's all right!" wailed the detective, fairly running toward the gate.

John made one more visit to Vernon that day. He called on the Chief of Police. He informed the Chief that he had taken the bonding company's detective through his house, but wouldn't the police consent to search it also? He wanted to expiate—The Chief patted John on the back, advised him not to feel responsible for his brother's guilt, and begged, "Skip along now—very busy."

As John walked to the Soul Hope meeting that evening dozens of people murmured that it was his brother who had robbed the Lumber National Bank. His head was bowed with the shame.

At the meeting he took Jasper's sin upon himself and prayed that Jasper would be caught and receive the blessed healing of punishment. The others begged John not to feel that he was guilty—was he not one of the Soul Hope brethren who alone in this wicked and perverse generation were assured of salvation?

On Thursday, on Saturday morning, on Tuesday, and on Friday, John went into the city to call on the president of the bank and the detective. Twice the president saw him and was infinitely bored by his sermons. The third time he sent word that he was out. The fourth time he saw John, but curtly explained that if John wanted to help them the best thing he could do was to stay away.

The detective was out all four times.

John smiled meekly and ceased to try to help them. Dust began to gather on certain candy boxes on the lower shelf of his bookcase, save for one of them, which he took out now and then. Always after he had taken it out a man with faded brown hair and a wrinkled black suit, a man signing himself R. J. Smith, would send a fair-sized money order from the post office at South Vernon to John Holt, at Rosebank—as he had been doing for more than six months.

These money orders could not have amounted to more than twenty-five dollars a week, but that was even more than an ascetic like John Holt needed. By day John sometimes cashed these at the Rosebank post office, but usually, as had been his custom, he cashed them at his favorite grocery when he went out in the evening.

In conversation with the commuter neighbor, who every evening walked about and smoked an after dinner cigar in the yard at the right, John was frank about the whole lamentable business of his brother's crime. He wondered, he said, if he had not shut himself up with his studies too much, and neglected his brother. The neighbor ponderously advised John to get out more. John let himself be persuaded, at least to the extent of taking a short walk every afternoon and of letting his literary solitude be disturbed by the delivery of milk, meat, and groceries. He also went to the public library, and in the reference room glanced at books on Central and

69

South America—as though he were planning to go south some day.

But he continued his religious studies. It may be doubted if previous to the embezzlement John had worked very consistently on his book about Revelation. All that the world had ever seen of it was a jumble of quotations from theological authorities. Presumably the crime of his brother shocked him into more concentrated study, more patient writing. For during the year after his brother's disappearance—a year in which the bonding company gradually gave up the search and came to believe that Jasper was dead—John became fanatically absorbed in somewhat nebulous work. The days and nights drifted together in meditation in which he lost sight of realities, and seemed through the clouds of the flesh to see flashes from the towered cities of the spirit.

It has been asserted that when Jasper Holt acted a role he veritably lived it. No one can ever determine how great an actor was lost in the smug bank teller. To him were imperial triumphs denied, yet he was not without material reward. For playing his most subtle part he received $97,000. It may be that he earned it. Certainly for the risk entailed it was but a fair payment, Jasper had meddled with the mystery of personality and was in peril of losing all consistent purpose, of becoming a Wandering Jew of the spirit, a strangled body walking.

The sharp-pointed willow leaves had twisted and fallen, after the dreary rains of October. Bark had peeled from the willow trunks, leaving gashes of bare wood that was a wet and sickly yellow. Through the denuded trees bulked the solid stone of John Holt's house. The patches of earth were greasy between the tawny knots of grass stems. The bricks of the walk were always damp now. The world was hunched up in this pervading chill.

As melancholy as the sick earth seemed the man who in a slaty twilight paced the willow walk. His step was slack, his lips moved with the intensity of his meditation. Over his wrinkled black suit and bleak shirt bosom was a worn overcoat, the velvet collar turned green. He was considering.

"There's something to all this. I begin to see—I don't know what it is I do see! But there are lights—a supernatural world that makes food and bed seem ridiculous. I am—I really am beyond the law! I make my own law! Why shouldn't I go beyond the law of vision and see the secrets of life? But I sinned, and I must repent—some day. I need not return the money. I see now that it was given me so that I could lead this life of contemplation. But the ingratitude to the president, to the people who trusted me! Am I but the most miserable of sinners, and as the blind? Voices —I hear conflicting voices—some praising me for my courage, some rebuking—"

He knelt on the slimy black surface of a wooden bench beneath the willows and as dusk clothed him round about he prayed. It seemed to him that he prayed not in words but in vast confusing dreams—the words of a language larger than human tongues.

When he had exhausted himself he slowly entered the house. He locked the door. There was nothing definite of which he was afraid, but he was never comfortable with the door unlocked.

By candlelight he prepared his austere supper—dry toast, an egg, cheap tea with thin milk. As always—as it had happened after every meal, now, for eighteen months—he wanted a cigarette when he had eaten, but did not take one.

He paced into the living room and through the long still hours of the evening he read an ancient book, all footnotes and cross references, about *The Numerology of the Prophetic Books, and the Number of the Beast.* He tried to make notes for his own book on Revelation—that scant pile of sheets covered with writing in a small finicky hand. Thousands of other sheets he had covered; through whole nights he had written; but always he seemed with tardy pen to be racing after thoughts that he could never quite catch, and most of what he had written he had savagely burned.

But some day he would make a masterpiece! He was feeling toward the greatest discovery that mortal man had encountered. Everything, he had determined, was a symbol—not just this holy sign and that, but all physical manifestations. With frightened exultation he tried his new power of divination. The hanging lamp swung tinily. He ventured: "If the arc of that moving radiance touches the edge of the bookcase, then it will be a sign that I am to go to South America, and spend my money."

He shuddered. He watched the lamp's unbearably slow swing. The moving light almost touched the bookcase. He gasped. Then it receded.

It was a warning; he quaked. Would he never leave this place of brooding and of fear, which he had thought so clever a refuge? He suddenly saw it all.

"I ran away and hid in a prison! Man isn't caught by justice—he catches himself!"

Again he tried. He speculated as to whether the number of pencils on the table was greater or less than five. If greater, then he had sinned; if less, then he was veritably beyond the law. He began

71

to lift books and papers, looking for pencils. He was coldly sweating with the suspense of the test.

Suddenly he cried, "Am I going crazy?"

He fled to his prosaic bedroom. He could not sleep. His brain was smoldering, with confused inklings of mystic numbers and hidden warnings.

He woke from a half sleep more vision-haunted than any waking thought, and cried, "I must go back and confess! But I can't! I can't, when I was too clever for them! I can't go back and let them win. I won't let those fools just sit tight and still catch me!"

It was a year and a half since Jasper had disappeared. Some times it seemed a month and a half; sometimes gray centuries. John's will power had been shrouded with curious puttering studies; long, heavy-breathing sittings with the ouija board on his lap, midnight hours when he had fancied that tables had tapped and crackling coals had spoken.

Now that the second autumn of his seclusion was creeping into winter he was conscious that he had not enough initiative to carry out his plans for going to South America. The summer before he had boasted to himself that he would come out of hiding and go South, leaving such a twisty trail as only he could make. But —oh, it was too much trouble. He hadn't the joy in play-acting which had carried his brother Jasper through his preparations for flight.

He had killed Jasper Holt, and for a miserable little pile of paper money he had become a moldy recluse!

He hated his loneliness, but still more did he hate his only companions, the members of the Soul Hope Fraternity—that pious shrill seamstress, that surly carpenter, that tight-lipped housekeeper, that old shouting man with the unseemly frieze of whiskers. They were so unimaginative. Their meetings were all the same; the same persons rose in the same order and made the same intimate announcements to the Deity that they alone were his elect.

At first it had been an amusing triumph to be accepted as the most eloquent among them, but that had become commonplace; he resented their daring to be familiar with him, who was, he felt, the only man of all men living who saw the strange beatitude of higher souls beyond the illusions of the world.

It was at the end of November, during a Wednesday meeting at which a red-faced man had for a half hour maintained that he couldn't possibly sin, that the cumulative ennui burst in John Holt's brain. He sprang up.

72

He snarled, "You make me sick, all of you! You think you're so certain of sanctification that you can't do wrong. So did I, once! Now, I know that we are all miserable sinners—really are! You all *say* you are, but you don't believe it. I tell you that you there that have just been yammering, and you, Brother Judkins, with the long twitching nose, and I—I—I, most unhappy of men, we must repent, confess, expiate our sins! And I will confess right now. I st-stole—"

Terrified he darted out of the hall, and hatless, coatless, tumbled through the main street of Rosebank, nor ceased till he had locked himself in his house. He was frightened because he had almost betrayed his secret, yet agonized because he had not gone on, really confessed, and gained the only peace he could ever know now—the peace of punishment.

He never returned to Soul Hope Hall. Indeed, for a week he did not leave his house except for midnight prowling in the willow walk. Quite suddenly he became desperate with the silence. He flung out of the house, not stopping to lock or even close the front door. He raced uptown, no topcoat over his rotting garments, only an old gardener's cap on his thick brown hair. People stared at him. He bore it with resigned fury.

He entered a lunchroom, hoping to sit inconspicuously and hear men talking normally. The attendant at the counter gaped. John heard a mutter from the cashier's desk: "There's that crazy hermit!"

All of the half dozen young men loafing in the place were looking at him. He was so uncomfortable that he could not eat even the milk and sandwich he had ordered. He pushed them away and fled, a failure in the first attempt to dine out that he had made in eighteen months; a lamentable failure to revive that Jasper Holt whom he had coldly killed.

He entered a cigar store and bought a pack of cigarettes. He took joy out of throwing away his asceticism. But when, on the street, he lighted a cigarette it made him so dizzy that he was afraid he was going to fall. He had to sit down on the curb. People gathered. He staggered to his feet and up an alley.

For hours he walked, making and discarding the most contradictory plans—to go to the bank and confess, to spend the money riotously and never confess.

It was midnight when he returned to his house.

Before it he gasped. The front door was open. He chuckled with relief as he remembered that he had not closed it. He sauntered in. He was passing the door of the living room, going directly up to his

73

bedroom, when his foot struck an object the size of a book, but hollow sounding.

He picked it up. It was one of the booklike candy boxes. And it was quite empty.

Frightened, he listened. There was no sound. He crept into the living room and lighted the lamp.

The doors of the bookcase had been wrenched open. Every book had been pulled out on the floor. All the candy boxes, which that evening had contained almost $96,000, were in a pile, and all were empty.

He searched for ten minutes, but the only money he found was one five-dollar bill, which had fluttered under the table. In his pocket he had one dollar and sixteen cents.

John Holt had $6.60, no job, no friends—and no identity.

When the president of the Lumber National Bank was informed that John Holt was waiting to see him he scowled.

"Lord, I'd forgotten that minor plague! Must be a year since he's been here. Oh, let him— No, hanged if I will! Tell him I'm too busy to see him. That is, unless he's got some news about Jasper. Pump him and find out."

The president's secretary sweetly confided to John: "I'm so sorry, but the president is in conference just now. What was it you wanted to see him about? Is there any news about—uh—about your brother?"

"There is not, miss. I am here to see the president on the business of the Lord."

"Oh. If that's all I'm afraid I can't disturb him."

"I will wait."

Wait he did, through all the morning, through the lunch hour—when the president hastened out past him—then into the afternoon, till the president was unable to work with the thought of that scarecrow out there, and sent for him.

"Well, well! What is it this time, John? I'm pretty busy. No news about Jasper, eh?"

"No news, sir, but—Jasper himself! I am Jasper Holt! His sin is my sin."

"Yes, yes, I know all that stuff—twin brothers, twin souls, share responsibility—"

"You don't understand. There isn't any twin brother. There isn't any John Holt. I am Jasper. I invented an imaginary brother and disguised myself— Why, don't you recognize my voice?"

While John leaned over the desk, his two hands upon it, and

74

smiled wistfully, the president shook his head and soothed, "No, I'm afraid I don't. Sounds, like good old religious John to me! Jasper was a cheerful, efficient sort of crook. Why, his laugh—"

"But I can laugh!" The dreadful croak which John uttered was the cry of an evil bird of the swamps. The president shuddered. Under the edge of the desk his fingers crept toward the buzzer by which he summoned his secretary.

They stopped as John urged. "Look—this wig—it *is* a wig. See, I *am* Jasper!"

He had snatched off the brown thatch. He stood expectant.

The president was startled, but he shook his head and sighed.

"You poor devil! Wig, all right. But I wouldn't say that hair was much like Jasper's!"

He motioned toward the mirror in the corner of the room.

John wavered to it. And he saw that his hair had turned from Jasper's thin sleek blackness to a straggle of damp gray locks writhing over a yellow skull.

He begged pitifully, "Oh, can't you see I *am* Jasper? I stole ninety-seven thousand dollars from the bank. I want to be punished! I want to do anything to prove— Why, I've been at your house. Your wife's name is Evelyn. My salary here was—"

"My dear boy, don't you suppose that Jasper might have told you all these interesting facts? I'm afraid the worry of this has—pardon me if I'm frank, but I'm afraid it's turned your head a little, John."

"There *isn't* any John! There isn't! There isn't!"

"I'd believe that a little more easily if I hadn't met you before Jasper disappeared."

"Give me a piece of paper. You know my writing—"

With clutching claws John seized a sheet of bank stationery and tried to write in the round script of Jasper. During the past year and a half he had filled thousands of pages with the small finicky hand of John. Now, though he tried to prevent it, the shaky letters became smaller, more pinched, less legible.

Even while John wrote the president looked at the sheet and said. "Afraid it's no use. That isn't Jasper's fist. See here, I want you to get away from Rosebank—go to some farm—work outdoors—cut out this fuming and fussing—get some fresh air in your lungs." The president rose and purred, "Now, I'm afraid I have some work to do."

He paused, waiting.

John fiercely crumpled the sheet and hurled it away. Tears were in his weary eyes.

He wailed, "Is there *nothing* I can do to prove I am Jasper?"

"Why, certainly! You can produce what's left of the ninety-seven thousand dollars!"

John took from his ragged waistcoat pocket a five-dollar bill and some change. "Here's all there is. Ninety-six thousand of it was stolen from my house last night."

Sorry though he was for the madman, the president could not help laughing. Then he tried to look sympathetic as he comforted: "Well, that's hard luck, old man. Uh, let's see. You might produce some parents or relatives or somebody to prove that Jasper never did have a twin brother."

"My parents are dead and I've lost track of their kin—I was born in England—Father came over when I was six. There might be some cousins or some old neighbors, but I don't know. Probably impossible to find out without going over there."

"Well, I guess we'll have to let it go, old man." The president was pressing the buzzer for his secretary and gently bidding her, "Show Mr. Holt out, please."

From the door John desperately tried to add, "You will find my car sunk—"

The door had closed behind him. The president had not even bothered to listen.

The president gave orders that never, for any reason, was John Holt, to be admitted to his office again. He telephoned to the bonding company that John Holt had now gone crazy, that they would save themselves trouble by refusing to admit him.

John did not try to see them. He went to the county jail. He entered the keeper's office and said, quietly, "I have stolen a lot of money, but I can't prove it. Will you put me in jail?"

The keeper shouted, "Get out of here! You hoboes always spring that when you want a good warm lodging for the winter! Why the devil don't you go to work with a shovel in the sand pits? They're paying two-seventy-five a day."

"Yes, sir," said John timorously. "Where are they?"

THE NEIGHBORS

BY JOHN GALSWORTHY

John Galsworthy was raised in comfortable circumstances and educated at Harrow, where he became captain in football, and Oxford, where he was graduated
with honors in law. Though called to the bar, he practiced
little, traveling widely instead. In 1904, he married his
cousin's ex-wife, who encouraged him to write. His first
works, published under the pen-name John Sinjohn,
were unsuccessful but with *The Man of Property* in 1906
Galsworthy emerged as a writer of power and influence.
His first play, *The Silver Box*, was produced in London the
same year.

IN THE REMOTE COUNTRY, NATURE, at first sight so serene, so simple, will soon intrude on her observer a strange discomfort; a feeling that some familiar spirit haunts the old lanes, rocks, wasteland, and trees, and has the power to twist all living things around into some special shape befitting its genius.

When moonlight floods the patch of moorland about the centre of the triangle between the little towns of Hartland, Torrington, and Holsworthy, a pagan spirit steals forth through the wan gorse; gliding round the stems of the lonely, gibbetlike fir trees, peeping out among the reeds of the white marsh. That spirit has the eyes of a borderer, who perceives in every man a possible foe. And, in fact, this high corner of the land has remained border to this day, where the masterful, acquisitive invader from the North dwells side by side with the unstable, proud, quick-blooded Celt-Iberian.

In two cottages crowning some fallow land two families used to live side by side. That long white dwelling seemed all one, till the eye, peering through the sweet-brier which smothered the right-hand half, perceived the rude, weather-beaten presentment of a Running Horse, denoting the presence of intoxicating liquors; and in a window of the left-hand half, that strange conglomeration of edibles and shoe-leather which proclaims the one shop of a primitive hamlet.

These married couples were by name Sandford at the eastern, and Leman at the western end; and he who saw them for the first time thought: "What splendid-looking people!"

They were all four above the average height, and all four as straight as darts. The innkeeper, Sandford, was a massive man, stolid, grave, light-eyed, with big fair mustaches, who might have stepped straight out of some Norseman's galley. Leman was lean and lathy, a regular Celt, with an amiable, shadowy, humorous face. The two women were as different as the men. Mrs. Sandford's fair, almost transparent cheeks colored easily, her eyes were gray, her hair pale brown; Mrs. Leman's hair was of a lustreless jet-black, her eyes the color of a peaty stream, and her cheeks had the close creamy texture of old ivory.

Those accustomed to their appearance soon noted the qualifications of their splendor. In Sandford, whom neither sun nor wind ever tanned, there was a look as if nothing would ever turn him from acquisition of what he had set his heart on; his eyes had the idealism of the worshipper of property, ever marching towards a heaven of great possessions. Followed by his cowering spaniel, he walked to his fields (for he farmed as well as kept the inn) with a tread that seemed to shake the lanes, disengaging an air of such heavy and complete insulation that even the birds were still. He rarely spoke. He was not popular. He was feared, no one quite knew why.

On Mrs. Sandford, for all her pink and white, sometimes girlish look, he had set the mark of his slow, heavy domination. Her voice was seldom heard. Once in a while, however, her reserve would yield to garrulity, as of water flowing through a broken dam. In these outbursts she usually spoke of her neighbors, the Lemans, deploring the state of their marital relations. "A woman," she would say, "must give way to a man sometimes; I've had to give way to Sandford myself, I have." Her lips, from long compression, had become thin as the edge of a teacup; all her character seemed to have been driven down below the surface of her long, china-white face. She had not broken, but she had chipped; her edges had become jagged, sharp. The consciousness, that she herself had been beaten to the earth, seemed to inspire in her that waspish feeling towards Mrs. Leman—"a woman with a proud temper," as she would say in her almost ladylike voice; "a woman who's never bowed down to a man—that's what she'll tell you herself. 'Tisn't the drink that makes Leman behave so mad, 'tis because she won't give way to him. We're glad to sell drink to anyone we can, of course; but 'tisn't that what's making Leman so queer. 'Tis her."

Leman, whose long figure was often to be seen seated on the wooden bench of his neighbor's stone-flagged little inn, had, indeed, begun to have the soaked look and scent of a man never quite drunk, and hardly ever sober. He spoke slowly, his tongue seemed thickening; he no longer worked; his humorous, amiable face had grown hangdog and clouded. All the village knew of his passionate outbreaks, and bursts of desperate weeping; and of two occasions when Sandford had been compelled to wrest a razor from him. People took a morbid interest in this rapid deterioration, speaking of it with misgiving and relish, unanimous in their opinion that— "summat'd 'appen about that; the drink wer duin' for George Leman, *that* it wer, praaperly!"

But Sandford—that blond, ashy-looking Teuton—was not easy of approach, and no one cared to remonstrate with him; his taciturnity was too impressive, too impenetrable. Mrs. Leman, too, never complained. To see this black-haired woman, with her

79

stoical, alluring face, come out for a breath of air, and stand in the sunlight, her baby in her arms, was to have looked on a very woman of the Britons. In conquering races the men, they say, are superior to the women; in conquered races, the women to the men. She was certainly superior to Leman. That woman might be bent and mangled, she could not be broken; her pride was too simple, too much a physical part of her. No one ever saw a word pass between her and Sandford. It was almost as if the old racial feelings of this borderland were pursuing in these two their unending conflict. For there they lived, side by side under the long, thatched roof, this great primitive, invading male, and that black-haired, lithe-limbed woman of an older race, avoiding each other, never speaking—as much too much for their own mates as they were, perhaps, worthy of each other.

In this lonely parish, houses stood far apart, yet news traveled down the May-scented lanes and over the whin-covered moor with a strange speed; blown perhaps by the west wind, whispered by the pagan genius of the place in his wanderings, or conveyed by small boys on large farm horses.

On Whit-Monday it was known that Leman had been drinking all Sunday; for he had been heard on Sunday night shouting out that his wife had robbed him, and that her children were not his. All next day he was sitting in the bar of the inn soaking steadily. Yet on Tuesday morning Mrs. Leman was serving in her shop as usual—a really noble figure, with that lustreless black hair of hers—very silent, and ever sweetening her eyes to her customers. Mrs. Sandford, in one of her bursts of garrulity, complained bitterly of the way her neighbors had "gone on" the night before. But unmoved, ashy, stolid as ever, Sandford worked in the most stony of his fields.

That hot, magnificent day wore to its end; a night of extraordinary beauty fell. In the gold moonlight the shadows of the lime-tree leaves lay, blacker than any velvet, piled one on the other at the foot of the little green. It was very warm. A cuckoo called on till nearly midnight. A great number of little moths were out; and the two broad meadows which fell away from the hamlet down to the stream were clothed in a glamorous haze of their own moonlit buttercups. Where that marvelous moonlight spread out across the moor it was all pale witchery; only the three pine trees had strength to resist the wan gold of their fair visitor, and brooded over the scene like the ghosts of three great gallows. The long white dwelling of "the neighbors," bathed in that vibrating glow, seemed to be exuding a refulgence of its own. Beyond the stream a night-jar hunted, whose fluttering harsh call tore the garment of the scent-laden still air. It was long before sleep folded her wings.

A little past 12 o'clock there was the sound of a double shot. By 5 o'clock next morning the news had already traveled far; and before 7, quite a concourse had gathered to watch two mounted constables take Leman on Sandford's pony to Bideford jail. The dead bodies of Sandford and Mrs. Leman lay—so report ran—in the locked bedroom at Leman's end of the neighbors' house. Mrs. Sandford, in a state of collapse, was being nursed at a neighboring cottage. The Leman children had been taken to the Rectory. Alone of the dwellers in those two cottages, Sandford's spaniel sat in a gleam of early sunlight under the eastern porch, with her nose fixed to the crack beneath the door.

It was vaguely known that Leman had "done for 'em"; of the how, the why, the when, all was conjecture. Nor was it till the assizes that the story of that night was made plain, from Leman's own evidence, read from a dirty piece of paper:

"I, George Leman, make this confession—so help me God! When I came up to bed that evening, I was far gone in liquor and so had been for two days off and on, which Sandford knows. My wife was in bed. I went up, and I said to her: 'Get up!' I said; 'do what I tell you for once!' 'I will not!' she said. So I pulled the bedclothes off her. When I saw her all white like that, with her black hair, it turned me queer, and I ran downstairs and got my gun, and loaded it. When I came upstairs again, she was against the door. I pushed, and she pushed back. She didn't call out, or say one word—but pushed; she was never one to be afraid. I was the stronger, and I pushed in the door. She stood up against the bed, defying me with her mouth tight shut, the way she had; and I put up my gun to shoot her. It was then that Sandford came running up the stairs and knocked the gun out of my hand with his stick. He hit me a blow over the heart with his fist, and I fell down against the wall, and couldn't move. And he said: 'Keep quiet!' he said, 'you dog!' Then he looked at her. 'And as for you,' he said, 'you bring it on yourself! You can't bow down, can't you? *I'll* bow you down for once!' And he took and raised his stick. But he didn't strike her, he just looked at her in her nightdress, which was torn at the shoulders, and her black hair ragged. She never said a word, but smiled at him. Then he caught hold of her by the arms, and they stood there. I saw her eyes; they were as black as two sloes. He seemed to go all weak of a sudden, and white as the wall. It was like as they were

81

struggling which was the better of them, meaning to come to one another at the end. I saw what was in them as clear as I see this paper. I got up and crept round, and I took the gun and pointed it, and pulled the triggers one after the other, and they fell dead, first him, then her; they fell quietly, neither of them made a noise. I went out, and lay down on the grass. They found me there when they came to take me. This is all I have to write, but it is true that I was far gone in liquor, which I had of him . . ."

RANSOM

BY PEARL BUCK

Pearl Buck, novelist, short-story writer and translator, was born in Hillsboro, West Virginia, on June 26, 1892. Her missionary parents brought her to China when she was five months old and she spent many years there, though she returned to the U.S. to attend Randolph-Macon College in Virginia. She taught English literature at universities in Nanking from 1921 to 1931 and in later years became active in world peace movements. She was awarded a Pulitzer Prize in 1932 and the Nobel in Literature in 1938. Her best-known novel is *The Good Earth*.

THE BEETHOVEN SYMPHONY stopped abruptly. A clear metallic voice broke across the melody of the third movement.

"Press radio news. The body of Jimmie Lane, kidnaped son of Mr. Headley Lane, has been found on the bank of the Hudson River near his home this afternoon. This ends the search of—"

"Kent, turn it off, please!" Allin exclaimed.

Kent Crothers hesitated a second. Then he turned off the radio.

In the silence Allin sat biting her lower lip. "That poor mother! All these days—not giving up hope."

"I suppose it is better to know something definite," he said quietly, "even though it is the worst."

Perhaps this would be a good time to talk with her, to warn her that she was letting this kidnaping business grow into an obsession. After all, children did grow up in the United States, even in well-to-do families like theirs. The trouble was that they were not quite rich enough and still too rich—not rich enough to hire guards for their children, but rich enough, because his father owned the paper mill, to make them known in the neighborhood, at least.

The thing was to take it for granted that they did not belong to the millionaire class and therefore were not prize for kidnapers. They should do this for Bruce's sake. He would be starting school next autumn. Bruce would have to walk back and forth on the streets like millions of other American children. Kent wouldn't have his son driven three blocks, even by Peter the outdoor man; it would do him more harm than . . . after all, it was a democracy they lived in, and Bruce had to grow up with the crowd.

"I'll go and see that the children are covered," Allin said. "Betsy throws off the covers whenever she can."

Kent knew that she simply wanted to make sure they were there. But he rose with her, lighting his pipe, thinking how to begin. They walked up the stairs together, their fingers interlaced. Softly she opened the nursery door. It was ridiculous how even he was being affected by her fears. Whenever the door opened his heart stood cold for a second, until he saw the two beds, each with a little head on the pillow.

They were there now, of course. He stood beside Bruce's bed and looked down at his son. Handsome little devil. He was sleeping so soundly that when his mother leaned over him he did not move.

84

His black hair was a tousle; his red lips pouted. He was dark, but he had Allin's blue eyes.

They did not speak. Allin drew the cover gently over his outflung arm, and they stood a moment longer, hand in hand, gazing at the child. Then Allin looked up at Kent and smiled, and he kissed her. He put his arm about her shoulder, and they went to Betsy's bed.

Here was his secret obsession. He could say firmly that Bruce must take his chances with the other children, because a boy had to learn to be brave. But this baby—such a tiny feminine creature, his little daughter. She had Allin's auburn coloring, but by some miracle she had his dark eyes, so that when he looked into them he seemed to be looking into himself.

She was breathing now, a little unevenly, through her tiny nose.

"How's her cold?" he whispered.

"It doesn't seem worse," Allin whispered back. "I put stuff on her chest."

He was always angry when anything happened to this baby. He didn't trust her nurse, Mollie, too much. She was good-hearted, maybe, but easy-going.

The baby stirred and opened her eyes. She blinked, smiled, and put up her arms to him.

"Don't pick her up darling," Allin counseled. "She'll only want it every time."

So he did not take her. Instead, he put her arms down, one and then the other, playfully, under the cover.

"Go to sleep-bye, honey," he said. And she lay, sleepily smiling. She was a good little thing.

"Come—let's put out the light," Allin whispered. They tiptoed out and went back to the living room.

Kent sat down, puffed on his pipe, his mind full of what he wanted to say to Allin. It was essential to their life to believe that nothing could happen to their children.

"Kidnaping's like lightning," he began abruptly. "It happens, of course—once in a million. What you have to remember is all the rest of the children who are perfectly safe."

She had sat down on the ottoman before the fire, but she turned to him when he said this. "What would you do honestly, Kent, if some night when we went upstairs—,"

"Nonsense!" he broke in. "That's what I've been trying to tell you. It's so unlikely as to be—it's these damned newspapers! When a thing happens in one part of the country, every little hamlet hears of it."

85

"Jane Eliot told me there are three times as many kidnapings as ever get into the newspapers," Allin said.

"Jane's a newspaperwoman," Kent said. "You mustn't let her sense of drama—"

"Still, she's been on a lot of kidnaping cases," Allin replied. "She was telling me about the Wyeth case—"

This was the time to speak, now when all Allin's secret anxiety was quivering in her voice. Kent took her hand and fondled it as he spoke. He must remember how deeply she felt everything, and this thing had haunted her before Bruce was born. He had not even thought of it until one night in the darkness she had asked him the same question, "What would we do, Kent, if—" Only then he had not known what she meant.

"If what?" he had asked.

"If our baby were ever kidnaped."

He had answered what he had felt then and believed now to be true. "Why worry about what will never happen?" he had said. Nevertheless, he had followed all the cases since Bruce was born.

He kissed her palm now. "I can't bear having you afraid," he said. "It isn't necessary, you know, darling. We can't live under the shadow of this thing. We have to come to some rational position on it."

"That's what I want, Kent. I'd be glad not to be afraid—if I knew how."

"After all," he went on, "most people bring up their families without thinking about it."

"Most mothers think of it," she said. "Most of the women I know have said something about it to me—some time or other—enough to make me know they think about it all the time."

"You'd be better off not talking about it," he said.

But she said, "We keep wondering what we would do, Kent."

"That's just it!" he exclaimed. "That's why I think if we decided now what we would do—always bearing in mind that it's only the remotest possibility—"

"What *would* we do, Kent?" she asked.

He answered half playfully, "Promise to remember it's as remote as—an airplane attack on our home?"

She nodded.

"I've always thought that if one of the children were kidnapped I'd simply turn the whole thing over to the police at once."

"What police?" she asked instantly. "Gossipy old Mike O'Brien, who'd tell the newspapers the first thing? It's fatal to let it get into the papers, Jane says."

86

"Well, the Federal police, then—the G-men."

"How does one get in touch with them?"

He had to confess he did not know. "I'll find out," he promised. "Anyway, it's the principle, darling, that we want to determine. Once we know what we'll do, we can put it out of our minds. No ransom, Allin—that I feel sure about. As long as we keep on paying ransoms, we're going to have kidnapings. Somebody has to be strong enough to take the stand. Then maybe other people will see what they ought to do."

But she did not look convinced. When she spoke, her voice was low and full of dread. "The thing is, Kent, if we decided not to pay ransom, we just couldn't stick to it—not really, I mean. Suppose it were Bruce—suppose he had a cold and it was winter—and he was taken out of his warm bed in his pajamas, we'd do anything. You know we would!" She rushed on. "We wouldn't care about other children, Kent. We would only be thinking of our own little Bruce—and no one else. How to get him back again, at whatever cost."

"Hush, darling," he said. "If you're going to be like this we can't talk about it, after all."

"No, Kent, please. I do want to talk. I want to know what we ought to do. If only I could be not afraid!" she whispered.

"Come here by me," he said. He drew her to the couch beside him. "First of all, you know I love the children as much as you do, don't you?" She nodded, and he went on, "Then, darling, I'd do anything I thought would be best for our children, wouldn't I?"

"You'd do the best you knew, Kent. The question is, do any of us know what to do?"

"I do know," he said gravely, "that until we make the giving and taking of ransoms unlawful we shall have kidnapers. And until somebody begins it, it will never be done. That's the law of democratic government. The people have to begin action before government takes a stand."

"What if they said not to tell the police?" she asked.

Her concreteness confounded him. It was not as if it could happen!

"It all depends," he retorted, "on whether you want to give in to rascals or stand on your principle."

"But if it were our own child?" she persisted. "Be honest, Kent. Please don't retire into principles."

"I am trying to be honest," he said slowly. "I think I would stick by principle and trust somehow to think of some way—" He looked waveringly into her unbelieving eyes. . . .

"Try to remember exactly what happened!" he was shouting at the silly nurse. "Where did you leave her?"

Allin was quieter than he, but Allin's voice on the telephone half an hour ago had been like a scream: "Kent, we can't find Betsy!"

He had been in the mill directors' meeting, but he'd risen instantly. "Sorry," he had said sharply. "I have to leave at once."

"Nothing serious, Kent?" His father's white eyebrows had lifted.

"I think not," he'd answered. He had sense enough not to say what Allin had screamed. "I'll let you know if it is."

He had leaped into his car and driven home like a crazy man. He'd drawn up in a spray of gravel at his own gate. Allin was there, and Mollie, the silly nurse. Mollie was sobbing.

"We was at the gate, sir, watchin' for Brucie to come home from school, like we do every day, and I put 'er down—she's heavy to carry—while I went in to get a clean hankie to wipe her little hands. She'd stooped into a puddle from the rain this morning. When I came back, she wasn't there. I ran around the shrubs, sir, lookin'—and then I screamed for the madam."

"Kent, I've combed the place," Allin whispered.

"The gate!" he gasped.

"It was shut, and the bar across," Mollie wailed. "I'd sense enough to see to that before I went in."

"How long were you gone?" he shouted at her.

"I don't know, sir," Mollie sobbed. "It didn't seem a minute!"

He rushed into the yard. "Betsy, Betsy!" he cried. "Come to Daddy! Here's Daddy!" He stooped under the big lilac bushes. "Have you looked in the garage?" he demanded of Allin.

"Peter's been through it twice," she answered.

"I'll see for myself," he said. "Go into the house, Allin. She may have got inside, somehow."

He tore into the garage. Peter crawled out from under the small car.

"She ain't hyah, suh," he whispered. "Ah done looked ev'ywheah."

But Kent looked again, Peter following him like a dog. In the back of his mind was a telephone number, National 7117. He had found out about that number the year before, after he and Allin had talked that evening. Only he wouldn't call yet. Betsy was sure to be somewhere.

The gate clicked, and he rushed out. But it was Bruce—alone.

"Why, what's the matter with you, Daddy?" Bruce asked.

Kent swallowed—no use scaring Bruce. "Bruce, did you—you didn't see Betsy on the way home, did you?"

"No, Daddy, I didn't see anybody except Mike to help me across the square 'cause there was a notomobile."

"Wha' dat?" Peter was pointing at something. It was a bit of white paper, held down by a stone.

As well as he knew anything, Kent knew what it was. He had read that note a dozen times in the newspaper accounts. He stooped and picked it up. There it was—the scrawled handwriting.

We been waiting this chanse. The handwriting was there, illiterate, disguised. *Fifty grand is the price. Your dads got it if you aint. Youll hear where to put it. If you tell the police we kill the kid.*

"Daddy, what's—" Bruce began.

"Bring him indoors," he ordered Peter.

Where was Allin? He had to—he had promised her it would not happen! The telephone number was—

"Allin!" he shouted.

He heard her running down from the attic.

"Allin!" he gasped. She was there, white and piteous with terror—and so helpless. God, they were both so helpless! He had to have help; he had to know what to do. But had not he—he *had* decided long ago what he must do, because what did he know about crooks and kidnapers? People gave the ransom and lost their children, too. He had to have advice he could trust.

"I'm going to call National 7117!" he blurted at her.

"No, Kent—wait!" she cried.

"I've got to," he insisted. Before she could move, he ran to the telephone and took up the receiver. "I want National 7117!" he shouted.

Her face went white. He held out his hand with the crumpled note. She read it and snatched at the receiver.

"No, Kent—wait. We don't know. Wait and see what they say!"

But a calm voice was already speaking at the other end of the wire: "This is National 7117." And Kent was shouting hoarsely, "I want to report a kidnaping. It's our baby girl. Kent Crothers, 134 Eastwood Avenue, Greenvale, New York."

He listened while the voice was telling him to do nothing, to wait until tomorrow, and then at a certain village inn, 50 miles away, to meet a certain man who would wear a plain gray suit and have a blue handkerchief in his pocket.

And all the time Allin was whispering, "They'll kill her—they'll kill her, Kent."

"They won't know," he whispered back. "Nobody will know." When he put the receiver down he cried at her angrily, "They won't tell anybody—those fellows in Washington! Besides, I've got to have help, I tell you!"

She stood staring at him with horrified eyes. "They'll kill her," she repeated.

He wanted to get somewhere to weep, only men could not weep. But Allin was not weeping, either. Then suddenly they flung their arms about each other, and together broke into silent terrible tears.

He was not used to waiting, but he had to wait. And he had to help Allin wait. Men were supposed to be stronger.

At first it had been a comfort to have the directions to follow. First, everybody in the house—that was easy: simply the cook Sarah, the maid Rose, and Mollie and Peter. They of course were beyond blame, except Mollie. Perhaps Mollie was more than just a fool. They all had to be told they were to say absolutely nothing.

"Get everybody together in the dining room," Kent had told Allin. He had gone into the dining room.

"Daddy!" He saw Bruce's terrified figure in the doorway. "What's the matter? Where's Betsy?"

"We can't find her, son," Kent said, trying to make his voice calm. "Of course we will, but just now nobody must know she isn't here."

"Shall I go out in the yard?" Bruce asked. "Maybe I could find her."

"No," Kent said sharply. "I'd rather you went upstairs to your own room. I'll be up—in a minute."

The servants were coming in, Allin behind them.

"I'll go with Bruce," she said.

She was so still and so controlled, but he could tell by the quiver about her lips that she was only waiting for him.

"I'll be up in a very few minutes," he promised her. He stood until she had gone, Bruce's hand in hers. Then he turned to the four waiting figures. Mollie was still crying. He could tell by their faces that they all knew about the note.

"I see you know what has happened," he said. Strange how all these familiar faces looked sinister to him! Peter and Sarah had been in his mother's household. They had known him for years. And Rose was Sarah's niece. But they all looked hostile, or he imagined they did. "And I want not one word said of this to anyone in the town," he said harshly. "Remember, Betsy's life depends on no one outside knowing."

He paused, setting his jaws. He would not have believed he could cry as easily as a woman, but he could.

He cleared his throat. "Her life depends on how we behave now—in the next few hours." Mollie's sobbing burst out into wails. He rose. "That's all," he said. "We must simply wait."

The telephone rang, and he hurried to it. There was no way of knowing how the next message would come. But it was his father's peremptory voice: "Anything wrong over there, Kent?"

He knew now it would never do for his father to know what had happened. His father could keep nothing to himself.

"Everything is all right, Dad," he answered. "Allin's not feeling very well, that's all."

"Have you had the doctor?" his father shouted.

"We will if it is necessary, Dad," he answered and put up the receiver abruptly.

He thought of Bruce and went to find him. He was eating his supper in the nursery, and Allin was with him. She had told Mollie to stay downstairs. She could not bear to see the girl anymore than he could.

But the nursery was unbearable, too. This was the time when Betsy, fresh from her bath . . .

"I'm—I'll be downstairs in the library," he told Allin hurriedly, and she nodded.

In the library the silence was torture. They could only wait.

And all the time who knew what was happening to the child? Tomorrow, the man had said an hour ago. Wait, he had said. But what about tonight? In what sort of place would the child be sleeping?

Kent leaped to his feet. Something had to be done. He would have a look around the yard. There might be another letter.

He went out into the early autumn twilight. He had to hold himself together to keep from breaking into foolish shouts and curses. It was the agony of not being able to do anything. Then he controlled himself. The thing was to go on following a rational plan. He had come out to see if he could find anything.

He searched every inch of the yard. There was no message of any sort.

Then in the gathering darkness he saw a man at the gate. "Mist' Crothers!" it was Peter's voice. "Fo' God, Mist' Crothers, Ah don' know why they should pick on mah ole 'ooman. When Ah come home fo' suppah, she give it to me—she cain't read, so she don' know what wuz in it."

Kent snatched a paper from Peter's shaking hand and ran to the house. In the lighted hall he read:

Get the dough ready all banknotes dont mark any or well get the other kid to. Dont try double-crossing us. You cant get away with nothing. Put it in a box by the dead oak at the mill creek. You know where. At twelve o'clock tomorrow night.

He knew where, indeed. He had fished there from the time he was a little boy. The lightning had struck that oak tree one summer when he had been only a hundred yards away, standing in the doorway of the mill during a thunderstorm. How did they know he knew?

He turned on Peter. "Who brought this?" he demanded.

"Ah don' know, suh," Peter stammered. "She couldn't tell me nothin' 'cep'n' it wuz a white man. He chuck it at 'er and say, 'Give it to yo' ole man.' So she give it to me, and Ah come a-runnin'."

Kent stared at Peter, trying to ferret into his brain. Was Peter being used by someone—bribed, perhaps, to take a part? Did he know anything?

"If I thought you knew anything about Betsy, I'd kill you myself," he said.

"Fo' God, Ah don', Mist' Crothers—you know me, suh! Ah done gyardened for yo' since yo' and Miss Allin got mah'ied. 'Sides, whut Ah want in such devilment? Ah got all Ah want—mah house and a sal'ry. Ah don' want nuthin'."

It was all true, of course. The thing was, you suspected everybody.

"You tell Flossie to tell no one," he commanded Peter.

"Ah done tole 'er," Peter replied fervently. "Ah tole 'er Ah'd split 'er open if she told anybody 'bout dat white man."

"Get along, then," said Kent. "And remember what I told you."

"Yassuh," Peter replied.

"Of course we'll pay the ransom!" Allin was insisting.

They were in their own room, the door open into the narrow passage, and beyond that the door into the nursery was open, too. They sat where, in the shadowy light of a night lamp, they could see Bruce's dark head on the pillow. Impossible, of course, to sleep. Sarah had sent up some cold chicken and they had eaten it here, and later Kent had made Allin take a hot bath and get into a warm robe and lie down on the chaise lounge. He did not undress. Someone might call.

"I'll have to see what the man says tomorrow," he answered.

Terrifying to think how he was pinning everything on that fellow tomorrow—a man whose name, even, he did not know. All he

knew was he'd wear a plain gray suit and he'd have a blue handkerchief in his pocket. That was all he had to save Betsy's life. No,
that wasn't true. Behind that one man were hundreds of others,
alert, strong, and ready to help.

"We've got to pay it," Allin was saying hysterically. "What's
money now?"

"Allin!" he cried. "You don't think I'm trying to save the money,
in God's name!"

"We have about twenty thousand, haven't we, in the bank?" she
said hurriedly. "Your father would have the rest, though, and we
could give him the securities. It isn't as if we didn't
have it."

"Allin, you're being absurd! The thing is to know how
to—"

But she flew at him fiercely. "The thing is to save Betsy—that's
all; there's nothing else—absolutely nothing. I don't care if it takes
everything your father has.

"Allin, be quiet!" he shouted at her. "Do you mean my father
would begrudge anything—?"

"You're afraid of him, Kent," she retorted. "Well, I'm not! If you
don't go to him, I will."

They were quarreling now, like two insane people.. They were
both stretched beyond normal reason.

Suddenly Allin was sobbing. "I can't forget what you said that
night," she cried. "All that standing on principle! Oh, Kent, she's
with strangers, horrible people, crying her little heart out; perhaps
they're even—hurting her, trying to make her keep quiet. Oh,
Kent, Kent!"

He took her in his arms. They must not draw apart now. He must
think of her.

"I'll do anything, darling," he said. "The first thing in the morning I'll get hold of Dad and have the money ready."

"If they could only *know* it," she said.

"I could put something in the paper, perhaps," he said. "I believe
I could word something that no one else would understand."

"Let's try, Kent!"

He took a pencil and envelope from his pocket and wrote.
"How's this?" he asked. "Fifty agreed by dead oak at twelve."

"I can't see how it could do any harm," she said eagerly. "And if
they see it, they'll understand we're willing to do anything."

"I'll go around to the newspaper office and pay for this in cash,"
he said. "Then I won't have to give names."

"Yes, yes!" she urged him. "It's something more than just sitting here!"

He drove through the darkness the two miles to the small town and parked in front of the ramshackle newspaper office. A red-eyed night clerk took his advertisement and read it off.

"This is a funny one," he said. "We get some, now and then. That'll be a dollar, Mr. —"

Kent did not answer. He put a dollar bill on the desk.

"I don't know what I've done, even so," he groaned to himself.

He drove back quietly through the intense darkness. The storm had not yet come, and the air was strangely silent. He kept his motor at its most noiseless, expecting somehow to hear through the sleeping stillness Betsy's voice, crying.

They scarcely slept, and yet when they looked at each other the next morning the miracle was that they had slept at all. But he had made Allin go to bed at last, and then, still dressed, he had lain down on his own bed near her. It was Bruce who waked them. He stood hesitatingly between their beds. They heard his voice.

"Betsy hasn't come back yet, Mommie."

The name waked them. And they looked at each other.

"How could we!" Allin whispered.

"It may be a long pull, dearest," he said, trying to be steady. He got up, feeling exhausted.

"Will she come back today?" Bruce asked.

"I think so, son."

At least it was Saturday, and Bruce need not go to school today.

"I'm going to get her tonight," Kent said after a moment.

Instantly he felt better. They must not give up hope—not by a great deal. There was too much to do: his father to see and the money to get. Secretly, he still reserved his own judgment about the ransom. If the man in gray was against it, he would tell Allin nothing—he simply would not give it. The responsibility would be his.

"You and Mommie will have to get Betsy's things ready for her tonight," he said cheerfully. He would take a bath and get into a fresh suit. He had to have all his wits about him today, every moment—listen to everybody, and use his own judgment finally. In an emergency, one person had to act.

He paused at the sight of himself in the mirror. Would he be able to keep it from Allin if he made a mistake? Suppose they never got Betsy back. Suppose she just—disappeared. Or suppose they found her little body somewhere.

This was the way all those other parents had felt—this sickness

94

and faintness. If he did not pay the ransom and *that* happened, would he be able *not* to tell Allin—or to tell her it was his fault? Both were impossible.

"I'll just have to go on from one thing to the next," he decided.

The chief thing was to try to be hopeful. He dressed and went back into the bedroom. Bruce had come in to dress in their room. But Allin was still in bed, lying against the pillows, white and exhausted.

He bent over her and kissed her. "I'll send your breakfast up," he said. "I'm going to see Father first. If any message comes through, I'll be there—then at the bank."

She nodded, glanced up at him, and closed her eyes. He stood looking down into her tortured face. Every nerve in it was quivering under the set stillness.

"Can't break yet," he said sharply. "The crisis is ahead."

"I know," she whispered. Then she sat up. "I can't lie here!" she exclaimed. "It's like lying on a bed of swords, being tortured. I'll be down, Kent—Bruce and I."

She flew into the bathroom. He heard the shower turned on instantly and strongly. But he could wait for no one.

"Come down with Mother, son," he said. And he went on alone.

"If you could let me have thirty thousand today," he said to his father, "I can give it back as soon as I sell some stock."

"I don't care when I get it back," his father said irritably. "Good God, Kent, it's not that. It's just that I—it's none of my business, of course, but thirty thousand in cold cash! I'd like to ask what on earth you've been doing, but I won't."

Kent had made up his mind at the breakfast table that if he could keep the thing out of the papers, he would also keep it from his father and mother. He'd turned to the personals in the morning paper. There it was, his answer to those scoundrels. Well, he wouldn't stick to it unless it were best for Betsy. Meanwhile, silence!

To Rose, bringing in the toast, he had said sharply, "Tell everybody to come in now before your mistress comes down."

They had filed in, subdued and drooping, looking at him with frightened eyes.

"Oh sir!" Mollie had cried hysterically.

"Please!" he had exclaimed, glancing at her. Maybe the man in gray ought to see her. But last night he had distrusted Peter. This morning Peter looked like a faithful old dog, and as incapable of evil.

95

"I only want to thank you for obeying me so far," he said wearily. "If we can keep our trouble out of the papers, perhaps we can get Betsy back. At least, it's the only hope. If you succeed in letting no one know until we know—the end, I shall give each of you a hundred dollars as a token of my gratitude."

"Thank you, sir," Sarah and Rose had said. Mollie only sobbed. Peter was murmuring, "Ah don' wan' no hundred dollahs, Mist' Crothers. All Ah wan' is dat little chile back."

How could Peter be distrusted? Kent had wrung his hand. "That's all I want, too, Peter," he had said fervently.

Strange how shaky and emotional he had felt!

Now, under his father's penetrating eyes, he held himself calm. "I know it sounds outrageous, Father," he admitted, "but I simply ask you to trust me for a few days."

"You're not speculating, I hope. It's no time for that. The market's uncertain."

It was, Kent thought grimly, the wildest kind of speculation —with his own child's life.

"It's not ordinary speculation, certainly," he said. "I can manage through the bank, Dad," he said. "Never mind. I'll mortgage the house."

"Oh, nonsense!" his father retorted. He had his checkbook out and was writing. "I'm not going to have it get around that my son had to go mortgaging his place. Here you are."

"Thanks," Kent said briefly.

Now for the bank . . .

Step by step the day went. It was amazing how quickly the hours passed. It was noon before he knew it, and in an hour he must start for the inn. He went home and found Allin on the front porch in the sunshine. She had a book in her hand, and Bruce was playing with his red truck out in the yard. Anyone passing would never dream there was tragedy here.

"Do you have it?" she asked him.

He touched his breast pocket. "All ready," he answered.

They sat through a silent meal, listening to Bruce's chatter. Allin ate nothing and he very little, but he was grateful to her for being there, for keeping the outward shape of the day usual.

"Good sport!" he said to her across the table in the midst of Bruce's conversation. She smiled faintly. "Thank you, no more coffee," he said to Rose. "I must be going, Allin."

"Yes," she said, and added. "I wish it were I—instead of waiting."

"I know," he replied, and kissed her.

Yesterday, waiting had seemed intolerable to him, too. But now

96

that he was going towards the hour for which he had been waiting, he clung to the hopefulness of uncertainty.

He drove alone to the inn. The well-paved roads, the tended fields and comfortable farmhouses were not different from the landscape any day. He would have said, only yesterday, that it was impossible that underneath all this peace and plenty there could be men so evil as to take a child out of its home, away from its parents, for money.

There was, he pondered, driving steadily west, no other possible reason. He had no enemies; none, that is, whom he knew. There were always discontented people, of course, who hated anyone who seemed successful. There was, of course, too, the chance that his father had enemies—he was ruthless with idle workers.

"I can't blame a man if he is born a fool," Kent had heard his father maintain stoutly, "but I can blame even a fool for being lazy." It might be one of these. If only it were not some perverted mind!

He drove into the yard of the inn and parked his car. His heart was thudding in his breast, but he said casually to the woman at the door, "Have you a bar?"

"To the right," she answered quickly. It was Saturday afternoon, and business was good. She did not even look at him as he sauntered away.

The moment he entered the door of the bar he saw the man. He stood at the end of the bar, small, inconspicuous, in a gray suit and a blue-striped shirt. He wore a solid blue tie, and in his pocket was the blue handkerchief. Kent walked slowly to his side.

"Whiskey and soda, please," he said to the bartender. The room was full of people at tables, drinking and talking noisily. He turned to the man in gray and smiled. "Rather unusual to find a bar like this in a village inn."

"Yes, it is," the little man agreed. He had a kind, brisk voice, and he was drinking a tall glass of something clear, which he finished. "Give me another of the same," he remarked to the bartender. "London Washerwoman's Treat, it's called," he explained to Kent.

It was hard to imagine that this small hatchet-faced man had any importance.

"Going my way?" Kent asked suddenly.

"If you'll give me a lift," the little man replied.

Kent's heart subsided. The man knew him, then. He nodded. They paid for their drinks and went out to the car.

"Drive due north into a country road," the little man said with sudden sharpness. All his dreaminess was gone. He sat beside

Kent, his arms folded. "Please tell me exactly what's happened, Mr. Crothers."

And Kent, driving along, told him.

He was grateful for the man's coldness; for the distrust of everything and everybody. He was like a lean hound in a life-and-death chase. Because of his coldness, Kent could talk without fear of breaking.

"I don't know your name," Kent said.

"Doesn't matter," said the man. "I'm detailed for the job."

"As I was saying," Kent went on, "we have no enemies—at least, none I know."

"Fellow always has enemies," the little man murmured.

"It hardly seems like a gangster would—" Kent began again.

"No, gangsters don't kidnap children," the little man told him. "Adults, yes. But they don't monkey with kids. It's too dangerous, for one thing. Kidnaping children's the most dangerous job there is in crime, and the smart ones know it. It's always some little fellow does it—him and a couple of friends, maybe."

"Why dangerous?" Kent demanded.

"Always get caught," the little man said, shrugging. "Always!"

There was something so reassuring about this strange sharp creature that Kent said abruptly, "My wife wants to pay the ransom. I suppose you think that's wrong, don't you?"

"Perfectly *right*," the man said. "Absolutely! We aren't magicians, Mr. Crothers. We got to get in touch somehow. The only two cases I ever knew where nothing was solved was where the parents wouldn't pay. So we couldn't get a clue."

Kent set his lips. "Children killed?"

"Who knows?" the little man said, shrugging again. "Anyway, one of them was. And the other never came back."

There might be comfort, then, in death, Kent thought. He had infinitely rather hold Betsy's dead body in his arms than never know . . .

"Tell me what to do and I'll do it," he said.

The little man lighted a cigarette. "Go on just as though you'd never told us. Go on and pay your ransom. Make a note of the numbers of the notes, of course—no matter what the letter says. How's he going to know? But pay it over—and do what he says next. You can call me up here." He took a paper out of his coat pocket and put it in Kent's pocket. "I maybe ought to tell you, though, we'll tap your telephone wire."

"Do anything you like," Kent said.

"That's all I need!" the man exclaimed. "That's our orders—to do what the parents want. You're a sensible one. Fellow I knew once walked around with a shotgun to keep off the police. Said he'd handle things himself."

"Did he get his child back?"

"Nope—paid the ransom, too. Paying the ransom's all right— that's the way we get 'em. But he went roarin' around the neighborhood trying to be his own law. We didn't have a chance."

Kent thought of one more thing. "I don't want anything spared—money or trouble. I'll pay anything, of course."

"Oh, sure," the man said. "Well, I guess that'll be all. You might let me off near the inn. I'll go in and get another drink."

He lapsed into dreaminess again, and in silence Kent drove back to the village.

"All right," the little man said. "So long. Good luck to you." He leaped out and disappeared into the bar.

And Kent, driving home through the early sunset, thought how little there was to tell Allin—really nothing at all, except that he liked and trusted the man in gray. No, it was much more than that: the fellow stood for something far greater than himself—he stood for all the power of the government organized against crimes like this. That was the comfort of the thing. Behind that man was the nation's police, all for him, Kent Crothers, helping him find his child.

When he reached home, Allin was in the hall waiting.

"He really said nothing, darling," Kent said, kissing her, "except you were right about the ransom. We have to pay that. Still, he was extraordinary. Somehow I feel—if she's still alive, we'll get her back. He's that sort of fellow." He did not let her break, though he felt her trembling against him. He said very practically, "We must check these banknotes, Allin."

And then, when they were checking them upstairs in their bedroom with doors locked, he kept insisting that what they were doing was right.

At a quarter to 12 he was bumping down the rutted road to the forks. He knew every turn the road made, having traveled it on foot from the time he was a little boy. But that boy out on holiday had nothing to do with himself as he was tonight, an anxious, harried man.

He drew up beneath the dead oak and took the cardboard box in which he and Allin had packed the money and stepped out of the car. There was not a sound in the dark night, yet he knew that somewhere not far away were the men who had his child.

He listened, suddenly swept again with the conviction he had had the night before, that she would cry out. She might even be this moment in the old mill. But there was not a sound. He stooped and put the box at the root of the tree.

And as he did this, he stumbled over a string raised from the ground about a foot. What was this? He followed it with his hands. It encircled the tree—a common piece of twine. Then it went under a stone, and under the stone was a piece of paper. He seized it, snapped on his cigarette lighter, and read the clumsy writing.

If everything turns out like we told you to do, go to your hired mans house at twelve tomorrow night for the kid. If you double-cross us you get it back dead.

He snapped off the light. He'd get her back dead! It all depended on what he did. And what he did, he would have to do alone. He would not go home to Allin until he had decided every step.

He drove steadily away. If he did not call the man in gray, Betsy might be at Peter's alive. If he called, and they did not find out, she might be alive anyway. But if the man fumbled and they did find out, she would be dead.

He knew what Allin would say: "Just so we get her home, Kent, nothing else! People have to think for themselves, first." Yes, she was right. He would keep quiet; anyway, he would give the kidnapers a chance. If she were safe and alive, that would be justification for anything. If she were dead . . .

Then he remembered that there was something courageous and reassuring about that little man. He alone had seemed to know what to do. And anyway, what about those parents who had tried to manage it all themselves? Their children had never come back, either. No, he had better do what he knew he ought to do.

He tramped into the house. Allin was lying upstairs on her bed, her eyes closed.

"Darling," he said gently. Instantly she opened her eyes and sat up. He handed her the paper and sat down on her bed. She lifted miserable eyes to him.

"Twenty-four more hours!" she whispered. "I can't do it, Kent."

"Yes, you can," he said harshly. "You'll do it because you damned well have to." He thought. She can't break now, if I have to whip her! "We've got to wait," he went on. "Is there anything else we can do? Tell Mike O'Brien? Let the newspapers get it and ruin everything?"

She shook her head. "No."

He got up. He longed to take her in his arms, but he did not dare.

If this was ever over, he would tell her what he thought of her—how wonderful she was, how brave and game—but he could not now. It was better for them both to stay away from that edge of breaking.

"Get up," he said. "Let's have something to eat. I haven't really eaten all day."

It would be good for her to get up and busy herself. She had not eaten either.

"All right, Kent," she said. "I'll wash my face in cold water and be down."

"I'll be waiting," he replied.

This gave him the moment he had made up his mind he would use—damned if he wouldn't use it! The scoundrels had his money now, and he would take the chance on that quiet little man. He called the number, and almost instantly he heard the fellow's drawl.

"Hello?" the man said.

"This is Kent Crothers," he answered. "I've had that invitation."

"Yes?" The voice was alert.

"Twelve tomorrow."

"Yes? Where? Midnight, of course. They always make it midnight."

"My gardener's house."

"Okay, Mr. Crothers. Go right ahead as if you hadn't told us." The phone clicked.

Kent listened, but there was nothing more. Everything seemed exactly the same, but nothing was the same. This very telephone wire was cut somewhere, by someone. Someone was listening to every word anyone spoke to and from his house. It was sinister and yet reassuring—sinister if you were the criminal.

He heard Allin's step on the stair and went out to meet her. "I have a hunch," he told her, smiling.

"What?" She tried to smile back.

He drew her towards the dining room. "We're going to win," he said.

Within himself he added, If she were still alive, that little heart of his life. Then he put the memory of Betsy's face away from him resolutely.

"I'm going to eat," he declared "and so must you. We'll beat them tomorrow."

But tomorrow very nearly beat them. Time stood still—there was no making it pass. They filled it full of a score of odd jobs about the house. Lucky for them it was Sunday; luckier that Kent's mother had a cold and telephoned that she and Kent's father would not be over for their usual weekly visit.

They stayed together, a little band of three. By mid-afternoon Kent had cleaned up everything—a year's odd jobs—and there were hours to go.

They played games with Bruce, and at last it was his supper-time and they put him to bed. Then they sat upstairs in their bedroom again, near the nursery, each with a book.

Sometime, after these hours were over, he would have to think about a lot of things again. But everything had to wait now, until this life ended at midnight. Beyond that no thought could reach.

At 11 he rose. "I'm going now," he said, and stooped to kiss her. She clung to him, and then in an instant they drew apart. In strong accord they knew it was not yet time to give way.

He ran the car as noiselessly as he could and left it at the end of the street, six blocks away. Then he walked past the few tumbledown bungalows, past two empty lots, to Peter's rickety gate. There was no light in the house. He went to the door and knocked softly. He heard Peter's mumble: "Who's dat?"

"Let me in, Peter," he called in a low voice. The door opened. "It's I, Peter—Kent Crothers. Let me in. Peter, they're bringing the baby here."

"To mah house? Lemme git de light on."

"No, Peter, no light. I'll just sit down here in the darkness, like this. Only don't lock the door, see? I'll sit by the door. Where's a chair? That's it." He was trembling so that he stumbled into the chair Peter pushed forward.

"Mist' Crothers, suh, will yo' have a drink? Ah got some corn likker."

"Thanks, Peter."

He heard Peter's footsteps shuffling away, and in a moment a tin cup was thrust into his hand. He drank the reeking stuff down. It burned him like indrawn flame, but he felt steadier for it.

"Ain't a thing Ah can do, Mist' Crothers?" Peter's whisper came ghostly out of the darkness.

"Not a thing. Just wait."

"Ah'll wait here, then. Mah ole 'ooman's asleep. Ah'll jest git thrashin' round if Ah go back to bed."

"Yes, only we mustn't talk," Kent whispered back.

"Nosuh."

This was the supremest agony of waiting in all the long agony that this day had been. To sit perfectly still, straining to hear, knowing nothing, wondering . . .

Suppose something went wrong with the man in gray, and they fumbled, and frightened the man who brought Betsy back. Suppose he just sat here waiting and waiting until dawn came. And at home Allin was waiting.

The long day had been nothing to this. He sat reviewing all his life, pondering on the horror of this monstrous situation in which he and Allin now were. A free country, was it? No one was free when his lips were locked against crime, because he dared not speak lest his child be murdered. If Betsy were dead, if they didn't bring her back, he'd never tell Allin he had telephoned the man in gray. He was still glad he had done it. After all, were respectable men and women to be at the mercy of—but if Betsy were dead, he'd wish he had killed himself before he had anything to do with the fellow!

He sat, his hands interlocked so tightly he felt them grow cold and bloodless and stinging, but he could not move. Someone came down the street roaring out a song.

"Thass a drunk man," Peter whispered.

Kent did not answer. The street grew still again.

And then in the darkness—hours after midnight, it seemed to him—he heard a car come up to the gate and stop. The gate creaked open and then shut, and the car drove away.

"Guide me down the steps," he told Peter.

It was the blackest night he had ever seen. But the stars were shining when he stepped out. Peter pulled him along the path. Then, by the gate, Peter stooped.

"She's here," he said.

And Kent, wavering and dizzy, felt her in his arms again, limp and heavy. "She's warm," he muttered. "That's something."

He carried her into the house, and Peter lighted a candle and held it up. It was she—his little Betsy, her white dress filthy and a man's sweater drawn over her. She was breathing heavily.

"Look lak she done got a dose of sumpin," Peter muttered.

"I must get her home," Kent whispered frantically. "Help me to the car, Peter."

"Yassah," Peter said, and blew out the candle.

They walked silently down the street, Peter's hand on Kent's arm. When he got Betsy home, he—he—

"Want I should drive you?" Peter was asking him.

"I—maybe you'd better," he replied.

He climbed into the seat with her. She was so fearfully limp. Thank God he could hear her breathing! In a few minutes he would put Betsy into her mother's arms.

"Don't stay, Peter," he said.

"Nosuh," Peter answered.

Allin was at the door, waiting. She opened it and without a word reached for the child. He closed the door behind them.

Then he felt himself grow sick. "I was going to tell you," he gasped, "I didn't know whether to tell you—" He swayed and felt himself fall upon the floor.

Allin was a miracle; Allin was wonderful, a rock of a woman. This tender thing who had endured the torture of these days was at his bedside when he woke next day, smiling, and only a little pale.

"The doctor says you're not to go to work darling," she told him.

"The doctor?" he repeated.

"I had him last night for both of you—you and Betsy. He won't tell anyone."

"I've been crazy," he said, dazed. "Where is she? How—"

"She's going to be all right," Allin said.

"No, but—you're not telling me!"

"Come in here and see," she replied.

He got up, staggering a little. Funny how his legs had collapsed under him last night!

They went into the nursery. There in her bed she lay, his beloved child. She was more naturally asleep now, and her face bore no other mark than pallor.

"She won't even remember it," Allin said. "I'm glad it wasn't Bruce."

He did not answer. He couldn't think—nothing had to be thought about now.

"Come back to bed, Kent," Allin was saying. "I'm going to bring your breakfast up. Bruce is having his downstairs."

He climbed back into bed, shamefaced at his weakness. "I'll be all right after a little coffee. I'll get up then, maybe."

But his bed felt wonderfully good. He lay back, profoundly grateful to it—to everything. But as long as he lived he would wake up to sweat in the night with memory.

The telephone by his bed rang, and he picked it up. "Hello?" he called.

"Hello, Mr. Crothers," a voice answered. It was the voice of the man in gray. "Say, was the little girl hurt?"

"No!" Kent cried. "She's all right!"

"Fine. Well, I just wanted to tell you we caught the fellow last night."

"You *did!*" Kent leaped up. "No! Why, that's extraordinary."

"We had a cordon around the place for blocks and got him. You'll get your money back, too."

"That—it doesn't seem to matter. Who was he?"

"Fellow named Harry Brown—a young chap in a drug store."

"I never heard of him!"

"No, he says you don't know him—but his dad went to school with yours, and he's heard a lot of talk about you. His dad's a poor stick, I guess, and got jealous of yours. That's about it, probably. Fellow says he figured you sort of owed him something. Crazy, of course. Well, it was an easy case—he wasn't smart, and scared to death, besides. You were sensible about it. Most people ruin their chances with their own fuss. So long, Mr. Crothers. Mighty glad."

The telephone clicked. That was all. Everything was incredible, impossible. Kent gazed around the familiar room. Had this all happened? It had happened, and it was over.

When he went downstairs he would give the servants their hundred dollars apiece. Mollie had had nothing to do with it, after all. The mystery had dissolved like a mist at morning.

Allin was at the door with his tray. Behind her came Bruce, ready for school. She said, so casually Kent could hardly catch the tremor underneath her voice, "What would you say, darling, if we let Peter walk to school with Bruce today?"

Her eyes pleaded with him: "No? Oughtn't we to? What shall we do?"

Then he thought of something else that indomitable man in gray had said, that man whose name he would never know, one among all those other men trying to keep the law for the nation.

"We're a lawless people," the little man had said that afternoon in the car. "If we made a law against paying ransoms, nobody would obey it any more than they did Prohibition. No, when the Americans don't like a law, they break it. And so we still have kidnapers. It's one of the prices you pay for a democracy."

Yes, it was one of the prices. Everybody paid—he and Allin; the child they had so nearly lost; that boy locked up in prison.

"Bruce has to live in his own country," he said. "I guess you can go alone, can't you, son?"

"'Course I can," Bruce said sturdily.

AN ERROR IN CHEMISTRY

BY WILLIAM FAULKNER

Beginning in 1936, William Faulkner, whose great-grandfather was a plantation owner, colonel in the Confederate army, railroad builder and novelist, often went to Hollywood to write scenarios. He was also sent by the State Department on cultural missions to France, Brazil and Japan. But until 1957 his home base was Oxford, Mississippi. From there he wrote his major works, including *Sartoris, The Sound and the Fury, As I Lay Dying, Sanctuary, Absalom, Absalom!* and *A Fable*. He was a master of the short story—many of his are the finest of our time.

IT WAS JOEL FLINT HIMSELF who telephoned the sheriff that he had killed his wife. And when the sheriff and his deputy reached the scene, drove the twenty-odd miles into the remote back-country region where old Wesley Pritchel lived, Joel Flint himself met them at the door and asked them in. He was the foreigner, the outlander, the Yankee who had come into our county two years ago as the operator of a pitch—a lighted booth where a roulette wheel spun against a bank of nickel-plated pistols and razors and watches and harmonicas, in a traveling street carnival—and who when the carnival departed had remained, and two months later was married to Pritchel's only living child: the dim-witted spinster of almost forty who until then had shared her irascible and violent-tempered father's almost hermit-existence on the good though small farm which he owned.

But even after the marriage, old Pritchel still seemed to draw the line against his son-in-law. He built a new small house for them two miles from his own, where the daughter was presently raising chickens for the market. According to rumor old Pritchel, who hardly ever went anywhere anyway, had never once entered the new house, so that he saw even this last remaining child only once a week. This would be when she and her husband would drive each Sunday in the second-hand truck in which the son-in-law marketed the chickens, to take Sunday dinner with old Pritchel in the old house where Pritchel now did his own cooking and housework. In fact, the neighbors said the only reason he allowed the son-in-law to enter his house even then was so that his daughter could prepare him a decent hot meal once a week.

So for the next two years, occasionally in Jefferson, the county seat, but more frequently in the little cross-roads hamlet near his home, the son-in-law would be seen and heard too. He was a man in the middle forties, neither short nor tall nor thin nor stout (in fact, he and his father-in-law could easily have cast that same shadow which later for a short time they did), with a cold, contemptuous intelligent face and a voice lazy with anecdote of the teeming outland which his listeners had never seen—a dweller among the cities, though never from his own accounting long resident in any one of them, who within the first three months of his residence among them had impressed upon the people whose way of life he had assumed, one definite personal habit by which he presently became known throughout the whole county, even by men who had never seen him. This was a harsh and contemptuous derogation, sometimes without even provocation or reason or opportunity, of our local southern custom of drinking whiskey by mixing sugar and water with it. He called it effeminacy, a pap for children, himself drinking even our harsh, violent, illicit and unaged homemade corn whiskey without even a sip of water to follow it.

Then on this last Sunday morning he telephoned the sheriff that he had killed his wife and met the officers at his father-in-law's door and said: "I have already carried her into the house. So you won't need to waste breath telling me I shouldn't have touched her until you got here."

"I reckon it was all right to take her up out of the dirt," the sheriff said. "It was an accident, I believe you said."

"Then you believe wrong," Flint said. "I said I killed her."

And that was all.

The sheriff brought him to Jefferson and locked him in a cell in the jail. And that evening after supper the sheriff came through the side door into the study where Uncle Gavin was supervising me in the drawing of a brief. Uncle Gavin was only county, not District, attorney. But he and the sheriff, who had been sheriff off and on even longer than Uncle Gavin had been county attorney, had been friends all that while. I mean friends in the sense that two men who play chess together are friends, even though sometimes their aims are diametrically opposed. I heard them discuss it once.

"I'm interested in truth," the sheriff said.

"So am I," Uncle Gavin said. "It's so rare. But I am more interested in justice and human beings."

"Ain't truth and justice the same thing?" the sheriff said.

"Since when?" Uncle Gavin said. "In my time I have seen truth that was anything under the sun but just, and I have seen justice using tools and instruments I wouldn't want to touch with a ten-foot fence rail."

The sheriff told us about the killing, standing, looming above the tablelamp—a big man with little hard eyes, talking down at Uncle Gavin's wild shock of prematurely white hair and his quick thin face, while Uncle Gavin sat on the back of his neck practically, his legs crossed on the desk, chewing the bit of his corncob pipe and spinning and unspinning around his finger his watch chain weighted with the Phi Beta Kappa key he got at Harvard.

"Why?" Uncle Gavin said.

108

"I asked him that, myself," the sheriff said. "He said, 'Why do men ever kill their wives? Call it for the insurance.'"

"That's wrong," Uncle Gavin said. "It's women who murder their spouses for immediate personal gain—insurance policies, or at what they believe is the instigation or promise of another man. Men murder their wives from hatred or rage or despair, or to keep them from talking since not even bribery not even simple absence can bridle a woman's tongue."

"Correct," the sheriff said. He blinked his little eyes at Uncle Gavin. "It's like he *wanted* to be locked up in jail. Not like he was submitting to arrest because he had killed his wife, but like he had killed her so that he would be locked up, arrested. Guarded."

"Why?" Uncle Gavin said.

"Correct too," the sheriff said. "When a man deliberately locks doors behind himself, it's because he is afraid. And a man who would voluntarily have himself locked up on suspicion of murder ..." He batted his hard little eyes at Uncle Gavin for a good ten seconds while Uncle Gavin looked just as hard back at him. "Because he wasn't afraid. Not then nor at any time. Now and then you meet a man that ain't ever been afraid, not even of himself. He's one."

"If that's what he wanted you to do," Uncle Gavin said, "why did you do it?"

"You think I should have waited a while?"

They looked at one another a while. Uncle Gavin wasn't spinning the watch chain now. "All right," he said. "Old Man Pritchel—"

"I was coming to that," the sheriff said. "Nothing."

"Nothing?" Uncle Gavin said. "You didn't even see him?" And the sheriff told that too—how as he and the deputy and Flint stood on the gallery, they suddenly saw the old man looking out at them through a window—a face rigid, furious, glaring at them through the glass for a second and then withdrawn, vanished, leaving an impression of furious exultation and raging triumph, and something else. . . .

"Fear?" the sheriff said. "No. I tell you, he wasn't afraid—Oh," he said. "You mean Pritchel." This time he looked at Uncle Gavin so long that at last Uncle Gavin said,

"All right. Go on." And the sheriff told that too: how they entered the house, the hall, and he stopped and knocked at the locked door of the room where they had seen the face and he even called old Pritchel's name and still got no answer. And how they went on and found Mrs. Flint on a bed in the back room with the shotgun wound in her neck, and Flint's battered truck drawn up beside the back steps as if they had just got out of it.

"There were three dead squirrels in the truck," the sheriff said. "I'd say they had been shot since daylight"—and the blood on the steps, and on the ground between the steps and the truck, as if she had been shot from inside the truck, and the gun itself, still containing the spent shell, standing just inside the hall door as a man would put it down when he entered the house. And how the sheriff went back up the hall and knocked again at the locked door—

"Locked where?" Uncle Gavin said.

"On the inside," the sheriff said—and shouted against the door's blank surface that he would break the door in if Mr. Pritchel didn't answer and open it, and how this time the harsh furious old voice answered, shouting:

"Get out of my house! Take that murderer and get out of my house."

"You will have to make a statement," the sheriff answered.

"I'll make my statement when the time comes for it!" the old man shouted. "Get out of my house, all of you!" And how he (the sheriff) sent the deputy in the car to fetch the nearest neighbor, and he and Flint waited until the deputy came back with a man and his wife. Then they brought Flint on to town and locked him up and the sheriff telephoned back to old Pritchel's house and the neighbor answered and told him how the old man was still locked in the room, refusing to come out or even to answer save to order them all (several other neighbors had arrived by now, word of the tragedy having spread) to leave. But some of them would stay in the house, no matter what the seemingly crazed old man said or did, and the funeral would be tomorrow.

"And that's all?" Uncle Gavin said.

"That's all," the sheriff said. "Because it's too late now."

"For instance?" Uncle Gavin said.

"The wrong one is dead."

"That happens," Uncle Gavin said.

"For instance?"

"That clay-pit business."

"What clay-pit business?" Because the whole county knew about old Pritchel's clay-pit. It was a formation of malleable clay right in the middle of his farm, of which people in the adjacent countryside made quite serviceable though crude pottery—those times they could manage to dig that much of it up before Mr. Pritchel saw them and drove them off. For generations, Indian and even aboriginal relics—flint arrow-heads, axes and dishes and skulls and thigh-bones and pipes—had been excavated from it by random boys, and a few years ago a party of archaeologists from the State University had dug into it until Old Man Pritchel got there, this time with a shotgun. But everybody knew this; this was not what the sheriff was telling, and now Uncle Gavin was sitting erect in the chair and his feet were on the floor now.

"I hadn't heard about this," Uncle Gavin said.

"It's common knowledge out there," the sheriff said. "In fact, you might call it the local outdoor sport. It began about six weeks ago. They are three northern men. They're trying to buy the whole farm from old Pritchel to get the pit and manufacture some kind of road material out of the clay, I understand. The folks out there are still watching them trying to buy it. Apparently the northerners are the only folks in the country that don't know yet old Pritchel aint got any notion of selling even the clay to them, let alone the farm."

"They've made him an offer, of course."

"Probably a good one. It runs all the way from two hundred and fifty dollars to two hundred and fifty thousand, depending on who's telling it. Them northerners just don't know how to handle him. If they would just set in and convince him that everybody in the county is hoping he won't sell it to them, they could probably buy it before supper tonight." He stared at Uncle Gavin, batting his eyes again. "So the wrong one is dead, you see. If it was that clay-pit, he's no nearer to it than he was yesterday. He's worse off than he was yesterday. Then there wasn't anything between him and his pa-in-law's money but whatever private wishes and hopes and feelings that dim-witted girl might have had. Now there's a penitentiary wall, and likely a rope. It don't make sense. If he was afraid of a possible witness, he not only destroyed the witness before there was anything to be witnessed but also before there was any witness to be destroyed. He set up a signboard saying 'Watch me and mark me,' not just to this county and this state but to all folks everywhere who believe the Book where it says *Thou Shalt Not Kill*—and then went and got himself locked up in the very place created to punish him for this crime and restrain him from the next one. Something went wrong."

"I hope so," Uncle Gavin said.

"You hope so?"

"Yes. That something went wrong. in what has already happened, rather than what has already happened is not finished yet."

"How not finished yet?" the sheriff said. "How can he finish whatever it is he aims to finish? Ain't he already locked up in jail, with the only man in the county who might make bond to free him being the father of the woman he as good as confessed he murdered?"

"It looks that way," Uncle Gavin said. "Was there an insurance policy?"

"I don't know," the sheriff said. "I'll find that out tomorrow. But that ain't what I want to know. I want to know why he *wanted* to be locked up in jail. Because I tell you he wasn't afraid, then nor at any other time. You already guessed who it was out there that was afraid."

But we were not to learn that answer yet. And there was an insurance policy. But by the time we learned about that, something else had happened which sent everything else temporarily out of mind. At daylight the next morning, when the jailer went and looked into Flint's cell, it was empty. He had not broken out. He had walked out, out of the cell, out of the jail, out of the town and apparently out of the country—no trace, no sign, no man who had seen him or seen anyone who might have been him. It was not yet sunup when I let the sheriff in at the side study door; Uncle Gavin was already sitting up in bed when we reached his bedroom.

"Old Man Pritchel!" Uncle Gavin said. "Only we are already too late."

"What's the matter with you?" the sheriff said. "I told you last night he was already too late the second he pulled that wrong trigger. Besides, just to be in position to ease your mind, I've already telephoned out there. Been a dozen folks in the house all night, sitting up with the—with Mrs. Flint, and old Pritchel's still locked in his room and all right too. They heard him bumping and blundering around in there just before daylight, and so somebody knocked on the door and kept on knocking and calling him until he finally opened the door wide enough to give them all a good cussing and order them again to get out of his house and stay out. Then he locked the door again. Old fellow's been hit pretty hard, I reckon. He must have seen it when it happened, and at his age, and having already druv the whole human race away from his house except that half-wit girl, until at last even she up and left him, even at any cost. I reckon it ain't any wonder she married even a man like Flint. What is it the Book says? 'Who lives by the sword, so shall he die.'?—the sword in old Pritchel's case being whatever it was he decided he preferred in place of human beings, while he was still young and hale and strong and didn't need them. But to keep your mind easy, I sent Bryan Ewell out there thirty minutes ago and told him not to let that locked door—or old Pritchel himself, if he comes out of it—out of his sight until I told him to, and I sent Ben Berry and some others out to Flint's house and told Ben to telephone me. And I'll call you when I hear anything. Which won't be anything, because that fellow's gone. He got caught yesterday because he made a mistake, and the fellow that can walk out of that jail like he did ain't going to make two mistakes within five hundred miles of Jefferson or Mississippi either."

"Mistake?" Uncle Gavin said. "He just told us this morning why he wanted to be put in jail."

"And why was that?"

"So he could escape from it."

"And why get out again, when he was already out and could have stayed out by just running instead of telephoning me he had committed a murder?"

"I don't know," Uncle Gavin said. "Are you sure Old Man Pritchel—"

"Didn't I just tell you folks saw and talked to him through that half-opened door this morning? And Bryan Ewell probably sitting in a chair tilted against that door right this minute—or he better be. I'll telephone you if I hear anything. But I've already told you that too—that it won't be nothing."

He telephoned an hour later. He had just talked to the deputy who had searched Flint's house, reporting only that Flint had been there sometime in the night—the back door open, an oil lamp shattered on the floor where Flint had apparently knocked it while fumbling in the dark, since the deputy found, behind a big, open, hurriedly ransacked trunk, a twisted spill of paper which Flint had obviously used to light his search of the trunk—a scrap of paper torn from a billboard—

"A what?" Uncle Gavin said.

"That's what I said," the sheriff said. "And Ben says, 'All right, then send somebody else out here, if my reading ain't good enough to suit you. It was a scrap of paper which was evidently tore from the corner of a billboard because it says on the scrap in English that even I can read—' and I says, 'Tell me exactly what it is you're holding in your hand.' And he did. It's a page, from a magazine or a small paper named *Billboard* or maybe *The Billboard*. There's some more printing on it but Ben can't read it because he lost his spectacles back in the woods while he was surrounding the house to catch Flint doing whatever it was he expected to catch him doing—cooking breakfast, maybe. Do you know what it is?"

"Yes," Uncle Gavin said.

"Do you know what it means, what it was doing there?"

"Yes," Uncle Gavin said. "But why?"

"Well, I can't tell you. And he never will. Because he's gone, Gavin. Oh, we'll catch him—somebody will, I mean, someday, somewhere. But it won't be here, and it won't be for this. It's like that poor, harmless, half-witted girl wasn't important enough for even that justice you claim you prefer above truth, to avenge her."

And that did seem to be all of it. Mrs. Flint was buried that afternoon. The old man was still locked in his room during the funeral, and even after they departed with the coffin for the churchyard, leaving in the house only the deputy in his tilted chair outside the locked door, and two neighbor women who remained to cook a hot meal for old Pritchel, finally prevailing on him to open the door long enough to take the tray from them. And he thanked them for it, clumsily and gruffly, thanking them for their kindness during all the last twenty-four hours. One of the women was moved enough to offer to return tomorrow and cook another meal for him, whereupon his old-time acerbity and choler returned and the kind-hearted woman was even regretting that she had made the offer at all when the harsh, cracked old voice from inside the half-closed door added: "I don't need no help. I ain't had no darter nohow in two years," and the door slammed in their faces and the bolt shot home.

Then the two women left, and there was only the deputy sitting in his tilted chair beside the door. He was back in town the next morning, telling how the old man had snatched the door suddenly open and kicked the chair out from beneath the dozing deputy before he could move and ordered him off the place with violent curses, and how as he (the deputy) peered at the house from around the corner of the barn a short time later, the shotgun blared from the kitchen window and the charge of squirrel shot slammed into the stable wall not a yard above his head. The sheriff telephoned that to Uncle Gavin too:

"So he's out there alone again. And since that's what he seems to want, it's all right with me. Sure I feel sorry for him. I feel sorry for anybody that has to live with a disposition like his. Old and alone, to have all this happen to him. It's like being snatched up by a tornado and whirled and slung and then slammed right back down where you started from, without even the benefit and pleasure of having taken a trip. What was it I said yesterday about living by the sword?"

"I don't remember," Uncle Gavin said. "You said a lot yesterday."

"And a lot of it was right. I said it was finished yesterday. And it is. That fellow will trip himself again someday, but it won't be here."

Only it was more than that. It was as if Flint had never been here at all—no mark, no scar to show that he had ever been in the jail cell. The meagre group of people who pitied but did not mourn, departing, separating, from the raw grave of the woman who had had little enough hold on our lives at best, whom a few of us had known without ever having seen her and some of us had seen without ever knowing her. . . . The childless old man whom most of us had never seen at all, once more alone in the house where, as he said himself, there had been no child anyway in two years. . . .

"As though none of it had ever happened," Uncle Gavin said. "As if Flint had not only never been in that cell but had never existed at all. That triumvirate of murderer, victim, and bereaved—not three flesh-and-blood people but just an illusion, a shadow-play on a sheet—not only neither men nor women nor young nor old but just three labels which cast two shadows for the simple and only reason that it requires a minimum of two in order to postulate the verities of injustice and grief. That's it. They have never cast but two shadows, even though they did bear three labels, names. It was as though only by dying did that poor woman ever gain enough substance and reality even to cast a shadow."

"But somebody killed her," I said.

"Yes," Uncle Gavin said. "Somebody killed her."

That was at noon. About five that afternoon I answered the telephone. It was the sheriff. "Is your uncle there?" he said. "Tell him to wait. I'm coming right over." He had a stranger with him—a city man, in neat city clothes.

"This is Mr. Workman," the sheriff said. "The adjustor. There was an insurance policy. For five hundred, taken out seventeen months ago. Hardly enough to murder anybody for."

"If it ever was a murder," the adjustor said. His voice was cold too, cold yet at the same time at a sort of seething boil. "That policy will be paid at once, without question or any further investigation. And I'll tell you something else you people here don't seem to know yet. That old man is crazy. It was not the man Flint who should have been brought to town and locked up."

Only it was the sheriff who told that too: how yesterday afternoon the insurance company's Memphis office had received a telegram, signed with Old Man Pritchel's name, notifying them of the insured's death, and the adjustor arrived at Old Man Pritchel's house about two o'clock this afternoon and within thirty minutes had extracted from Old Man Pritchel himself the truth about his daughter's death: the facts of it which the physical evidence—the truck and the three dead squirrels and the blood on the steps and on the ground—supported. This was that while the daughter was cooking dinner, Pritchel and Flint had driven the truck down to Pritchel's woods lot to shoot squirrels for supper—"And that's correct," the sheriff said. "I asked. They did that every Sunday morning. Pritchel wouldn't let anybody but Flint shoot his squirrels, and he wouldn't even let Flint shoot them unless he was along"—and they shot the three squirrels and Flint drove the truck back to the house and up beside the back steps and the woman came out to take the squirrels and Flint opened the door and picked up the gun to get out of the truck and stumbled, caught his heel on the edge of the running-board and flinging up the hand carrying the gun to break his fall, so that the muzzle of the gun was pointing right at his wife's head when it went off. And Old Man Pritchel not only denied having sent the wire, he violently and profanely repudiated any and all implication or suggestion that he even knew the policy existed at all. He denied to the very last that the shooting had been any part of an accident. He tried to revoke his own testimony as to what had happened when the daughter came out to get the dead squirrels and the gun went off, repudiating his own story when he realized that he had cleared his son-in-law of murder, snatching the paper from the adjustor's hand, which he apparently believed was the policy itself, and attempting to tear it up and destroy it before the adjustor could stop him.

"Why?" Uncle Gavin said.

"Why not?" the sheriff said. "We had let Flint get away; Mr. Pritchel knew he was loose somewhere in the world. Do you reckon he aimed to let the man that killed his daughter get paid for it?"

"Maybe," Uncle Gavin said. "But I don't think so. I don't think he is worried about that at all. I think Mr. Pritchel knows that Joel Flint is not going to collect that policy or any other prize. Maybe he knew a little country jail like ours wasn't going to hold a wide-travelled ex-carnival man, and he expected Flint to come back out there and this time he was ready for him. And I think that as soon as people stop worrying him, he will send you word to come out there, and he will tell you so."

"Hah," the adjustor said. "Then they must have stopped worrying him. Listen to this. When I got there this afternoon, there were three men in the parlor with him. They had a certified check. It was a big check. They were buying his farm from him—lock, stock and barrel—and I didn't know land in this country was worth that much either, incidentally. He had the deed all drawn and signed, but when I told them who I was, they agreed to wait until I could get back to town here and tell somebody—the sheriff, probably. And I left, and that old lunatic was still standing in the door, shaking that deed at me and croaking: 'Tell the sheriff, damn you! Get a lawyer, too! Get that lawyer Gavin. I hear tell he claims to be pretty slick!'"

"We thank you," the sheriff said. He spoke and moved with that deliberate, slightly florid, old-fashioned courtesy which only big men can wear, except that his was constant; this was the first time I ever saw him quit anyone shortly, even when he would see them again tomorrow. He didn't even look at the adjustor again. "My car's outside," he told Uncle Gavin.

So just before sunset we drove up to the neat picket fence enclosing Old Man Pritchel's neat, bare little yard and neat, tight little house, in front of which stood the big, dust-covered car with its city license plates and Flint's battered truck with a strange Negro youth at the wheel—strange because Old Man Pritchel had never had a servant of any sort save his daughter.

"He's leaving too," Uncle Gavin said.

"That's his right," the sheriff said. We mounted the steps. But before we reached the door, Old Man Pritchel was already shouting for us to come in—the harsh, cracked old man's voice shouting at us from beyond the hall, beyond the door to the dining room where a tremendous old-fashioned telescope bag, strapped and bulging, sat on a chair and the three northerners in dusty khaki stood watching the door and Old Man Pritchel himself sat at the table. And I saw for the first time (Uncle Gavin told me he had seen him only twice) the uncombed thatch of white hair, a fierce tangle of eyebrows above steel-framed spectacles, a jut of untrimmed mustache and a scrabble of beard stained with chewing tobacco to the color of dirty cotton.

"Come in," he said. "That lawyer Gavin, heh?"

"Yes, Mr. Pritchel," the sheriff said.

"Hehm," the old man barked. "Well, Hub," he said. "Can I sell my land, or can't I?"

"Of course, Mr. Pritchel," the sheriff said. "We hadn't heard you aimed to."

"Heh," the old man said. "Maybe this changed my mind." The check and the folded deed both lay on the table in front of him. He pushed the check toward the sheriff. He didn't look at Uncle Gavin again; he just said: "You, too." Uncle Gavin and the sheriff moved to the table and stood looking down at the check. Neither of them touched it. I could see their faces. There was nothing in them. "Well?" Mr. Pritchel said.

"It's a good price," the sheriff said.

This time the old man said "Hah!" short and harsh. He unfolded the deed and spun it to face, not the sheriff but Uncle Gavin. "Well?" he said. "You, lawyer?"

"It's all right, Mr. Pritchel," Uncle Gavin said. The old man sat back, both hands on the table before him, his head tilted back as he looked up at the sheriff.

"Well?" he said. "Fish, or cut bait."

"It's your land," the sheriff said. "What you do with it is no man's business else."

"Hah," Mr. Pritchel said. He didn't move. "All right, gentlemen." He didn't move at all; one of the strangers came forward and took up the deed. "I'll be out of the house in thirty minutes. You can take possession then, or you will find the key under the mat tomorrow morning." I don't believe he even looked after them as they went out, though I couldn't be sure because of the glare on his spectacles. Then I knew that he was looking at the sheriff, had been looking at him for a minute or more, and then I saw that he was trembling, jerking and shaking as the old tremble, although his hands on the table were as motionless as two lumps of the clay would have been.

"So you let him get away," he said.

"That's right," the sheriff said. "But you wait, Mr. Pritchel. We'll catch him."

"When?" the old man said. "Two years? Five years? Ten years? I am seventy-four years old; buried my wife and four children. Where will I be in ten years?"

"Here, I hope," the sheriff said.

"Here?" the old man said. "Didn't you just hear me tell that fellow he could have this house in thirty minutes? I own a automobile truck now; I got money to spend now, and something to spend it for."

"Spend it for what?" the sheriff said. "That check? Even this boy here would have to start early and run late to get shut of that much money in ten years."

"Spend it running down the man that killed my Ellie!" He rose suddenly, thrusting his chair back. He staggered, but when the sheriff stepped quickly toward him, he flung his arm out and seemed actually to strike the sheriff back a pace. "Let be," he said, panting. Then he said, harsh and loud in his cracked shaking voice: "Get out of here! Get out of my house all of you!" But the sheriff didn't move, nor did we, and after a moment the old man stopped trembling. But he was still holding to the table edge. But his voice was quiet. "Hand me my whiskey. On the sideboard. And three glasses." The sheriff fetched them—an old-fashioned cut-glass decanter and three heavy tumblers—and set them before him. And when he spoke this time, his voice was almost gentle and I knew what the woman had felt that evening when she offered to come back tomorrow and cook another meal for him: "You'll have to excuse me. I'm tired. I've had a heap of trouble lately, and I reckon I'm wore out. Maybe a change is what I need."

"But not tonight, Mr. Pritchel," the sheriff said.

And then again, as when the woman had offered to come back and cook, he ruined it. "Maybe I won't start tonight," he said. "And then maybe again I will. But you folks want to get on back to town, so we'll just drink to goodbye and better days." He unstoppered the decanter and poured whiskey into the three tumblers and set the decanter down and looked about the table. "You, boy," he said, "hand me the water bucket. It's on the back gallery shelf." Then, as I turned and started toward the door, I saw him reach and take up the sugar bowl and plunge the spoon into the sugar and then I stopped too. And I remember Uncle Gavin's and the sheriff's faces and I could not believe my eyes either as he put the spoonful of sugar into the raw whiskey and started to stir it. Because I had not only watched Uncle Gavin, and the sheriff when he would come to play chess with Uncle Gavin, but Uncle Gavin's father too who was my grandfather, and my own father before he died, and all the other men who would come to Grandfather's house who drank cold toddies as we call them, and even I knew that to make a cold toddy you do not put the sugar into the whiskey because sugar will not dissolve in raw whiskey but only lies in a little intact swirl like sand at the bottom of the glass; that you first put the water into the glass and dissolve the sugar into the water, in a ritual almost; then you add the whiskey, and that anyone like Old Man Pritchel who must have been watching men make cold toddies for nearly seventy years and had been making and drinking them himself for at least fifty-three, would know this too. And I remember how the man we had thought was Old Man Pritchel realized too late what he was doing and jerked his head up just as Uncle Gavin sprang toward him, and swung his arm back and hurled the glass at Uncle Gavin's head, and the thud of the flung glass against the wall and the dark splash it made and the crash of the table as it went over and the raw stink of the spilled whiskey from the decanter and Uncle Gavin shouting at the sheriff: "Grab him, Hub! Grab him!"

Then we were all three on him. I remember the savage strength

119

and speed of the body which was no old man's body; I saw him duck beneath the sheriff's arm and the entire wig came off; I seemed to see his whole face wrenching itself furiously free from beneath the makeup which bore the painted wrinkles and the false eyebrows. When the sheriff snatched the beard and mustache off, the flesh seemed to come with it, springing quick and pink and then crimson, as though in that last desperate cast he had had to beard, disguise, not his face so much as the very blood which he had spilled.

It took us only thirty minutes to find old Mr. Pritchel's body. It was under the feed room in the stable, in a shallow and hurried trench, scarcely covered from sight. His hair had not only been dyed, it had been trimmed, the eyebrows trimmed and dyed too, and the mustache and beard shaved off. He was wearing the identical garments which Flint had worn to the jail and he had been struck at least one crushing blow on the face, apparently with the flat of the same axe which had split his skull from behind, so that his features were almost unrecognizable and, after another two or three weeks underground, would perhaps have been even unidentifiable as those of the old man. And pillowed carefully beneath the head was a big ledger almost six inches thick and weighing almost twenty pounds and filled with the carefully pasted clippings which covered twenty years and more. It was the record and tale of the gift, the talent, which at the last he had misapplied and betrayed and which had then turned and destroyed him. It was all there: inception, course, peak, and then decline—the handbills, the theatre programs, the news clippings, and even one actual ten-foot poster:

SIGNOR CANOVA
Master of Illusion
He Disappears While You Watch Him
*Management offers One Thousand
Dollars in Cash To Any Man or
Woman or Child Who . . .*

Last of all was the final clipping, from our Memphis-printed daily paper, under the Jefferson date line, which was news and not press-agentry. This was the account of that last gamble in which he had cast his gift and his life against money, wealth, and lost—the clipped fragment of news-sheet which recorded the end not of one life but of three, though even here two of them cast but one shadow: not only that of the harmless dim-witted woman but of Joel Flint and Signor Canova too, with scattered among them and marking the date of that death too, the cautiously worded advertisements in *Variety* and *Billboard*, using the new changed name and no takers probably, since Signor Canova the Great was already dead then and already serving his purgatory in this circus for six months and that circus for eight—bandsman, ringman, Bornean wild man, down to the last stage where he touched bottom: the travelling from country town to country town with a roulette wheel wired against imitation watches and pistols which would not shoot, until one day instinct perhaps showed him one more chance to use the gift again.

"And lost this time for good," the sheriff said. We were in the study again. Beyond the open side door fire-flies winked and drifted across the summer night and the crickets and tree-frogs cheeped and whirred. "It was that insurance policy. If that adjustor hadn't come to town and sent us back out there in time to watch him try to dissolve sugar in raw whiskey, he would have collected that check and taken that truck and got clean away. Instead, he sends for the adjustor, then he practically dares you and me to come out there and see past that wig and paint—"

"You said something the other day about his destroying his witness too soon," Uncle Gavin said. "She wasn't his witness. The witness he destroyed was the one we were supposed to find under that feed room."

"Witness to what?" the sheriff said. "To the fact that Joel Flint no longer existed?"

"Partly. But mostly to the first crime, the old one: the one in which Signor Canova died. He intended for that witness to be found. That's why he didn't bury it, hide it better and deeper. As soon as somebody found it, he would be at once and forever not only rich but free, free not only of Signor Canova who had betrayed him by dying eight years ago, but of Joel Flint too. Even if we had found it before he had a chance to leave, what would he have said?"

"He ought to have battered the face a little more," the sheriff said.

"I doubt it," Uncle Gavin said. "What would he have said?"

"All right," the sheriff said. "What?"

"'Yes, I killed him. He murdered my daughter.' And what would you have said, being, as you are, the Law?"

"Nothing," the sheriff said after a time.

"Nothing," Uncle Gavin said. A dog was barking somewhere, not

121

a big dog, and then a screech-owl flew into the mulberry tree in the back yard and began to cry, plaintive and tremulous, and all the little furred creatures would be moving now—the field mice, the possums and rabbits and foxes and the legless vertebrates— creeping or scurrying about the dark land which beneath the rainless summer stars was just dark: not desolate. "That's one reason he did it," Uncle Gavin said.

"One reason?" the sheriff said. "What's the other?"

"The other is the real one. It had nothing to do with the money; he probably could not have helped obeying it if he had wanted to. That gift he had. His first regret right now is probably not that he was caught, but that he was caught too soon, before the body was found and he had the chance to identify it as his own; before Signor Canova had had time to toss his gleaming tophat vanishing behind him and bow to the amazed and stormlike stac- cato of adulant palms and turn and stride once or twice and then himself vanish from the pacing spotlight—gone, to be seen no more. Think what he did: he convicted himself of murder when he could very likely have escaped by flight; he acquitted himself of it after he was already free again. Then he dared you and me to come out there and actually be his witnesses and guarantors in the consummation of the very act which he knew we had been trying to prevent. What else could the possession of such a gift as his have engendered, and the successful practising of it have increased, but a supreme contempt for mankind? You told me yourself that he had never been afraid in his life."

"Yes," the sheriff said. "The Book itself says somewhere, *Know thyself*. Ain't there another book somewhere that says, *Man, fear thyself, thine arrogance and vanity and pride?* You ought to know; you claim to be a book man. Didn't you tell me that's what that luck- charm on your watch chain means? What book is that in?"

"It's in all of them," Uncle Gavin said. "The good ones, I mean, It's said in a lot of different ways, but it's there."

THE CORSICAN ORDEAL
OF MISS X

BY BERTRAND RUSSELL

Bertrand Russell, 3rd Earl Russell, was born in Wales. He was orphaned at three and succeeded to the title in 1931 on the death of his brother. He was a fellow at Trinity when he was sentenced to prison for pacifism during World War I. Later he taught in Peking and at various U.S. universities. With his second wife he ran a progressive school for children in Sussex. Logic was the basis of his philosophy. Edmund Wilson called him an eighteenth-century philosopher, "ironic, elegant, dry, humanitarian, and anti-mystic."

I HAD OCCASION RECENTLY to visit my good friend, Professor N, whose paper on pre-Celtic Decorative Art in Denmark raised some points that I felt needed discussing. I found him in his study, but his usually benign and yet slightly intelligent expression was marred by some strange bewilderment. The books which should have been on the arm of the chair, and which he supposed himself to be reading, were scattered in confusion on the floor. The spectacles which he imagined to be on his nose lay idle on his desk. The pipe which was usually in his mouth lay smoking in his tobacco bowl, though he seemed completely unaware of its not occupying its usual place. His mild and somewhat silly philanthropy and his usually placid gaze had somehow dropped off him. A harassed, distracted, bewildered, and horrified expression was stamped upon his features.

"Good God!" I said, "what has happened?"

"Ah," said he, "it is my secretary, Miss X. Hitherto, I have found her level-headed, efficient, cool, and destitute of those emotions which are only too apt to distract youth. But in an ill-advised moment I allowed her to take a fortnight's holiday from her labours on decorative art, and she, in a still more ill-advised moment, chose to spend the fortnight in Corsica. When she returned I saw at once that something had happened. 'What *did* you do in Corsica?' I asked. 'Ah! What indeed!' she replied."

The secretary was not in the room at the moment, and I hoped that Professor N might enlarge a little upon the misfortune that had befallen him. But in this I was disappointed. Not another word, so at least he assured me, had he been able to extract from Miss X. Horror piled upon horror glared from her eyes at the mere recollection, but nothing more specific could he discover.

I felt it my duty to the poor girl, who, so I had been given to understand, had hitherto been hard-working and conscientious, to see whether anything could be done to relieve her of the dreadful weight which depressed her spirits. I bethought me of Mrs. Menhennet, a middle-aged lady of considerable bulk, who, so I was informed by her grandchildren, had once had some pretences to beauty. Mrs. Menhennet, I knew, was the granddaughter of a Corsican bandit; in one of those unguarded moments, too frequent, alas, in that rough island, the bandit had assaulted a thoroughly respectable young lady, with the result that she had given birth, after a due interval, to the redoubtable Mr. Gorman.

Mr. Gorman, though his work took him into the City, pursued there the same kind of activities as had led to his existence. Eminent financiers trembled at his approach. Well-established bankers of unblemished reputation had ghastly visions of prison. Merchants who imported the wealth of the gorgeous East turned pale at the thought of Customs House officers at the dead of night. All of which misfortunes, it was well understood, were set in motion by the machinations of the predacious Mr. Gorman.

His daughter, Mrs. Menhennet, would have heard of any strange and unwonted disturbance in the home of her paternal grandfather. I therefore asked for an interview, which was graciously accorded. At four o'clock on a dark afternoon in November I presented myself at her tea table.

"And what," she said, "brings you here? Do not pretend that it is my charms. The day for such pretence is past. For ten years it would have been true; for another ten I should have believed it. Now it is neither true nor do I believe it. Some other motive brings you here, and I palpitate to know what it may be."

This approach was somewhat too direct for my taste. I find a pleasure in a helicoidal approach to my subject. I like to begin at a point remote from that at which I am aiming, or on occasion, if I begin at a point near my ultimate destination, I like to approach the actual point by a boomerang course, taking me at first away from the final mark and thereby, I hope, deceiving my auditor. But Mrs. Menhennet would permit no such finesse. Honest, downright, and straightforward, she believed in the direct approach, a characteristic which she seemed to have inherited from her Corsican grandfather. I therefore abandoned all attempt at circumlocution and came straight to the core of my curiosity.

"Mrs. Menhennet," I said, "it has come to my knowledge that there have been in recent weeks strange doings in Corsica, doings which, as I can testify from ocular demonstration, have turned brown hairs grey and young springy steps leaden with the weariness of age. These doings, I am convinced, owing to certain rumours which have reached me, are of transcendent international importance. Whether some new Napoleon is marching to the conquest of Moscow, or some younger Columbus to the discovery of a still unknown Continent, I cannot guess. But something of this sort, I am convinced, is taking place in those wild mountains, something of the sort is being plotted secretly, darkly, dangerously, something of the sort is being concealed tortuously, ferociously, and criminally from those who rashly seek to pierce the veil. You, dear lady, I am convinced, in spite of the correctness of your tea table and the elegance of your china and the fragrance of your Lapsang Souchong, have not lost touch with the activities of your revered father. At his death, I know, you made yourself the guardian of those interests for which he stood. His father, who had ever been to him a shining light on the road towards swift success, inspired every moment of his life. Since his death, although perhaps some of your less perspicacious friends may not have pierced your very efficient disguise, you, I know, have worn his mantle. You, if anyone in this cold and dismal city, can tell me what is happening in that land of sunshine, and what plots, so dark as to cause eclipse even in the blaze of noon, are being hatched in the minds of those noble descendants of ancient greatness. Tell me, I pray you, what you know. The life of Professor N, or if not his life at least his reason, is trembling in the balance. He is, as you are well aware, a benevolent man, not fierce like you and me, but full of gentle lovingkindness. Owing to this trait in his character he cannot divest himself of responsibility for the welfare of his worthy secretary, Miss X, who returned yesterday from Corsica transformed completely from the sunny carefree girl that once she was to a lined, harassed, and weary woman weighed down by all the burdens of the world. What it was that happened to her she refuses to reveal, but if it cannot be discovered it is much to be feared that that great genius, which has already all but solved the many and intricate problems besetting the interpretation of pre-Celtic decorative art, will totter and disintegrate and fall a heap of rubble, like the old Campanile in Venice. You cannot, I am sure, be otherwise than horrified at such a prospect, and I therefore beseech you to unfold, so far as lies in your power, the dreadful secrets of your ancestral home."

Mrs. Menhennet listened to my words in silence, and when I ceased to speak she still for a while abstained from all reply. At a certain point in my discourse the colour faded from her cheeks and she gave a great gasp. With an effort she composed herself, folded her hands, and compelled her breathing to become quiet.

"You put before me," she said, "a dreadful dilemma. If I remain silent, Professor N, not to mention Miss X, must be deprived of reason. But if I speak . . ." Here she shuddered, and no further word emerged.

At this point, when I had been at a loss to imagine what the next development would be, the parlour maid appeared and mentioned that the chimney sweep, in full professional attire, was waiting at the door, as he had been engaged to sweep the chimney of the drawing room that very afternoon.

"Good heavens!" she exclaimed. "While you and I have been engaged in small talk and trivial badinage this proud man with his great duties to perform has been kept waiting at my doorstep. This will never do. For now this interview must be at an end. One last word, however. I advise you, if you are in earnest, but only if you are, to pay a visit to General Prz."*

General Prz, as everybody remembers, greatly distinguished himself in the First World War by his exploits in defence of his native Poland. Poland, however, in recent years had shown herself ungrateful, and he had been compelled to take refuge in some less unsettled country. A long life of adventure had made the old man, in spite of his grey hairs, unwilling to sink into a quiet life. Although admirers offered him a villa at Worthing, a bijou residence at Cheltenham, or a bungalow in the mountains of Ceylon, none of these took his fancy. Mrs. Menhennet gave him an introduction to some of the more unruly of her relatives in Corsica, and among them he found once more something of the *élan*, the fire and the wild energy, which had inspired the exploits of his earlier years.

But although Corsica remained his spiritual home, and his physical home during the greater part of the year, he would allow himself on rare occasions to visit such of the capitals of Europe as were still west of the Iron Curtain. In these capitals he would converse with the elder statesmen, who would anxiously ask his opinion on all the major trends of recent policy. Whatever he deigned to say in reply they listened to with the respect justly owing to his years and valour. And he would carry back to his mountain fastness the knowledge of the part that Corsica—yes, even Corsica—could play in the great events to come.

As the friend of Mrs. Menhennet, he was at once admitted to the innermost circle of those who, within or without the law, kept alive the traditions of ancient liberty which their Ghibelline ancestors had brought from the still vigorous republics of Northern Italy. In the deep recesses of the hills, hidden from the view of the casual tourist, who saw nothing but rocks and shepherd's huts and a few stunted trees, he was allowed to visit old palaces full of medieval splendour, the armour of ancient Gonfalonieri,

*Pronounced "Pish."

and the jewelled swords of world-famous Condottieri. In their magnificent halls these proud descendants of ancient chieftains assembled and feasted, not perhaps always wisely but always too well. Even in converse with the General their lips were sealed as to some of the great secrets of their order, except indeed, in those moments of exuberant conviviality, when the long story of traditional hospitality overcame the scruples which at other times led to a prudent silence.

It was in these convivial moments that the General learned of the world-shaking design that these men cherished, a design that inspired all their waking actions and dominated the dreams in which their feasts too often terminated. Nothing loath, he threw himself into their schemes with all the ardour and all the traditional recklessness of the ancient Polish nobility. He thanked God that at a period of life when to most men nothing remains but reminiscence he had been granted the opportunity to share in great deeds of high adventure. On moonlight nights he would gallop over the mountains on his great charger, whose sire and dam alike had helped him to shed immortal glory upon the stricken fields of his native land. Inspired by the rapid motion of the night wind, his thoughts flowed through a mingled dream of ancient valour and future triumph, in which past and future blended in the alembic of his passion.

At the time when Mrs. Menhennet uttered her mysterious suggestion it happened that the General was engaged in one of his periodic rounds of visits to the elder statesmen of the Western world. He had in the past entertained a somewhat anachronistic prejudice against the Western hemisphere, but since he had learned from his island friends that Columbus was a Corsican he had endeavoured to think better than before of the consequences of that adventurer's somewhat rash activities. He could not quite bring himself actually to imitate Columbus, since he felt that there would be a slight taint of trade about any such journey, but he would call after due notice on the American Ambassador to the Court of St. James's, who always took pains to have a personal message from the President in readiness for his distinguished guest. He would, of course, visit Mr. Winston Churchill, but he never demeaned himself so far as to recognize the existence of the Socialist ministers.

It was after he had been dining with Mr. Churchill that I had the good fortune to find him at leisure in the ancient club of which he was an honorary member. He honoured me with a glass of his pre-1914 Tokay, which was part of the *spolia opima* of his encounter with the eminent Hungarian general whom he left dead upon the field of honour with a suitable eulogy for his bravery. After due acknowledgment of the great mark of favour which he was bestowing upon me—a notable mark, for after all not even Hungarian generals go into battle with more than a few bottles of Tokay bound to their saddles—I led the conversation gradually towards Corsica.

"I have heard," I said, "that that island is not what it was. Education, they tell me, has turned brigands into bank clerks, and stilettos into stylographic pens. No longer, so they tell me, do ancient vendettas keep alive through the generations. I have even heard dreadful tales of inter-marriage between families which had had a feud lasting eight hundred years, and yet the marriage was not accompanied by bloodshed. If all this is indeed true, I am forced to weep. I had always hoped, if fortune should favour my industry, to exchange the sanitary villa which I inhabit in Balham for some stormy peak in the home of ancient romance. But if romance even there is dead, what remains to me as a hope for old age? Perhaps you can reassure me; perhaps something yet lingers there. Perhaps amid thunder and lightning the ghost of Farinata degli Uberti is still to be seen looking around with great disdain. I have come to you tonight in the hope that you can give me such reassurance, since without it I shall not know how to support the burden of the humdrum years."

As I was speaking his eyes gleamed. I saw him clench his fists and close his jaws fiercely. Scarcely could he wait for the end of my periods. And as soon as I was silent he burst forth.

"Young man," he said, "were you not a friend of Mrs. Menhennet I should grudge you that noble nectar which I have allowed your unworthy lips to consume. I am compelled to think that you have been associating with the ignoble. Some few there may be among the riff-raff of the ports, and the ignoble gentry who concern themselves with the base business of bureaucracy—some few there may be, I repeat, of whom the dreadful things at which you have been hinting may be true. But they are no true Corsicans. They are but bastard Frenchmen, or gesticulating Italians, or toad-eating Catalans. The true Corsican breed is what it always was. It lives the free life, and emissaries of governments who seek to interfere die the death. No, my friend, all is yet well in that happy home of heroism."

I leapt to my feet and took his right hand in both of mine.

"O happy day," said I, "when my faith is restored, and my doubts are quenched! Would that I might see with my own eyes the noble breed of men whom you have brought so forcibly before my imagination. Could you permit me to know even one of them I should live a happier life, and the banalities of Balham would become more bearable."

"My young friend," said he, "your generous enthusiasm does you credit. Great though the favour may be, I am willing, in view of your enthusiasm, to grant the boon you ask. You shall know one of these splendid survivors of the golden age of man. I know that one of them, indeed one of my closest friends among them—I speak of the Count of Aspramonte—will be compelled to descend from the hills to pick up in Ajaccio a consignment of new saddles for his stallions. These saddles, you will of course understand, are made specially for him by the man who has charge of the racing stables of the Duke of Ashby-de-la-Zouche. The Duke is an old friend of mine, and as a great favour allows me occasionally to purchase from him a few saddles for the use of such of my friends as I deem worthy of so priceless a gift. If you care to be in Ajaccio next week, I can give you a letter to the Count of Aspramonte, who would be more accessible there than in his mountain fastness."

With tears in my eyes I thanked him for his great kindness. I bowed low and kissed his hand. As I left his presence, my heart filled with sorrow at the thought of the nobility that is perishing from our ignoble earth.

Following the advice of General Prz, I flew the following week to Ajaccio, and inquired at the principal hotels for the Count of Aspramonte. At the third place of inquiry I was informed that he was at the moment occupying the Imperial Suite, but that he was a busy man with little time for unauthorized visitors. From the demeanour of the hotel servants I inferred that he had earned their most profound respect. In an interview with the proprietor I handed over the letter of introduction from General Prz with the request that it should be put as soon as possible into the hands of the Count of Aspramonte, who, I learned, was at the moment engaged in business in the town.

The hotel was filled with a chattering throng of tourists of the usual description, all of them, so far as I could observe, trivial and transitory. Coming fresh from the dreams of General Prz I felt the atmosphere a strange one, by no means such as I could have wished. It was not in this setting that I could imagine the realization of the Polish nobleman's dreams. I had, however, no other clue, and was compelled to make the best of it.

After an ample dinner, totally indistinguishable from those provided in the best hotels of London, New York, Calcutta, and

Johannesburg, I was sitting somewhat disconsolate in the lounge, when I saw approaching me a brisk gentleman of young middle-age whom I took at first to be a successful American executive. He had the square jaw, the firm step and the measured speech which I have learned to associate with that powerful section of society. But to my surprise, when he addressed me it was in English English with a Continental accent. To my still greater surprise he mentioned that he was the Count of Aspramonte.

"Come," he said, "to the sitting room of my suite, where we can talk more undisturbed than in this mêlée."

His suite, when we reached it, turned out to be ornate and palatial in a somewhat garish style. He gave me a stiff whisky and soda and a large cigar.

"You are, I see," so he began the conversation, "a friend of that dear old gentleman, General Prz. I hope you have never been tempted to laugh at him. For us who live in the modern world the temptation undoubtedly exists, but out of respect for his grey hairs I resist it.

"You and I, my dear sir," he continued, "live in the modern world and have no use for memories and hopes that are out of place in an age dominated by dollars. I for my part, although I live in a somewhat out of the way part of the world, and although I might, if I let myself be dominated by tradition, be as lost in misty dreams as the worthy General, have decided to adapt myself to our time. The main purpose of my life is the acquisition of dollars, not only for myself but for my island. 'How,' you may ask, 'does your manner of life conduce to this end?' In view of your friendship with the General I feel that I owe you an answer to this not unnatural query.

"The mountains in which I have my home afford an ideal ground for the breeding and exercising of race horses. The Arab stallions and mares which my father collected in the course of his wide travels gave rise to a breed of unexampled strength and swiftness. The Duke of Ashby-de-la-Zouche, as you of course are aware, has one great ambition. It is to own three successive Derby winners, and it is through me that he hopes to realize this ambition. His vast wealth is devoted mainly to this end. On the ground that the Derby offers an attraction to American tourists he is allowed to deduct the expenses of his stud from his income in his tax returns. He is thus able to retain that wealth which too many of his peers have lost. The Duke is not alone among my customers. Some of my best horses have gone to Virginia, others to Australia. There is no part of the world in which the royal sport is

131

known where my horses are not famous. It is owing to them that I am able to keep up my palace and to preserve intact the sturdy human stock of our Corsican mountains.

"My life, as you will see, unlike that of General Prz, is lived on the plane of reality. I think more frequently of the dollar exchange than of Ghibelline ancestry, and I pay more attention to horse dealers than to even the most picturesque aristocratic relics. Nevertheless, when I am at home, the need to preserve the respect of the surrounding population compels me to conform to tradition. It is just possible that if you visit me in my castle you will be able to pick up some clue to the enigma which, as I see from the General's letter, is the cause of your visit to me. I shall be returning to my castle on horseback the day after tomorrow. It is a long journey, and an early start will be necessary, but if you care to present yourself at six o'clock in the morning I shall be happy to provide you with a horse on which you can accompany me to my home."

Having by this time finished the whisky and the cigar, I thanked him somewhat effusively for his courtesy, and accepted his invitation.

It was still pitch dark when on the next day I presented myself at the door of the Count's hotel. It was a raw and gusty morning and bitterly cold, with a hint of snow in the air. But the Count seemed impervious to meteorological conditions when he appeared upon his magnificent steed. Another, almost equally magnificent, was led to the door by his servant, and I was bidden to mount him. We set off, soon leaving the streets of the town and then, by small roads which only long experience could have enabled a man to find, we wound up and up to ever greater heights, at first through woodlands and then through open country, grass and rocks.

The Count, it appeared, was incapable of fatigue, or hunger, or thirst. Throughout a long day, with only a few moments' intermission during which we munched dry bread, ate some dates, and drank icy water from a stream, he conversed intelligently and informatively about this and that, showing a wide knowledge of the world of affairs and an acquaintance with innumerable rich men who found leisure for an interest in horses. But not one word did he utter throughout the whole of that long day on the matter which had brought me to Corsica. Gradually, in spite of the beauty of the scenery and the interest of his multi-lingual anecdotes, impatience mastered me.

"My dear Count," I said, "I cannot express to you how grateful I am for this chance to visit your ancestral home. But I must venture to remind you that I have come upon an errand of mercy, to save the life, or at least the reason, of a worthy friend of mine for whom I have the highest regard. You are leaving me in doubt as to whether I am serving this purpose by accompanying you on this long ride."

"I understand your impatience," he said, "but you must realize that, however I adapt myself to the modern world, I cannot in these uplands accelerate the tempo which is immemorially customary. You shall, I promise you, be brought nearer to your goal before the evening ends. More than that I cannot say, for the matter does not rest with me."

With these enigmatic words I had to be content.

We reached his castle as the sun was setting. It was built upon a steep eminence, and to every lover of architecture it was obvious that every part of it, down to the minutest detail, dated from the Thirteenth Century. Crossing the drawbridge we entered a Gothic gateway into a large courtyard. Our horses were taken by a groom, and the Count led me into a vast hall, out of which, by a narrow doorway, he conducted me into the chamber that I was to occupy for the night. A huge canopied bed and heavy carved furniture of ancient design filled much of the space. Out of the window a vast prospect down innumerable winding valleys enticed the eye to a distant glimpse of sea.

"I hope," he said, "that you will succeed in being not too uncomfortable in this somewhat antiquated domicile."

"I do not think that will be difficult," said I, glancing at the blazing fire of enormous logs that spread a flickering light from the vast hearth. He informed me that dinner would be ready in an hour, and that after dinner, if all went well, something should be done to further my inquiries.

After a sumptuous dinner, he led me back to my room, and said, "I will now introduce you to an ancient servant of this house, who, from the long years of his service here, has become a repository of all its secrets. He, I have no doubt, will be able to help you towards the solution of your problem."

He rang the bell, and when it was answered requested the manservant to ask the seneschal to join in our conversation. After a short interval the seneschal approached. I saw before me an old man, bent double with rheumatism, with white locks, and the grave air of one who has lived through much.

"This man," said my host, "will give you as much enlightenment as this place can afford."

With that he withdrew.

"Old man," said I, "I do not know whether at your great age I may hope that your wits are what they were. I am surprised, I must confess, that the Count should refer me to you. I had fondly imagined myself worthy to deal with equals, and not only with serving men in their dotage."

As I uttered these words a strange transformation occurred. The old man, as I had supposed him to be, suddenly lost his rheumatic appearance, drew himself up to his full height of six-foot three, tore from his head the white wig which concealed his ample coal-black hair, threw off the ancient cloak he had been wearing, and revealed beneath it the complete costume of a Florentine noble of the period when the castle was built. Laying his hand upon the sword, he turned upon me with flashing eyes, and said, "Young man, were you not brought here by the Count, in whose sagacity I have much confidence, I should here and now order you to be cast into the dungeons, as an impertinent upstart, unable to perceive noble blood through the disguise of a seedy cloak."

"Sir," I said, with all due humility, "I must humbly beg your pardon for an error which I cannot but think was designed both by you and by the Count. If you will accept my humble excuses, I shall be happy to learn who it is in whose presence I have the honour to be."

"Sir," said he, "I will accept your speech as in some degree making amends for your previous impertinence, and you shall know who I am and what I stand for. I, sir, am the Duke of Ermocolle. The Count is my right-hand man, and obeys me in all things. But in these sad times there is need of the wisdom of the serpent. You have seen him as a businessman, adapting himself to the practices of our age, blaspheming for a purpose against the noble creed by which he and I alike are inspired. I decided to present myself to you in disguise in order to form some estimate of your character and outlook. You passed the test, and I will now tell you the little that I have a right to reveal concerning the trouble which has come into the life of your unworthy professorial friend."

In reply to these words I spoke long and eloquently about the professor and his labours, about Miss X and her youthful innocence, and about the obligation which I felt that friendship had placed upon my inadequate shoulders. He listened to me in grave silence. At the end he said, "There is only one thing that I can do for you, and that I will do."

He thereupon took in his hand an enormous quill pen, and on a large sheet of parchment he wrote these words: "To Miss X. You are hereby released from a part of the oath you swore. Tell all to the bearer of this note and to Professor N. Then *ACT*." To this he appended his signature in full magnificence.

"That, my friend, is all that I can do for you."

I thanked him and bade him a ceremonial good-night.

I slept little. The wind howled, the snow fell, the fire died down. I tossed and turned upon my pillow. When at last a few moments of uneasy slumber came to me, strange dreams wearied me even more than wakefulness. When dawn broke, a leaden oppression weighed me down. I sought the Count and acquainted him with what had passed.

"You will understand," I said, "that in view of the message which I bear, it is my duty to return to England with all speed."

Thanking him once more for his hospitality I mounted the same steed upon which I had come and, accompanied by a groom whom he sent with me to help me in finding the road, I slowly picked my way through snow and sleet and tempest until I reached the shelter of Ajaccio. From there next day I returned to England.

On the morning after my return I presented myself at the house of Professor N. I found him sunk in gloom, decorative art forgotten, and Miss X absent.

"Old friend," I said, "it is painful to see you in this sad state. I have been active on your behalf, and returned but last night from Corsica. I was not wholly successful, but I was also not wholly unsuccessful. I bear a message, not to you, but to Miss X. Whether this message will bring relief or the opposite I cannot tell. But it is my plain duty to deliver it into her hands. Can you arrange that I may see her here in your presence, for it is in your presence that the message must be delivered."

"It shall be done," said he.

He called to him his aged housekeeper, who with sorrowful countenance approached to know his wishes.

"I wish you," said he, "to find Miss X, and request her presence urgently, imperatively, and at no matter what inconvenience."

The housekeeper departed, and he and I sat in gloomy silence. After an interval of some two hours she returned and replied that Miss X had fallen into a lethargy which had caused her to keep to her bed, but on receipt of Professor N's message some spark of doleful animation had returned to her and she had promised to be with him within a very short time. Scarcely had the house-keeper uttered this message when Miss X herself appeared, pale, distraught, with wild eyes and almost lifeless movements.

"Miss X," I said, "it is my duty, whether painful or not I do not yet know, to deliver to you this message from one who I believe is known to you."

I handed over the piece of parchment. She suddenly came to life, and seized it eagerly. Her eyes ran over its few lines in a moment.

"Alas!" she said. "This is not the reprieve for which I had hoped. It will not remove the cause of sorrow, but it does enable me to lift the veil of mystery. The story is a long one, and when I have finished it you will wish it had been longer. For when it is ended, it can be succeeded only by horror."

The Professor, seeing that she was on the verge of collapse, administered a strong dose of brandy. He then seated us round a table and in a calm voice said, "Proceed, Miss X."

"When I went to Corsica," she began, "and how long ago that seems, as though it had been in another existence, I was happy and carefree, thinking only of pleasure, of the light enjoyments which are considered suitable to my age, and of the delight of sunshine and new scenes. Corsica from the first moment enchanted me. I acquired the practice of long rambles in the hills, and each day I extended my rambles a little further. In the golden October sunshine, the leaves of the forest shone in their many bright colours. At last I found a path that led me beyond the forest on to the bare hills.

"In all-day rambles I caught a glimpse, to my immense surprise, of a great castle on a hill top. My curiosity was aroused. Ah! would that it had been otherwise. I was too late that day to approach any nearer to this astonishing edifice. But next day, having supplied myself with some simple sustenance, I set out early in the morning, determined, if it were possible, to discover the secret of this stately pile. Higher and higher I climbed through the sparkling autumn air. I met no human soul, and as I approached the castle it might have belonged to the Sleeping Beauty for all the signs of life that I saw about it.

"Curiosity, that fatal passion which misled our first mother, lured me on. I wandered round the battlements, seeking for a mode of ingress. For a long time my search was vain. Ah! would that it had remained so! But a malign fate willed otherwise. I found at last a little postern gate which yielded to my touch. I entered a dark abandoned out-house. When I had grown accustomed to the gloom, I saw at the far end a door standing ajar. I tiptoed to the door and glanced through. What met my gaze caused me to gasp, and I nearly emitted a cry of amazement.

"I saw before me a vast hall, in the very centre of which, at a long wooden table, were seated a number of grave men, some old, some young, some middle-aged, but all bearing upon their countenances the stamp of resolution, and the look of men born to do great deeds. 'Who may these be?' I wondered. You will not be surprised to learn that I could not bring myself to withdraw, and that standing behind that little door I listened to their words. This was my first sin on that day on which I was to sink to unimaginable depths of wickedness.

"At first I could not distinguish their words, though I could see that some portentous matter was being debated. But gradually, as my ears became attuned to their speech, I learned to follow what they were saying, and with every word my amazement grew.

"'Are we all agreed as to the day?' said the President.

"'We are,' many voices replied.

"'So be it,' said he. 'I decree that Thursday, the 15th of November, is to be the day. And are we all agreed as to our respective tasks?' he asked.

"'We are,' replied the same voices.

"'Then,' he said, 'I will repeat the conclusions at which we have arrived, and when I have done so, I will formally put them to the meeting and you will vote. All of us here are agreed that the human race is suffering from an appalling malady, and that the name of this malady is *GOVERNMENT*. We are agreed that if man is to recover the happiness that he enjoyed in the Homeric Age and which we, in this fortunate island, have in some measure retained, abolition of government is the first necessity. We are agreed also that there is only one way in which government can be abolished, and that is by abolishing governors. Twenty-one of us are here present, and we have agreed that there are twenty-one important states in the world. Each one of us on Thursday, the 15th of November, will assassinate the head of one of these twenty-one states. I, as your President, have the privilege of assigning to myself the most difficult and dangerous of these twenty-one enterprises. I allude, of course, to . . . but it is needless for me to pronounce the name. Our work, however, will not be quite complete when these twenty-one have suffered the fate that they so richly deserve. There is one other person, so ignoble, so sunk in error, so diligent in the propagation of falsehood, that he also must die. But as he is not of so exalted a status as these other twenty-one victims, I appoint my squire to effect his demise. You will all realize that I speak of Professor N, who has had the temerity to maintain in many learned journals and in a vast work which, as our secret service has informed us, is nearing completion, that it

137

was from Lithuania, and not, as all of us know, from Corsica, that pre-Celtic decorative art spread over Europe. He also shall die.'

"At this point," Miss X continued, amid sobs, "I could contain myself no longer. The thought that my benevolent employer was to die so soon afflicted me profoundly, and I gave an involuntary cry. All heads looked towards the door. The henchmen to whom the extermination of Professor N had been assigned was ordered to investigate. Before I could escape he seized me and led me before the twenty-one. The President bent stern eyes upon me and frowned heavily.

"'Who are you,' said he, 'that has so rashly, so impiously, intruded upon our secret councils? What has led you to eavesdrop upon the most momentous decision that any body of men has ever arrived at? Can you offer any reason whatever why you should not, here and now, die the death which your temerity has so richly merited?'"

At this point hesitation overcame Miss X, and she was scarcely able to continue her account of the momentous interview in the castle. At length she pulled herself together and resumed the narrative.

"I come now," she said, "to the most painful part of my story. It is a merciful dispensation of Providence that the future is concealed from our gaze. Little did my mother think, as she lay exhausted, listening to my first cry, that it was to this that her newborn daughter was destined. Little did I think as I entered the Secretarial College that it was to lead to this. Little did I dream that Pitman's was but the gateway to the gallows. But I must not waste time in vain repining. What is done is done, and it is my duty to relate the plain unvarnished tale without the trimmings of futile remorse.

"As the President spoke to me of swift death, I glimpsed the pleasant sunshine without. I thought of the carefree years of my youth. I thought of the promise of happiness which but that very morning had accompanied me as I climbed the lonely hills. Visions of summer rain and winter firesides, of spring in meadows and autumn in the beech woods haunted my imagination. I thought of the golden years of innocent childhood, fled never to return. And I thought fleetingly and shyly of one in whose eyes I fancied that I had seen the light of love. All this in a moment passed through my mind. 'Life,' I thought, 'is sweet. I am but young, and the best of life is still before me. Am I to be cut off thus, before I have known the joys, and the sorrows too, which make the warp and woof of human life? No,' I thought, 'this is too much. If there yet remains a means by which I may prolong my life I will seize it, even though it be at the price of dishonour.' When Satan had led me to this dreadful resolve I answered with such calmness as I could command: 'Oh, reverend Sir, I have been but an unwitting and unintentional offender. No thought of evil was in my mind as I strayed through that fatal door. If you will but spare my life I will do your will, whatever it may be. Have mercy, I pray you. You cannot wish that one so young and fair should perish prematurely. Let me but know your will and I will obey.' Although he still looked down upon me with no friendly eye, I fancied I saw some slight sign of relenting. He turned to the other twenty, and said, 'What is your will? Shall we execute justice, or shall we submit her to the ordeal? I will put it to the vote.' Ten voted for justice, ten for the ordeal. 'The casting vote is mine,' he said. 'I vote for the ordeal.'

"Then turning again to me, he continued, 'You may live, but on certain terms. What these terms are I will now explain to you. First of all you must swear a great oath—never to reveal by word or deed, by any hint or by any turn of demeanour, what you have learned in this hall. The oath which you must fulfil I will tell you, and you must repeat the words after me: I SWEAR BY ZOROASTER AND THE BEARD OF THE PROPHET, BY URIENS, PAYMON, EGYN, AND AMAYMON, BY MARBUEL, ACIEL, BARBIEL, MEPHISTOPHIEL, AND APADIEL, BY DIRACHIEL, AMNODIEL, AMUDIEL, TAGRIEL, GELIEL, AND REQUIEL, AND BY ALL THE FOUL SPIRITS OF HELL, THAT I WILL NEVER REVEAL OR IN ANY MANNER CAUSE TO BE KNOWN ANY SLIGHT HINT OF WHAT I HAVE SEEN AND HEARD IN THIS HALL.'

"When I had solemnly repeated this oath, he explained to me that this was but the first part of the ordeal, and that perhaps I might not have grasped its full immensity. Each of the infernal names that I had invoked possessed its own separate power of torture. By the magician's power invested in himself he was able to control the actions of these demons. If I infringed the oath, each separate one would, through all eternity, inflict upon me the separate torture of which he was master. But that, he said, was but the smallest part of my punishment.

"'I come now,' said he, 'to graver matters.'

"Turning to the henchman, he said, 'The goblet, please.'

"The henchman, who knew the ritual, presented the goblet to the President.

"'This,' he said, turning again to me, 'is a goblet of bull's blood. You must drink every drop, without taking breath while you drink. If you fail to do so, you will instantly become a cow, and be pursued forever by the ghost of the bull whose blood you will have failed to drink in due manner.' I took the goblet from him, drew a

139

long breath, closed my eyes and swallowed the noxious draught.

"'Two-thirds of the ordeal,' he said, 'are now fulfilled. The last part is slightly more inconvenient. We have decreed, as you are unfortunately aware, that on the 15th of November, twenty-one heads of state shall die. We decided also that the glory of our nation demands the death of Professor N. But we felt that there would be a lack of symmetry if one of us were to undertake this just execution. Before we discovered your presence, we delegated this task to my henchman. But your arrival, while in many ways inopportune, has in one respect provided us with an opportunity for neatness which it would be unwise and inartistic to neglect. You, and not my henchman, shall carry out this execution. And this to do you shall swear by the same oath by which you swore secrecy.'

"'Oh, sir!' I said, 'do not put upon me this terrible burden. You know much, but I doubt whether you know that it has been both my duty and my pleasure to assist Professor N in his researches. I have had nothing but kindness from him. It may be that his views on decorative art are not all that you could wish. Can you not permit me to continue serving him as before, and gradually I could wean him from his errors. I am not without influence upon the course of his thoughts. Several years of close association have shown me ways of guiding his inclinations in this direction or that, and I am pursuaded that if you will but grant me time I can bring him round to your opinions on the function of Corsica in pre-Celtic decorative art. To slay this good old man, whom I have regarded as a friend and who has hitherto, and not unjustly, regarded me in not unlike manner, would be almost as terrible as the pursuit of the many fiends whom you have caused me to invoke. Indeed, I doubt whether life is worth purchasing at such a price.'

"'Nay, my good maiden,' said he, 'I fear you are still indulging in illusions. The oath you have already taken was a sinful and blasphemous oath, and has put you forever in the power of the fiends, unless I, by my magic art, choose to restrain them. You cannot escape now. You must do my will or suffer.' I wept, I implored him, I knelt and clasped his knees. 'Have mercy,' I said, 'have mercy.' But he remained unmoved. 'I have spoken,' he said. 'If you do not wish to suffer forever the fifteen separate kinds of torment that will be inflicted by each of the fifteen fiends you have invoked, you must repeat after me, using the same dread names, the oath that on the 15th of November you will cause the death of Professor N.'

"Alas! dear Professor. It is impossible that you should pardon me, but in my weakness I swore this second oath. The 15th is rapidly approaching, and I see not how I am to escape, when that day comes, the dread consequences of my frightful oath. As soon as I got away from that dreadful castle, remorse seized me and has gnawed at my vitals ever since. Gladly would I suffer the fifteen diverse torments of the fifteen fiends, could I but persuade myself that in doing so I should be fulfilling the behests of duty. But I have sworn, and honour demands that I should fulfil my oath. Which is the greater sin, to murder the good man whom I revere, or to be false to the dictates of honour? I know not. But you, dear Professor, you who are so wise, you, I am sure, can resolve my doubts and show me the clear path of duty."

The Professor, as her narrative advanced towards its climax, somewhat surprisingly recovered cheerfulness and calm. With a kindly smile, with folded hands and a completely peaceful demeanour, he replied to her query.

"My dear young lady," he said, "nothing, nothing on earth, should be allowed to override the dictates of honour. If it lies in your power you must fulfil your oath. My work is completed, and my remaining years, if any, could have little importance. I should therefore tell you in the most emphatic manner that it is your duty to fulfil your oath if it is in any way possible. I should regret, however, I might even say I should regret deeply, that as a consequence of your sense of honour you should end your life upon the gallows. There is one thing, and one thing only, which can absolve you from your oath, and that is physical impossibility. You cannot kill a dead man."

So saying, he put his thumb and forefinger into his waistcoat pocket and with a lightning gesture conveyed them to his mouth. In an instant he was dead.

"Oh, my dear master," cried Miss X, throwing herself upon his lifeless corpse, "how can I bear the light of day now that you have sacrificed your life for mine? How can I endure the shame that every hour of sunshine and every moment of seeming happiness will generate in my soul? Nay, not another moment can I endure this agony."

With these words, she found the same pocket, imitated his gesture, and expired.

"I have not lived in vain," said I, "for I have witnessed two noble deaths."

But then I remembered that my task was not done, since the world's unworthy rulers must, I supposed, be saved from extinction. Reluctantly I bent my footsteps towards Scotland Yard.

THE MURDER

BY JOHN STEINBECK

John Steinbeck set some of his most vivid scenes in Monterey, California, where he was born and lived much of his life. His second book, *Pastures of Heaven* (1932), was a collection of stories that showed the first evidence of the author's interest in half-wits, "the unfinished children of nature," the simple man uncorrupted by money-grubbing civilization, the relationship of man to land and man to man. His major works include *Tortilla Flat, Of Mice and Men, East of Eden*, the motion picture *Viva Zapata!* and the Pulitzer Prize-winning *Grapes of Wrath*.

THIS HAPPENED A NUMBER OF YEARS AGO in Monterey County, in central California. The Cañon del Castillo is one of those valleys in the Santa Lucia range which lie between its many spurs and ridges. From the main Cañon del Castillo a number of little arroyos cut back into the mountains, oak-wooded canyons, heavily brushed with poison oak and sage. At the head of the canyon there stands a tremendous stone castle, buttressed and towered like those strongholds the Crusaders put up in the path of their conquests. Only a close visit to the castle shows it to be a strange accident of time and water and erosion working on soft stratified sandstone. In the distance the ruined battlements, the gates, the towers, even the arrow slits require little imagination to make out.

Below the castle, on the nearly level floor of the canyon, stand an old ranch house, a weathered and mossy barn and a warped feeding shed for cattle. The house is empty and deserted; the doors, swinging on rusted hinges, squeal and bang on nights when the wind courses down from the castle. Not many people visit the house. Sometimes a crowd of boys tramp through the rooms, peering into empty closets and loudly defying the ghosts they deny.

Jim Moore, who owns the land, does not like to have people about the house. He rides up from his new house, farther down the valley, and chases the boys away. He has put "No Trespassing" signs on his fences to keep curious and morbid people out. Sometimes he thinks of burning the old house down, but then a strange and powerful relation with the swinging doors, the blind and desolate windows forbids the destruction. If he should burn the house he would destroy a great and important piece of his life. He knows that when he goes to town with his plump and still pretty wife, people turn and look at his retreating back with awe and some admiration.

Jim Moore was born in the old house and grew up in it. He knew every grained and weathered board of the barn, every smooth, worn manger rack. His mother and father were both dead when he was thirty. He celebrated his majority by raising a beard. He sold the pigs and decided never to have any more. At last he bought a fine Guernsey bull to improve his stock, and he began to go to

Monterey on Saturday nights, to get drunk and to talk with the noisy girls of the Three Star.

Within a year Jim Moore married Jelka Sepić, a Jugo-Slav girl, daughter of a heavy and patient farmer of Pine Canyon. Jim was not proud of her foreign family, of her many brothers and sisters and cousins, but he delighted in her beauty. Jelka had eyes as large and questioning as a doe's eyes. Her nose was thin and sharply faceted, and her lips were deep and soft. Jelka's skin always startled Jim, for between night and night he forgot how beautiful it was. She was so smooth and quiet and gentle, such a good housekeeper, that Jim often thought with disgust of her father's advice on the wedding day. The old man, bleary and bloated with festival beer, elbowed Jim in the ribs and grinned suggestively, so that his little dark eyes almost disappeared behind puffed and wrinkled lids.

"Don't be big fool now," he said. "Jelka is Slav girl. He's not like American girl. If he is bad, beat him. If he's good too long, beat him too. I beat his mama. Papa beat my mama. Slav girl! He's not like a man that don't beat hell out of him."

"I wouldn't beat Jelka," Jim said.

The father giggled and nudged him again with his elbow. "Don't be big fool," he warned. "Sometime you see." He rolled back to the beer barrel.

Jim found soon enough that Jelka was not like American girls. She was very quiet. She never spoke first, but only answered his questions, and then with soft short replies. She learned her husband as she learned passages of Scripture. After they had been married a while, Jim never wanted for any habitual thing in the house but Jelka had it ready for him before he could ask. She was a fine wife, but there was no companionship in her. She never talked. Her great eyes followed him, and when he smiled, sometimes she smiled too, a distant and covered smile. Her knitting and mending and sewing were interminable. There she sat, watching her wise hands, and she seemed to regard with wonder and pride the little white hands that could do such nice and useful things. She was so much like an animal that sometimes Jim patted her head and neck under the same impulse that made him stroke a horse.

In the house Jelka was remarkable. No matter what time Jim came in from the hot dry range or from the bottom farm land, his dinner was exactly, steamingly ready for him. She watched while he ate, and pushed the dishes close when he needed them, and filled his cup when it was empty.

Early in the marriage he told her things that happened on the

144

farm, but she smiled at him as a foreigner does who wishes to be agreeable even though he doesn't understand.

"The stallion cut himself on the barbed wire," he said.

And she replied, "Yes," with a downward inflection that held neither question nor interest.

He realized before long that he could not get in touch with her in any way. If she had a life apart, it was so remote as to be beyond his reach. The barrier in her eyes was not one that could be removed, for it was neither hostile nor intentional.

At night he stroked her straight black hair and her unbelievably smooth golden shoulders, and she whimpered a little with pleasure. Only in the climax of his embrace did she seem to have a life apart and fierce and passionate. And then immediately she lapsed into the alert and painfully dutiful wife.

"Why don't you ever talk to me?" he demanded. "Don't you want to talk to me?"

"Yes," she said. "What do you want me to say?" She spoke the language of his race out of a mind that was foreign to his race.

When a year had passed, Jim began to crave the company of women, the chattery exchange of small talk, the shrill pleasant insults, the shame-sharpened vulgarity. He began to go again to town, to drink and to play with the noisy girls of the Three Star. They liked him there for his firm, controlled face and for his readiness to laugh.

"Where's your wife?" they demanded.

"Home in the barn," he responded. It was a never failing joke.

Saturday afternoons he saddled a horse and put a rifle in the scabbard in case he should see a deer. Always he asked, "You don't mind staying alone?"

"No. I don't mind."

And once he asked, "Suppose some one should come?"

Her eyes sharpened for a moment, and then she smiled. "I would send them away," she said.

"I'll be back about noon tomorrow. It's too far to ride in the night." He felt that she knew where he was going, but she never protested nor gave any sign of disapproval. "You should have a baby," he said.

Her face lighted up. "Sometime God will be good," she said eagerly.

He was sorry for her loneliness. If only she visited with the other women of the canyon she would be less lonely, but she had no gift for visiting. Once every month or so she put horses to the buckboard and went to spend an afternoon with her mother, and with the brood of brothers and sisters and cousins who lived in her father's house.

"A fine time you'll have," Jim said to her. "You'll gabble your crazy language like ducks for a whole afternoon. You'll giggle with that big grown cousin of yours with the embarrassed face. If I could find any fault with you, I'd call you a damn foreigner." He remembered how she blessed the bread with the sign of the cross before she put it in the oven, how she knelt at the bedside every night, how she had a holy picture tacked to the wall in the closet.

On Saturday of a hot dusty June, Jim cut hay in the farm flat. The day was long. It was after six o'clock when the mower tumbled the last band of oats. He drove the clanking machine up into the barnyard and backed it into the implement shed, and there he unhitched the horses and turned them out to graze on the hills over Sunday. When he entered the kitchen Jelka was just putting his dinner on the table. He washed his hands and face, and sat down to eat.

"I'm tired," he said, "but I think I'll go to Monterey anyway. There'll be a full moon."

Her soft eyes smiled.

"I'll tell you what I'll do," he said. "If you would like to go, I'll hitch up a rig and take you with me."

She smiled again and shook her head. "No, the stores would be closed. I would rather stay here."

"Well all right, I'll saddle a horse then. I didn't think I was going. The stock's all turned out. Maybe I can catch a horse easy. Sure you don't want to go?"

"If it was early, and I could go to the stores—but it will be ten o'clock when you get there."

"Oh, no—well, anyway, on horseback I'll make it a little after nine."

Her mouth smiled to itself, but her eyes watched him for the development of a wish. Perhaps because he was tired from the long day's work, he demanded, "What are you thinking about?"

"Thinking about? I remember, you used to ask that nearly every day when we were first married."

"But what are you?" he insisted irritably.

"Oh—I'm thinking about the eggs under the black hen." She got up and went to the big calendar on the wall. "They will hatch tomorrow or maybe Monday."

It was almost dusk when he had finished shaving and putting on his blue serge suit and his new boots. Jelka had the dishes washed and put away. As Jim went through the kitchen he saw that she had taken the lamp to the table near the window, and that she sat beside it knitting a brown wool sock.

"Why do you sit there tonight?" he asked. "You always sit over here. You do funny things sometimes."

Her eyes arose slowly from her flying hands. "The moon," she said quietly. "You said it would be full tonight. I want to see the moon rise."

"But you're silly. You can't see it from that window. I thought you knew direction better than that."

She smiled remotely. "I will look out of the bedroom window then."

Jim put on his black hat and went out. Walking through the dark empty barn, he took a halter from the rack. On the grassy sidehill he whistled high and shrill. The horses stopped feeding and moved slowly in toward him, and stopped twenty feet away. Carefully he approached his bay gelding and moved his hand from its rump along its side and up and over its neck. The halterstrap clicked in its buckle. Jim turned and led the horse back to the barn. He threw his saddle on and cinched it tight, put his silver-bound bridle over the stiff ears, buckled the throat latch, knotted the tie-rope about the gelding's neck and fastened the neat coil-end to the saddle string. Then he slipped the halter and led the horse to the house. A radiant crown of soft red light lay over the eastern hills. The full moon would rise before the valley had completely lost the daylight.

In the kitchen Jelka still knitted by the window. Jim strode to the corner of the room and took up his 30-30 carbine. As he rammed shells into the magazine, he said, "The moon glow is on the hills. If you are going to see it rise, you better go outside now. It's going to be a good red one at rising."

"In a moment," she replied, "when I come to the end here." He went to her and patted her sleek head.

"Good night. I'll probably be back by noon tomorrow." Her dusty black eyes followed him out the door.

Jim thrust the rifle into his saddle-scabbard, and mounted and swung his horse down the canyon. On his right, from behind the blackening hills, the great red moon slid rapidly up. The double light of the day's last afterglow and the rising moon thickened the outlines of the trees and gave a mysterious new perspective to the hills. The dusty oaks shimmered and glowed, and the shade under them was black as velvet. A huge, long-legged shadow of a horse and half a man rode to the left and slightly ahead of Jim. From the ranches near and distant came the sound of dogs tuning up for a night of song. And the roosters crowed, thinking a new dawn had come too quickly. Jim lifted the gelding to a trot. The spattering hoofsteps echoed back from the castle behind him. He thought of blonde May at the Three Star in Monterey. "I'll be late. Maybe some one else'll have her," he thought. The moon was clear of the hills now.

Jim had gone a mile when he heard the hoofbeats of a horse coming toward him. A horseman cantered up and pulled to a stop. "That you, Jim?"

"Yes. Oh, hello, George."

"I was just riding up to your place. I want to tell you—you know the springhead at the upper end of my land?"

"Yes. I know."

"Well, I was up there this afternoon. I found a dead campfire and a calf's head and feet. The skin was in the fire, half burned, but I pulled it out and it had your brand."

"The hell," said Jim. "How old was the fire?"

"The ground was still warm in the ashes. Last night, I guess. Look, Jim, I can't go up with you. I've got to go to town, but I thought I'd tell you, so you could take a look around."

Jim asked quietly, "Any idea how many men?"

"No. I didn't look close."

"Well, I guess I better go up and look. I was going to town too. But if there are thieves working, I don't want to lose any more stock. I'll cut up through your land if you don't mind, George."

"I'd go with you, but I've got to go to town. You got a gun with you?"

"Oh yes, sure. Here under my leg. Thanks for telling me."

"That's all right. Cut through any place you want. Good night." The neighbor turned his horse and cantered back in the direction from which he had come.

For a few moments Jim sat in the moonlight, looking down at his stilted shadow. He pulled his rifle from its scabbard, levered a shell into the chamber, and held the gun across the pommel of his saddle. He turned left from the road, went up the little ridge, through the oak grove, over the grassy hog-back and down the other side into the next canyon.

In half an hour he had found the deserted camp. He turned over the heavy, leathery calf's head and felt its dusty tongue to judge by the dryness how long it had been dead. He lighted a match and looked at his brand on the half-burned hide. At last he

148

mounted his horse again, rode over the bald grassy hills and crossed into his own land.

A warm summer wind was blowing on the hilltops. The moon, as it quartered up the sky, lost its redness and turned the color of strong tea. Among the hills the coyotes were singing, and the dogs at the ranch houses below joined them with broken-hearted howling. The dark green oaks below and the yellow summer grass showed their colors in the moonlight.

Jim followed the sound of the cow-bells to his herd, and found them eating quietly, and a few deer feeding with them. He listened long for the sound of hoofbeats or the voices of men on the wind.

It was after eleven when he turned his horse toward home. He rounded the west tower of the sandstone castle, rode through the shadow and out into the moonlight again. Below, the roofs of his barn and house shone dully. The bedroom window cast back a streak of reflection.

The feeding horses lifted their heads as Jim came down through the pasture. Their eyes glinted redly when they turned their heads.

Jim had almost reached the corral fence—he heard a horse stamping in the barn. His hand jerked the gelding down. He listened. It came again, the stamping from the barn. Jim lifted his rifle and dismounted silently. He turned his horse loose and crept toward the barn.

In the blackness he could hear the grinding of the horse's teeth as it chewed hay. He moved along the barn until he came to the occupied stall. After a moment of listening he scratched a match on the butt of his rifle. A saddled and bridled horse was tied in the stall. The bit was slipped under the chin and the cinch loosened. The horse stopped eating and turned its head toward the light.

Jim blew out the match and walked quickly out of the barn. He sat on the edge of the horse trough and looked into the water. His thoughts came so slowly that he put them into words and said them under his breath.

"Shall I look through the window? No. My head would throw a shadow in the room."

He regarded the rifle in his hand. Where it had been rubbed and handled, the black gun-finish had worn off, leaving the metal silvery.

At last he stood up with decision and moved toward the house. At the steps, an extended foot tried each board tenderly before he put his weight on it. The three ranch dogs came out from under the house and shook themselves, stretched and sniffed, wagged their tails and went back to bed.

The kitchen was dark, but Jim knew where every piece of furniture was. He put out his hand and touched the corner of the table, a chair-back, the towel hanger, as he went along. He crossed the room so silently that even he could hear only his breath and the whisper of his trousers legs together, and the beating of his watch in his pocket. The bedroom door stood open and spilled a patch of moonlight on the kitchen floor. Jim reached the door at last and peered through.

The moonlight lay on the white bed. Jim saw Jelka lying on her back, one soft bare arm flung across her forehead and eyes. He could not see who the man was, for his head was turned away. Jim watched, holding his breath. Then Jelka twitched in her sleep and the man rolled his head and sighed—Jelka's cousin, her grown embarrassed cousin.

Jim turned and quickly stole back across the kitchen and down the back steps. He walked up the yard to the water trough again, and sat down on the edge of it. The moon was white as chalk, and it swam in the water, and lighted the straws and barley dropped by the horses' mouths. Jim could see the mosquito wigglers, tumbling up and down, end over end, in the water, and he could see a newt lying in the sun moss in the bottom of the trough.

He cried a few dry, hard, smothered sobs, and wondered why, for his thought was of the grassed hilltops and of the lonely summer wind whisking along.

His thought turned to the way his mother used to hold a bucket to catch the throat blood when his father killed a pig. She stood as far away as possible and held the bucket at arm's length to keep her clothes from getting spattered.

Jim dipped his hand into the trough and stirred the moon to broken, swirling streams of light. He wetted his forehead with his damp hands and stood up. This time he did not move so quietly, but he crossed the kitchen on tiptoe and stood in the bedroom door. Jelka moved her arm and opened her eyes a little. Then the eyes sprang wide, then they glistened with moisture. Jim looked into her eyes; his face was blank of expression. A little drop ran out of Jelka's nose and lodged in the hollow of her upper lip. She stared back at him.

Jim cocked the rifle. The steel click sounded through the house. The man on the bed stirred uneasily in his sleep. Jim's hands were quivering. He raised the gun to his shoulder and held it tightly to keep from shaking. Over the sights he saw the little white square between the man's brows and hair. The front sight wavered a moment and then came to rest.

The gun crash tore the air. Jim, still looking down the barrel, saw the whole bed jolt under the blow. A small, black, bloodless hole was in the man's forehead. But behind, the hollow-point bullet took brain and bone and splashed them on the pillow.

Jelka's cousin gurgled in his throat. His hands came crawling out from under the covers like big white spiders, and they walked for a moment, then shuddered and fell quiet.

Jim looked slowly back at Jelka. Her nose was running. Her eyes had moved from him to the end of the rifle. She whined softly, like a cold puppy.

Jim turned in panic. His boot-heels beat on the kitchen floor, but outside he moved slowly toward the watering trough again. There was a taste of salt in his throat, and his heart heaved painfully. He pulled his hat off and dipped his head into the water, then he leaned over and vomited on the ground. In the house he could hear Jelka moving about. She whimpered like a puppy. Jim straightened up, weak and dizzy.

He walked tiredly through the corral and into the pasture. His saddled horse came at his whistle. Automatically he tightened the cinch, mounted and rode away, down the road to the valley. The squat black shadow traveled under him. The moon sailed high and white. The uneasy dogs barked monotonously.

At daybreak a buckboard and pair trotted up to the ranch yard, scattering the chickens. A deputy sheriff and a coroner sat in the seat. Jim Moore half reclined against his saddle in the wagon-box. His tired gelding followed behind. The deputy sheriff set the brake and wrapped the lines around it. The men dismounted.

Jim asked, "Do I have to go in? I'm too tired and wrought up to see it now."

The coroner pulled his lip and studied. "Oh, I guess not. We'll tend to things and look around."

Jim sauntered away toward the watering trough. "Say," he called, "kind of clean up a little, will you? You know."

The men went on into the house.

In a few minutes they emerged, carrying the stiffened body between them. It was wrapped up in a comforter. They eased it up into the wagon-box. Jim walked back toward them. "Do I have to go in with you now?"

"Where's your wife, Mr. Moore?" the deputy sheriff demanded.

"I don't know," he said wearily. "She's somewhere around."

"You sure you didn't kill her too?"

"No. I didn't touch her. I'll find her and bring her in this

151

afternoon. That is, if you don't want me to go in with you now."

"We've got your statement," the coroner said. "And by God, we've got eyes, haven't we, Will? Of course there's a technical charge of murder against you, but it'll be dismissed. Always is in this part of the country. Go kind of light on your wife, Mr. Moore."

"I won't hurt her," said Jim.

He stood and watched the buck-board jolt away. He kicked his feet reluctantly in the dust. The hot June sun showed its face over the hills and flashed viciously on the bedroom window.

Jim went slowly into the house, and brought out a nine-foot, loaded bull whip. He crossed the yard and walked into the barn. And as he climbed the ladder to the hayloft, he heard the high, puppy whimpering start.

When Jim came out of the barn again, he carried Jelka over his shoulder. By the watering trough he set her tenderly on the ground. Her hair was littered with bits of hay. The back of her shirtwaist was streaked with blood.

Jim wetted his bandana at the pipe and washed her bitten lips, and washed her face and brushed back her hair. Her dusty black eyes followed every move he made.

"You hurt me," she said. "You hurt me bad."

He nodded gravely. "Bad as I could without killing you."

The sun shone hotly on the ground. A few blowflies buzzed about, looking for the blood.

Jelka's thickened lips tried to smile. "Did you have any breakfast at all?"

"No," he said. "None at all."

"Well, then I'll fry you up some eggs." She struggled painfully to her feet.

"Let me help you." he said. "I'll help you get your waist off. It's drying stuck to your back. It'll hurt."

"No. I'll do it myself." Her voice had a peculiar resonance in it. Her dark eyes dwelt warmly on him for a moment, and then she turned and limped into the house.

Jim waited, sitting on the edge of the watering trough. He saw the smoke start up out of the chimney and sail straight up into the air. In a very few moments Jelka called him from the kitchen door.

"Come, Jim. Your breakfast."

Four fried eggs and four thick slices of bacon lay on a warmed plate for him. "The coffee will be ready in a minute," she said.

"Won't you eat?"

"No. Not now. My mouth's too sore."

He ate his eggs hungrily and then looked up at her. Her black hair was combed smooth. She had on a fresh white shirtwaist. "We're going to town this afternoon," he said. "I'm going to order lumber. We'll build a new house farther down the canyon."

Her eyes darted to the closed bedroom door and then back to him. "Yes," she said. "That will be good." And then, after a moment, "Will you whip me any more—for this?"

"No, not any more, for this."

Her eyes smiled. She sat down on a chair beside him, and Jim put out his hand and stroked her hair, and the back of her neck.

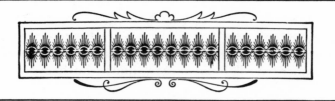

CORONER'S INQUEST

BY MARC CONNELLY

Marc Connelly was born in McKeesport, Pennsylvania, on December 13, 1890. He made his living at journalism and writing humorous verse and occasional sketches and lyrics for musical comedies before achieving success with the play *Dulcy*, his first collaboration with George S. Kaufman, in 1921. Eight years later he won the Pulitzer Prize for *The Green Pastures*, adapted from Roark Bradford's *Ol' Man Adam and His Chillun*. "Coroner's Inquest" earned him the O. Henry Prize for best short story of 1930. He is one of the founders of *The New Yorker*.

WHAT is your name?"

"Frank Wineguard."

"Where do you live?"

"A hundred and eighty-five West Fifty-fifth Street."

"What is your business?"

"I'm stage manager for Hello, America."

"You were the employer of James Dawle?"

"In a way. We both worked for Mr. Bender, the producer, but I have charge backstage."

"Did you know Theodore Robel?"

"Yes, sir."

"Was he in your company, too?"

"No, sir. I met him when we started rehearsals. That was about three months ago, in June. We sent out a call for midgets and he and Jimmy showed up together, with a lot of others. Robel was too big for us. I didn't see him again until we broke into their room Tuesday."

"You discovered their bodies?"

"Yes, sir. Mrs. Pike, there, was with me."

"You found them both dead?"

"Yes, sir."

"How did you happen to be over in Jersey City?"

"Well, I'd called up his house at curtain time Monday night when I found Jimmy hadn't shown up for the performance. Mrs. Pike told me they were both out, and I asked her to have either Jimmy or Robel call me when they came in. Then Mrs. Pike called me Tuesday morning and said she tried to get into the room but she'd found the door was bolted. She said all her other roomers were out and she was alone and scared.

"I'd kind of suspected something might be wrong. So I said to wait and I'd come over. Then I took the tube over and got there about noon. Then we went up and I broke down the door."

"Did you see this knife there?"

"Yes, sir. It was on the floor, about a foot from Jimmy."

"You say you suspected something was wrong. What do you mean by that?"

"I mean I felt something might have happened to Jimmy. Nothing like this, of course. But I knew he'd been feeling very depressed lately, and I knew Robel wasn't helping to cheer him up any."

"You mean that they had had quarrels?"

"No, sir. They just both had the blues. Robel had had them for a long time. Robel was Jimmy's brother-in-law. He'd married Jimmy's sister—she was a midget, too—about five years ago, but she died a year or so later. Jimmy had been living with them and after the sister died he and Robel took a room in Mrs. Pike's house together."

"How did you learn this?"

"Jimmy and I were pretty friendly at the theater. He was a nice little fellow and seemed grateful that I'd given him his job. We'd only needed one midget for an Oriental scene in the second act and the agencies had sent about fifteen. Mr. Gehring, the director, told me to pick one of them as he was busy and I picked Jimmy because he was the littlest.

"After I got to know him he told me how glad he was I'd given him the job. He hadn't worked for nearly a year. He wasn't little enough to be a featured midget with circuses or in museums so he had to take whatever came along. Anyway, we got to be friendly and he used to tell me about his brother-in-law and all."

"He never suggested that there might be ill-feeling between him and his brother-in-law?"

"No, sir. I don't imagine he'd ever had any words at all with Robel. As a matter of fact from what I could gather I guess Jimmy had quite a lot of affection for him and he certainly did everything he could to help him. Robel was a lot worse off than Jimmy. Robel hadn't worked for a couple of years and Jimmy practically supported him. He used to tell me how Robel had been sunk ever since he got his late growth."

"His what?"

"His late growth. I heard it happens among midgets often, but Jimmy told me about it first. Usually a midget will stay as long as he lives at whatever height he reaches when he's fourteen or fifteen, but every now and then one of them starts growing again just before he's thirty, and he can grow a foot or even more in a couple of years. Then he stops growing for good. But of course he don't look so much like a midget any more.

"That's what had happened to Robel about three years ago. Of course he had trouble getting jobs and it hit him pretty hard.

"From what Jimmy told me and from what Mrs. Pike says, I guess he used to talk about it all the time. Robel used to come over and see his agent in New York twice a week, but there was never anything for him. Then he'd go back to Jersey City. Most of the week he lived alone because after the show started Jimmy often stayed in New York with a cousin or somebody that lived uptown.

"Lately Robel hadn't been coming over to New York at all. But every Saturday night Jimmy would go over to Jersey City and stay till Monday with him, trying to cheer him up. Every Sunday they'd take a walk and go to a movie. I guess as they walked along the street Robel realized most the difference in their heights. And I guess that's really why they're both dead now."

"How do you mean?"

"Well, as I told you, Jimmy would try to sympathize with Robel and cheer him up. He and Robel both realized that Jimmy was working and supporting them and that Jimmy would probably keep right on working, according to the ordinary breaks of the game, while Robel would always be too big. It simply preyed on Robel's mind.

"And then three weeks ago Monday Jimmy thought he saw the ax fall.

"I was standing outside the stage door—it was about seven-thirty—and Jimmy came down the alley. He looked down in the mouth, which I thought was strange seeing that he usually used to come in swinging his little cane and looking pretty cheerful. I said, 'How are you feeling, Jimmy?' and he said, 'I don't feel so good, Mr. Wineguard.' So I said, 'Why, what's the matter, Jimmy?' I could see there really was something the matter with him by this time.

"'I'm getting scared,' he said, and I says, 'Why?'

"'I'm starting to grow again,' he says. He said it the way you'd say you just found out you had some disease that was going to kill you in a week. He looked like he was shivering.

"'Why, you're crazy, Jimmy,' I says. 'You ain't growing.'

"'Yes, I am,' he says. 'I'm thirty-one and it's that late growth like my brother-in-law has. My father had it, but his people had money, so it didn't make much difference to him. It's different with me. I've got to keep working.'

"He went on like that for a while and then I tried to kid him out of it.

"'You look all right to me,' I said. 'How tall have you been all along?'

"'Thirty-seven inches,' he says. So I says, 'Come on into the prop-room and I'll measure you.'

"He backed away from me. 'No,' he says, 'I don't want to know how much it is.' Then he went up to the dressing-room before I could argue with him.

157

"All week he looked awful sunk. When he showed up the next Monday evening he looked almost white.

"I grabbed him as he was starting upstairs to make up.

"'Come on out of it,' I says. I thought he'd make a break and try to get away from me, but he didn't. He just sort of smiled as if I didn't understand. Finally he says, 'It ain't any use, Mr. Wineguard.'

"'Listen,' I says, 'you've been over with that brother-in-law of yours, haven't you?' He said yes, he had. 'Well,' I says, 'that's what's bothering you. From what you tell me about him he's talked about his own tough luck so much that he's given you the willies, too. Stay away from him the end of this week.'

"He stood there for a second without saying anything. Then he says, 'That wouldn't do any good. He's all alone over there and he needs company. Anyway, it's all up with me, I guess. I've grown nearly two inches already.'

"I looked at him. He was pretty pathetic, but outside of that there wasn't any change in him as far as I could see.

"I says, 'Have you been measured?' He said he hadn't. Then I said, 'Then how do you know? Your clothes fit you all right, except your pants, and as a matter of fact they seem a little longer.'

"'I fixed my suspenders and let them down a lot farther,' he says. 'Besides they were always a little big for me.'

"'Let's make sure,' I says. 'I'll get a yard-stick and we'll make absolutely sure.'

"But I guess he was too scared to face things. He wouldn't do it.

"He managed to dodge me all week. Then, last Saturday night, I ran into him as I was leaving the theater. I asked him if he felt any better.

"'I feel all right,' he says. He really looked scared to death.

"That's the last time I saw him before I went over to Jersey City after Mrs. Pike phoned me Tuesday."

"Patrolman Gorlitz has testified that the bodies were in opposite ends of the room when he arrived. They were in that position when you forced open the door?"

"Yes, sir."

"The medical examiner has testified that they were both dead of knife wounds, apparently from the same knife. Would you assume the knife had fallen from Dawle's hand as he fell?"

"Yes, sir."

"Has it been your purpose to suggest that both men were driven to despondency by a fear of lack of employment for Dawle, and that they might have committed suicide?"

"No, sir. I don't think anything of the kind."

"What do you mean?"

"Well, when Mrs. Pike and I went in the room and I got a look at the knife, I said to Mrs. Pike that that was a funny kind of a knife for them to have in the room. You can see it's a kind of a butcher knife. Then Mrs. Pike told me it was one that she'd missed from her kitchen a few weeks before. She'd never thought either Robel or Jimmy had taken it. It struck me as funny Robel or Jimmy had stolen it, too. Then I put two and two together and found out what really happened. Have you got the little broken cane that was lying on the bed?"

"Is this it?"

"Yes, sir. Well, I'd never been convinced by Jimmy that he was really growing. So when Mrs. Pike told me about the knife I started figuring. I figured that about five minutes before that knife came into play Jimmy must have found it, probably by accident."

"Why by accident?"

"Because Robel had gone a little crazy, I guess. He'd stolen it and kept it hidden from Jimmy. And when Jimmy found it he wondered what Robel had been doing with it. Then Robel wouldn't tell him and Jimmy found out for himself. Or maybe Robel did tell him. Anyway, Jimmy looked at the cane. It was the one he always carried. He saw where, when Jimmy wasn't looking, Robel had been *cutting little pieces off the end of it!*"

A JURY OF HER PEERS

BY SUSAN GLASPELL

After working for native Iowa newspapers, Susan Glaspell (b. July 1, 1882) began to write short stories and then the first of her novels, *The Glory of the Conquered*. She and writer George Cram Cook married in 1913 and moved to Cape Cod, where they organized the experimental Provincetown Players. They encouraged young dramatists like Eugene O'Neill and wrote plays strikingly different from the stereotyped dramas of the time. Miss Glaspell's play *Alison's House* (1930), based on the life of Emily Dickinson, won her the Pulitzer Prize. She died in Greece in 1948.

WHEN MARTHA HALE OPENED the storm-door and got a cut of the north wind, she ran back for her big woolen scarf. As she hurriedly wound that round her head her eye made a scandalized sweep of her kitchen. It was no ordinary thing that called her away—it was probably farther from ordinary than anything that had ever happened in Dickson County. But what her eye took in was that her kitchen was in no shape for leaving: her bread all ready for mixing, half the flour sifted and half unsifted.

She hated to see things half done; but she had been at that when the team from town stopped to get Mr. Hale, and then the sheriff came running in to say his wife wished Mrs. Hale would come too—adding, with a grin, that he guessed she was getting scarey and wanted another woman along. So she had dropped everything right where it was.

"Martha!" now came her husband's impatient voice. "Don't keep folks waiting out here in the cold."

She again opened the storm-door, and this time joined the three men and the one woman waiting for her in the big two-seated buggy.

After she had the robes tucked around her she took another look at the woman who sat beside her on the back seat. She had met Mrs. Peters the year before at the county fair, and the thing she remembered about her was that she didn't seem like a sheriff's wife. She was small and thin and didn't have a strong voice. Mrs. Gorman, sheriff's wife before Gorman went out and Peters came in, had a voice that somehow seemed to be backing up the law with every word. But if Mrs. Peters didn't look like a sheriff's wife, Peters made it up in looking like a sheriff. He was to a dot the kind of man who could get himself elected sheriff—a heavy man with a big voice, who was particularly genial with the law-abiding, as if to make it plain that he knew the difference between criminals and non-criminals. And right there it came into Mrs. Hale's mind, with a stab, that this man who was so pleasant and lively with all of them was going to the Wrights' now as a sheriff.

"The country's not very pleasant this time of year," Mrs. Peters at last ventured, as if she felt they ought to be talking as well as the men.

Mrs. Hale scarcely finished her reply, for they had gone up a little hill and could see the Wright place now, and seeing it did not make her feel like talking. It looked very lonesome this cold March morning. It had always been a lonesome-looking place. It was down in a hollow, and the poplar trees around it were lonesome-looking trees. The men were looking at it and talking about what had happened. The county attorney was bending to one side of the buggy, and kept looking steadily at the place as they drew up to it.

"I'm glad you came with me," Mrs. Peters said nervously, as the two women were about to follow the men in through the kitchen door.

Even after she had her foot on the door-step, her hand on the knob, Martha Hale had a moment of feeling she could not cross that threshold. And the reason it seemed she couldn't cross it now was simply because she hadn't crossed it before. Time and time again it had been in her mind, "I ought to go over and see Minnie Foster"—she still thought of her as Minnie Foster, though for twenty years she had been Mrs. Wright. And then there was always something to do and Minnie Foster would go from her mind. But *now* she could come.

The men went over to the stove. The women stood close together by the door. Young Henderson, the county attorney, turned around and said:

"Come up to the fire, ladies."

Mrs. Peters took a step forward, then stopped. "I'm not—cold," she said.

The men talked for a minute about what a good thing it was the sheriff had sent his deputy out that morning to make a fire for them, and then Sheriff Peters stepped back from the stove, unbuttoned his outer coat, and leaned his hands on the kitchen table in a way that seemed to mark the beginning of official business. "Now, Mr. Hale," he said in a sort of semi-official voice, "before we move things about, you tell Mr. Henderson just what it was you saw when you came here yesterday morning."

The county attorney was looking around the kitchen.

"By the way," he said, "has anything been moved?" He turned to the sheriff. "Are things just as you left them yesterday?"

Peters looked from cupboard to sink; from that to a small worn rocker a little to one side of the kitchen table.

"It's just the same."

"Somebody should have been left here yesterday," said the county attorney.

"Oh—yesterday," returned the sheriff, with a little gesture as of yesterday having been more than he could bear to think of. "When I had to send Frank to Morris Center for that man who went crazy—let me tell you, I had my hands full *yesterday*. I knew you could get back from Omaha by today, George, and as long as I went over everything here myself—"

"Well, Mr. Hale," said the county attorney, in a way of letting what was past and gone go, "tell just what happened when you came here yesterday morning."

Mrs. Hale, still leaning against the door, had that sinking feeling of the mother whose child is about to speak a piece. Lewis often wandered along and got things mixed up in a story. She hoped he would tell this straight and plain, and not say unnecessary things that would just make things harder for Minnie Foster. He didn't begin at once, and she noticed that he looked queer—as if standing in that kitchen and having to tell what he had seen there yesterday morning made him almost sick.

"Harry and I had started to town with a load of potatoes," Mrs. Hale's husband began.

Harry was Mrs. Hales's oldest boy. He wasn't with them now, for the very good reason that those potatoes never got to town yesterday and he was taking them this morning, so he hadn't been home when the sheriff stopped to say he wanted Mr. Hale to come over to the Wright place and tell the county attorney his story there, where he could point it all out.

"We came along this road," Hale was going on, with a motion of his hand to the road over which they had just come, "and as we got in sight of the house I says to Harry, 'I'm goin' to see if I can't get John Wright to take a telephone.' You see," he explained to Henderson, "unless I can get somebody to go in with me they won't come out this branch road except for a price *I* can't pay. I'd spoke to Wright about it once before; but he put me off, saying folks talked too much anyway, and all he asked was peace and quiet—guess you know about how much he talked himself. But I thought maybe if I went to the house and talked about it before his wife, and said all the women-folks liked the telephones, and that in this lonesome stretch of road it would be a good thing—well, I said to Harry that that was what I was going to say—though I said at the same time that I didn't know as what his wife wanted made much difference to John—"

Now, there he was!—saying things he didn't need to say. Mrs. Hale tried to catch her husband's eye, but fortunately the county attorney interrupted with:

"Let's talk about that a little later, Mr. Hale. I do want to talk about that, but I'm anxious now to get along to just exactly what happened when you got here."

When he began this time, it was very deliberately and carefully:

"I didn't see or hear anything. I knocked at the door. And still it was all quiet inside. I knew they must be up—it was past eight o'clock. So I knocked again, louder, and I thought I heard somebody say, 'Come in.' I wasn't sure—I'm not sure yet. But I opened the door—this door," jerking a hand toward the door by which the two women stood, "and there, in that rocker"—pointing to it—"sat Mrs. Wright."

Everyone in the kitchen looked at the rocker. It came into Mrs. Hale's mind that that rocker didn't look in the least like Minnie Foster—the Minnie Foster of twenty years before. It was a dingy red, with wooden rungs up the back, and the middle rung was gone, and the chair sagged to one side.

"How did she—look?" the county attorney was inquiring.

"Well," said Hale, "she looked—queer."

"How do you mean—queer?"

As he asked it he took out a notebook and pencil. Mrs. Hale did not like the sight of that pencil. She kept her eye fixed on her husband, as if to keep him from saying unnecessary things that would go into that notebook and make trouble.

Hale did speak guardedly, as if the pencil had affected him too.

"Well, as if she didn't know what she was going to do next. And kind of—done up."

"How did she seem to feel about your coming?"

"Why, I don't think she minded—one way or other. She didn't pay much attention. I said, 'Ho' do, Mrs. Wright? It's cold, ain't it?' And she said, 'Is it?'—and went on pleatin' at her apron.

"Well, I was surprised. She didn't ask me to come up to the stove, or to sit down, but just set there, not even lookin' at me. And so I said: 'I want to see John.' And then she laughed. I guess you would call it a laugh.

"I thought of Harry and the team outside, so I said, a little sharp, 'Can I see John?' 'No,' says she—kind of dull like. 'Ain't he home?' says I. Then she looked at me. 'Yes,' says she, 'he's home.' 'Then why can't I see him?' I asked her, out of patience with her now. ''Cause he's dead,' says she, just as quiet and dull—and fell to pleatin' her apron. 'Dead?' says I, like you do when you can't take in what you've heard.

"She just nodded her head, not getting a bit excited, but rockin' back and forth.

"'Why—where is he?' says I, not knowing *what* to say.

"She just pointed upstairs—like this"—pointing to the room above.

"I got up, with the idea of going up there myself. By this time I—didn't know what to do. I walked from there to here; then I says: 'Why, what did he die of?'

"'He died of a rope round his neck' says she; and just went on pleatin' at her apron."

Hale stopped speaking, and stood staring at the rocker, as if he were still seeing the woman who had sat there the morning before. Nobody spoke; it was as if everyone were seeing the woman who had sat there the morning before.

"And what did you do then?" the county attorney at last broke the silence.

"I went out and called Harry. I thought I might—need help. I got Harry in, and we went upstairs." His voice fell almost to a whisper. "There he was—lying over the—"

"I think I'd rather have you go into that upstairs," the county attorney interrupted, "where you can point it all out. Just go on now with the rest of the story."

"Well, my first thought was to get that rope off. It looked—"

He stopped, his face twitching.

"But Harry, he went up to him, and he said, 'No, he's dead all right, and we'd better not touch anything.' So we went downstairs. She was still sitting the same way. 'Has anybody been notified?' I asked. 'No,' said she, unconcerned.

"'Who did this, Mrs. Wright?' said Harry. He said it business-like, and she stopped pleatin' at her apron. 'I don't know,' she says. 'You don't *know?*' says Harry. 'Weren't you sleepin' in the bed with him?' 'Yes,' says she, 'but I was on the inside.' 'Somebody slipped a rope round his neck and strangled him, and you didn't wake up?' says Harry. 'I didn't wake up,' she said after him.

"We may have looked as if we didn't see how that could be, for after a minute she said, 'I sleep sound.'

"Harry was going to ask her more questions, but I said maybe that weren't our business; maybe we ought to let her tell her story first to the coroner or the sheriff. So Harry went fast as he could over to High Road—the Rivers' place, where there's a telephone."

"And what did she do when she knew you had gone for the coroner?" The attorney got his pencil in his hand all ready for writing.

"She moved from that chair to this one over here"—Hale pointed to a small chair in the corner—"and just sat there with her hands held together and looking down. I got a feeling that I

165

ought to make some conversation, so I said I had come in to see if John wanted to put in a telephone; and at that she started to laugh, and then she stopped and looked at me—scared."

At the sound of a moving pencil the man who was telling the story looked up.

"I dunno—maybe it wasn't scared," he hastened; "I wouldn't like to say it was. Soon Harry got back, and then Dr. Lloyd came, and you, Mr. Peters, and so I guess that's all I know that you don't."

He said that last with relief, and moved a little, as if relaxing. Everyone moved a little. The county attorney walked toward the stair door.

"I guess we'll go upstairs first—then out to the barn and around."

He paused and looked around the kitchen.

"You're convinced there was nothing important here?" he asked the sheriff. "Nothing that would—point to any motive?"

The sheriff too looked all around, as if to re-convince himself.

"Nothing here but kitchen things," he said, with a little laugh for the insignificance of kitchen things.

The county attorney was looking at the cupboard—a peculiar, ungainly structure, half closet and half cupboard, the upper part of it being built in the wall, and the lower part just the old-fashioned kitchen cupboard. As if its queerness attracted him, he got a chair and opened the upper part and looked in. After a moment he drew his hand away sticky.

"Here's a nice mess," he said resentfully.

The two women had drawn nearer, and now the sheriff's wife spoke.

"Oh—her fruit," she said, looking to Mrs. Hale for sympathetic understanding. She turned back to the county attorney and explained: "She worried about that when it turned so cold last night. She said the fire would go out and her jars burst."

Mrs. Peters' husband broke into a laugh.

"Well, can you beat the women! Held for murder, and worrying about her preserves!"

The young attorney set his lips.

"I guess before we're through she may have something more serious than preserves to worry about."

"Oh, well," said Mrs. Hale's husband, with good-natured superiority, "women are used to worrying over trifles."

The two women moved a little closer together. Neither of them spoke. The county attorney seemed suddenly to remember his manners—and think of his future.

"And yet," said he, with the gallantry of a young politician, "for all their worries, what would we do without the ladies?"

The women did not speak, did not unbend. He went to the sink and began washing his hands. He turned to wipe them on the roller towel—whirled it for a cleaner place.

"Dirty towels! Not much of a housekeeper, would you say, ladies?"

He kicked his foot against some dirty pans under the sink.

"There's a great deal of work to be done on a farm," said Mrs. Hale stiffly.

"To be sure. And yet"—with a little bow to her—"I know there are some Dickson County farm-houses that do not have such roller towels."

"Those towels get dirty awful quick. Men's hands aren't always as clean as they might be."

"Ah, loyal to your sex, I see," he laughed. He stopped and gave her a keen look. "But you and Mrs. Wright were neighbors. I suppose you were friends, too."

Martha Hale shook her head.

"I've seen little enough of her of late years. I've not been in this house—it's more than a year."

"And why was that? You didn't like her?"

"I liked her well enough," she replied with spirit. "Farmers' wives have their hands full, Mr. Henderson. And then—" She looked around the kitchen.

"Yes?" he encouraged.

"It never seemed a very cheerful place," said she, more to herself than to him.

"No," he agreed; "I don't think anyone would call it cheerful. I shouldn't say she had the home-making instinct."

"Well, I don't know as Wright had, either," she muttered.

"You mean they didn't get on very well?" he was quick to ask.

"No; I don't mean anything," she answered, with decision. As she turned a little away from him, she added: "But I don't think a place would be any the cheerfuller for John Wright's bein' in it."

"I'd like to talk to you about that a little later, Mrs. Hale," he said. "I'm anxious to get the lay of things upstairs now."

He moved toward the stair door, followed by the two men.

"I suppose anything Mrs. Peters does'll be all right?" the sheriff inquired. "She was to take in some clothes for her, you know—and a few little things. We left in such a hurry yesterday."

The county attorney looked at the two women whom they were leaving alone there among the kitchen things.

"Yes—Mrs. Peters," he said, his glance resting on the woman who was not Mrs. Peters, the big farmer woman who stood behind the sheriff's wife. "Of course Mrs. Peters is one of us," he said, in a manner of entrusting responsibility. "And keep your eye out, Mrs. Peters, for anything that might be of use. No telling; you women might come upon a clue to the motive—and that's the thing we need."

Mr. Hale rubbed his face after the fashion of a showman getting ready for a pleasantry.

"But would the women know a clue if they did come upon it?" he said; and, having delivered himself of this, he followed the others through the stair door.

The women stood motionless and silent, listening to the footsteps, first upon the stairs, then in the room above.

Then, as if releasing herself from something strange, Mrs. Hale began to arrange the dirty pans under the sink, which the county attorney's disdainful push of the foot had deranged.

"I'd hate to have men comin' into my kitchen," she said testily—"snoopin' round and criticizin'."

"Of course it's no more than their duty," said the sheriff's wife, in her manner of timid acquiescence.

"Duty's all right," replied Mrs. Hale bluffly; "but I guess that deputy sheriff that come out to make the fire might have got a little of this on." She gave the roller towel a pull. "Wish I'd thought of that sooner! Seems mean to talk about her for not having things slicked up, when she had to come away in such a hurry."

She looked around the kitchen. Certainly it was not "slicked up." Her eye was held by a bucket of sugar on a low shelf. The cover was off the wooden bucket, and beside it was a paper bag—half full.

Mrs. Hale moved toward it.

"She was putting this in there," she said to herself—slowly.

She thought of the flour in her kitchen at home—half sifted. She had been interrupted, and had left things half done. What had interrupted Minnie Foster? Why had that work been left half done? She made a move as if to finish it—unfinished things always bothered her—and then she glanced around and saw that Mrs. Peters was watching her—and she didn't want Mrs. Peters to get that feeling she had got of work begun and then—for some reason—not finished.

"It's a shame about her fruit," she said, and walked toward the cupboard that the county attorney had opened, and got on the chair, murmuring: "I wonder if it's all gone."

It was a sorry enough looking sight, but "Here's one that's all right," she said at last. She held it toward the light. "This is cherries, too." She looked again. "I declare I believe that's the only one."

With a sigh, she got down from the chair, went to the sink, and wiped off the bottle.

"She'll feel awful bad, after all her hard work in the hot weather. I remember the afternoon I put up my cherries last summer."

She set the bottle on the table, and, with another sigh, started to sit down in the rocker. But she did not sit down. Something kept her from sitting down in that chair. She straightened—stepped back, and, half turned away, stood looking at it, seeing the woman who had sat there "pleatin' at her apron."

The thin voice of the sheriff's wife broke in upon her: "I must be getting those things from the front room closet." She opened the door into the other room, started in, stepped back. "You coming with me, Mrs. Hale?" she asked nervously. "You—you could help me get them."

They were soon back—the stark coldness of that shut-up room was not a thing to linger in.

"My!" said Mrs. Peters, dropping the things on the table and hurrying to the stove.

Mrs. Hale stood examining the clothes the woman who was being detained in town had said she wanted.

"Wright was close!" she exclaimed, holding up a shabby black skirt that bore the marks of much making over. "I think maybe that's why she kept so much to herself. I s'pose she felt she couldn't do her part; and then, you don't enjoy things when you feel shabby. She used to wear pretty clothes and be lively—when she was Minnie Foster, one of the town girls, singing in the choir. But that—oh, that was twenty years ago."

With a carefulness in which there was something tender, she folded the shabby clothes and piled them at one corner of the table. She looked up at Mrs. Peters, and there was something in the other woman's look that irritated her.

"She don't care," she said to herself. "Much difference it makes to her whether Minnie Foster had pretty clothes when she was a girl."

Then she looked again, and she wasn't so sure; in fact, she hadn't at any time been perfectly sure about Mrs. Peters. She had that shrinking manner, and yet her eyes looked as if they could see a long way into things.

"This all you was to take in?" asked Mrs. Hale.

"No," said the sheriff's wife; "she said she wanted an apron. Funny thing to want," she ventured in her nervous little way, "for there's not much to get you dirty in jail, goodness knows. But I suppose just to make her feel more natural. If you're used to wearing an apron—. She said they were in the bottom drawer of this cupboard. Yes—here they are. And then her little shawl that always hung on the stair door."

She took the small gray shawl from behind the door leading upstairs.

Suddenly Mrs. Hale took a quick step toward the other woman. "Mrs. Peters!"

"Yes, Mrs. Hale?"

"Do you think she—did it?"

A frightened look blurred the other thing in Mrs. Peters' eyes.

"Oh, I don't know," she said, in a voice that seemed to shrink away from the subject.

"Well, I don't think she did," affirmed Mrs. Hale stoutly. "Asking for an apron, and her little shawl. Worryin' about her fruit."

"Mr. Peters says—." Footsteps were heard in the room above; she stopped, looked up, then went on in a lowered voice: "Mr. Peters says—it looks bad for her. Mr. Henderson is awful sarcastic in a speech, and he's going to make fun of her saying she didn't— wake up."

For a moment Mrs. Hale had no answer. Then, "Well, I guess John Wright didn't wake up—when they was slippin' that rope under his neck," she muttered.

"No, it's *strange*," breathed Mrs. Peters. "They think it was such a—funny way to kill a man."

"That's just what Mr. Hale said," said Mrs. Hale, in a resolutely natural voice. "There was a gun in the house. He says that's what he can't understand."

"Mr. Henderson said, coming out, that what was needed for the case was a motive. Something to show anger—or sudden feeling."

"Well, I don't see any signs of anger around here," said Mrs. Hale. "I don't—"

She stopped. It was as if her mind tripped on something. Her eye was caught by a dish-towel in the middle of the kitchen table. Slowly she moved toward the table. One half of it was wiped clean, the other half messy. Her eyes made a slow, almost unwilling turn to the bucket of sugar and the half empty bag beside it. Things begun—and not finished.

After a moment she stepped back, and said, in that manner of releasing herself: "Wonder how they're finding things upstairs? I hope she had it a little more red up there. You know"—she paused, and feeling gathered—"it seems kind of *sneaking:* locking her up in town and coming out here to get her own house to turn against her!"

"But, Mrs. Hale," said the sheriff's wife, "the law is the law."

"I s'pose 'tis," answered Mrs. Hale shortly.

She turned to the stove, worked with it a minute, and when she straightened up she said aggressively:

"The law is the law—and a bad stove is a bad stove. How'd you like to cook on this?"—pointing with the poker to the broken lining. She opened the oven door and started to express her opinion of the oven; but she was swept into her own thoughts, thinking of what it would mean, year after year, to have that stove to wrestle with. The thought of Minnie Foster trying to bake in that oven—and the thought of her never going over to see Minnie Foster—

She was startled by hearing Mrs. Peters say:

"A person gets discouraged—and loses heart."

The sheriff's wife had looked from the stove to the pail of water which had been carried in from outside. The two women stood there silent, above them the footsteps of the men who were looking for evidence against the woman who had worked in that kitchen. That look of seeing into things, of seeing through a thing to something else, was in the eyes of the sheriff's wife now. When Mrs. Hale next spoke to her, it was gently:

"Better loosen up your things, Mrs. Peters. We'll not feel them when we go out."

Mrs. Peters went to the back of the room to hang up the fur tippet she was wearing. A moment later she exclaimed, "Why, she was piecing a quilt," and held up a large sewing basket piled high with quilt pieces.

Mrs. Hale spread some of the blocks out on the table.

"It's log-cabin pattern," she said, putting several of them together. "Pretty, isn't it?"

They were so engaged with the quilt that they did not hear the footsteps on the stairs. Just as the stair door opened Mrs. Hale was saying:

"Do you suppose she was going to quilt it or just knot it?"

The sheriff threw up his hands.

"They wonder whether she was going to quilt it or just knot it!" he cried.

There was a laugh for the ways of women, a warming of hands over the stove, and then the county attorney said briskly:

"Well, let's go right out to the barn and get that cleared up."

"I don't see as there's anything so strange," Mrs. Hale said

resentfully, after the outside door had closed on the three men—
"our taking up our time with little things while we're waiting for
them to get the evidence. I don't see as it's anything to laugh about."

"Of course they've got awful important things on their minds,"
said the sheriff's wife apologetically.

They returned to an inspection of the block for the quilt. Mrs.
Hale was looking at the fine, even sewing, and preoccupied with
thoughts of the woman who had done that sewing, when she heard
the sheriff's wife say, in a queer tone:

"Why, look at this one."

She turned to take the block held out to her.

"The sewing," said Mrs. Peters, in a troubled way. "All the rest of
them have been so nice and even—but—this one. Why, it looks as if
she didn't know what she was about!"

Their eyes met—something flashed to life, passed between
them; then, as if with an effort, they seemed to pull away from each
other. A moment Mrs. Hale sat there, her hands folded over that
sewing which was so unlike all the rest of the sewing. Then she had
pulled a knot and drawn the threads.

"Oh, what are you doing, Mrs. Hale?" asked the sheriff's wife.

"Just pulling out a stitch or two that's not sewed very good," said
Mrs. Hale mildly.

"I don't think we ought to touch things," Mrs. Peters said, a little
helplessly.

"I'll just finish up this end," answered Mrs. Hale, still in that mild,
matter-of-fact fashion.

She threaded a needle and started to replace bad sewing with
good. For a little while she sewed in silence. Then, in that thin,
timid voice, she heard:

"Mrs. Hale!"

"Yes, Mrs. Peters?"

"What do you suppose she was so—nervous about?"

"Oh, *I* don't know," said Mrs. Hale, as if dismissing a thing not
important enough to spend much time on. "I don't know as she
was—nervous. I sew awful queer sometimes when I'm just tired."

She cut a thread, and out of the corner of her eye looked up at
Mrs. Peters. The small, lean face of the sheriff's wife seemed to
have tightened up. Her eyes had that look of peering into something. But next moment she moved, and said in her indecisive
way:

"Well, I must get these clothes wrapped. They may be through
sooner than we think. I wonder where I could find a piece of
paper—and string."

"In that cupboard, maybe," suggested Mrs. Hale, after a glance around.

One piece of the crazy sewing remained unripped. Mrs. Peters' back turned, Martha Hale now scrutinized that piece, compared it with the dainty, accurate sewing of the other blocks. The difference was startling. Holding this block made her feel queer, as if the distracted thoughts of the woman who had perhaps turned to it to try and quiet herself were communicating themselves to her.

Mrs. Peters' voice roused her.

"Here's a bird-cage," she said. "Did she have a bird, Mrs. Hale?"

"Why, I don't know whether she did or not." She turned to look at the cage Mrs. Peters was holding up. "I've not been here in so long." She sighed. "There was a man last year selling canaries cheap—but I don't know as she took one. Maybe she did. She used to sing real pretty herself."

"Seems kind of funny to think of a bird here." She half-laughed—an attempt to put up a barrier. "But she must have had one—or why would she have a cage? I wonder what happened to it."

"I suppose maybe the cat got it," suggested Mrs. Hale, resuming her sewing.

"No; she didn't have a cat. She's got that feeling some people have about cats—being afraid of them. When they brought her to our house yesterday, my cat got in the room, and she was real upset and asked me to take it out."

"My sister Bessie was like that," laughed Mrs. Hale.

The sheriff's wife did not reply. The silence made Mrs. Hale turn around. Mrs. Peters was examining the bird-cage.

"Look at this door," she said slowly. "It's broke. One hinge has been pulled apart."

Mrs. Hale came nearer.

"Looks as if someone must have been—rough with it."

Again their eyes met—startled, questioning, apprehensive. For a moment neither spoke nor stirred. Then Mrs. Hale, turning away, said brusquely:

"If they're going to find any evidence, I wish they'd be about it. I don't like this place."

"But I'm awful glad you came with me, Mrs. Hale." Mrs. Peters put the bird-cage on the table and sat down. "It would be lonesome for me—sitting here alone."

"Yes, it would, wouldn't it?" agreed Mrs. Hale, a certain very determined naturalness in her voice. She had picked up the sewing, but now it dropped in her lap, and she murmured in a different voice: "But I tell you what I *do* wish, Mrs. Peters. I wish I had come over sometimes when she was here. I wish—I had."

"But of course you were awful busy, Mrs. Hale. Your house—and your children."

"I could've come," retorted Mrs. Hale shortly. "I stayed away because it weren't cheerful—and that's why I ought to have come. I"—she looked around—"I've never liked this place. Maybe because it's down in a hollow and you don't see the road. I don't know what it is, but it's a lonesome place, and always was. I wish I had come over to see Minnie Foster sometimes. I can see now—" She did not put it into words.

"Well, you mustn't reproach yourself," counseled Mrs. Peters. "Somehow, we just don't see how it is with other folks till—something comes up."

"Not having children makes less work," mused Mrs. Hale, after a silence, "but it makes a quiet house—and Wright out to work all day—and no company when he did come in. Did you know John Wright, Mrs. Peters?"

"Not to know him. I've seen him in town. They say he was a good man."

"Yes—good," conceded John Wright's neighbor grimly. "He didn't drink, and kept his word as well as most, I guess, and paid his debts. But he was a hard man, Mrs. Peters. Just to pass the time of day with him—" She stopped, shivered a little. "Like a raw wind that gets to the bone." Her eye fell upon the cage on the table before her, and she added, almost bitterly: "I should think she would've wanted a bird!"

Suddenly she leaned forward, looking intently at the cage. "But what do you s'pose went wrong with it?"

"I don't know," returned Mrs. Peters; "unless it got sick and died."

But after she said it she reached over and swung the broken door. Both women watched it as if somehow held by it.

"You didn't know—her?" Mrs. Hale asked, a gentler note in her voice.

"Not till they brought her yesterday," said the sheriff's wife.

"She—come to think of it, she was kind of like a bird herself. Real sweet and pretty, but kind of timid and—fluttery. How—she—did—change."

That held her for a long time. Finally, as if struck with a happy thought and relieved to get back to everyday things, she exclaimed:

"Tell you what, Mrs. Peters, why don't you take the quilt in with you? It might take up her mind."

"Why, I think that's a real nice idea, Mrs. Hale," agreed the sheriff's wife, as if she too were glad to come into the atmosphere of a simple kindness. "There couldn't possibly be any objection to that, could there? Now, just what will I take? I wonder if her patches are in here—and her things."

They turned to the sewing basket.

"Here's some red," said Mrs. Hale, bringing out a roll of cloth. Underneath that was a box. "Here, maybe her scissors are in here—and her things." She held it up. "What a pretty box! I'll warrant that was something she had a long time ago—when she was a girl."

She held it in her hand a moment; then, with a little sigh, opened it.

Instantly her hand went to her nose.

"Why—!"

Mrs. Peters drew nearer—then turned away.

"There's something wrapped up in this piece of silk," faltered Mrs. Hale.

Her hand not steady, Mrs. Hale raised the piece of silk. "Oh, Mrs. Peters!" she cried, "it's—"

Mrs. Peters bent closer.

"It's the bird," she whispered.

"But, Mrs. Peters!" cried Mrs. Hale. "*Look* at it! Its *neck*—look at its neck! It's all—other side *to*."

The sheriff's wife again bent closer.

"Somebody wrung its neck," said she, in a voice that was slow and deep.

And then again the eyes of the two women met—this time clung together in a look of dawning comprehension, of growing horror. Mrs. Peters looked from the dead bird to the broken door of the cage. Again their eyes met. And just then there was a sound at the outside door.

Mrs. Hale slipped the box under the quilt pieces in the basket, and sank into the chair before it. Mrs. Peters stood holding to the table. The county attorney and the sheriff came in.

"Well, ladies," said the county attorney, as one turning from serious things to little pleasantries, "have you decided whether she was going to quilt it or knot it?"

"We think," began the sheriff's wife in a flurried voice, "that she was going to—knot it."

He was too preoccupied to notice the change that came in her voice on that last.

"Well, that's very interesting, I'm sure," he said tolerantly.

He caught sight of the cage. "Has the bird flown?"

"We think the cat got it," said Mrs. Hale in a voice curiously even.

He was walking up and down, as if thinking something out.

"Is there a cat?" he asked absently.

Mrs. Hale shot a look up at the sheriff's wife.

"Well, not *now*," said Mrs. Peters. "They're superstitious, you know; they leave."

The county attorney did not heed her. "No sign at all of anyone having come in from the outside," he said to Peters, in the manner of continuing an interrupted conversation. "Their own rope. Now let's go upstairs again and go over it, piece by piece. It would have to have been someone who knew just the—"

The stair door closed behind them and their voices were lost.

The two women sat motionless, not looking at each other, but as if peering into something and at the same time holding back. When they spoke now it was as if they were afraid of what they were saying, but as if they could not help saying it.

"She liked the bird," said Martha Hale, low and slowly. "She was going to bury it in that pretty box."

"When I was a girl," said Mrs. Peters, under her breath, "my kitten—there was a boy took a hatchet, and before my eyes—before I could get there—" She covered her face an instant. "If they hadn't held me back I would have"—she caught herself, looked upstairs where footsteps were heard, and finished weakly—"hurt him."

Then they sat without speaking or moving.

"I wonder how it would seem," Mrs. Hale at last began, as if feeling her way over strange ground—"never to have had any children around." Her eyes made a slow sweep of the kitchen, as if seeing what that kitchen had meant through all the years. "No, Wright wouldn't like the bird," she said after that—"a thing that sang. She used to sing. He killed that too." Her voice tightened.

Mrs. Peters moved uneasily.

"Of course we don't know who killed the bird."

"I knew John Wright," was Mrs. Hale's answer.

"It was an awful thing was done in this house last night, Mrs. Hale," said the sheriff's wife. "Killing a man while he slept—slipping a thing round his neck that choked the life out of him."

Mrs. Hale's hand went out to the bird-cage.

"His neck. Choked the life out of him."

"We don't *know* who killed him," whispered Mrs. Peters wildly. "We don't *know*."

Mrs. Hale had not moved. "If there had been years and years of—nothing, then a bird to sing to you, it would be awful—still—after the bird was still."

It was as if something within her not herself had spoken, and it found in Mrs. Peters something she did not know as herself.

"I know what stillness is," she said, in a queer, monotonous voice. "When we homesteaded in Dakota, and my first baby died—after he was two years old—and me with no other then—"

Mrs. Hale stirred.

"How soon do you suppose they'll be through looking for the evidence?"

"I know what stillness is," repeated Mrs. Peters, in just that same way. Then she too pulled back. "The law has got to punish crime, Mrs. Hale," she said in her tight little way.

"I wish you'd seen Minnie Foster," was the answer, "when she wore a white dress with blue ribbons, and stood up there in the choir and sang."

The picture of that girl, the fact that she had lived neighbor to that girl for twenty years, and had let her die for lack of life, was suddenly more than she could bear.

"Oh, I *wish* I'd come over here once in a while!" she cried. "That was a crime! That was a crime! Who's going to punish that?"

"We mustn't take on," said Mrs. Peters with a frightened look toward the stairs.

"I might 'a' *known* she needed help! I tell you, it's *queer*, Mrs. Peters. We live close together, and we live far apart. We all go through the same things—it's all just a different kind of the same thing! If it weren't—why do you and I *understand*? Why do we *know*—what we know this minute?"

She dashed her hand across her eyes. Then, seeing the jar of fruit on the table, she reached for it and choked out:

"If I was you I wouldn't *tell* her her fruit was gone! Tell her it *ain't*. Tell her it's all right—all of it. Here—take this in to prove it to her! She—she may never know whether it was broke or not."

Mrs. Peters reached out for the bottle of fruit as if she were glad to take it—as if touching a familiar thing, having something to do, could keep her from something else. She got up, looked about for something to wrap the fruit in, took a petticoat from the pile of clothes she had brought from the front room, and nervously started winding that round the bottle.

"My!" she began, in a high, false voice, "it's a good thing the men couldn't hear us! Getting all stirred up over a little thing like a—dead canary." She hurried over that. "As if that could have anything to do with—with—My, wouldn't they *laugh?*"

Footsteps were heard on the stairs.

"Maybe they would," muttered Mrs. Hale—"maybe they wouldn't."

"No, Peters," said the county attorney incisively; "it's all perfectly clear, except the reason for doing it. But you know juries when it comes to women. If there was some definite thing—something to show. Something to make a story about. A thing that would connect up with this clumsy way of doing it."

In a covert way Mrs. Hale looked at Mrs. Peters. Mrs. Peters was looking at her. Quickly they looked away from each other. The outer door opened and Mr. Hale came in.

"I've got the team round now," he said. "Pretty cold out there."

"I'm going to stay here awhile by myself," the county attorney suddenly announced. "You can send Frank out for me, can't you?" he asked the sheriff. "I want to go over everything. I'm not satisfied we can't do better."

Again, for one brief moment, the two women's eyes found one another.

The sheriff came up to the table.

"Did you want to see what Mrs. Peters was going to take in?"

The county attorney picked up the apron. He laughed. "Oh, I guess they're not very dangerous things the ladies have picked out."

Mrs. Hale's hand was on the sewing basket in which the box was concealed. She felt that she ought to take her hand off the basket. She did not seem able to. He picked up one of the quilt blocks which she had piled on to cover the box. Her eyes felt like fire. She had a feeling that if he took up the basket she would snatch it from him.

But he did not take it up. With another little laugh, he turned away.

"No; Mrs. Peters doesn't need supervising. For that matter, a sheriff's wife is married to the law. Ever think of it that way, Mrs. Peters?"

Mrs. Peters was standing beside the table. Mrs. Hale shot a look up at her; but she could not see her face. Mrs. Peters had turned away. When she spoke, her voice was muffled.

"Not—just that way," she said.

"Married to the law!" chuckled Mrs. Peters' husband. He moved toward the door into the front room, and said to the county attorney:

"I just want you to come in here a minute, George. We ought to take a look at these windows."

"Oh—windows," said the county attorney scoffingly.

"We'll be right out, Mr. Hale," said the sheriff to the farmer.

Hale went to look after the horses. The sheriff followed the county attorney into the other room. Again—for one final moment—the two women were alone in that kitchen.

Martha Hale sprang up, her hands tight together, looking at that other woman, with whom it rested. At first she could not see her eyes, for the sheriff's wife had not turned back since she turned away at that suggestion of being married to the law. But now Mrs. Hale made her turn back. Her eyes made her turn back. Slowly, unwillingly, Mrs. Peters turned her head until her eyes met the eyes of the other woman. There was a moment when they held each other in a steady, burning look in which there was no evasion nor flinching.

Then Martha Hale's eyes pointed the way to the basket in which was hidden the thing that would make certain the conviction of the other woman—that woman who was not there and yet who had been there with them all through that hour.

For a moment Mrs. Peters did not move. And then she did it. With a rush forward, she threw back the quilt pieces, got the box, tried to put it in her handbag. It was too big. Desperately she opened it, started to take the bird out. But there she broke—she could not touch the bird. She stood there helpless, foolish.

There was the sound of a knob turning in the inner door. Martha Hale snatched the box from the sheriff's wife, and got it in the pocket of her big coat just as the sheriff and the county attorney came back.

"Well, Henry," said the county attorney facetiously, "at least we found out that she was not going to quilt it. She was going to—what is it you call it, ladies?"

Mrs. Hale's hand was against the pocket of her coat.

"We call it—knot it, Mr. Henderson."

IT TAKES A THIEF

BY ARTHUR MILLER

Arthur Miller's first successful play, *All My Sons*, was produced when he was 32, in New York, the city of his birth. *Death of a Salesman* followed in 1947. His *The Crucible*, written during the McCarthy era, dealt with the question of freedom of conscience. *A View from the Bridge* in 1955 won the Pulitzer Prize as well as the N.Y. Drama Critics Circle Award. The scenario for his film, *The Misfits* (1961), which starred his wife Marilyn Monroe, evolved from a story he had written for *Esquire* in 1957.

SOME PEOPLE ARE LAUGHING IN OUR neighborhood these nights, but most of us are just waiting, like the Sheltons. It is simply unbelievable, it came out so right.

Here is this man, Mr. Shelton, a middle-aged man with what they call a nice family and a nice home. Ordinary kind of businessman, tired every night, sits around on Sundays, pinochle and so on. The point is, he's been doing all right the past few years. Automobiles. His used cars were shipped to California, Florida—wherever the war plants were springing up. Did fine. Then the war ended. The new cars started coming through and then the strikes made them scarce. But people wanted them very badly. Very, very badly. He did fine. Very, very fine.

One night not long ago he and his wife decided to take in a night club, and she put on her two diamond rings, the bracelet, and some of her other frozen cash, and they locked up the house—the children are all married and don't live home any more—and they were off for a trip to the city.

Nobody knows what they did in the city, but they stayed out till 3 in the morning. Late enough for Shelton to get a headful. The drive home was slow and careful because the car was one of his brand-new ones and he couldn't see well in his condition. Nevertheless, when he put the key in the front-door lock he was able to notice that the door swung open at a touch, whereas it usually took some jiggling of the latch. They went in and turned on the living-room lights, and then they saw it.

The drawer of the desk was lying on the floor, and the rug was littered with check stubs and stationery. The Sheltons rushed into the dining room and saw at once that the sterling-silver service was gone from the massive serving table. Shelton clutched at his heart as though he were going to suffocate, and Mrs. Shelton thrust her fingers into her hair and screamed. At this stage, of course, there was only the sensation that an alien presence had passed through their home. Perhaps they even imagined that the thief was still there. In wild fright they ran to the stairs and up to their bedroom, and Shelton tripped and fell over a bureau drawer that the thief had left on the threshold. Mrs. Shelton helped him up and made him lie down on the colonial bed and she massaged his heart while they both looked anxiously toward the closet door, which stood open.

When he had caught his breath, he pushed her aside and went into the closet and turned on the light. She crowded in beside him as soon as she saw the terrible expression on his face. The safe. The little steel safe that had always stood in the corner of the closet covered with dress boxes and old clothes, the safe was looking up at them from the corner with its door open. Shelton simply stood there panting. It was Mrs. Shelton who got to her knees and felt inside.

Nothing. Nothing was left. The safe was empty. Mrs. Shelton, on her knees in the closet, screamed again. Perhaps they felt once more the presence, the terrifying presence of the thief, for they rushed one behind the other down the stairs, and Shelton picked up the telephone.

The instrument shook in his hand as he bent over close to the dial and spun it around. Mrs. Shelton moved up and down beside him, clasping and unclasping her hands and weeping. "Oh, my God!"

"Police!" Shelton roared into the telephone as soon as he heard the operator's calm voice. "My house has been robbed. We just got home and—"

His voice caught Mrs. Shelton just as she was about to dig her fingers into her hair again. For an instant she stood perfectly still, then she turned suddenly and swung her arm out and clapped her hand over Shelton's mouth. Infuriated, he attempted to knock her hand away. Then his eyes met hers. They stood that way, looking into each other's eyes; and then Shelton's hand began to shake violently and he dropped the telephone with a loud bang onto the marble tabletop and collapsed into a high-backed, Italian-type chair. Mrs. Shelton replaced the telephone on its cradle as the operator's anxious voice flowed out of it.

They were both too frightened to speak for a few minutes. The same thing was rushing through their heads and there was no need to say what it was. Only a solution was needed, and neither of them could find it. At last Mrs. Shelton said, "You didn't give the operator the name or address. Maybe—"

"We'll see," he said, and went into the living room and stretched out on the couch.

Mrs. Shelton went to the front windows and drew the shades. Then she came back to the couch and proceeded to walk up and down beside it, her breasts rising and falling with the heavy rhythm of her breathing.

Nothing happened for nearly an hour. They even made a pass at undressing, just as though he had not shouted frantically into the telephone that his house had been robbed. But they were hardly out of their clothes when the doorbell rang. In dressing gown and slippers Shelton went down the stairs with his wife behind him. In the presence of strangers he always knew how to look calm, so much so that when he opened the door and let the two policemen in, he appeared almost sleepy.

The question of his having hung up without giving his name was cleared away first: He had been too excited to give that detail to the operator. The officers then went about inspecting the premises. That completed, Shelton and his wife sat in the living room with them and gave a detailed description of the seven pieces of jewelry that had been taken from the safe, and the silver service, and the old Persian lamb coat, and the other items, all of which were noted in a black-covered pad that one policeman wrote in. When Shelton had closed the door behind the two officers, he stood thinking for a while, and his wife waited for his word. Finally he said, "We'll report the jewelry to the insurance company tomorrow."

"What about the money?"

"How can I mention the money?"

She knew there was no answer to that one, but it was hard, nevertheless, to give up $91,000 without a complaint.

In bed they lay without moving. Thinking. "What'll we do," she asked, "if they find the crook and he's still got the money?"

A long time later, Shelton said, "They never catch thieves."

Eight days passed, in fact, before Shelton's opinion was proved wrong. The telephone rang at dinnertime. He covered the mouthpiece with his palm and turned to his wife. "They want me to come down and identify the stuff." There was a quavering note in his voice.

"What about the money?" she whispered.

"They didn't mention the money," he said, questioning her with his eyes.

"Maybe tell them you're too sick to go now."

"I'll have to go sometime."

"Try to find out first if they found the money."

"I can't *ask* them, can I?" he said angrily, and turned again to the telephone and said he would be right over.

He drove slowly. The new, purring engine, the $1900 car for which he could easily get 4,000 cash carried him effortlessly toward the police station. He drove slumped in the seat. As though to rehearse, he kept repeating the same sentence in his mind: I am simply a dealer, I am simply a dealer; I keep that much cash on hand to buy cars with. It sounded all right, businesslike. But was it possible they were that dumb? Maybe. They were just plain cops. Plain cops might not realize that 91,000 was too much to have in a safe for that purpose. And still, it was possible they would not stumble on the truth at all, not know that cash in a home safe was probably not entered on any ledger or income-tax form. Cops did not know much about big money, he felt. And yet—$91,000. Oh! $91,000! His insides grew cool at the thought of it. Not 20,000, or 40,000, not even 75,000, but $91,000. His retirement, his whole future ease, his very sureness of gait lay entirely in that money. It had become a tingling sensation for him, a smell, a feeling, a taste—$91,000 cash money in his safe at home. He had even stopped bothering to read the papers in the past year. Nothing that happened in the world could touch him while he had $91,000 in his closet.

There were three policemen sitting in the room when he entered. He identified himself, and they asked him to sit down. One of them went out. The remaining two were in shirt-sleeves and seemed to be merely waiting around. In a little while a gray-haired man entered, followed by a detective who carried a cheap canvas zipper bag which he set on a desk near the door. The detective introduced himself to Shelton, and asked him to repeat his description of the jewelry. Shelton did so in some detail, answering more specific questions as they occurred to the detective.

The gray-haired man had slumped into a chair. Now he sat staring at the floor. Shelton slowly realized, as he described the jewelry, that this was the thief; for the man seemed resigned, very tired, and completely at home in the situation.

The detective went at last to the desk and opened the zipper bag and laid out the jewelry for Shelton to inspect. Shelton glanced at it and said it was his, picking up a wedding ring which had his name and his wife's engraved on the inside.

"We'll have the coat for you by tomorrow and maybe the silver, too," the detective said, idly arranging the jewelry in a pattern on the desk as he spoke. Shelton felt that the detective was getting at something from the way he played with the jewelry. The detective completed the pattern on the desk and then turned his broad, dark face toward Shelton and said, "Is there anything else you lost?"

Shelton's hand, of its own accord, moved toward his heart as he said, "That's all I can remember."

The detective turned his whole body now and sat easily on the edge of the desk. "You didn't lose any money?"

The gray-haired thief raised his head, a mystified look clouding his face.

184

"Money?" asked Shelton. And yet he could not help adding, "What money?" Just curiously.

"We found this on him," the detective said, reaching into the bag and taking out five rolled-up wads of money wrapped in red rubber bands. Shelton's heart hurt him when he saw the rubber bands, because they, more than any of the other items, were peculiarly his. They were the rubber bands he always used in his office.

"There's $91,000 here," the detective said.

The thief was looking up at Shelton from his chair, an expression of wounded bewilderment drawing his brows together. The detective merely sat on the desk, an observer; the moment suddenly belonged only to Shelton and the thief.

Shelton stared at the money without any expression on his face. It was too late to think fast; he had no idea what sort of mind this stolid detective had and he dared not hesitate long enough to sound the man out. A detective, Shelton knew, is higher than a cop; is more like a businessman, knows more. This one looks smart, and yet maybe . . .

Shelton broke into a smile and touched one of the wads of bills that lay on the desk. (Oh, the 91,000; oh, the touch of it!) Sweat was running down his back; his heart pained like a wound. He smiled and stalled for time. "That's a lot of money," he said softly, frantically studying the detective's eyes for a sign.

But the detective was impassive, and said, "Is it yours?"

"Mine?" Shelton said, with a weak laugh. Longingly he looked at the solid wads. "I wish it were, but it isn't. I don't keep 91 thou—"

The thief, a tall man, stood up quickly and pointed to the money. "What the hell is *this?*" he shouted, amazed.

The detective moved toward him, and he sat down again. "It's his. I took it out of the safe with the other stuff."

"Take it easy," the detective said.

"Where did I get it, then?" the thief demanded in a more frightened tone. "What're you trying to do, pin another job on me? I only pulled one, that's all! You asked me and I told you." And, pointing directly up at Shelton's face, he said, "He's pullin' something!"

The detective, as he turned to Shelton, was an agonizingly expressionless man who seemed to have neither pulse nor point of view. He simply stood there, the law with two little black eyes. "You're sure," he said, "that this is not your money?"

"I ought to know," Shelton said, laughing calmly.

The detective seemed to catch the absurdity of it, and very nearly smiled. Then he turned to the thief and, with a nod of his head, motioned him outside. The two policemen walked out behind him.

They were alone. The detective, without a word, returned to the desk and put the jewelry back into the zipper bag. Without turning his head, he said that they would return the stuff to Shelton in the morning. And then he picked up one of the heavy wads, but instead of dropping it into the bag he hefted it thoughtfully in his palm and turned his head to Shelton. "Lot of dough," he said.

"I'll say," Shelton agreed.

The detective continued placing the wads in the bag. Shelton stood a little behind him and to one side, watching as best he could for the slightest change in the man's expression. But there was none; the detective might have been asleep but for his open eyes. Shelton wanted to leave—immediately. It was impossible to know what was happening in the detective's head.

And yet Shelton dared not indicate his desperation. He smiled again, and shifted his weight easily to one foot and started to button his coat, and said—as if the question were quite academic—"What do you fellas do with money like that?"

The detective zipped the bag shut. "Money like what?" he asked evenly.

A twinge of pain shot through Shelton's chest at the suspicious reserve in the detective's question. "I mean, money that's not claimed," he amended.

The detective walked past him toward the door. "We wait," he said, and opened the door.

"I mean, supposing it's never claimed?" Shelton asked, following him, still smiling as though with idle curiosity.

"Hot money is never claimed," the detective said. "We'll just wait. Then we'll start looking around."

"I see."

Shelton walked with the detective to the door of the precinct station, and he even talked amiably, and then they said a pleasant good night.

Staring at the pavement rolling under the wheels of his car, he could summon neither feeling nor thought. It was only when he opened the door of his house, the house that had once contained the fortune of his life, that his numbness flowed away, and he felt weak and ill.

"There must be a way to get it back," she began.

"How?"

"You mean to tell me—?"

"I mean to tell you!" he shouted, and got to his feet. "What'll I do, break into the station house?"

"But they've got laws against robbery!"

In reply, Shelton pulled his collar open and climbed the stairs and went to bed.

These days, Shelton rides to business very slowly. The few friends he has on the block have grown accustomed to the gray and haunted stare in his eyes. The children seem to quiet down as he guides his car through their street games.

Sometimes he goes by the police station, and passing it he slows down and peers through the car window at it, but he always continues on.

And when a police car rolls into the block on its ordinary tour, people can be seen stopping to watch until it passes his house. Nobody has said anything, of course, but we are waiting with Shelton for that awful moment when the white coupé pulls up at his door. And it must, of course.

Thirty days, maybe two months from now, it will turn the corner and slow down, and gradually, ominously, come to a stop.

The house is very quiet these nights—almost silent. The shades are drawn, and it is seldom that you see anyone going in or out. The Sheltons are waiting.

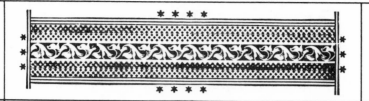

THE MURDER IN
THE FISHING CAT

BY EDNA ST. VINCENT MILLAY

Edna St. Vincent Millay was born in Rockland, Maine, on February 22, 1892, and attended Barnard and Vassar before settling down in Greenwich Village. For a while she acted with the Provincetown Players (*see Susan Glaspell*) who produced some of her plays. She won the Pulitzer Prize in 1923 for *The Harp-Weaver and Other Poems*. That same year she married Eugen Boissevain, an importer, and moved with him to a farm in Austerlitz, N.Y., where they lived for the rest of their lives and where some of her finest poetry was written.

NOBODY CAME any more to the *Restaurant du Chat qui Peêche*. It was difficult to say just why.

The popularity of a restaurant does not depend on the excellence of its cuisine or the cobwebs on the bottles in its cellar. And you might have in the window ten glass tanks instead of one in which moved obscurely shadowy eels and shrimps, yet you could be no surer of success. Jean-Pierre knew this, and he did not reproach himself for his failure. It is something that may happen to the best of us.

For fourteen years he had served as good *lapin sauté* as was to be found in Paris; and if the *petits pois* were rather big and hard, and the Vouvray rather like thin cider, and you got no more than a teaspoonful of sugar with your strawberries, well, what could you expect for seven francs, all told? Not the world, surely. As for the rest, where else might you, while sitting comfortably at your table under a red-and-white awning, choose your eel, and see it captured for you deftly in a napkin, and borne off, writhing muscularly, to the kitchen, to be delivered to you five minutes later on a platter, fried? That was more than you could do at Ciro's.

It might be, of course, because Margot had scolded him much too audibly. But where was the man among his clients whose wife had not at some time or other addressed him as *saligaud,* or *espèce de soupe au lait?* Let him stand forth.

And, anyway, she had gone now. After fourteen years at his side, stamping the butter, whacking the long loaves of bread, sitting down with a sigh to a bowl of onion soup after nine o'clock, she had gone. She had run off with a taxi-driver who had red mustaches that curled naturally. And the place was very still.

Jean-Pierre stood in the doorway with a damp cloth in his hand, and watched the people go by. They all went by. Once he had been sure that all were coming in, but now he knew better. They were going to the *Rendezvous des Cochers et Camionneurs,* next door.

"*J'ai pas la veine,*" said Jean-Pierre. He stepped out upon the pavement and busily passed the damp cloth over a table which was not yet dry.

A man and girl went by. Two men went by. A woman went past, selling papers: "*L'Intran*'! L'Intransigeant! La Liberté—troisième édition! L'Intran'! L'Intransigeant!*" Two young men went by;

one was wearing a smock, the other had a painted picture under his arm. A man and a girl went past with their arms about each other. The man was saying, "*Si, si, c'est vrai.*" A very little girl came along, carrying a basket of small fringe-petaled pinks and fading roses. She had a serious face. She held out the flowers earnestly to a woman, with a coat over her arm, pushing a baby-carriage; to an old man reading a newspaper as he walked; to two young women, dressed precisely alike, who were hurrying some-where, chattering.

A priest went by, taking long steps, his black gown flapping about his large shoes, his stiff, shallow hat on the back of his head. He was trying to catch a bus. He began to run. The little girl watched him go by, seriously. Still watching him, she held out her flowers to a soldier in a uniform of horizon-blue. Then she went to the restaurant next door and moved among the tables.

"*Sentez, madame.*" she said without emotion, and impassively thrust a bunch of pinks under the nose of a young woman, with a very red mouth, whose fork dangled languidly from her hand as she conversed with the man across from her.

"*Merci, merci,*" said the woman, and motioned her away without looking at her.

An American boy was dining alone, reading from a yellow book. He looked up from his book, and followed the little girl with his eyes as she moved about the terrace. As she approached him he spoke to her.

"*C'est combien, ça, ma petite?*" he asked.

She came up to him, and pressed her small stomach against the table.

"*Dix sous,*" she answered lispingly, staring at his forehead.

He put an arm about her while he selected a nosegay from the basket, stood it up in his empty wine-glass, and poured Vichy for it. Then he gave her a franc and told her to keep the change.

She stared at him, and went off up the street, holding out her basket to the passers-by.

Jean-Pierre came to himself with a start: the proprietor of a flourishing café does not stand all the afternoon gaping at the goings-on in the café next door. No wonder people did not come to the *Restaurant du Chat*: it had an absent-minded *patron*. He hur-riedly passed the damp cloth over two of the iron-legged tables, plucked a brown leaf from the laurel which hedged the terrace from the pavement proper, and went back into the restaurant.

"*Ça, va, Philippe?*" he questioned jovially of the large eel which was now the sole occupant of the tank.

Not for the life of him could Jean-Pierre have told you why he had addressed the eel as Philippe; but having done so, he was glad. For from the moment he had given the creature a name, it possessed an identity, it was a person, something he could talk to.

He went to the kitchen, and returned with a morsel of lobster from a salad of the night before and tossed it into the pool.

Two men and two women, finding the *Rendezvous des Cochers* crowded, turned in at the *Restaurant du Chat qui Pêche* and seated themselves.

They heard Jean-Pierre singing:
"Oh, madame, voilà du bon fromage!
Oh, madame, voilà du bon fromage!
Voilà du bon fromage au lait!"

One of the men rapped on the table with his stick. Jean-Pierre stopped short in his song, caught up the *carte du jour*, smoothed down his black beard, and hurried out.

"Very good, the rabbit," he suggested. And, "What will you have, sirs, in the way of wine?"

For half a year there had been only three of them to do the work—he, his wife, and Maurice, the waiter. Maurice had come to them when he was sixteen; but very soon he was nineteen, and the War Department, which knows about everything, had found out about that also, and had taken him away to put him into the army.

Then for two months there had been only two of them, but it was quite enough. Now Margot was gone, and he was alone. But business was worse and worse, and very rarely was he hurried with all the cooking and the serving and the cleaning-up.

Jean-Pierre had made few friends in Paris in these fourteen years. He had dealt pleasantly with his clients, his neighbors, and the tradespeople with whom he had to do; but he had been content with his wife. She was a pretty woman from the frontier of Spain and more Spanish than French. He had met her for the first time right over there, in the Luxembourg Gardens. He could almost see from his doorway the very tree under which she had been sitting. She was wearing a hat of pink straw sloping down over her forehead, with many little roses piled high under the back of it; and she was very small about the waist. She was embroidering something white.

Several times he passed the chair in which she was sitting, and every time she looked up, and then looked down again. When she arose to go, he fell into step beside her.

"Mademoiselle, may I accompany you?" he asked.

"No, please," she answered hurriedly, without looking at him, and quickened her step.

He kept pace with her, however, and bent over her and spoke again more softly.

"It is wrong for one so beautiful to be so cruel."

"*Veux-tu me laisser!*" she scolded, tossing her head, and hastened out of sight.

But the next afternoon she was there again.

"You remember my wife, Philippe?" said Jean-Pierre. "Margot of the naughty eyes and the pretty ankles?"

Philippe said nothing.

"You do, all the same," Jean-Pierre averred. "She used to stir the water to make you mad." After a moment he said again, "Philippe, you remember Margot, don't you?"

Philippe said nothing.

"Well, anyhow," said Jean-Pierre, "she's gone."

For three months now Philippe had been alone in the tank. Nobody ate eels any more. The few customers that came ordered rabbit, mutton, or beefsteak and potatoes. It would be foolish to have more eels sent in from the basin in the country. Jean-Pierre had explained that he would need for a time no more eels or shrimps, that he was making some changes.

Every morning when the proprietor of the *Chat qui Pêche* came down to open the door and put the tables and chairs out upon the pavement, Philippe lay sluggishly on the green bottom of his tank, the sunshine bringing out colors on his back that one had not known were there.

It was an oblong glass tank with brass edges. Fresh water came up through a little spout in the middle of it, and the stale water was sucked away through a pipe in one corner, which was covered with a bubble-shaped piece of netting. Looking into the tank one day, Jean-Pierre wondered why the netting was shaped like that; then he reflected that if the wire had been flat over the mouth of the pipe, it would have been clogged always with bits of dirt and food, which would float up to settle on it. He felt very proud when he had come to this conclusion.

Philippe had been at one time gray-green in color, and thin and very active. Now he was green-black, with a valance standing up along his spine of transparent purple, and with two little pale-green fins behind his head. He was big now, but as lithe as ever.

Jean-Pierre had heard queer tales about eels; he did not know how much truth there was in them. He had heard that their mothers came ashore to give birth to them; that they were born, like little animals, not laid, like eggs. And when they were small they were called "elvers." And he had been told that after they were born, their mothers left them, and went away. And in a little while the elvers started out for themselves in search of pools to live in. And if it so happened that the pools nearby had dried up with the heat, they went farther. And it was said that they have gone as far as twenty miles, across the land, in search of water, thousands of them, an army of little eels. And no human eye had witnessed their sinuous migration. Only from time to time there was found a dead elver in the grass, and people knew the eels had passed that way.

"*Dis-moi un peu, Philippe.*" said Jean-Pierre. "You are a droll one, aren't you?"

The days went by, and nothing happened in them. Every day a few people came to eat there. Once there had been ten at a time, and Jean-Pierre had said to himself that if this kept on, he would have to get a waiter. But it did not keep on.

Every day he missed his wife more keenly. One day he went across the *rue de Médicis* into the Luxembourg Gardens, and walked up and down past the place where he had first seen her. A young woman was sitting under the tree, embroidering, but she was not Margot. She had two children with her, two little girls, dressed just alike, in very short dresses made all of pale blue silk ruffles. They were chasing one another up and down the walk and calling in shrill voices. One of them lost her hair-ribbon, a pale blue silk bow, and ran sidewise up to her mother, holding in one hand the ribbon and lifting with the other a lock of straight blonde hair at the top of her head; but all the time calling to her sister, and pawing the earth with brown, impatient legs.

Jean-Pierre wished very much that his only child, his and Margot's, had not died of diphtheria. She would have been much prettier than either of these little girls; she had looked like her mother. And she would be a companion for him now. If she were here this afternoon, he would take her to the *Jardin des Plantes* and show her all the different-colored birds. And after that they would go to the *Café des Deux Magots* and sit outside, and he would have a half-blond beer, and she would have a grenadine. And he would buy her one of those small white-and-brown rabbits made all of real fur that hop when you press a bulb, such as old men are always peddling along the pavement from trays suspended in front of their stomachs by a cord about their necks.

The days went by and went by. May passed, and June passed. One day there came a postcard from Maurice, a picture bearing the title, *Panorama de Metz*. On it was written carefully in pencil, *Bon souvenir d'un nouveau poilu aviateur*. Jean-Pierre was very excited about the postcard. Four times that day he drew it from his pocket and read it aloud, then turned it over and read with happiness his own name on the front of it. Late in the afternoon it occurred to him with pleasure that he had not yet read it to Philippe, and he hastened to do so. But from his wife there had come no word.

It seemed to Jean-Pierre that he would give everything he had in the world if he might once again hear Margot wail from the terrace, *"Un-e sou-u-u-u-u-pe!"* And, oh, to be called once more a dirty camel, a robber, or a species of dog!

He went to the tank and leaned over the quivering water.

"You are my wife, Philippe. You know?" said Jean-Pierre. "You are a *salope*!"

Having delivered himself of which genial insult, he felt happier, and stood for some moments in his doorway with his arms folded, looking boldly out upon the world.

"Ça va, mon vieux?" he accosted the eel one morning, and stirred the top of the water with a lobster-claw. But Philippe scarcely moved. Jean-Pierre reached down with the lobster-claw and tickled his back. The flat tail flapped slightly, but that was all. Jean-Pierre straightened up and pulled at his beard in astonishment. Then he leaned far over, so that his head made a shadow in which the eel was clearly visible, and shouted down to him:

"Philippe, Philippe, my friend, you are not sick, are you?"

He waited eagerly, but there was no responsive motion. The eel lay still.

"Oh, my God!" cried the *patron* of the *Chat qui Pêche*, and clutched his hair in his hands. Then for the first time he noticed that the surface of the water was unusually quiet. No fresh water bubbled up from the tap in the middle.

"Oh, my God!" cried Jean-Pierre again, and rushed to the kitchen.

There was nothing there with which to clean a clogged water-pipe. Everything that was long enough was much too thick. One tine of a fork would go in, but was probably not long enough. Nevertheless, he would try.

He ran back to the window and prodded the tube with a tine of the fork. Then he straightened up and waited, breathless. The water did not come. He rushed again to the kitchen, and scratched about among the cooking utensils. Was there no piece of wire anywhere in the world? A pipecleaner! That was it! He searched feverishly through all his pockets, but he knew all the time that he had none. It occurred to him that if Margot were there, she would have a hair-pin, which could be straightened out, and he cursed her savagely that she had gone.

Suddenly his eye fell on the broom, which was standing in a corner. He went over to it and tore forth a handful of splints, with which he rushed back to the tank.

"Wait, wait, Philippe!" he called as he approached. "Don't die! Wait just a very little minute!" And he thrust a splint down into the tube. It broke, and he had difficulty in extracting it. Sweat came out on his forehead. He put two splints together, and inserted them with care.

"Don't die! don't die!" he moaned, but softly, lest the splints should break.

Suddenly, incredibly, the water came, and dust and particles of food began to travel slowly toward the outlet. Jean-Pierre thrust his hands in up to the wrists, and shooed the stale water down the tank.

The next morning Philippe was quite himself again. Fearfully, Jean-Pierre crept into the room and approached the window.

"*Comment ça va ce matin?*" he questioned in a timid voice, and put a finger into the pool.

The eel aroused, and wriggled sullenly to the other end of the glass.

Jean-Pierre giggled sharply with delight, and all that morning he went about with a grin on his face, singing, "*Madame, voilà du bon fromage!*"

Jean-Pierre hated the room in which he slept. It seemed to have become, since Margot left, every day dirtier and more untidy. For one thing, of course, he never made the bed. When he crawled into it at night it was just as he had crawled out of it in the morning. The thin blanket dragged always to the floor on one side, the counter-pane on the other. The sheets grew grayer and grayer, and the bolster flatter. And he seemed always to have fallen asleep on the button side of the square pillow.

Infrequently he drew off the soiled sheets and put on clean ones. But at such times he became more than usually unhappy; he missed Margot more. She had been used to exclaim always over the fresh bed that it smelled sweet, and to pass her hand with pleasure over the smooth old linen. Often she would say with pride: "I tell you frankly, my little cabbage, in many of the big hotels today, rich hotels, full of Americans, they make up the beds with cotton. I don't see how the clients sleep. I could not."

Every morning on awaking, Jean-Pierre groaned once and turned heavily. Then he rubbed the back of his wrist across his eyes, and stared out at the daylight. He saw on the shelf above the narrow fireplace a pale photograph of himself and his brother when they were children. They were seated in an imitation row-boat. Into his hand had been thrust an imitation oar, which it supported without interest; from the hand of his brother dangled listlessly a handsome string of imitation fish.

He saw also the swathed and ghostly bulk of what he knew to be a clock—a clock so elegant and fine, so ornamented with whorls of shiny brass, that his wife had kept it lovingly wrapped in a towel. To be sure, the face of the clock could not be seen; but what will you? One cannot have everything. Between the clock and the photograph was a marvelous object—a large melon growing serenely in a small-necked bottle. A great trick, that. But Jean-Pierre was very tired of the melon.

He was tired of everything in the room, everything in his life, but particularly of the things on the mantelpiece. And most of all was he tired of the candlestick that stood between the clock and the wreath of wax gardenias—a candlestick which had never known a candle, a flat lily-pad with a green frog squatting on it. Jean-Pierre did not know that it was a green frog squatting on a lily-pad. It had been there so long that when he looked at it he no longer saw it. It was only one of the things on the mantelpiece.

One morning, however, as he awoke and groaned and turned and looked out with dull eyes on still another yesterday, it so happened that he stared for some moments at the candlestick. And presently he said, *"Tiens! tiens!"* and laid his forefinger alongside his nose.

That morning he dressed hurriedly, with a little smile going and coming at his lips. And when he was dressed he thrust the candle-stick into his pocket and ran downstairs.

"Bonjour, Philippe!" he called as he entered the restaurant. "Re-gard, species of wild man, I bring you a little friend!"

Happily, and with excessive care, he installed the green frog at the bottom of the tank. The eel moved away from it in beautiful curves.

"There is somebody for you to talk to, Philippe," said Jean-Pierre, "as you are for me."

He went to the door and opened it. The morning air came freshly in from the trees and fountains of the Luxembourg.

The days went by and went by, and nothing happened in them. One afternoon Jean-Pierre stood for a long time outside the window of a shop which had the sign up, *Fleurs Naturelles*. It was unfortunate for Margot, he told you frankly, that she had left him, because otherwise on this day she would be receiving a bouquet of flowers, *pois de senteur*, purple, pink, and mauve, and big white *pivoines*. It was the anniversary of their wedding. There were water-lilies in the window, too.

Suddenly Jean-Pierre burst into the flower shop with the face of a boy in love, and after much shrugging and gesticulation and interchange of commonplace insults, he parted from the shop-keeper, and went home to Philippe, bearing a long-stemmed lily.

At twenty minutes to one of an afternoon a week later a man might have been seen to walk along the *quai* of the Seine to the *Place St. Michel*, and then up the *Boulevard St. Michel* to the *rue de Médicis*. On the corner of the *rue de Médicis* he hesitated and looked both ways. Just then a very little girl came up the *boulevard* and held out to him a basket of pinks and roses. He shook his head.

It happened that for that moment these two were the only people on that corner. The little girl stood for a moment beside him, hesitating, looking both ways. Then she tucked her basket under her arm and started up the *rue de Médicis*. And because she had turned that way, the man turned that way, too, letting her decision take the place of his own.

He walked slowly, glancing as he passed at the many people taking their luncheon under the awnings in front of the cafés. He was looking for a place to eat, and it happened that he wished to be alone.

Before the *Restaurant du Chat qui Pêche* there were six oblong, iron-legged tables, on each of which stood a warted blue-glass vase containing a sprig of faded sweet-william and the wilted stamens of a rose from which the petals had dropped. The place was deserted. There was no sign of life anywhere about, saving only that in one of the windows there was a glass tank filled with slightly quivering water, on the surface of which floated a lily, and on the bottom of which, beside an artificial bright-green frog, dozed a large and sluggish eel.

The man seated himself at one of the tables and tapped upon the table with the vase. There was no response. He tapped again.

"*Voilà!*" called Jean-Pierre from the back of the restaurant, and came eagerly out, holding in his hand the *carte du jour*.

"The rabbit is very good," he suggested, "also the *gigot*. And what will you have, sir, in the way of wine?"

"White wine," said the man, "a half-bottle. A salad of tomatoes, an onion soup, and an *anguille*."

"*Oui, monsieur.*" said Jean-Pierre. "And after the *andouilles*, what?" *Andouilles* are a kind of sausage.

"Not *andouilles*," replied the man, with some impatience, "*anguille*."

"*Oui, monsieur*," said Jean-Pierre, trembling. He passed his damp cloth over the table and went back into the restaurant. He sat down upon a chair, and his head dropped to one side, his eyes bulging. "*O-o, là là!*" said Jean-Pierre.

Several moments passed. The man on the terrace outside rapped sharply on the table.

"*Voilà!*" called Jean-Pierre, leaping to his feet. Hurriedly he gathered up a folded napkin, a thick white plate, a knife, fork, and spoon, two round bits of bread, and an unlabeled bottle of white wine. With these he issued forth.

When the table was fairly set, he curved one hand behind his ear and leaned down to listen.

"Will *monsieur* kindly repeat his order?" he requested in a half-whisper.

The gentleman did so, with annoyance, glanced up into the face bending over him, frowned, and reached for the wine.

Jean-Pierre went away and returned with the tomato salad. It was very pretty. There were green bits of chopped onion scattered over it. Presently he brought the onion soup. This was not very good. It was composed chiefly of soaked bits of bread, and it was not hot; but with grated cheese it could be made to do.

When the soup was finished, Jean-Pierre appeared again and cleared away the dishes.

"And for the rest, sir," said he, fixing the eyes of his client with his own, which glittered meaningly, "it will be necessary to wait a few moments, you understand."

"Yes, yes," said the man, and shrugged. He wished vaguely he had gone elsewhere for his food.

"Because he is living," Jean-Pierre pursued in a clear voice of unaccountable pride, "and it will be necessary first to kill him. See, he lives!" And pulling the man by the sleeve, he pointed with his thumb to the brassbound tank in the window.

The man glanced askance at the window, and twitched his sleeve free.

"*Encore une demi-bouteille de vin blanc,*" he replied.

Jean-Pierre stood for a moment looking down into the water. The eel was stretched along the bottom of the tank, dozing in the sunshine. Once he idly flipped his thick tail, then lay still again. His dark back shone with a somber iridescence.

"*Philippe*," whispered Jean-Pierre, thrusting his face close to the surface of the pool—"*Philippe, mon petit, adieu!*"

At this, tears rushed from his eyes, and his neck and chest tried horridly to sob, working out and in like the shoulders of a cat that is sick.

"O Holy Virgin!" he moaned, and wound the clean white napkin firmly about his hand.

The eel came writhing out into the air. It was muscular and strong. It struck backward with its heavy body. It wound itself about Jean-Pierre's wrist. It was difficult to hold. It was difficult to shift from one hand to the other while one rushed to the kitchen.

Jean-Pierre held the eel to the table and reached for the knife. The knife was gone. Sweat rolled from his forehead, down his cheeks, and into his beard.

He ran wildly from one end of the kitchen to the other, the eel all the time plunging and twisting in his hand. He could not think what it was he was looking for.

The broom! But, no, it was not that. At length he saw the handle of the knife, Margot's knife, with which she used to kill the bread. It was peering at him from under a clutter of red and white onion skins. It had been watching him all this time.

He walked slowly past it, then turned sharply, and snatched it with his hand. He held Philippe firmly down upon the table, turned away his face, and struck with closed eyes. When he looked again, the knife was wedged in the table; Philippe had not been touched. He eased the knife free; the eel struck it with his lashing tail, and it fell to the floor. He stooped to pick it up; the eel reared in his grasp and smote him across the face.

"Ah-h-h!" cried Jean-Pierre, "you would, would you!" Smarting and furious from the blow, he clutched the knife and rose.

"You would, would you!" he said again, between his teeth. His throat thickened. Flames danced before his eyes. "*Eh bien, on verra!* Name of a name! We shall see, my little pigeon!" The flames roared and crackled. His eyes smarted, and his lungs were full of smoke. His heart swelled, burst, and the stored resentment and pain of his long isolation raced through his body, poisoning his blood.

"Take *that* for your lying face!" he cried. "Spaniard!"

"Take *that* for your ankles! *That* for your red mustaches! Take *that!* Take *that!*"

199

Kneeling on the floor, he beat in the head of Philippe with the handle of the knife.

All the time that the stranger was eating, Jean-Pierre watched him slyly from the door. Twice a small giggle arose to his lips, but he caught at his beard and pulled it down. He was happy for the first time in many months. He had killed the taxi-driver with the red mustaches, he had fried him in six pieces that leaped, and the stranger was eating him.

When the stranger had gone, Jean-Pierre gathered up the dishes and bore them to the kitchen, chuckling as he did so. He saw the head of the eel in the corner whither he had kicked it, and he spat upon it. But when he came back for the wine bottles and the salt and pepper and vinegar and oil, his eyes fell on the tank in the window, with its bright-green frog and its floating lily and its quiet emptiness. Then he remembered that it was Margot that he had killed.

He put his hand to his throat and stared. Margot! Now, how had that happened? He was sure that he had never intended to kill Margot. What a terrible mistake! But, no, it was not true that he had killed Margot. It was an ugly and tiresome dream. There was sun on the trees in the Gardens of the Luxembourg. Was not that proof enough that Margot was not dead, if one had needed proof?

Still, come to think of it, it was a long time since she had been about the house. It was fully a year, if you pressed the point, since he had heard her voice. There was something very dead about her, come to think of it.

But certainly he had killed Margot! How silly of him! He remembered the circumstances now perfectly. They had been out together in a rowboat on a river whose banks were brass. In Margot's hand was an oar, in his a handsome string of fish. At one end of the river was a dam covered by a dome of netted wire. At the other end water bubbled up continuously from a hidden spring.

He looked at Margot. As he looked, the oar slipped softly from her hand into the water; on the other side of the boat the string of fish slipped softly from his hand into the water. Then he noted with disquiet that the water in the river was steadily receding. He looked at the banks; they were like high walls of brass. He looked at them again; they were like tall cliffs of brass. He looked at the river; it was as shallow as a plate of soup.

It occurred to him that if he wanted to drown Margot, he would best be quick about it, as soon there would be no water in which to drown her. "But I do not wish to drown Margot!" he protested. But the man kept rapping on the table with a sprig of sweet-william. And even as he said it, he stepped from the boat, seized her by the waist with both hands, and plunged her beneath the surface.

Her lithe body doubled powerfully in his grasp. He was astonished at the litheness of her body. Her feet, in elegant shoes of patent-leather with six straps, appeared above the water, the ankles crossed. The top of her head was not even wet. Yet, for all that, the life came out of her. It rose to the surface in a great colored bubble, and floated off into the sunshine.

Jean-Pierre gazed across at the Luxembourg. A child in a white dress passed through a gate into the garden, holding in its hand by a string a blue balloon. Jean-Pierre smiled, and watched the balloon float off.

Over there, under a tree whose blossoms of white and mauve wire drifted like lilies on the air, wearing a white dress and a pink hat with roses piled beneath the brim, forever and ever sat Margot. Over her head, tethered to her wrist by its string, floated forever and ever the blue balloon.

She was very near to him. It was a matter of a moment only to go across to her and lift the hat and say, "*Mademoiselle*, may I accompany you?"

Save that between them, flowing level with its brassy banks past the curb before his door, forever and ever ran the sunny river, full of rolling motor-buses and rocking red taxicabs, too broad, too broad to swim. People went paddling past the window, this way and that way. A priest sailed by in a flapping gown, square boats upon his feet. A little girl went drifting by in a basket; her eyes were closed; her hands were full of brown carnations. Two gendarmes passed, their short capes winging in thick folds.

At the sight of the gendarmes Jean-Pierre started violently and stepped back from the window. There was something he must be about, and that without more delay, but he could not think what it was. Memories of Margot flew at his mind with sharp beaks. He waved his arms about his head to scare them off. There was something he must be about, and that at once.

Something touched him lightly on the shoulder. He uttered an indrawn scream, and swung on his heel. It was only the wall. He had backed into the wall. Yet even as he said to himself, "It is only the wall," and wiped his sleeve across his forehead, he saw them beside him, the two gendarmes, one on the left of him and one on the right. The one on the right of him said to the other:

"This is he, the man who drowned his wife in a plate of soup."

201

But the other answered: "Not at all. He beat in her head with a knife. Do you not see the onion skins?"

Then for the first time Jean-Pierre saw that both had red mustaches, and he knew that he was lost.

"Come, my man," they said, and stepped back, and he was left standing alone.

Suddenly that part of the floor on which he was standing slipped backward like a jerked rug under his feet, and he was thrown forward on his face. There came a rush of cold wind on the nape of his neck.

"No, you don't!" he shrieked, and, rolling over violently, leaped into the kitchen and bolted the door.

He knelt behind the door, and addressed them craftily through the keyhole.

"*Messieurs*," he said, "upstairs in my chamber is a melon as big as my head, in a bottle with a neck the size of a pipe-stem. It is the marvel of all Paris. I will give ten thousand francs to the man who can divine me how it came there."

Then he put his ear to the hole and listened, with difficulty restraining himself from chuckling aloud.

In a moment he heard their feet upon the stairs.

He counted the stairs with them as they ascended, nodding his head at each. When he knew that they were at the top, he slipped quietly forth, and bolted the stairway door.

His head was very clear; it was as light as a balloon on his shoulders. He knew precisely what he must do. He must bury the body, remove all traces of his guilt, and get away. And he must lose no time. He took his hat and coat from the peg where they were hanging, and placed them in readiness over a chair by the street door. Then he went softly and swiftly into the kitchen.

He gathered up from the table six sections of a broken backbone, a large knife, and an unwashed platter; from the stove a greasy frying-pan; and from the floor a crushed and blood-stained head. These objects he wrapped in a newspaper, laid upon a chair, and then covered with a cloth.

Hark! Was that a step in the room above? No.

Hastily, he washed the table, scrubbing feverishly until the last stain was removed, scrubbed a wide stain from the floor, and set the kitchen in order.

Hark! Was that a step on the stair? No.

He lifted the newspaper parcel from the chair and bore it, shielded from sight by his apron, into the small backyard behind the restaurant, a yard bare save for a tree of empty bottles, some flower-pots full of dry earth and withered stalks, and a rusted birdcage with crushed and dented wires.

There he laid his burden down, and after an hour of terror and sweating toil buried it in a hole much bigger than was required.

The afternoon advanced, and evening came. A light flashed on in the *Rendezvous des Cochers et Camionneurs*; farther up the street another light. The street was ablaze. Gay people walked up and down, sat at tables eating, talked eagerly together.

In the *Restaurant du Chat qui Pêche* the dusk thickened into dark, the darkness into blackness, and no lights came on. The door was wide open. The night wind came in through the door, and moved about the empty rooms.

At midnight a gendarme, seeing that the door was open and the restaurant in darkness, approached, rapped sharply on the open door, and called. There was no answer.

He closed the door, and went on.

BY LOUIS BROMFIELD

Louis Bromfield was born in Ohio on December 27, 1896. His Pulitzer Prize novel, *Early Autumn*, was published in 1926. He lived for many years in France with his wife and three daughters, their home there a gathering place for artists and writers. He returned to Ohio before World War II and bought a farm he named Malabar after the Indian coastal region that was the setting for his book, *The Rains Came*. Bromfield's factual accounts of life on his farm have been compared to Thomas Jefferson's notes on Monticello.

HOMER DILWORTH WAS BORN IN 1881 and they hanged him by the neck until dead only last Tuesday, so he was only 50 when he died in the prime of life. He was younger than most men of 50. He was solider, rosier, clearer-eyed. His voice was alive, and his skin was soft and young. And the funny thing is that he was younger at 50 than he was at 40.

He was even younger when he died than he was at 30. He'd always been rather sour-faced and dry and bony, like a handsome tree withered by blight. And then, all at once, when he was 48 he suddenly turned young.

In a way, to have hanged him was worse than killing most young fellows, because Homer had his youth so late in life. He turned young all of a sudden, like an old apple tree blossoming carelessly in October.

His parents were respectable folk and very religious. The old woman was a little queer, and they lived in a little town called Hanover, and Homer was an only child. 'Way back when he was a boy, little towns like that didn't have theaters or movies or automobiles or radios, and everything centered about the church. There was going to church on Sunday, and church sociables and strawberry festivals, and then, about once a year, a big revival meeting, when everything broke loose.

It was like that in Hanover. They were awful strict but just as much love-making went on there as anywhere else, only they made it nasty in Hanover.

His mother and father wanted Homer, their only son, to be a preacher, and Homer thought he wanted to be one. He took it all seriously and talked a lot about purity and the devil. He used to harangue me a good deal. We had a kind of Damon and Pythias friendship.

The other night I was thinking back over his story and I remembered a few things, mostly in pictures, the way you remember things when you're beginning to grow old. There was a swimming hole about three miles from town where we used to go swimming together. It was a clear stream and in the middle of a wide pasture it spread out into a kind of pond.

A couple of hundred feet away there was a low hill with a house on it, but nobody lived in the house and it was falling into ruin. It was partly log cabin and partly clapboard and all the windows were broken and the bushes had grown up high around it.

There was a story about the house which happened before my time. They said that a certain old man known as Elder Sammis had lived there once and that he'd beaten his daughter to death when he found that she'd got into trouble.

He didn't mean to beat her as bad as that, but when he found she was dead he put her body in a box under the bed and ran away, and they found the dead girl there two weeks later. They tried to catch him but they never did, because about a month later he jumped off a river boat and was drowned.

So nobody lived in the house and everybody was scared of it, so there wasn't any reason why we couldn't swim there in peace.

After Homer was hanged, one of the pictures I remembered was that swimming hole on an afternoon in early June when he'd come over from the Theological Seminary to spend Sunday with his folks. The water was clear and the sunlight was hot, and after we'd swum about a bit and splashed at each other like a couple of kids, we got out of the water and lay on the grass and talked.

We lay there almost in the shadow of the empty old home and for a long time we didn't say anything. It was beautiful, with the sun on our bodies and the soft grass under us and a warm breeze blowing over us.

A calf came up and sniffed at me and went away again, and it struck me all of a sudden how beautiful Homer was lying there in the sun. He was like the ideas some people have about the Greeks, which aren't true probably but are kind of idealized.

That afternoon he was preachier than ever. He went after me for going on buggy rides at night with old man Fisher's girl, and for not believing in God. And he began to hash over a lot of ideas about purity that didn't make any sense, and all the time I wanted to get up and laugh and dance, because it seemed so funny to hear all that claptrap coming out of the mouth of a young fellow, sitting on the grass beside that clear stream.

I wanted to laugh but I kept my mouth shut, and then he said something that made me want to cry. I'm not emotional or sentimental, but I guess it must have been the feel of the grass and the sun and the warm breeze that made me feel that way. He said, "I don't care for myself, Buck. It's because when I go to heaven I want to find you there, too."

And then the sun disappeared. It had slipped down behind the desolate Sammis house and was shining through the empty holes where the windows used to be, and the breeze wasn't so warm any more and I began to pull on my clothes; and then Homer, seeing that all his talk wasn't having any effect, began to dress, too.

After we dressed we sat around for a while and Homer said presently, "Let's go up and look through old Sammis's house."

We'd never done it as kids on account of the story that Hester Sammis's ghost was always in the house. I don't believe in ghosts, and that afternoon I knew for the first time that it wasn't really the thought of ghosts which had scared me but something else. I knew that it was because of the sadness that clung to the old house itself.

We didn't go into the house, but all the way home he kept kidding me about being afraid of ghosts and I didn't try to explain to him. Lately, I've been thinking I was wrong not to have talked about it and that if I'd tried as hard to convert him as he tried to convert me, they mightn't have hanged him last Tuesday.

The trouble was that I was finding my heaven right here on earth and not worrying much about what happened afterwards, and he was afraid of this earth and worrying himself about the next and he wanted me to be in heaven with him. I guess he cared a lot more for me than I knew in those days.

It was that afternoon that he told me he was going to get married as soon as he was out of college. I was glad, because I thought it would be good for him.

But I didn't see the girl until after they were married and came back to Hanover to live. He didn't become a preacher, after all, because his uncle died and left his hardware store to Homer's father and Homer's father thought it over and decided the cash drawer of a good-paying hardware store was better than the rewards of saving souls.

So Homer came back to Hanover to live and set up his wife in a house alongside his parents' house and took over the hardware store.

The hardware business flourished because Homer was honest and reliable and sold only the best hardware, and his father kind of looked after the business, because Homer wasn't very good about things like that. He was really romantic and all that squeezing into a hard pious shell couldn't change that in him. It was always bursting out somewhere.

After he got married he took to reading all kinds of romantic novels like *The Three Musketeers*. He really wanted to travel to places alone, looking for adventures, but he'd got himself married when he was twenty-one and his wife had twins, and after that there was a baby about every eighteen months until there were five, so he couldn't very well do anything but look after the store and take care of the children when his wife Etta was doing church work.

And his wife wasn't much. I'm kind of an idealist, and before he got married, I always pictured him taking up with a woman who was as fine and beautiful as himself. There was something wonderful in the idea of a beautiful girl marrying such a handsome fellow as Homer and in their having a lot of beautiful children.

But when he came back and invited me to supper one night to meet Etta, I felt kind of sick when I saw her. I knew right away that Homer had been up to his old tricks. He'd married the kind of woman he'd been brought up to marry and not the kind he'd been meant by Nature to marry.

She didn't take to me and I certainly didn't like her, and after that first meeting, Homer and I began to see less and less of each other. She was the kind of woman who wasn't going to let her husband have any friends.

It wasn't just women. She wouldn't let him have men friends, either. And I guess she thought I was the devil himself, so she wouldn't even let Homer go on trying to save my soul so I could be in heaven with him.

Once she buttonholed me on the street and called me a sot and harangued me until I got away from her, and after that Homer was ashamed and he'd walk around a block or go into a store if he saw me coming. I guess there's lots of women like her in America.

Of course, with all that going on, she didn't have much time for housework. The children were always sick and the dishes were never washed, and Homer used to have to stay at home to look after the children and take care of the house while she went to meetings and traveled about lecturing and haranguing.

I always thought he had too much character to do things like that, but I guess she just wore him down with abuse and whining and nagging. But he did have enough character to preserve a kind of dignity in spite of everything. He just gave up going out anywhere and lived between his house and the hardware store. He was crazy about his children.

But marriage didn't do him much good. Instead of growing fat on it like most men, he seemed to grow dry. He looked older than he was and there were hard lines in his face that oughtn't to have been there, and I only found out the reason when he sent for me at the Mitchellville jail after he got into trouble.

When I got word that he wanted to see me, I could have died of surprise, because he hadn't seen me in fifteen years for more than long enough to say "Howdydo" when we passed in the street. I guess his mind must have gone back a long way, beyond Etta and all she'd done to him, to that day when we went swimming together for the last time and lay on the soft grass behind the haunted Sammis house.

Sitting there in the cell of the Mitchellville jail, he told me all about Etta and about everything else, too. After the fifth child was born, she told him the doctor said if she had another child it would kill her, so they couldn't live together as man and wife any more. And that happened before Homer was 30. So for seventeen years they lived together as if they weren't married.

The summer that Homer was 48 Etta said she had to have a rest because she was all worn out. Homer didn't want to go away but she kept nagging him, and at last he left the hardware store with his clerk and his oldest boy and they went up to La Vallette. He was looking bad himself, all gray and dried-up.

He hardly spoke to anybody any more, and just lived between his home and the store. He'd just given up all his old friends, and somehow he'd got all bitter inside.

La Vallette is a little town up on the lake where all sorts of religious cranks go for a cheap rest. There are some cottages and three or four cheap hotels and a wooden tabernacle.

Homer and Etta were just like all the others. Etta, of course, knew most of the dreary lot. She'd made herself into a kind of celebrity. They all knew the crusader, Mrs. Etta Dallet Dilworth. I guess she enjoyed it a great deal, holding court in a rocking chair on the hotel porch and speaking now and then at the tabernacle, but Homer got a bit fed up being just *Mister* Etta Dallet Dilworth and he took to going for long walks along the lake front.

It was a desolate country but beautiful in a wild way. There were miles and miles of dunes with the whitest sand glittering in the sunlight. And here and there were marshes and inlets where wild birds settled.

Homer went walking along the shore in and out among the dunes, skirting the marshes. At first he'd go off for an hour or two, and then he began to go off in the morning and stay until lunch time, and then one day he began taking a box lunch with him.

He'd been unhappy for so long that he liked to get away from people and hide. I guess getting away from Etta and the pack of gabblers who surrounded her was kind of a relief, too. And being away all day like that got him to thinking.

It's dangerous for a man of 48 to think too much about his own happiness, especially when he's had a life like Homer's. And the marshes and the lake and the sunlight and the wild birds began to do things to him.

He said it was like slipping backwards. He kept going back and back until he got to feeling a little the way he used to feel when we went swimming together. And one day he found himself taking off all his clothes and lying down on the clean white sand among the dunes to eat his lunch. And all at once he was kind of frightened.

It was the first time the sun had touched his body since that day he lay on the grass by the haunted house, and the feel of it began to do funny things to him. He sat up and looked at his body and saw suddenly that it wasn't old and soft and fat. It was dry and the muscles were sharp and hard but not rounded the way they'd been when he was young. But it struck him suddenly that he wasn't old. He was 48, though, and wouldn't have many more years of health and vigor. And the feel of the sun and the soft warm breeze made him kind of dizzy.

He said he felt as if he was beginning to grow all over again inside himself. Suddenly he saw that he was happy for the first time in twenty years; but that frightened him and he began to be afraid of sin again, and he got up quickly and put on his clothes.

He tried to give up his long walks but when he stayed at the hotel all he saw were gabbing old women and skinny men, and soon he began going off again for the day among the dunes, and after a day or two he began taking off his clothes again and lying in the sun.

He began to grow tanned all over. His muscles began to grow round and plump and solid again.

He felt happier, and once or twice he got up at 4 in the morning to go out to the lake and see the sun rise. The sun became the center of all his existence. It was kind of as if he had a rendezvous every day with the sun out there among the white dunes.

Sometimes on cloudy days he thought he was going crazy, but as soon as the sun came out he felt all right again, and sure of himself. After a time he began to be troubled because the more he thought of it the more it seemed impossible ever to go back to live at Hanover in that untidy house that Etta kept so badly.

Etta noticed that he went off alone a good deal and she began to nag him about leaving her alone so much and not going to the tabernacle. But he didn't seem to mind even that. He just didn't hear her and managed to endure it until he could escape to the dunes.

One day she made a terrible scene in the dining room because she said he was being too kind to the waitress and looked at her too often.

After it was over she went to the management and demanded that the girl be discharged, but the management wouldn't do it because Etta couldn't prove the girl had done anything at all. They couldn't discharge a girl just because she "looked" at a man. They just transferred her to another table and put an ugly old woman to wait on him and Etta.

After that he really took to noticing the girl for the first time, and he saw that she was big and blonde and voluptuous, and in spite of himself, he began stealing glances at her across the room. Once or twice she saw him and smiled. He knew that what he was doing was sinful and tried to put her out of his mind.

Etta grew more and more difficult. He said he thought it was because she couldn't bear to see him looking well and happy. And one day she said she'd told the hotel they were going to leave at the end of the week.

The idea terrified him because it meant the end of the only happiness he'd known since he married her and it meant a return to the awful house in Hanover. He'd been so used to doing what she wanted that he didn't say anything, but that afternoon, while he was lying in the sun, he made up his mind that he wasn't going to leave and go back to Hanover. As he dressed himself, he made up the speech he was going to say to her, repeating it over and over to himself in the silence of the dunes to give himself courage.

He was walking home through the dunes, kicking the white sand and thinking how he meant to defy Etta, when he heard a curlew crying, and looking up to see it, he saw something else. Just ahead of him, lying in a hollow between two dunes, he saw the figures of a man and woman. They were asleep in the sun.

At first he wanted to run, and then he was overcome suddenly by a return of his old bitterness. He was outraged and indignant. And then he saw that, like himself, they had thought themselves alone among the dunes because it was a spot never visited by the people who came to La Vallette.

He tried to run away and could not. He was only able to stand there, his feet fixed in the white sand, staring.

Suddenly he was no longer shocked. These two people were like himself. They weren't like Etta. Like him, they worshipped the sun!

He did not know how long he stood there. The sun slipped down towards the blue lake and the girl stirred, and he saw then for the first time that the Venus of the sands with the golden hair was the waitress over whom Etta had made the scene.

He turned and ran, fearful lest they should discover him, and as he ran he knew that he meant to stay on at La Vallette, and that maybe he would never go back to Hanover at all. When he got home he went to Etta and told her he meant to stay, and when she couldn't find out any reason she tried everything to gain control over him again. She even flung the washbowl on the floor and broke it and dashed her head against the door, but all her hysterics seemed to have no effect upon him.

That night he dared not look for the waitress, because he saw her in a new way and looking at her became intolerable to him.

I imagine she was good-hearted and easy-going and meant well to everybody, and was just born to be good to men and make them happy. She felt sorry for Homer, I guess, being married to a dried-up whiner like Etta.

Anyway whenever he did look at her, she looked back and smiled, and that set Homer to thinking of everything he'd missed and that he was 48 and pretty soon he'd be dead without ever having lived at all.

After that day when he went to walk he tried not to go past the place where he'd seen them lying in the sun among the white dunes, but always, in spite of anything he could do, he'd find himself moving towards the spot. Sometimes he found them there and sometimes he didn't. And they never knew that all the time there was someone watching their rendezvous.

And then one day on the streets he saw the boy dressed in a shirt and an old pair of trousers and looking for all the world like himself 30 years ago, and when he asked who he was, they told him that the boy's name was Henry Landis and that he came to La Vallette in the summer to take the baggage of the summer people to and from the train.

Then one day the boy disappeared, and Homer asked what had become of him, and they said he'd gone away because his mother had died in Appleton and that he wouldn't be back until next summer.

So Homer went out and bought a cheap handbag and wrote a note and put it inside and asked one of the waitresses to give it to Frieda, the big blonde girl.

Just before he died he told me that he thought he must have been going crazy all that time. Up to the very end he couldn't make out whether he'd been crazy all those years he'd been married to Etta and only began to be sane when he took to lying in the sun among the dunes.

At night he always went to the tabernacle with Etta, but that night right after the second hymn he told Etta he would have to get some air. So she stayed and he went outside and walked down to the boat landing, and there in the shadow of some bushes stood Frieda waiting for him and carrying the handbag he'd sent her.

At first he thought he was going to die of excitement and of fear. He began to shake all over. His teeth chattered and he waited for a little while till he got control of himself before he went forward to meet her.

For a long time they stood looking at each other in the darkness talking awkwardly about the cheap handbag and the moon. He said it was kind of as if all that he'd missed all these years had been rolled up and burst out of him at last. There was so much he wanted to say that he couldn't say anything at all.

They sat down on the grass and all he could do was sit and look at her. The moonlight came through the trees on her hair. I guess she was a pretty swell looker. The people I talked to at the trial told me so. She wasn't very bright and she didn't have any ambition or she could have had almost anything she wanted.

While he was looking at her, he suddenly remembered Etta sitting at the tabernacle waiting for him to return, and he said to Frieda, "Will you meet me tomorrow afternoon?" And he told her where to meet him, among the dunes not very far from where he'd seen her and the boy.

He didn't sleep any that night and went off early to spend the day among the dunes. It was a brilliant day, late in September, with wonderful sunlight, but it seemed to him the time would never pass until he'd see Frieda coming along the shore.

She came at last, dressed all in white in her waitress' clothes, with her gold hair shining against the blue lake.

And for the first time in his life Homer knew what it was to be free and happy. When he told me about it, it all sounded simple and beautiful. I wanted to cry.

Two days before the hotel closed, Etta came up from the front porch and found a note pinned to the pillow. It said that Homer had gone away and that she needn't try to look for him and that she'd never see him again. He wrote that he'd taken the money that was in the bank at Hanover and left her and the children the hardware store, which would keep them all well enough.

At first they thought he'd committed suicide and Etta fainted and screamed a good deal. They tried dragging the water by the boat landing, but about 6 o'clock one of the waitresses said it wasn't any use because he'd run off with Frieda.

Then Etta screamed and fainted a lot more and took the next train for Hanover, and about two days later the newspapers ran them to ground in a little town up in northern Michigan and printed a lot of stuff about the elopement, so they had to run away again. They kept running from town to town till the newspapermen got tired hounding them, and at last they disappeared.

Etta tried to have them arrested, but nobody could or would do anything about it. She wouldn't divorce him—she just got more and more righteous and martyred. It made an awful scandal in Hanover, but it died down pretty soon.

I was glad because I'd always wanted to see Homer have a little fun in life, but I couldn't say anything. He'd been a stranger to me for twenty years, all dried-up and sour from living with Etta. I couldn't understand how he did manage to do it until two years afterwards when I opened the paper one morning and read that a girl called Frieda Hemyers had been killed with some man and that Homer Dilworth, who had been living with her, was arrested for both murders; and a week later I got a letter from a town called Mitchellville, in Missouri, where they had him in jail.

It was from Homer himself, asking me to come and see him and help him. I went right off, and that was when he told me everything.

I expected to find a dried-up man on the verge of old age, but when they opened the door of the cell I saw a vigorous man of about 35 or 40. I couldn't have believed it was Homer except that he looked like himself when he was young.

He must have grown 15 years younger since I last saw him on the street in Hanover. He was always a good-looking fellow and he'd got handsome again, just as I said, like an apple tree that suddenly blossoms in October.

And when he spoke, it was harder still to believe that he was Homer Dilworth.

He looked at me and sort of grinned and said, "Well, Jim, I guess you thought I was the last person in the world you'd ever find in a fix like this." I saw that he had a kind of manliness about him he'd never had even in the days before he married Etta, because then he was always kind of soft and good.

He told me to sit down on his cot. He didn't seem to be discouraged. He just said, "I did it, Jim. I didn't mean to do it, but I did it. They can do with me whatever they like."

The funny thing was that he didn't seem to care.

He told me he'd sent for me because I was the only one he knew who'd understand. It wasn't any good sending for church people because they'd just lecture him and pray over him, and he didn't want to see Etta, even if she would have come.

She never did come and she wouldn't let any of the children come to see him. And in the two years since he'd run away with Frieda they'd had to go from place to place, so they'd never stopped

214

anywhere long enough to make friends. In the end he went back 30 years, to that last afternoon we'd gone swimming together, and sent for me.

He told me all the story of what happened to him at La Vallette up to the time he ran off with Frieda, and then he told me what happened afterwards—how they were followed from town to town by newspapermen, and then how they'd always get found out and be forced to move on. He said they'd been to 27 little towns in two years.

He had the money he'd drawn out of the bank, and when that gave out he worked, sometimes as dishwasher, sometimes as farm-hand, doing anything he could find to do. And he was happy all the time because Frieda was easy-going and good-natured.

He spoke about her as if she wasn't dead at all. Sometimes he was jealous of her, and once or twice they'd quarreled when she spoke to a man younger than himself.

It seemed he was frightened of younger men. He knew that he was getting old and that some day he'd lose her to a younger man because she was still young. It got to be a kind of obsession with him.

And finally they came to that little town in Missouri, and nobody found them out. He had a job checking off grain bags and hogs at the river landing and it looked as if they were going to be safe and happy at last, because there weren't even any men in the place more vigorous than himself.

They had a little house and were furnishing it from a furniture catalogue. And then one day he came home when she was out and found a letter addressed to "Miss Frieda Hemyers care of Mrs. John Slade," which was the name they were living under.

It was postmarked "Appleton, Wisconsin," and when he asked her about it she said it was from the boy who'd wrestled the baggage at the hotel in La Vallette, the same one he'd seen with her among the dunes. Later, when he asked her what was in it, she said she'd burned it and told him there was nothing in it—the fellow only wanted to know how she was.

But the thing stuck in Homer's brain. It wasn't, he said, that he was jealous. He had a kind of funny affection for the boy, even though he'd never spoken to him.

He kind of felt that Frieda really belonged to the boy if he wanted her. It was all mixed up in his head and he kept trying to think it out.

And then one day the river boat was a day late and he went back to the house an hour or two after he'd left it. He opened the back door but there wasn't anybody in and when he called Frieda's name she didn't answer, so he went to their bedroom and found the door was locked, and all at once he knew what had happened.

For a moment he just stood still, feeling that he was going to die. He turned cold all over, and then for a moment he couldn't see. It seemed to him that it was the end of everything, because he'd got to feel that all his life that went before was nothing at all and that he'd been alive only since he ran off with Frieda.

In his brain the thought was born that the only thing to do was to finish it then and there, and to finish it, he'd have to kill Frieda and the man who was in there with her, and then himself.

The funny thing was how clearly he remembered it all, because he was certainly insane at that moment. He took a chair and smashed down the door, and then, with a revolver, he just fired blindly into the dark room until the revolver clicked empty. And when he tried to shoot himself there wasn't any bullet left.

It was an awful moment when he stood there in the doorway. The emptiness of the pistol seemed to bring him to himself, and suddenly, because he was really a good man, he wanted to save them both.

But it was too late. Frieda was unconscious and dying, and the man was dead.

It was only then that he discovered it was the boy who had wrestled the baggage at La Vallette. He'd come all the way to Missouri to find her and run off with her.

It made him sick, and the funny thing was that the remorse he felt wasn't so great because he'd killed two people, but because the two people were Frieda and the boy. If he'd known that Frieda had the boy with her, he'd have gone away quietly and left them together forever.

They were young and love belonged to them. He was old and finished, and he was left alive. And it was terrible, too, that he'd killed the two people who had set him free. They were the two who had given him life and he'd killed them. For a moment he said he had a horrible feeling that instead of killing the boy, he shot himself as he was 30 years before.

After a long time he got up and laid the two bodies on the bed and covered them with a sheet, and then went into the kitchen and put his head into the oven of the stove and turned on the gas. One of the neighbors who ran in to borrow some eggs from Frieda found him there.

He wasn't dead yet. They dragged him out and brought him to and then found the bodies.

I stayed with him up to the end.

He didn't make the least effort to save himself. If Frieda had been his wife they'd have let him off maybe with manslaughter, but of course, all their story came out at the trial and he didn't have a chance.

But Homer didn't give them any satisfaction. He was sorry he'd killed Frieda and the boy, but he wasn't repentant about anything else, and he was glad of the two years of happiness he'd had with Frieda. He just sort of smiled when the judge sentenced him.

I took his body back to Hanover and buried it alongside my grandfather, because Etta wouldn't have anything to do with it. In Hanover, he became a great Example. The wages of sin is death, they said, but they never said anything about the wages of the way Homer was brought up, or the wages of living with Etta.

Last week Martha and I drove out to Ontario to see about buying our winter apples and before I thought about it we were passing the old Sammis house. The roof had fallen in and it was almost hid by bushes, and the pasture where Homer and I had lain in the sun was muddy and frozen. The cattle stood with their heads together and their tails towards the November wind.

THE AMATEUR OF CRIME

BY STEPHEN VINCENT BENÉT

Stephen Vincent Benét began his career with several modestly successful collections of verse. He attended Yale and the Sorbonne. In Paris on a Guggenheim fellowship he completed his epic *John Brown's Body*, which won a Pulitzer Prize in 1929. His greatest triumph in the field of prose was *The Devil and Daniel Webster*. Benét's early death in 1943 at 44 was attributed to overwork on war propaganda. His brother William Rose Benét said of him that "poetry was from the first a bright valor in his blood."

And what is *your* hobby, Mr. Scarlet?" queried Mrs. Culverin kindly of her shyest guest. Her long, pendent earrings of antique crystal winked like tiny stars as she turned upon him the full battery of her celebrated smile.

"Murder," said the owlish young man in the English dinner-jacket, serenely. Mrs. Culverin gave a slight, pleased scream.

In a day of hostesses who were famous for rules, and hostesses who were notorious for breaking them, Mrs. Culverin achieved unique celebrity as a hostess who seemed to recognize no rules at all. At the moment she was opening her Long Island house for the summer, and the company gathered to celebrate the event could hardly have been more diverse had Mrs. Culverin deliberately planned it so. But Mrs. Culverin never planned anything deliberately.

This particular house party included, among others, Prince Mirko, of Ruritania, head of the Ruritanian debt commission to the United States; his extraordinarily beautiful wife; Baron Kossovar, the Ruritanian Ambassador; Daisy Delight, the cinema star; a bishop; a banker; a bandmaster; the most celebrated dance expert of the moment; two débutantes; the woman's Olympic diving champion; a blind pianist; a Mr. Lang, who was vaguely spoken of as a big-game hunter, and Peter Scarlet—the last, a pink-cheeked youth with surprised, mouse-colored hair which, together with his enormous horn rimmed spectacles, gave him much of the innocent downiness of a very young owl.

Mrs. Culverin could not remember exactly what he did, or exactly why she had asked him; but, as she was often in the same quandary about many of her guests, the fact perturbed her not at all. He neither smoked opium in his bedroom nor attempted to secrete small articles of silverware about his person—and as these were the only two social solecisms her generous heart admitted, she felt satisfied enough with him, whoever he might be.

But when he spoke of murder, she viewed him with a new and acquisitive eye. So far, it must be admitted, her Long Island house-warming had leaned perilously toward the verge of failure. The bishop, though a liberal bishop, had lifted episcopal eyebrows at the dancer. The banker had insisted on talking statistics. The Olympic diving champion had had too much of a cold to exhibit

219

her skill—and the Ruritanians had been so freezingly polite to each other that a pall of gentility had descended upon the whole assemblage. Mrs. Culverin suddenly remembered, with that vagueness that characterized her memories, having heard of some tiresome, political feud between Prince Mirko and Baron Kossovar.

Now, however, young Mr. Scarlet's unexpected admission of his unusual hobby seemed to give her a heaven-sent opportunity of redeeming her dinner party. She raised her voice to carry to the end of the table.

"How quaint!" she said, with relish. "Mr. Scarlet knows all about murders—or murdering—which was it, Mr. Scarlet? Do tell us lots about them, anyhow!" And she patted him approvingly on the arm.

The young man, thus abruptly singled out as the object for the stares of the whole company, looked more owlish than ever. A faint pink flush mounted slowly toward his ears.

"Mrs. Culverin flatters me," he said, looking at his plate. "I don't know all about murders—or murderers, either. But, yes, I am—interested in them."

"You are a detective, Mr. Scarlet, yes?" queried Prince Mirko, in his careful English.

"No, Your Highness. Merely an amateur of crime."

The princess laughed—a long, beautiful ripple of laughter. "An amateur of crime!" she said, giving the words a foreign twist. "Think of it, Mirko! At his age—an amateur of crime! But I thought you were—what is it?—undergraduate at an American university, Mr. Scarlet?"

"I am, Madame. I'm going back to college Monday," muttered Scarlet, obviously abashed. "But, well—you ought to start in young at any profession, oughtn't you? And—I've had certain opportunities, in a way. At least, my father was in the diplomatic service, so we traveled around a lot when I was a kid—"

A pleased expression crossed Prince Mirko's face: "If I am right, your father was *chargé d'affaires* at our capital, Mr. Scarlet—let me see—in my father's time?"

Scarlet nodded rapidly. "Yes, Your Highness. I was only so high, then; but I remember your father." He smiled. "I used to be terrified by his beard."

"And Baron Kossovar—you remember him too?" asked the prince, with an acid smile.

"I'm afraid not, sir," said Scarlet pleasantly. "I think Baron Kossovar was away from Ruritania at the time."

"I was in exile—a very unjust exile," said the tall baron, coldly.

His glance and Prince Mirko's were two rapiers clashing together. Again a constraint fell on the party.

"But, Mr. Scarlet, do tell us all about your murders!" said Mrs. Culverin brightly.

Scarlet grinned boyishly: "They aren't really my murders, Mrs. Culverin. I've just studied a bit—thing fascinated me. I mean—the queer kinds of people who are murderers, and the even queerer kinds who are murderees."

"Murderees?" breathed Mrs. Culverin. "Murderees?"

"Yes—that's what Pearson calls them, in his book." His spectacles flashed. "The people who seem just born and bound to be murdered. Who have the same irresistible attraction for a murderer that—a nice, plump goat has for a hungry tiger."

"I think it's all perfectly horrid!" said Mrs. Culverin delightedly. "Do go on!"

"Well," said Peter Scarlet, "there was the Jamison case, in London. Mrs. Jamison was an ideal murderee. She had an acquaintance, Mrs. Wheen. She knew Mrs. Wheen hated her. She often said so to her friends. She even said, several times, that she was sure Mrs. Wheen would murder her if she got a chance. And yet, for some unfathomable reason, she kept on going to tea with Mrs. Wheen until, finally, of course, Mrs. Wheen did murder her."

"Served her right," said Mrs. Culverin, with a beaming smile. "I'm sure, if I ever got the idea that anyone would murder me, I—I'd never so much as ask them to dinner again!"

A general chuckle followed her pronouncement. But Peter Scarlet stuck to his guns. "You wouldn't—because you're not a murderee," he said. "Most people aren't—most people never contract elephantiasis, either. But there is a certain proportion of people who do both, and a very definite proportion. Of course,"—he spread out his hands—"there are the normal, casual murders, too. But I'm talking of this one peculiar tendency."

"And you think," said the somber Mr. Lang, "that you could diagnose—a tendency to be murdered, in an otherwise normal person, as a doctor could diagnose illness in a person who looked perfectly well?"

"That's what I'd like to do," said Peter Scarlet ingenuously. "Oh, I know it sounds fantastic, especially from me. But if you could do that and safeguard the murderee, as modern science safeguards the diabetic, why, half our present murders would never occur at all!"

Mrs. Culverin struck in. "But this is marvelous!" she said, her eyes very wide. "Just like numerology and reading your fate in tea leaves, only so much more exciting! Do tell us, dear Mr. Scarlet, because you can, of course—are any of us—murderees?"

Peter Scarlet looked very unhappy. "I couldn't, honestly," he managed to reply at last. "I mean—even if some of you did have murderee tendencies—well, you'd allow a doctor some time for a diagnosis and some rather intimate information, wouldn't you? Well—" He obviously did not wish to go on.

Mrs. Culverin, however, was insistent. "But you could just give us a hint?" she persisted. "The tiniest hint! It would be too wonderful!"

Peter Scarlet's eyes roved nervously up and down the table. "Well—" he said dolefully, and paused.

"You need not be afraid to say it!" said Prince Mirko, abruptly, with unexpected grimness. "I know there would be rejoicing—in many quarters—if I were to die by violence."

"And there are others whose murder would please certain men in my country. Myself, for one," said Baron Kossovar instantly. Again his eyes and the prince's met, with the impact of steel upon steel. The princess's hand went nervously to her breast.

Scarlet did his best to smooth over the awkward moment. "Any statesman's life is always at the mercy of a fanatic's bullet," he said, with a little bob at both Ruritanians. "But, oddly enough, if I had to decide at first glance upon the one person in this room who stood the likeliest chance of meeting a violent end, I should select—Mr. Lang!" he ended unexpectedly, with a nod in that gentleman's direction.

Mr. Lang gave a slight but definite start. For a moment his eyes blazed with anger. Then he gave a loud laugh—and the tension in the room relaxed.

"Not bad at all, for getting out of a hole," he said, still laughing: "I suppose you could be murdered by a lion—if you'd want to call it that—and my last trip out from Nairobi—" He plunged into a big-game reminiscence, and the talk grew general again.

"Only, I wasn't thinking about lions," murmured Peter Scarlet to his plate. But no one at the table overheard him.

Some time later, after the ladies had left the room, Scarlet found himself near the banker.

"You nearly put your foot in it then, my boy," said the latter, in a low voice, glancing down the table at Prince Mirko and Baron Kossovar. "You know what this Ruritanian debt commission means, I suppose?"

"I know the prince and the baron are old enemies," admitted Scarlet, "and that the baron is supposed to look for a return of the monarchy—in Ruritania—while the prince is entirely committed to the new republic."

"Just so," said the banker. "And if Mirko succeeds in his mission, he and the republic win—and Kossovar's political future isn't worth *that*! On the other hand, if he fails, the republic will undoubtedly go to pot, and Kossovar will be the power behind the return of the throne. The way things are at present, the prince seems sure to win, too," he added thoughtfully. "He's going down to Washington, Monday, to clinch it."

On their way to the lesser drawing-room where the Royal Russian Midgets, especially brought down for the occasion, were to perform their celebrated though Lilliputian feats of acrobatics before the dancing began, Peter Scarlet was accosted by the saturnine Mr. Lang.

"What the dickens did you mean by picking me out as a likely target for murder?" he queried, in a tone whose attempted lightness was not wholly successful.

Peter Scarlet looked at him steadily. "I wonder," he said. "Have you ever shot a Lipmann's gazelle, Mr. Lang?"

Mr. Lang seemed both amazed and piqued by the odd query. "Lipmann's gazelle?" he said. "Well, I have, as it happens—managed to bag a brace near Victoria Nyanza. But what the deuce has that got to do with my being murdered?"

"It might have a good deal, under certain circumstances," said Peter Scarlet cryptically, and turned away.

He watched with apparent interest the agile feats of the Russian midgets, and the little pantomime of "Beauty and the Beast" that concluded their performance. But within his mind, all the while, certain dim, half-remembered pictures were beginning to take on form and color and perspective. He shook his head, wearily—the pictures weren't very pleasant pictures; and yet he must fit them together, somehow. Only he couldn't quite recollect a few of the most important ones—yet.

At the end of the little entertainment, as the Blue Boy Blue Blowers began to blare out their invitation to the dance from the larger ballroom, he unobtrusively sought the princess.

She looked drawn and tired—the continual friction between her husband and the baron was obviously telling upon her. He made some compliment, to which she replied mechanically; then his glance fell upon an ornament in her hair.

"I am glad you still keep up the old Ruritanian custom, Madame," he said.

She laughed a little. "The dagger, you mean? Yes—all our girls

223

pin their hair with a little dagger on feastdays—you must remember." She withdrew the small, needle-pointed, silver stiletto
from the dark coils of her coiffure, so that he might examine it. "It
is a family thing," she said, the weariness returning to her face.
"You must have seen many like it in Ruritania."

Her expression changed, she lowered her voice. "Did you mean
what you said tonight—that Mr. Lang was in greater danger of his
life here than my husband?" she asked with a sudden, queer intensity, as they paused on their way to the door.

Peter Scarlet looked at her with an expression of humble surprise. "I didn't say quite that," he said embarrassedly. "Do you
mean that you have any reason to suspect that . . . your husband is
in danger here?"

She made a nervous, pathetic little gesture with her hands. "Oh
no, no, no!" she said hurriedly. "Oh no—it is impossible—
inpossible—and yet—"

Baron Kossovar came up to them. "May I have the honor of the
first dance, Madame?" he asked, bowing profoundly as the princess
replaced the dagger in her hair.

The evening wore on, the Blue Boy Blue Blowers outdid themselves in miracles of syncopation; at last Peter Scarlet found himself
ready for bed. Alone in his room, he undressed for the night.
Then, with the same neat, unhurried swiftness, he dressed himself
completely again. It was no use—he couldn't sleep till one question
at least had been decided in his mind. He left his room and, walking
with a singular lack of noise for so ingenuous and blundering a
young man, made his way toward the wing of the house where the
Ruritanians were quartered.

Prince and Princess Mirko's suite was on the second floor; Baron
Kossovar's, above, on the third. The house itself was a curious
example of architectural misalliance between Long Island and
Spain. Odd, useless balconies jutted from it at unexpected
corners; there was one at the end of the corridor which
Scarlet now traversed, and another, he knew, outside the princess's
bedroom.

As Scarlet came down the corridor, walking more loudly now, a
low voice challenged him suddenly. "Who's that?" said a fierce
whisper.

Scarlet stood perfectly still. "It's Scarlet, Mr. Lang."

There was a sound of breath taken in. "How in—" said the low
voice. Then it changed its tone. "I thought your room was in the
other wing of the house," it said.

Scarlet smiled to himself in the dim shadows of the corridor. "I

224

thought yours was too, Mr. Lang," he said easily. "But I felt restless, couldn't get to sleep."

"So did I," said Lang, unconvincingly. "Well—I suppose we'd both of us better get back to bed."

"I suppose so," admitted Scarlet, strolling on to the end of the corridor. He stepped out upon the balcony for a moment and glanced up.

"H'm," he said, "that iron stair must go to the third-floor balcony. Convenient little dingus for a burglar, wouldn't you say?"

"Infernally convenient," admitted Lang, with a certain tenseness. "Well—" This time his hand fell definitely upon Scarlet's shoulder, and the latter permitted himself to be led back toward his own wing of the house. Mr. Lang paused outside a door halfway down the Ruritanian corridor.

"Well, here I am," he said. "Good night, Scarlet. And I wouldn't go wandering about at night if I were you. It isn't done—take the word of an older man."

Scarlet seemed entirely unperturbed by the rebuke. He walked noisily back to his own room and waited there for some time. Then he emerged again, slipped up to the third floor, retraced his way to the Ruritanian wing, and concealed himself on the third-floor balcony. He had hardly done so when the tall figure of Baron Kossovar ascended from the second floor and entered his quarters. Scarlet smiled, and devoted his attention to another point. A little while later his vigil was rewarded by a curious sight that gave him much food for thought. But it was not until half an hour at least had passed that he heard the scream from the second floor.

Twenty seconds later he was outside the door of Prince Mirko's suite—but the mysterious Mr. Lang was there before him, now rapping upon the door with a sort of muffled fury, now trying to force the lock with what looked suspiciously like a skeleton key.

He saw Scarlet and wheeled. A revolver glittered suddenly in his other hand. "You infernal meddler—" he began furiously, motioning him back; but Scarlet continued to advance.

"Oh, shut up!" he said, somewhat tiredly. "I know you're a detective—known it for hours. You get in that room—I'll keep the others back."

Lang gave him one sharp, very searching glance, then turned back to his work with the key. After a moment the lock yielded— the door flew open.

Scarlet, glancing in at the room over Lang's shoulder, felt the bristles at the back of his neck begin to rise. Prince Mirko of

Ruritania lay on his face in the middle of the luxurious sitting-room, dead, with the hilt of a silver dagger protruding from his neck. The princess knelt beside him. Her hands were stained with his blood, her eyes were staring, and the silver dagger ornament was gone from her hair. A tiny handkerchief lay on the floor, and a little white dog ran in circles about the body, moaning and whining.

As Scarlet was turning away, the princess succeeded in rolling the body over on its back. There was a curious incision on the dead man's forehead—two little slashes that formed a capital T.

When the initial confusion of the event had somewhat subsided, a strange court of inquiry met in the disfigured sitting-room. Luckily, Mrs. Culverin's house was huge, and many of the guests had not been aroused at all. Those who had, Peter Scarlet sent back to bed again, with the news that Princess Mirko's maid had suffered a minor accident. As for Mrs. Culverin herself, she had risen to the crisis astonishingly, and she now sat patting Princess Mirko's limp hand with a certain sturdy kindliness that made Peter Scarlet like her better than he ever had before. Baron Kossovar, Lang, and Scarlet completed the party.

Mrs. Culverin rose at last. "Well, Mr. Lang," she said, "the matter is entirely in your hands. I'll do and say whatever you tell me. Meanwhile, I'll go back to my room, unless, Your Highness, you—" She turned to the princess.

"No," murmured the latter weakly. "No, thank you. You are very kind. But—"

"I know," said Mrs. Culverin. She gathered her wrapper about her. "Oh, one thing," she said to Lang, "if I might make a suggestion?"

"Yes, Mrs. Culverin?"

"You'll find that young man useful," she said, indicating Scarlet. "His talk about murders may be all bosh—but he knows Ruritanian." She swept away.

Lang turned to Scarlet. "You do speak and understand Ruritanian?"

Scarlet nodded. "Yes, I've kept it up fairly well."

Lang considered. "Well, I suppose you'd better stay," he said at last. "Only—no interference—no amateur detecting! And, naturally, if your father was in the Service, you understand the gravity of—"

Scarlet's face was very grave. "I do. And I shouldn't think of—interfering. But—I could make a suggestion? If one occurred to me?"

"You could," said Lang grimly. Scarlet's spectacles blinked.

Lang turned to the baron and the princess. "I have no wish to put impertinent questions," he said, with a good deal of dignity. "But you must realize, as I do, the very delicate position in which this murder has placed not only everyone in this house but the Governments of two countries. Prince Mirko was in this country under the protection of the United States. He was murdered while under that protection. Naturally, in view of the diplomatic issues involved, this inquiry cannot follow the normal course of such inquiries. But—I take it you both are willing to help me in finding the murderer?"

The princess stared at him, dry-eyed. "My husband's murderer must be found," she said in a dry, toneless voice.

Baron Kossovar stiffened. "Prince Mirko was my political enemy," he said; "but I am no less anxious than you, Mr. Lang, to find his murderer."

Lang received their statements gravely. "Thank you," he said. "Now—you'll pardon me if I'm frank—there are three ways in which Prince Mirko might have been murdered: He might have been murdered by an intruder from without. He might have been murdered by a servant or a guest. Or—"

"Say it," said the princess, in a dry, terrible voice. "He might have been murdered by me, his wife."

"Or me," said Baron Kossovar rigidly.

Lang made a little bow. "I regret the necessity," he said; "but we must take every supposition into account. First: the intruder from without. In the first place, my men—and they're skilled men—have been guarding the gates and so forth since Prince Mirko's arrival. It would have been practically impossible for an intruder to get past them. In addition,"—he stepped toward the window—"the windows of this room and of Prince Mirko's bedroom were all locked on the inside when we found the body; and it is a sheer fifteen-foot drop from the windows to the ground."

"Also," said the princess, still in that toneless voice, "I had locked the door from my part of the suite earlier in the evening. When I unlocked it again, it was to find my husband dead." She shuddered.

"I remember," said Lang noncommittally. "You wished to be alone?"

"For a time, yes—my husband and the baron were talking business; I did not wish to disturb them. Then later, I heard the dog barking and came to say good night to my husband—and then—"

"Yes," said Lang. "But even supposing the intruder had flown through the walls and got in—how did he get out? We made a thorough search. Of course he might have jumped from one of your bedroom windows, Princess, supposing you did not lock the door as you say you did."

"I did lock the door," said the Princess. "And—my maid, and myself, of course, were in our part of the suite the whole time. He could not have concealed himself or escaped."

"Exactly," said Lang. "Therefore, if there was an intruder, he is still here. But he isn't here. Therefore, Prince Mirko was not murdered by an intruder from without."

He paused. The logic of his explanation seemed inevitable. Scarlet took the opportunity to emerge from his silence.

"May I ask a question?" he said diffidently. Lang nodded.

"You didn't hear any sound of a struggle—a fall—either you or your maid?" he queried owlishly.

The princess seemed greatly perturbed. "No," she muttered. "That is strange—strange—yet the door was thick."

"Very thick," said Scarlet agreeably. "I wonder you heard the dog through it. Yet you did hear the dog barking."

The princess moved her hands. "Yes," she said weakly. "But that was the first we heard. It is—strange—yes, strange!"

It did not seem so strange to Lang. By the expression on his face it obviously seemed either impossible or untrue. But he resumed his questioning, with a scrupulous, heavy fairness.

"Then," he said, "we come to the valet and the maid. The valet's room did not communicate directly with the rest of the suite. I saw him go out before Baron Kossovar came to talk with Prince Mirko. He could not have entered again without my seeing him. So we may dismiss the valet. As for the maid—you insist, Princess, that she was under your eye all the time?"

"I do," said the Princess, in a ghost of a voice.

"Very well," said Lang. "Then we must dismiss the maid. As for another guest, or servant, getting in from the corridor—I was there on guard. I would have stopped and questioned anyone who came."

"Yes," said Scarlet; "you stopped and questioned me."

"And so you come to us," said the princess bluntly. Her voice rose. "Oh, it is terrible—terrible!" she said. "You suspect me—you have reason to suspect me! My husband is killed with the little dagger I wear in my hair—I do not hear him killed, though I hear a dog bark afterward—you find me beside his body when you come—you find a handkerchief too, a woman's handkerchief— you find—" her voice broke—"the mark on his face—And yet, I swear before God, I did not murder my husband!"

Baron Kossovar rose, his eyes burning. "But if you must suspect her, you must suspect me more!" he cried. "I was with him and we were talking, sometimes angrily, till half an hour before you found him dead. I had reason to kill him if I wished. I might have killed him—pretended to say good night to him at the door, so you could hear me and think he was still alive, and then gone back to my room, to be aroused by the news of his murder!"

"Only," said Scarlet quietly, "in that case, after you had said good night to the dead man, the dead man got up and locked the door after you."

"Well, he might have had strength enough left to do that," said the baron impatiently. "Or it might have been done somehow else, or—" Then his head drooped suddenly. "No, it is useless," he said; "I did not kill Mirko; I cannot pretend I did. But you should not suspect her, when you have better reason to suspect me."

"Ah, my friend, you are very noble," said the princess, lightly touching his hand with hers.

"You're both noble," said Scarlet dispassionately; "but you're both very silly. There is another possible murderer that Mr. Lang has not mentioned."

"And that is?" said the latter with a dangerous calm.

"Mr. Lang," said Scarlet demurely. "He might have got in with his masterkey after the baron left, murdered the prince, relocked the door, and—"

"But what reason would I have to murder Prince Mirko?"

"Oh, you might have had a dozen reasons," said Scarlet airily. "But you didn't. Because you wouldn't have used a dagger. You'd have shot him—or killed him with your hands—in the good old Anglo-Saxon way. On the other hand," he continued reflectively, "Madame is a Ruritanian and might very possibly use a dagger—especially this one." He lifted the stained weapon delicately from the table. "But Madame asserts that she lost her dagger-ornament earlier in the evening and did not see it again till she found it in her husband's body."

"Yes," said the princess desperately, "that is true. The dagger fell from my hair. I do not know where. I do not know how. But at first, when I found it again"—she shivered—"I did not see how it could be mine."

Scarlet blinked. "I see. And then—the handkerchief." He replaced the dagger and took up a tiny square of fine linen. "Obviously not a man's handkerchief, from its size, and"—he sniffed it—"scented. But Madame asserts that the handkerchief is not hers, that she found it beside the body."

"Yes, I have never seen it before. It is not mine," said the princess, in the voice of an automaton, staring down at her feet as if she saw them already enmeshed in the net which Scarlet's diffident sentences slowly wove about her. Scarlet went on:

"Third point. The slash on the prince's forehead—the slash like a capital T. Well, that rather points to the baron, on the whole. At least, Mr. Lang, who has had great experience with Italian criminals, has informed us that a similar T-shaped slash is a common occurrence in political assassinations—the "T" being for 'Traddi-tore' or 'Traitor.' Now, the baron's political views might easily lead him to consider the prince a traitor to their mutual country. On the other hand, the T might be a blind—employed for the purposes of argument by Madame. Curious clues all of them; and yet the most curious thing of all is—that every one points in the same direction—"

"I'm afraid they do," said Mr. Lang heavily. "Princess Mirko—" he began in an official voice.

"But I did not murder my husband!" said the princess, with a terrified gasp.

"One moment," said Scarlet bashfully. "Think of the nature of the wound. The prince was a tall man—the wound was high on his neck and slanted down—such a wound as would suggest a tall assassin—woman or man. Now the baron and madame are both tall, but—"

"Stop!" said the baron suddenly. He turned to the princess. "It's no use, Nadja," he said. "One of us must speak to protect you. Gentlemen—Prince Mirko's wife was not even in this suite when her husband was murdered. She was on the balcony of my suite; I had asked her to come there—to talk of a private matter—"

The princess put her head in her hands with a gesture of utter defeat. "Oh, Stanislas, Stanislas!" she sobbed, "you have ruined everything. They will never believe me now!"

"Yes; I think that clinches it, if that's true," said Lang with austere triumph. "Gives a better motive than politics. And they both killed him. Princess Mirko—"

But Scarlet cut in before he could finish his sentence. "Oh, what the baron says is true enough," he said briskly. "I saw and heard them from the other balcony. Only your deduction's wrong Lang. It wasn't a love affair—she went because she was worried about her husband. But why do you keep on calling her 'Princess Mirko'? She isn't really Princess Mirko, you know," he went on in tones of shy patience.

The princess raised terror-stricken eyes to his. Lang gasped.

"You mean that woman isn't the prince's wife?"

"Oh, yes; she was the prince's wife, right enough—she merely isn't and wasn't Princess Mirko. Have you never heard of a morganatic marriage? If she had been a princess," he concluded thoughtfully, "the murder, most probably, would never have been committed."

"I don't see why?" said Lang, with the air of a baited bull. "And I don't see why it makes any difference whether the princess was a princess or not. Someone murdered Prince Mirko—if it wasn't this woman here—what woman was it?"

"No woman murdered Prince Mirko," said Scarlet quietly.

"A man, then? What man? The baron?"

"Nor was the murderer of Prince Mirko a man, as we think of men."

"Well, then, in heaven's name, what was it?" cried Lang, in a sort of fury. "A ghost that walks through the walls? A gorilla? An act of God?"

Scarlet's eyes, behind his spectacles, danced with little points of light. "On that point," he said, with deceptive meekness, "I should like to take the evidence of the dog." He turned quickly to the princess. "The little white dog your husband was so fond of," he said. "The dog we found running about when we came in—do you remember when he was brought back to your suite this evening?"

"Why, yes," said the princess, with obvious bewilderment. "Stepan, the valet, brought him up from the kennels when we came back after the dancing; my husband liked to have him in his room at night."

"Ah," said Scarlet, obviously laboring under some mounting excitement. He flung open the door of the princess's room and whistled. The dog came bounding in, ran about for a moment, sniffing, then, lifting his head toward the ceiling, gave a long, doleful howl. The princess burst into tears.

"What in thunder do you think you'll get from the dog?" queried Lang. "And we know he's tracked up the carpet," he added as Scarlet stooped to examine certain dull red paw marks on the floor.

Scarlet straightened up, his whole body alive and tense. "Yes, we know he's tracked up the carpet," he said, in a voice like a trumpet; "but what we don't know is how he tracked up the wall!" And he pointed at a spot on the glazed wallpaper above a tall painted wardrobe—a muddy spot, near the ceiling, that looked singularly like the imprint of a dog's muddy paw.

For a moment none of the others could believe their eyes—and the world seemed to slide and alter into a distorted and monstrous cosmos, where a little white dog could run up a wall like a fly, and a tall prince might be struck dead with a dagger wielded by neither a man's nor a woman's hand. Then Scarlet threw open the doors of the painted wardrobe. There was nothing there but an overcoat on a hook, some hats on a shelf above, and a large leather hat trunk beside the hats.

"We've looked through that wardrobe already," called Lang.

"No," said Scarlet; "you've only looked *at* it. For instance,"—he shook out the overcoat—"here are the same kind of paw marks there are on the wall, only here the marks are bloody. While, as for the hat trunk—"

The dog burst into a fury of barking that drowned the rest of the sentence.

"For heaven's sake!" shouted Lang, in a final exasperation, "you don't expect to find the murderer of Prince Mirko inside a brown leather hatbox, do you?"

"That," said Scarlet, quite unruffled, "is precisely what I expect to find!"

He started gingerly to lift the hat trunk down from its shelf. As he did so, its lid popped open like the lid of a jack-in-the-box, and something bright and tiny struck at his eyes. There was an intense little scuffle for an instant; then Scarlet was holding out for Lang's inspection a kicking, fighting little creature hardly three feet high. The thing was grotesquely disguised in the stage-garb of a midget Beast, and its distorted lips poured forth a stream of denunciation in a hissing, clucking language that Lang did not understand.

"Permit me to present the murderer of Prince Mirko," said Scarlet, with a boyish flourish.

"Well, I'll be—" said Lang, with a long whistle. "One of those Russian midgets that played the pantomime! But what is he talking—Russian?"

"No," said Scarlet pensively, "Ruritanian. He's telling the princess—if we may give her her title—that she was always a bad sister to him, and he's glad he killed her husband; and she's telling him she hopes he hangs, if he *is* her brother. You see, the whole was what one might call a family affair," he added, with a touch of embarrassment.

Some time later, over cigarettes and full glasses, Lang and Peter Scarlet watched the dawn brighten the window of the latter's chamber, and discussed the extraordinary events of the night.

"But I don't see yet—" said Lang, and paused.

"Oh, I was very lucky," said Scarlet. "Very. Knowing Ruritanian—and some of the previous story. And then, hearing the princess and the baron on the balcony. Though, of course, the minute I saw the weapon I knew the baron hadn't committed the crime."

"Why?" said Lang, with heavy patience. Scarlet considered. He flushed.

"Sounds absurd—my trying to lay down the law to you," he said. "But—the baron had motive enough; but he wouldn't have killed that way. He might hack his enemy to bits with a cavalry saber; he wouldn't stab him with a toy. It wasn't in character—as I'd heard of it, and knew it in other Ruritanian nobles of his sort."

"The princess might have stabbed, though," said Lang thoughtfully.

"Oh yes—she'd be a stabber, if she'd be anything," agreed Scarlet promptly. "But I also happened to know that she was devoted to her husband. In fact, she'd as much as told me that she was worried for his safety, earlier in the evening. I know now she was worried on two counts: Baron Kossovar, and the brother she thought she'd recognized among the midgets. She wasn't quite sure it was he—she hadn't seen him for years and he was made up as the Beast in the play. That was the real reason she had her talk with the baron above—though the baron used to be in love with her, right enough. She wanted to try and find out if the baron had recognized any of the midgets, either. She didn't dare ask her husband."

"Why not?"

"Well, that's a long story. I'll cut it as short as possible. But they *are* blood brother and sister."

"That beautiful woman and the little deformity? It seems incredible."

"Not as incredible as it sounds. There have been numerous cases—one or two normal children in a family of giants or dwarfs, and vice versa. But Nadja was the only normal one in her family, except for a brother who died. The other two were midgets—two brothers. The family were small farmers, but proud as Lucifer. They'd been great people, long back. Well, Mirko came along and fell in love with Nadja, so much in love he was ready to make her is morganatic wife; but he couldn't stick her family—one can see why. And she was in love with him; so she married him. But her being willing to be his morganatic wife struck her family in their sorest point—their pride."

"They got ready to make trouble; and Mirko, very quietly, had them shipped to England—saw they got an allowance, but were never to come back to Ruritania. This was just the midget brothers, the old people were dead. So the midget brothers—they hadn't thought much of Nadja when they had her; in fact, they'd been pretty spiteful to her; but now she was their wronged sister—they were going to get Mirko if they ever had a chance. Then the war came along, and one brother died. The one who was left organized a troupe of performing midgets—when Mirko's allowance stopped coming after Ruritania was invaded by the Germans—and brought them over to America after the war."

"And—he got into the room—"

"With the help of the others. Bribed them, probably. You saw them do their living tower on each other's shoulders. Well, they did it for him under the window, and it was just high enough to get him up to the window sill. The window was open—the valet locked it later. Then our friend hid on top of that wardrobe—he's an excellent acrobat for his size—and he probably swarmed up to the shelf by way of the overcoat and so on. That was how he got the mark on the wall. It looked like a paw mark because he was still wearing his Beast's costume from the pantomime—perhaps for a blind, perhaps because he didn't bother to change."

"While the marks on the carpet?"

"Were some of them his and some of them the dog's. The handkerchief was his, too; it was scented, because, like many midgets, he was very vain. And the dagger that actually killed Mirko was his—one of a pair of family heirlooms. The princess was speaking the truth when she said she lost hers—it fell from her hair while she was on Kossovar's balcony. She got up there without your seeing her, by the same sort of little stair there was on the balcony you and I visited. And her maid was waiting for her on her own balcony. That's why neither of them heard the prince fall when he was killed—or cry out, if he did."

"I see; and, of course, the actual attack was entirely unexpected."

"Entirely. The little fiend waited with monumental patience till the prince was alone. Then, at some moment when the prince passed fairly near the wardrobe, he jumped at the back of his neck like a striking snake. You see, we deduced that, because the wound was high and slanted downward, it must have been made by someone tall. But put a short man on stilts and he's as tall as a giant. Our friend, with the aid of the wardrobe, was much taller than the prince. Then, when he'd killed his man, he marked him with the T—used his own pocketknife that time."

"'T for traitor?'"

"No; that was where your Italians misled you. The Ruritanian word for traitor begins with a J. But the Ruritanian word for seducer does begin with a T—and that was what he meant. That was what finally put me on the right track—that and the dog."

"I couldn't see why you made so much fuss about the dog!"

"I didn't see it for a long time—and then everything hitched together, with a sort of flash. The dog hadn't been there when the midget first got in the room, he was brought into the bedroom by the valet when the Mirkos returned. And he stopped our little murderer from getting away by the bedroom window—his friends must have been ready to catch him in a blanket or something. Your men wouldn't have found them, except by great luck; they were too small.

"Well, after the murder, the midget made for the bedroom and the dog jumped at him—there are paw marks on the bedroom door. He couldn't get to the window—the dog wouldn't let him—so he scuttled back to the wardrobe, climbed up the overcoat, and stowed away in the hatbox. The dog found his master's body and stopped to whine at it; then he turned back to the midget, who had shut the wardrobe doors from the inside and was safe. But the dog kept barking—and the next minute or so, the princess came back and heard him. Then—you know the rest."

Lang smiled a trifle dubiously. "And I used to have a fairly good conceit of my own reasoning powers," he said somberly. "Well—but there's just one more thing—"

"Yes?"

"For heaven's sake tell me how I gave myself away to you—on the big-game-hunter stuff. It passed everyone else."

Scarlet blushed to the tips of his ears. "Well, there had to be somebody like you guarding Prince Mirko," he said. "And you were the likeliest candidate—the rest were too old or too flabby. So I tried you on the murderee idea. Naturally, if you were what I thought you were, you'd run into more chances of being murdered than the rest of us. And you played up marvelously—but you couldn't help blinking for just a second. So then I asked you about Lipmann's gazelle—and when you said you'd shot a couple I knew, whatever you hunted, it wasn't African big-game!"

"But what the dickens is the matter with Lipmann's gazelle?" queried Lang heatedly. "Isn't it an animal you shoot? It sounded all right."

"Old man," said Scarlet a trifle sadly, "it isn't an animal at all, at least to my knowledge. I made it up that minute—out of my own little head!

A DAYLIGHT ADVENTURE

BY T. S. STRIBLING

Thomas Sigismund Stribling, who signed himself T. S.
Stribling, was born in Clifton, Tennessee. He trained as a
teacher at the normal school in Florence, Alabama, then,
after an unsuccessful attempt at teaching, he received an
LL.B. degree from the University of Alabama. He practiced law for only one year before going to work for a
magazine in Nashville. When he lost that job, he turned
to writing. In 1932 he won the Pulitzer Prize for his novel,
The Store, one of an historical trilogy on a country town.

THE FOLLOWING NOTES CONCERNING Mrs. Cordy Cancy were not made at the time of her alleged murder of her husband, James Cancy. Worse than that, they were not taken even at the time of her trial, but seven or eight months later at the perfectly hopeless date when Sheriff Matheny of Lanesburg, Tennessee, was in the act of removing his prisoner from the county jail to the state penitentiary in Nashville.

Such a lapse of time naturally gave neither Professor Henry Poggioli nor the writer opportunity to develop those clues, fingerprints, bullet wounds, and psychological analyses which usually enliven the story of any crime.

Our misfortune was that we motored into Lanesburg only a few minutes before Sheriff Matheny was due to motor out of the village with his prisoner. And even then we knew nothing whatever of the affair. We simply had stopped for lunch at the Monarch café in Courthouse Square, and we had to wait a few minutes to get stools at the counter. Finally, two men vacated their places. As Poggioli sat down, he found a copy of an old local newspaper stuck between the paper-napkin case and a ketchup bottle. He unfolded it and began reading. As he became absorbed almost at once in its contents, I was sure he had found a murder story, because that is about all the professor ever reads.

I myself take no interest in murders. I have always personally considered them deplorable rather than entertaining. The fact that I make my living writing accounts of Professor Poggioli's criminological investigations, I consider simply as an occupational hazard and hardship.

The square outside of our café was crowded with people and filled with movement and noise. In the midst of this general racket I heard the voice of some revivalist preacher booming out through a loudspeaker, asking the Lord to save Sister Cordy Cancy from a sinner's doom, and then he added the rather unconventional phrase that Sister Cordy was not the "right" sinner but was an innocent woman, or nearly so.

That of course was faintly puzzling—why a minister should broadcast such a remark about one of his penitents. Usually the Tennessee hill preacher makes his converts out to be very bad persons indeed, and strongly in need of grace, which I suppose most of us really are. Now to hear one woman mentioned in a prayer as "nearly innocent" was a sharp break from the usual.

I suppose Poggioli also caught the name subconsciously, for he looked up suddenly and asked me if the name "Cancy" had been called. I told him yes, and repeated what I had just heard over the megaphone.

The criminologist made some sort of silent calculation, then said, "Evidently Mrs. Cancy has had her baby and the sheriff is starting with her to the penitentiary in Nashville."

I inquired into the matter. Poggioli tapped his paper. "Just been reading a stenographic account of the woman's trial which took place here in Lanesburg a little over seven months ago. She was sentenced to life imprisonment, but she was pregnant at the time, so the judge ruled that she should remain here in Lanesburg jail until the baby was born and then be transferred to the state penitentiary in Nashville. So I suppose by this noise that the baby has arrived and the mother is on her way to prison."

Just as my companion explained this the preacher's voice boomed out, "Oh, Lord, do something to save Sister Cordy! Sheriff Matheny's fixin' to start with her to Nashville. Work a miracle, Oh, Lord, and convince him she is innocent. You kain't desert her, Lord, when she put all her faith an' trust in You. She done a small crime as You well know, but done it with a pyure heart and for Yore sake. So come down in Yore power an' stop the sheriff and save an innocent woman from an unjust sentence. Amen." Then in an aside which was still audible over the megaphone, "Sheriff Matheny, give us five minutes more. He's bound to send Sister Cordy aid in the next five minutes."

Now I myself am a Tennessean, and I knew how natural it was for a hill-country revivalist to want some special favor from the Lord, and to want it at once; but I had never before heard one ask the rescue of a prisoner on her way to Nashville. I turned to Poggioli and said, "The minister admits the woman has committed some smaller crime. What was that?"

"Forgery," he replied. "She forged her husband's will in favor of herself, then applied the proceeds to build a new roof on the Leatherwood church. That's part of the court record."

"And what's the other crime—the one she claims to be innocent of?"

"The murder of her husband, Jim Cancy. She not only claims to be innocent, she really is. The testimony in the trial proved that beyond a doubt."

I was shocked. "Then why did the judge condemn . . ."

The criminologist drew down his lips. "Because the proof of her innocence is psychological. Naturally, that lay beyond the comprehension of the jury, and the judge too, as far as that goes."

I stared at my companion. "Can you prove her innocence, now, at this late date?"

"Certainly, if this paper has printed the court reporter's notes correctly, and I'm sure it has."

"Why, this is the most amazing thing I ever heard of—hitting in like this!"

"What do you mean 'hitting in like this'?"

"Good heavens, don't you see? Just as the sheriff is starting off with an innocent woman, just as the preacher is asking the Lord to send down some power to save her, here you come along at exactly the right moment. You know she is innocent and can prove it!"

Poggioli gave the dry smile of a scientific man. "Oh, I see. You think my coming here is providential."

"Certainly. What else is there to think?"

"I regret to disillusion you, but it is not. It couldn't be. It is nothing more than an extraordinary coincidence—and I can prove that, too." With this my friend returned to his paper.

This left me frankly in a nervous state. It seemed to me we ought to do something for the woman outside. I looked at the man sitting next to us at the counter. He nodded his head sidewise at Poggioli. "He don't live around here, does he?"

I said he didn't.

"If he don't live here, how does he know what's happened in these parts?"

"You heard him say he read it in the paper."

"He didn't do no such thing. I watched him. He didn't read that paper a tall, he jest turned through it, like I would a picture book."

I told him that was Poggioli's way of reading. It is called sight-reading—just a look and he knew it.

The hill man shook his head, "Naw, Mister, I know better'n that. I've watched hundreds of men read that paper sence it's laid thar on the counter, and the fassest one tuk a hour an twelve minutes to git through."

I nodded. I was not interested, so I said, "I daresay that's true."

"Of course hit's so," he drawled truculently, "ever'thing I say is so."

"I'm not doubting your word," I placated, "it is you who are doubting mine. You see I know my friend's ability at sight-reading."

This silenced him for a few moments, then he said shrewdly,

239

"Looky here, if he gits what he knows out'n that paper, how come him to say Cordy Cancy is innocent when the paper says she's guilty?"

"Because the judgment in the paper doesn't agree with the evidence it presents. My friend has gone over the evidence and has judged for himself that the woman is guilty of forgery but innocent of murder."

This gave the hill man pause. A certain expression came into his leathery face. "He's a detectif, ain't he?"

"Well, not exactly. He used to be a teacher in the Ohio State University, and he taught detectives how to detect."

"Mm—mm. Who hard [hired] him to come hyar?"

"Nobody," I said, "he just dropped in by chance."

"Chanst, huh? You expeck me to b'leve that?"

"Yes, I must say I do."

"Well, jest look at it frum my stan'point—him comin' hyar the very minnit the preacher is prayin' fer he'p and the shurrf startin' with her to the penitentiary—a great detectif like him jest drap in by chanst. Do you expeck me to b'leve that?"

All this was delivered with the greatest heat and my seat-mate seemed to hold me personally responsible for the situation.

"Well, what do you believe?" I asked in an amiable tone which gave him permission to believe anything he wanted to and no hard feelings.

"Why, jess what I said. I b'leve he wuz hard."

His suspicion of Poggioli, who would never accept a penny for his criminological researches, amused me. "Well, that's your privilege, but if it would strengthen your faith in me I will say that to the best of my knowledge and belief Professor Henry Poggioli's arrival in Lanesburg, Tennessee, on the eve of Mrs. Cordy Cancy's committal to the Nashville penitentiary, was a coincidence, a whole coincidence, and nothing but a coincidence, so help me, John Doe."

I had hoped to lighten my companion's dour mood, but he arose gloomily from his stool.

"I hope the Lord forgives you fer mawkin' His holy words."

"They are not the Lord's holy words," I reminded him, "they're the sheriff's words when he swears in a witness."

"Anyway, you tuk His name in vain when you said 'em."

"Didn't mention His name, sir. I said 'John Doe'."

"Anyway, Brother," he continued in his menacing drawl, "you shore spoke with lightness. The Bible warns you aginst speakin' with lightness—you kain't git aroun' that." With this he took himself out of the café, scraping his feet in the doorway as a symbol of shaking my dust from his shoes.

As I watched the saturnine fellow go, Poggioli turned from his paper.

"Poses quite a riddle, doesn't he?"

"Not for me," I said. "I was born here in the hills."

"You understand him?"

"I think so."

"You didn't observe any more precise and concrete contradiction about him?"

I tried to think of some simple contradiction in the man, something plain. I knew when Poggioli pointed it out it would be very obvious, but nothing came to my mind. I asked him what he saw.

"Two quite contradictory reactions: he was disturbed about my being a detective and about your near profanity."

"I am afraid I don't quite see what you mean."

"I'll make it simpler. He evidently was a deacon in some church."

"Why do you say that?"

"Because he reproved the 'lightness' of your language. The scriptures instruct deacons to reprove the faults of the brethren, and lightness of language is one of them. So he was probably a deacon."

"All right, say he was. What does that contradict?"

"His disturbance over my being a detective. Deacons are supposed to ally themselves with law and order."

I laughed. "You don't know your Tennessee hill deacons. That contradiction in them is historical. Their ancestors came here before the Revolution to worship God as they pleased and escape the excise tax. They have been for the Lord and against the law ever since."

At this point another man hurried from the square into the Monarch café. I noted the hurry because under ordinary circumstances hill men never hurry, not even in the rain. He glanced up and down the counter, immediately came to my companion, and lifted a hand. "Excuse me, Brother, but you're not a preacher?"

"No, I'm not," said my companion.

"Then you are the detective that was sent. Will you come with me?"

"Just what do you mean by 'sent'?", asked the criminologist.

"Why the Lord sent you," explained the man hurriedly but earnestly. "Brother Johnson was jest prayin' to the Lord to send somebody to prove Sister Cordy Cancy innocent and keep her from going to the pen. Jim Phipps heard you-all talkin' an' hurried out an' told us there was a detectif in here. So He's bound to have sent ye."

Poggioli reflected. "I am sure I can prove the woman innocent—from the evidence printed in this paper. But what good will that do, when the trial is over and the woman already sentenced?"

"Brother," said the countryman, "if the Lord started this work, don't you reckon He can go on an' finish it?"

"Look here, Poggioli," I put in, "we're here for some reason or other."

"Yes, by pure chance, by accident," snapped the psychologist. "Our presence has no more relation to this woman than . . ."

He was looking for a simile when I interrupted, "If you know she is innocent don't you think it your duty to—"

The psychologist stopped me with his hand and his expression. "I believe I do owe a duty . . . yes . . . yes, I owe a duty. I'll go do what I can."

The man who came for him was most grateful; so were all the people in the café, for they had overheard the conversation. Everybody was delighted except me. I didn't like Poggioli's tone, or the expression on his face. I wondered what he really was going to do.

Well, by the time we got out of the restaurant everybody in the square seemed to know who we were. There was a great commotion. The preacher's prayer for help had been answered instantly. It was a miracle.

The sound-truck which had been booming stood in front of the county jail on the south side of the square. Beside the truck was the sheriff's car with the woman prisoner handcuffed in the back seat. Near the car stood another woman holding a young baby in her arms. This infant, I gathered, was the prisoner's child, and would be left behind in the Lanesburg jail while its mother went on to the penitentiary in Nashville. The crowd naturally was in sympathy with the woman and expected us immediately to deliver her from her troubles. I heard one of the men say as we pushed forward, "That heavy man's the detective and that slim 'un's his stooge; he writes down what the big 'un does."

Frankly, I was moved by the situation, and I was most uneasy about the outcome. I asked Poggioli just what he meant to do.

He glanced at me as we walked. "Cure them of an illusion."

"Just what do you mean—cure them of an . . ."

He nodded at the crowd around us. "I will prove to these people the woman is innocent, but at the same time show that my proof can be of no benefit to the prisoner. This ought to convince the crowd that providence had nothing to do with the matter, and it ought to make them, as a group, a little more rationalistic and matter-of-fact. That is what I consider it my duty to do."

His whole plan appeared cruel to me. I said, "Well, thank goodness, you won't be able to do that in five minutes, and the sheriff gave them only that much more time before he starts out."

My hope to avoid Poggioli's demonstration was quashed almost at once. I saw the sheriff, a little man, climb out of his car, walk across to the sound-truck, and take the microphone from the minister. Then I heard the sheriff's voice boom out.

"Ladies and gentlemen, I understand there really is help on the way for Mrs. Cancy. Whether it is miraculous help or jest human help, I don't know. But anyway I'm extendin' Mrs. Cancy's time to prove her innocence one more hour before we start to Nashville."

A roar of approval arose at this. The minister in the truck then took over the loudspeaker, "Brothers and Sisters," he began in his more solemn drawl, "they ain't one ounce of doubt in my soul as to who sent this good man. I'll introduce him to you. He is Dr. Henry Poggioli the great detective some of you have read about in the magazines. The Lord has miraculously sent Dr. Poggioli to clear Sister Cordy Cancy from her troubles. And now I'll introduce Sister Cordy to Dr. Poggioli. Doctor, Sister Cordy don't claim complete innocence, but she's a mighty good woman. She did, however, forge her husban's will by takin' a carbon paper and some of his old love letters and tracin' out a will, letter by letter. She sees now that was wrong, but she was workin' for the glory of the Lord when she done it."

Shouts of approval here—"Glory be!" "Save her, Lord!" and so forth. The divine continued, "Jim Cancy, her husban', was a mawker and a scoffer. He wouldn't contribute a cent to the Lord's cause nor bend his knee in prayer. So Sister Cordy forged his will for religious ends. Now I guess the Lord knew Jim was goin' to git killed. But Sister Cordy didn't have a thing in the world to do with that. He jest got killed. And you all know what she done with his money—put a new roof on the Leatherwood churchhouse. Save her, Oh, Lord, from the penitentiary!" (Another uproar of hope and sympathy here) "And Brothers and Sisters, look how she acted in the trial, when suspicion fell on her for Jim's murder. She didn't spend one cent o' that money for a lawyer. She said it wasn't hers to spend, it was the Lord's and He would save her. She said she didn't need no lawyer on earth when she had one in Heaven. She said He would send her aid. And now, praise His name, He has sent it here at this eleventh hour." Again he was interrupted by shouts and applause. When a semi-silence was restored, he said, "Dr. Poggioli, you can now prove Sister Cordy innocent of her husband's murder and set her free."

In the renewed uproar the minister solemnly handed the microphone down to Poggioli on the ground. I have seldom been more nervous about any event in Poggioli's eventful career. I didn't suppose he would be in any actual danger from the irate hill people when they found out what he was trying to do, but on the other hand a mob can be formed in the South in about three minutes. And they are likely to do anything—ride a man out of town on a rail, tar and feather him, give him a switching, depending on how annoyed they are. Poggioli never lived in the South, he had no idea what he was tampering with.

He began, "Ladies and gentlemen, I have little to say. I have just read the report of Mrs. Cancy's trial in your county paper. From it I have drawn absolute proof of her innocence of her husband's murder, but unfortunately that proof can be of no benefit to her."

Cries of "Why won't it?" "What's the matter with it?" "What makes you talk like that?"

"Because, my friends, of a legal technicality. If I could produce new evidence the trial judge could reopen her case and acquit Mrs. Cancy. But a reinterpretation of old evidence is not a legal ground for a rehearing. All I can do now is to demonstrate to you from the evidence printed in your county paper that Mrs. Cancy is innocent of murder, but still she must go with the Sheriff to the penitentiary in Nashville."

Despair filled the square; there arose outcries, pleas, oaths. The revivalist quashed this. He caught up his microphone and thundered, "Oh, ye of little faith, don't you see Sister Cordy's salvation is at hand? Do you think the Lord would send a detectif here when it wouldn't do no good? I'm as shore of victory as I'm standin' here. Brother Poggioli, go on talkin' with a good heart!"

The irony of the situation stabbed me: for Poggioli to intend a purely materialistic solution to the situation, and the minister who had besought his aid to hope for a miracle. It really was ironic. Fortunately, no one knew of this inner conflict except me or there would have been a swift outbreak of public indignation. The scientist began his proof:

"Ladies and gentlemen, your minister has recalled to your memory how Mrs. Cordy Cancy forged her husband's will by tracing each letter of it with a carbon paper from a package of her husband's old love letters. But he did not mention the fact that after she did this—she had underscored and overscored these letters and made them the plainest and most conclusive proof of her forgery—she still kept those love letters! She did not destroy them. She put them in a trunk whose key was lost, and kept them in the family living room. Now every man, woman, and I might almost say child, sees clearly what this proves!"

Of course in this he was wrong. He overestimated the intelligence of his audience. Those nearer to him, who could make themselves heard, yelled for him to go on and explain.

"Further explanation is unnecessary," assured the psychologist. "If she felt sufficiently sentimental about her husband to preserve his love letters, obviously she did not mean to murder him. Moreover, she must have realized her marked-over letters would constitute absolute proof of the minor crime of forgery. She must have known that if her husband were murdered, her home would be searched and the tell-tale letters would be found. Therefore, she not only did not murder her husband herself but she had no suspicion that he would be murdered. Those letters in her unlocked trunk make it impossible that she should be either the principal or an accessory to his assassination."

A breath of astonishment went over the crowd at the simplicity of Poggioli's deduction. Everyone felt that he should have thought of that for himself.

Poggioli made a motion for quiet and indicated that his proof was not concluded. Quiet returned and the psychologist continued.

"Your minister tells us, and I also read it in the evidence printed in your county paper, that Mrs. Cancy did not hire an attorney to defend her in her trial. She used the entire money to place a new roof on the old Leatherwood church, and she told the court the reason she did this was because God would defend her."

Here shouts arose. "He did! He's doin' it now! He's sent you here to save her!"

Poggioli held up a hand and shook his head grimly. This was the point of his whole appearance in the square—the materialistic point by which he hoped to rid these hill people of too great a reliance on providential happenings and place them on the more scientific basis of self-help. He intoned slowly.

"I regret to say, ladies and gentlemen, that my appearance here is pure accident. Why? Because I have come too late. If a supernal power had sent me here to save an innocent woman—and she is an innocent woman—if a supernal power had sent me, it would certainly have sent me in time. But I am not in time. The trial is over.

245

All the proof is in. We cannot possibly ask a new trial on the ground of a reinterpretation of old proof, which is what I am giving you. That is no ground for a new trial. So this innocent woman who is on her way to the penitentiary must go on and serve out her unjust term. My appearance here today, therefore, can be of no service to anyone and can be attributed to nothing but pure chance."

At this pitiful negation an uproar arose in the square. Men surged toward the sheriff, yelling for him to turn the woman free or they would do it for him. Cooler heads held back the insurgents and voices shouted out,

"Dr. Poggioli, who did do the murder? You know ever' thing— who done it!"

The criminologist wagged a negative hand. "I have no idea."

"The devil!" cried a thick-set fellow. "Go ahead an' reason out who killed Jim Cancy—jest like you reasoned out his wife was innocent!"

"I can't do that. It's impossible. I haven't studied the evidence of the murder, merely the evidence that proves non-murder—a completely different thing."

"Go ahead! Go ahead!" yelled half a dozen voices. "The Lord has he'ped you so fur—He'll stan by you!"

It was amusing, in a grim fashion, for the crowd to twist the very materialistic point Poggioli was making into a logical basis for a spiritualistic interpretation. However, I do not think Pogggioli was amused. He held up his hands.

"Friends, how could I know anything about this when I stopped over for lunch in this village only one hour ago?"

A dried-up old farmer, whose face had about the color and texture of one of his own corn shucks, called out, "Somebody shot Jim, didn't they Dr. Poggioli?"

"Oh, yes, somebody shot him."

"Well, have you got any idyah of the kind of man who shot Jim Cancy?"

"Oh, certainly. I have a fairly clear idea of the kind of man who murdered Cancy."

"I allowed you had, Brother, I allowed you had," nodded the old fellow with satisfaction. "The Lord put it into my heart to ast you exactly that question." The old fellow turned to the officer, "Shurrf Matheny, has he got time to tell what kind of a fellow murdered Jim before you start with Sister Cordy to the pen?"

The officer held up his hand. "I am extendin' Sister Cordy's startin' time two more hours—so we can find out who murdered her husban' instid of her."

"O.K." called a woman's voice, "go ahead and tell us the kind of skunk that done that!"

"Well, Madam, I would say it was a man who shot Jim Cancy."

"Oh, yes, we all know that," shouted several listeners. "Women don't shoot nobody, they pisen 'em . . . as a rule." "Go on, tell us somp'm else."

"Well, let me see," pondered Poggioli aloud. "Let us begin back with the forgery itself. Mrs. Cancy did this. She admits it. But she did not originate the idea, because that is a highly criminal idea and she does not have a highly criminal psychology. She has, in fact, a very religious and dutiful psychology. I also know that if she had been bright enough to think of tracing the will from her old love letters, she would have realized how dangerous they were to keep in her unlocked trunk and would have destroyed them immediately. Therefore, I know somebody suggested to her how she could forge the will."

More angry shouts interrupted here, as if the crowd were reaching for the real criminal. Some voices tried to hush the others so the psychologist could proceed. Eventually Poggioli went on.

"All right, Mrs. Cancy did not originate the idea of forgery. Then she was used as a tool. But she is not a hard, resolute woman. Just look at her there in the sheriff's car and you can see that. She is a soft, yielding woman and would not carry any plan through to its bitter end. But in her trial she did carry a plan through to its bitter end, and this end, odd to say, was to put a new roof on the Leatherwood church. Ladies and gentlemen, a new roof on Leatherwood church was the basic motive for Cancy's murder. It is fantastic, but it is the truth. Mrs. Cancy refused to hire a lawyer when she came to trial. Why? To save the money to put a roof on Leatherwood church. So the person who persuaded her to commit the forgery must also have persuaded her to withhold the money for the church roof, and that God would come down and set her free from the charge of murder."

At this the enthusiasm of the crowd knew no bounds. They flung up their hats, they yelled, they cried out that now the Lord had come to help Sister Cordy just like He had promised. The sheriff arose in his car and shouted that he extended Sister Cordy's leaving time for the rest of the day. He yelled that they were hot on the trail of the man who done it and he would remain in town to make the arrest.

I could see Poggioli was unnerved. It would take a cleverer psychologist than I am to explain why he should be. Of course, his demonstration was going awry. He was not getting where he had intended to go. He lifted up his hands and begged the crowd.

"My friends, please remember this. I do not know the man. I have no idea who he is. I can only give you his type."

"All right," shouted many voices, "go on and give us his type, so Sheriff Matheny can arrest him!"

The criminologist collected himself. "As to his type: I ate lunch in the Monarch café a little while ago and was reading an account of Mrs. Cancy's trial in your county paper. As I read, a gentleman beside me said that he had been watching strangers read the story of that trial for months, as it lay there on the lunch counter. It is possible such a man might have some connection with the murder; or he may have been morbidly curious about crime in general—"

Shouts of satisfaction here—"Go ahead, now you're gittin' somewhere!"

Poggioli stopped them. "Wait! Wait! I by no means incriminate this gentleman. I am trying to show you the various hypotheses which a criminologist must apply to every clue or piece of evidence."

"All right, Doctor, if he didn't kill Jim Cancy, who did?"

Poggioli mopped his face. "That I do not know, nor do I know anything whatever about the man in the café. I am simply trying to give you a possible psychological description of the murderer. Now, this man at my table also reprimanded my friend here for what he considered to be an infraction of a religious formality. In fact, he became quite angry about it. That would link up with the fact that Jim Cancy was reported to be a free-thinker. A free-thinker would have irritated such a man very deeply. If Cancy had jibed at this man's faith, the fellow would have felt that any punishment he could inflict on the mocker would be justified, even unto death. Also, he could have persuaded himself that any money he might receive from Cancy's death should be devoted to the welfare of the church—as for example, to put a new roof on the Leatherwood church. Following these plans, he could have easily influenced Mrs. Cancy to forge Cancy's will, with the understanding that the money would go to the church. Then he could have waylaid and shot Cancy, and made the will collectible. This would have accomplished two things; gratify his private revenge and make a contribution to the church. . . . The murderer could be of that type or he could be of a completely different type which I shall now try to analyze. . . ."

How many more types Poggioli would have described nobody knew, for at this juncture the sheriff discovered that his prisoner had fainted. This created a tremendous commotion. For a hill woman to faint was almost as unparalleled as for a horse to faint. Sheriff Matheny arose in his car and hallooed that he would carry no sick woman to the Nashville pen, and that Mrs. Cancy should remain here with her baby until she was completely recovered, even if it took a week. After making this announcement, the officer climbed out of his car and disappeared in the throng.

Everybody was gratified. They came pouring around Poggioli to congratulate him on his speech. A fat man elbowed up, seized Poggioli by the arm, motioned at me, too, and shouted at us to come to dinner in his hotel. Poggioli said we had just eaten at the Monarch café.

"Then you-all are bound to be hungry. Come on, my wife sent me over here to bring ye. She feeds all the revivalists and their singers who come to preach in the square."

The criminologist repeated that we were not hungry, but the fat man came close to him and said in what was meant for an undertone:

"Don't make no diff'runce whether you are hungry or not—my wife wants you to come inside while you and your buddy are alive!"

"Alive!" said my friend.

"Shore, alive. Do you think Deacon Sam Hawley will let any man stand up in the public square and accuse him of waylayin' Jim Cancy, and then not kill the man who does the accusin?"

My friend was shocked. "Why, I never heard of Deacon Sam Hawley!"

"He's the man you et by, and he knows you. Come on, both of you!"

"But I was simply describing a type—"

"Brother, when you go to a city you find men in types—all dentists look alike, all bankers look alike, all lawyers look alike, and so on; but out here in these Tennessee hills we ain't got but one man to a type. And when you describe a man's type, you've described the man. Come on in to my hotel before you git shot. We're trying to make Lanesburg a summer resort and we don't want it to get a bad name for murderin' tourists."

We could see how a hotel owner would feel that way and we too were anxious to help preserve Lanesburg's reputation for peace and friendliness. We followed our host rather nervously to his hotel across the square and sat down to another lunch.

There was a big crowd in the hotel and they were all talking about the strange way the Lord had brought about the conviction of Deacon Sam Hawley, and rescued a comparatively innocent woman from an unjust sentence. Poggioli pointed out once or twice that the woman was not out of danger yet, but all the diners around us were quite sure that she soon would be.

The whole incident seemed about to end on a kind of unresolved anticlimax. The diners finally finished their meal and started out of the hotel. We asked some of the men if they thought it would be safe for us to go to our car. They said they didn't know, we would have to try it and see. Poggioli and I waited until quite a number of men and women were going out of the hotel and joined them. We were just well out on the sidewalk when a brisk gunfire broke out from behind the office of the *Lane County Weekly Herald*, which was just across the street from the hotel. It was not entirely unexpected. Besides, that sort of thing seemed to happen often enough in Lanesburg to create a pattern for public action. Everybody jumped behind everybody else, and holding that formation made for the nearest doors and alleys. At this point Sheriff Matheny began his counterattack. It was from a butcher's shop close to the hotel. How he knew what point to pick out, I don't know; whether or not he was using us for bait, I still don't know.

At any rate, the sheriff's fourth or fifth shot ended the battle. Our assailant, quite naturally, turned out to be Deacon Sam Hawley. He was dead when the crowd identified him. In the skirmish the sheriff was shot in the arm, and everybody agreed that now he would not be able to take Mrs. Cancy to the penitentiary for a good three months to come. She was reprieved at least for that long.

As we got into our car and drove out of Lanesburg, the crowd was circulating a petition to the Governor to pardon Mrs. Cordelia Cancy of the minor crime of forgery. The petition set forth Mrs. Cancy's charity, her purity of heart, her generosity in using the proceeds of her crime for the church, and a number of her other neighborly virtues. The village lawyer put in a note that a wife cannot forge her husband's signature. He argued that if she cannot steal from him, then she cannot forge his name, which is a form of theft. She simply signs his name for him, she does not forge it.

The petition was signed by two hundred and forty-three registered Democratic voters. The Governor of Tennessee is a Democrat.

At this point we drove out of Lanesburg . . .

GOODBYE, PICCADILLY

BY JOHN. P. MARQUAND

John P. Marquand was born in Delaware but grew up in Newburyport, Massachusetts. He attended Harvard on scholarship, then worked on the Boston *Transcript* and the New York *Tribune*. He saw action as a first lieutenant in World War I and afterward began to write, with time off for visits to the Orient. His most memorable characters, with the notable exception of Mr. Moto, were the socially prominent Northeasteners he knew so well—George Apley, H. M. Pulham, Esq., B. F.'s daughter and Melville Goodwin. He died on July 16th, 1960.

THERE WAS NO LONGER ANY doubt that Dr. Francis Barnwelder was going to take the London plane. Even after Dr. Barnwelder had checked his baggage and cleared his passport, Jim Briscoe had remained doubtful, because it was never wise to underestimate anyone on the Barnwelder level.

Jim Briscoe glanced across the passengers' waiting space at Idlewild airport. The small man in the dark coat was still standing near the barber shop reading his newspaper. It began now to look as though Jim would spend a quiet evening at home, since he might not need to follow Dr. Barnwelder. If Dr. Barnwelder had suspected he was being watched, he gave no sign of it; but then, why should he? There had been a routine check on him during all the years he had worked in secret installations, and no doubt anyone gradually became immune to personal attention.

If he had been Barnwelder, Jim Briscoe was thinking—granted that Barnwelder was the man he was almost sure he was—he would not have done anything so obvious as to take Flight 401. The man must have known it was very dangerous for him to go direct to London if things were the way Jim Briscoe believed. All he could think was that Dr. Barnwelder did not know how far the investigation had gone. If this was so, Jim Briscoe felt personally flattered, but it never paid to be too sure of anything.

He would not be alive today, he was thinking, if he had not learned never to indulge in overconfidence. There was a time in Rio, he recalled, when he had taken the precaution to brush clumsily against a room waiter only because he had not been overconfident; and owing to his sense of doubt he had learned, while there was still time to do something about it, that the waiter carried a knife. He would have been garroted in Singapore if he had not been impressed by the striking agility of the Arab who drove his taxi. It never paid to be too sure of anything just as it never paid to let your mind wander too long in reminiscence; but, even so, Jim Briscoe was finally growing certain that he and Dr. Barnwelder were about to cross the Atlantic together.

Of course, it was barely conceivable there might be trouble of some sort in Grander, yet this contingency might reasonably be discarded, since there were few places to go and a limited variety of things to do in Newfoundland.

Perhaps, after all, Jim Briscoe thought, the most obvious course was the safest, and Dr. Barnwelder was blatantly indicating that he had nothing to conceal. Mrs. Barnwelder was accompanying him, a stout, kind-looking, middle-aged woman, and she really was Mrs. Barnwelder, because a check had been made, even down to her Swedish-immigrant grandparents in Minnesota. Men seldom looked for trouble when accompanied by their wives. If obviousness could be classed as an art, Dr. Barnwelder had managed very well. He was off to a meeting of the Learned Societies in Geneva, with no doubt whatever about the Learned Societies or the Barnwelder connection.

There had been a time, Jim Briscoe was thinking, when he had not believed in all this checking and paper passing; but after Delhi, in 1946, he realized how unexpectedly revelation could spring out of routine. Suddenly, if you kept checking, some detail did not ring true—like a foreigner's error in syntax—but there had not been any discrepancy in the dossier of Dr. Francis Barnwelder, B.S., Leland Stanford, 1920; M.S., University of Chicago; and Ph.D., Columbia.

After all, as someone in Washington had said some months before, what was there so funny about Barnwelder's being learned? The trouble was as this individual in Washington had remarked, everyone was checking on everyone else since the nuclear scientist, Fuchs, had jumped the fence. Of course, the individual who had made these remarks has not been involved with the problem as long as Jim Briscoe.

At any rate, Dr. Barnwelder was close to being distractingly transparent. He had given his business and home address as Los Alamos, and now he was buying razor blades and toothpaste at the airport drug store while Mrs. Barnwelder sat waiting for him reading a copy of a large-circulation women's magazine.

It was possible, Jim Briscoe finally thought, that Dr. Barnwelder's carefree actions indicated that he had professional protection. But as Jim Briscoe examined the prospective passengers of Flight 401, he could discover no sign of a body-guard, and he knew enough to be almost infallible at spotting the type, which was conventionally someone who would never be looked at twice. Also, the passengers had all been identified as thoroughly as time had permitted. There were a handful of businessmen and the rest were American tourists, most of whom were now in the cocktail lounge waiting for Flight 401 to be called. One of the attendants behind the British airline counter had picked up a hand microphone.

"Passengers for Flight Four-oh-one to London," he was saying, "will now board at Gate Four B. Have your clearance cards ready."

It was not advisable to display undue curiosity as the passengers gathered, carrying their overnight luggage, but Jim Briscoe watched them carefully while he appeared to be searching through his brief case for his gate card. Their faces had already been matched against the thousands of photographic faces with which he was familiar. As they moved toward Gate 4B, there was no eccentricity in anyone's walk and no indefinable aura that might awaken intuition. They were all honest travelers on straight errands, whose anticipatory excitement stamped them all as genuine.

Dr. Barnwelder also was very natural. He came hurrying out of the drug store, hastily thrusting his purchases into his brief case, a stoutish, round-faced man, with heavy lips and thick-lensed, rimless glasses, whose baldness showed at the back of his gray felt hat. His careless handling of his brief case looked almost as though he were trying to prove to anyone who might be watching that he carried no secret papers; but then, why should he?

Dr. Barnwelder was equipped to write down anything he wished to communicate in a series of equations that could reside in his brain tissue until the final minute of recording. For the purpose of communication he needed only another brain as competent as his. There would be no papers. All Dr. Barnwelder had to do was to communicate with an individual who according to word that had arrived that afternoon, had appeared unexpectedly in London. Jim Briscoe had been one of the few people who had predicted this appearance, which explained why he too was leaving on Flight 401.

Dr. Barnwelder had found his card, and now he passed through beside him. Jim Briscoe lingered a moment beside the airline counter.

"Are you all cleared, sir?" the clerk asked.

"Oh, yes, thanks," Jim Briscoe answered, "now that I've found my card."

The attendant was a very reliable young man, who, Jim Briscoe was beginning to believe, might possibly have a professional future—if he lived long enough. His question, according to previous agreement, meant that there had been no last-minute changes in the list.

"I see you've got me in seat thirty-six," Jim Briscoe said. "I hope you have me sitting next to some very pretty girl!"

Jim Briscoe spoke loudly because it was time to be in character. He had used the same cover successfully several times before. He was using his own preparatory school and college. He was known as an ex-officer of the Marine Corps, and this detail was also true.

The name Briscoe was also his own, which made things easier; but also he had suddenly acquired independent means, with a bank account and securities to prove it, and he had also acquired an enthusiasm for medieval sculpture. There had been some talk, when the cover was being discussed, that he should be a well-to-do New Yorker trying to write, but this had seemed to him lacking in imagination. Besides, he had a good working knowledge of art.

"Yes, Mr. Briscoe," the airline clerk said, and for a second the mask dropped. "The prettiest girl on the flight, Mr. Briscoe, according to my judgment. Miss Edith Olmstead, from Bryn Mawr, Pennsylvania. She's a real pin-up girl."

"Flight Four-oh-one for London," the loudspeaker was calling, "is now loading at Gate Four B."

There was nothing to keep Jim Briscoe any longer. He remembered the name and notes. Miss Edith Olmstead was twenty-six years of age; height, five feet nine; weight, one hundred thirty; graduate of Bucknell University, Lewisburg, Pennsylvania. She resided with her parents, Mr. and Mrs. R. L. Olmstead, at 82 Frizell Street, Bryn Mawr, Pennsylvania and she was going abroad as a tourist. Mr. R. L. Olmstead was fifty-five years old, height, five feet ten and a half; weight, one eighty-six; Independent voter; and a partner in a real-estate-and-insurance firm. Jim Briscoe's mind had already gone back to special lists, but there had been no interest recently in any Olmstead.

Jim Briscoe had grown so accustomed in the last ten years to being two people at once that he was no longer very conscious of the effort. He was in his late thirties; height, six feet; weight, one seventy-five; complexion, fair; athletic and well-groomed. He was careful with his dress; and his speech was not markedly influenced by any section of the country.

His features were regular and his expression was amiable. Anyone seeing him in Europe always recognized him immediately as an American of good average background. He had a happy, anticipatory look as he climbed the steps to the plane, and he greeted the stewardess with a genial, warm interest that showed he was an eligible bachelor.

Dr. and Mrs. Barnwelder were sitting where he had directed, to his left, just across the aisle, five seats ahead—where he could check on them readily without their even noticing him. Dr. Barnwelder was reading the evening paper, and Mrs. Barnwelder was still reading her magazine. Miss Edith Olmstead was already in the seat near the window and Jim Briscoe smiled at her.

"Good afternoon," he said. "I see we're crossing the ocean together."

Jim Briscoe had developed his own methods of evaluating and remembering faces. He had trained himself never to be distracted by superficial peculiarities, because he believed an observer's attention should first be concentrated on bone structure. Jim Briscoe had observed that Miss Olmstead's forehead was broad and high, her eyes were hazel-gray, large and well separated, her cheek- and jawbones were photogenic, her teeth were even, that she had a small mole on her right cheek, and that the wave in the light brown hair above her forehead was natural. He had made mental notes of all these facts before he realized that Miss Olmstead was a very pretty girl.

Grades of beauty had only a minor bearing in Jim Briscoe's profession, but he discovered himself mentally admitting, when he seated himself beside Miss Olmstead and put his brief case securely beneath his seat, that beauty had very little to do with measurements or symmetry. Beauty, in the end, he supposed, was a matter of spirit and emotional adjustment. Miss Olmstead's mouth was too large and her nose too short for academic perfection, but there was a freshness and vigor about her, and an impression of high spirits and generosity that threatened to make one forget identifiable detail.

She had taken off her white gloves, which now lay in her lap neatly folded over a black leather handbag, which she must have purchased especially for the trip, judging by its newness—a roomy, competent bag, large enough to carry bills, a change purse, lipstick, a compact, passport, other papers, and possibly a small automatic.

This last idea came to him involuntarily, because he had no reason in the world to suspect that Miss Olmstead might be armed. Her hands, which were also folded in her lap, though delicate and with nails decorated by an unusually red polish, struck him as being strong, like those of a sculptress or a laboratory technician. She wore no rings and showed no trace of a ring hastily removed. She did, however, wear a small gold bracelet on her left wrist, and the way it hung indicated that it was not hollow.

She was dressed in a smoke-gray traveling suit and a white blouse—silk, not nylon—which was fastened at the throat by a gold-and-diamond clip. The stones were small, which made Jim Briscoe conclude that they were genuine. It was undoubtedly a present for graduating from that college in Pennsylvania—Bucknell. He could not recall that any personalities under observation had been graduated from Bucknell University.

256

"Of course I hope you're right about our crossing the ocean," Miss Olmstead said, and she laughed. "I hope we do get all the way over."

Her voice did not sound like Philadelphia. Each of her words was as clear as a newly minted coin. For just a moment he had the impression that she sounded like a foreigner who had spent years of her childhood in a boarding school in England, but there was not the requisite self-consciousness. She might have studied dramatics at Bucknell, but she was not a professional actress. Her skin showed none of the corrosive effects of stage make-up.

Jim Briscoe laughed reassuringly.

"You sound as though this were your first trip abroad," he said.

"Oh, no," Miss Olmstead answered. "I used to go to school in Switzerland, but this is the first time I've ever flown. My parents have always been against flying."

The boarding school in Switzerland explained the voice.

"I think you'll find," he said, "that statistically this trip is a good deal safer than if you and I were motoring from New York to—"

He hesitated. He had almost said from New York to Washington, but he had checked himself in time. Once you mentioned Washington, people always asked if you were in Government. As he hesitated he saw that Miss Olmstead looked curious.

"From New York to where?" she asked.

"Well," Jim Briscoe said, "let's say from New York to Buffalo."

"Oh," she said, "do you live in Buffalo?"

"No," he said. "I'm just naming it as a convenient location."

"But you must know Buffalo," she said. "You must have been up that way quite recently if you've motored on the thru-way."

"That's true." he said. "I was up near Buffalo once this summer."

"Well," she said, "I'm glad you were, because I like putting two and two together." She raised her voice because the first of the port motors was turning over. "Please don't think I'm worried about planes. It's my father who's against them."

"Well," Jim Briscoe answered, "planes may have their drawbacks, but they get you from one place to another pretty fast."

"It's my brother who made him feel that way," she said. "He was a flier. He was killed in the war."

"Oh," Jim Briscoe said, and the starting motors were an adequate excuse for not saying anything more. He was listening to the motors as though he were personally responsible for them. He glanced at his wrist watch.

"It looks as though we're starting out on time," Jim Briscoe said. "May I hold your bag for you while you fasten your seat belt?"

257

"Oh," she said. "Thank you. I forgot. I suppose it's just the same over the ocean as it is on land—I mean, seat belts at the take-off."

He wished that he could avoid balancing scraps of conversation. That remark of Miss Olmstead's about seat belts sounded unusually naive; but then she had not hesitated at all with her handbag. It seemed heavier than was necessary, that would indicate a heavy object. His instinctive precautions reminded Jim Briscoe of an old friend of his in Washington named Mr. Henry, who had quite recently retired from the Bureau.

Mr. Henry now lived in a small tapestry-brick house on Woodley Road, with his daughter, the widow of a naval commander. He was a plump, elderly man, with a thatch of white hair reminiscent of Mr. Carl Sandburg's and light-blue eyes that had what you might call a merry twinkle; and Mr. Henry's Cupid's-bow mouth wore an expression of amiability that Jim Briscoe had never seen it lose.

In spite of this jolly, though humdrum, exterior, Jim Briscoe had admired Mr. Henry from the very first moment they had met at the beginning of the war. Mr. Henry knew everything worth knowing about their subject. Instead of dying unexpectedly or developing digestive disturbances like some others high up in the agency, years of experience had mellowed him, and his remarkably broad understanding of people had finally developed into something that was a keen comprehension of human failings.

"If there is one thing we all must learn, Jim," Mr. Henry had said the last time Jim Briscoe had seen him, "it is not to be tense. Keep in mind the end result, and don't worry too much about the middle, except as regards women. Don't trust any of them when you're on a problem, particularly like the one on which you're working. Do you recall what Pope said?"

"Yes," Jim Briscoe had answered. "'Ev'ry woman is at heart a rake'—is that what you're thinking of?"

When Mr. Henry nodded, he looked like a teacher applauding the recitation of a favorite pupil, and Jim Briscoe could not help being flattered. Once, like other novices in the agency, Jim Briscoe had thought of Mr. Henry as being only another elderly authority on intelligence evaluation—until Mr. Henry had given him a lesson on strangulation with piano wire. Mr. Henry's technique had seemed considerably superior to that of an instructor at the secret installation who had been taught in Burma and Tokyo.

Mr. Henry had sighed and lighted his pipe. While in the Bureau he had never allowed anyone under him to use tobacco except when necessary for cover purposes, because it slowed the reflexes

and could not help but leave traces, and never under any circumstances to use a pipe.

"I do enjoy this," Mr. Henry said. "You must try a pipe, Jim, if the
time ever comes when circumstances permit you. Personally, I have
never greatly admired the ideas of any poet regarding women. The
thing that makes any woman a problem in our work are her violent
loyalties. Hers are much more emotional than those of the
average man, with a more personal connotation. She can be
loyal at any given time both to one man and to some other
man's beliefs."

Mr. Henry tamped down the tobacco in his pipe and lighted it
again, and Jim remembered his having said once that you could
always tell a pipe smoker from the number of matches he left
behind him.

"When you are in the field, always have the greatest reservation
about any woman you may meet. No matter if you are sure you
understand her, there's the danger of your mistaking her loyalty. I
am still a believer in the adage that a woman's place is in the home."

"I check with everything you say," Jim Briscoe said.

The corners of Mr. Henry's mouth tilted downward, but he still
gave the impression of smiling.

"Now, Jim," he said, "you must not be personally bitter. You see
your boy now and then, don't you?"

"Oh, yes, every now and then," Jim Briscoe said. "Helen is always
glad to have me see him."

"Well, he must be quite a little shaver by now," Mr. Henry said.
"Let's see, ten years if he's a day, isn't he?"

"That's right," Jim Briscoe answered, "he's ten and quite a boy."

"Let's see," Mr. Henry said, "what is it that Helen's present
husband does?"

"As a matter of fact, he's a dentist," Jim Briscoe said.

Mr. Henry laughed.

"Well," he said, "please forgive my little joke. His occupation is
more boring than yours is Jim."

Whatever reservations Jim Briscoe might have regarding the
British, he had never lost his admiration for what one might call
their flag-carrying capacities. There was no doubt the plane was
British the moment they were aloft.

The flight steward in his monkey jacket, had developed a new,
uncompromising cheerfulness, and the complexions of the two
stewardesses looked fresher. The passengers were already passengers, to be tended and preserved with kindness; they weren't

playmates, as they would have been on an American ship, any more than the stewardesses were hostesses.

The plane would level off at 18,000 feet, dinner would be served in one hour. The lounge bar would be opened in half an hour. In a very few minutes passengers would be free to move about; in the meanwhile they would receive instructions on what must be done in case of a forced landing on the water.

There was less joviality about these instructions, less feverish effort to stave off reality, than there would have been on an American ship. The steward demonstrated briskly and accurately the fitting and inflation of a Mae West life jacket, and he took pains to point out the flashlight with which one might signal at night and the whistle that one could blow in the daytime in case one needed assistance. Jim Briscoe noticed that Miss Edith Olmstead gave the talk such undivided attention that he was sure she could not have heard it before.

"If we have to ditch—" she said. "That's what you say if a plane has to land on the ocean, isn't it?"

"Why, yes," Jim Briscoe answered, "that's one way of putting it."

"If we have to ditch," she said, "how long will the plane float?"

As far as he could tell from her voice, she was not apprehensive but only academically curious. In this respect, he was thinking, she was a typical American girl of her generation, so sure of herself that she was incapable of envisaging ugly possibilities.

"Not more than a minute or two," Jim Briscoe said, "and the chances are somewhere around half a minute, but don't let it spoil your trip."

Miss Olmstead laughed easily, and he was faintly surprised at the quality of her laughter.

"Oh, things like that don't worry me," she said. "I only like to know what's in front of me; I don't like things that are hidden. Do you feel that way?"

"Yes, I do," Jim Briscoe said. Their glances met, and he was impressed again by the wide intentness of her eyes.

"How do you know so much about planes?" she asked. "How long they float and things like that."

Jim Briscoe weighed what he was to answer quickly, because any long pause would have been suspicious.

"Oh," he said, "I've been in airplanes a lot since nineteen forty-one."

"Did you ever land on the water?"

"Yes," Jim Briscoe answered, "but it was the Pacific, nice warm water. I was in the Marines at the time."

She did not speak when he paused. She was a nice girl and she must have known that she was asking too many questions.

"You know, I should have introduced myself long ago," Jim Briscoe said. "My name's Briscoe, Jim Briscoe. I'm just going over to London for the ride."

"My name's Edith Olmstead," she answered. "Over for the ride too, but I hope to end up with some friends in Rome."

Jim Briscoe smiled, and his smile was completely genuine. "I wish I could see Rome this time," he said, "but it's going to be nice to look at London now that some of the austerity has worn off. Let's see, you didn't have a brother named Bill Olmstead back at Princeton in nineteen forty?" He knew very well there had been no Bill Olmstead at Princeton, but still it was a good question.

"No," she said, "that must be some other Olmstead."

"I used to see him on the freshman football squad at Princeton," Jim Briscoe said. "I've sort of lost touch with Bill."

"Do you know we have a very important person with us on the plane?" Miss Olmstead asked.

"Why, no," Jim Briscoe said. "Who is it? I didn't know we were carrying any VIPs."

"It's Dr. Francis Barnwelder, the atomic scientist," Miss Olmstead said. "He's that heavy-looking, bald-headed man, five seats up on the left."

"Is he really?" Jim Briscoe said. "How did you happen to find out?"

Her answer was so prompt that he could not doubt its genuineness.

"Why, everyone knows," she said. "All the passengers were talking about him. Didn't you hear them?"

"I was pretty busy," he said, before he could check himself.

"You didn't look busy," she said, and she laughed. It was a natural and friendly laugh. "You were just staring wishfully into the window of the drug store."

"Well, well," Jim Briscoe said, hoping his own laugh sounded as carefree. "I didn't see you hanging around the drug store."

"Of course you didn't," she said. "I was looking at you from the bar."

"Oh," he said, "the bar." Nothing could have been more natural than her explanation. It annoyed him that he had momentarily forgotten that the bar at Idlewild airport, with its plate-glass windows, was as public as a goldfish bowl and that it was as easy to look out through those windows as it was to look in. "Your mentioning it brings up an interesting association of ideas. How would it be if we went to the smoking lounge and tried to induce the steward to give us something, even if the half hour isn't up?"

"I'd love to go and try," she said "but I don't believe we'll get anywhere. The British are always so incorruptible."

This was another remark of hers that he thought, for a second, was unduly precocious; but then if she had gone to school in Switzerland, she had more than likely spent vacationtime in England.

"We can only try," he said, "and hope. Occasionally one of them does break down."

In fact, the bar steward did break down, and there was every reason he should. His name was Jameson, and the C.I.D., at the request of the Foreign Office, had assigned him especially for the trip.

Once they were in the smoking lounge, Jim Briscoe felt entirely at ease. The first minutes of breaking into an acquaintance with either a man or woman were always difficult, but now he could relax and allow himself to appreciate the charm of Miss Olmstead. It was most agreeable to discover that she cared as much as he did for early Gothic architecture, especially the eccentricities of its ornamental sculpture as exemplified by the gargoyles of Notre Dame and Chartres.

It was true that he had a moment's fear that he might not like her when she said that she simply adored Chartres. In his previous experience women who said they adored Chartres knew nothing whatever about that great cathedral, but it was different with Miss Olmstead. As they talked, he wished for a few stabbing seconds that he was not always dealing with uncertainties. Could it be possible, he thought, that she knew that he specialized in Gothic architecture and that she had taken some intensive lessons in order to appear agreeable to him? Such a possibility was worth considering. Yet as far as Jim Briscoe could tell, Miss Olmstead's enthusiasm was genuine, with a depth derived from much more than superficial reading. He was pleased when she expressed admiration at the extent of his knowledge, although he was habitually careful to discount flattery.

"I never dreamed you'd know so much about this," she said.

Jim Briscoe smiled and offered her a cigarette. He was carrying a handsome gold cigarette case inscribed with his name as a winner of a squash-racquets tournament in 1946. He had never won such a tournament, but small mementos always helped cover.

"I don't feel very flattered that you should be surprised," he said. "Why shouldn't I know a little about medieval sculpture?"

"Oh, no reason," she answered, "except that you look more like the outdoor, athletic type, someone who wins prizes like your cigarette case."

"Oh, that," Jim Briscoe said. "I shouldn't have brought it along except that people very seldom notice the inscription."

"It's a bad habit of mine," she said. "I'm always noticing small, useless details."

"I wouldn't blame myself for that if I were you," Jim Briscoe said. "It can be a useful habit sometimes."

"I wish I'd never found it so," she said. "Everybody only thinks of me as being inquisitive—just the way I am about you now. For instance, I'm terribly anxious to know when you first saw a gargoyle."

There was no doubt at all that Miss Olmstead was a very pretty girl with a genuine and lively sense of humor. It was a real delight to watch her eyes narrow when she smiled. Her lips were conventionally red, but with very little lipstick, or else it was not the kind that came off on a cigarette and not the kind that stained her teeth when she laughed.

There was a little powder on her nose, but only a very little. He was thinking that her complexion was very clear, with a sort of Old World clarity. All at once she reminded him of a White Russian girl whom he had met once in Shanghai, who had had that same kind of complexion—delicate, pink and white, slightly reminiscent of a shepherdess done in French porcelain. Miss Olmstead had been to school in Switzerland, had lived for at least a few years in that clear, neutral atmosphere, and was doubtless an enthusiast at winter sports. He could draw a mental picture of her on skis, poised and beautiful. He could see her smiling on a mountaintop, full of the joy of living, anticipating the breathlessness of swift descent.

"I'm not embarrassed by your question about gargoyles," he said. "I first saw one when I was about eight years old." His mind worked smoothly, and the artificial past under which he traveled became almost genuine to him. "It happened I was residing with my parents at Great Neck, Long Island, and I saw a picture in a school geography—the one of the lad brooding over Paris from the roof of Notre Dame. He must have appealed to my emotions rather than my reason, because I couldn't get his face out of my mind, and I never have been able to since. I am still fascinated by the mental climate that made people think up gargoyles."

"Would you like to have lived then rather than now?" she asked.

"Oh no," he said. "I don't really think so. Would you?"

"Things might have been simpler in some ways," she said. "But

I'd rather be living now. I don't want to miss any of the show. By the way, why don't we have another drink?"

"That's a very good idea," Jim Briscoe said, and he waved to the bar steward. "Two double whiskeys, please."

Alcohol always demanded deep thought in his profession and kept cropping up as the unknown quantity in almost any problem. Aside from those questions of knockout drops and shifted glasses, which, though tiresome, were subtler than most amateurs realized, there was always the question of how much to drink and of what one's tolerance to alcohol might be at any given moment.

Was it ever worth attempting to get someone tipsy? On the whole he doubted it. Yet, on the other hand, he often thought of Sorgi, in Japan, for whose memory he had an inordinate respect. Sorgi had never refused a drink—or two or three or four, and this was surely one of the reasons why he had so long escaped suspicion. It was dangerous to refuse a drink, and even more dangerous not to finish if you accepted one.

"Doubles?" Miss Olmstead said.

"It was only a whim of mine," Jim Briscoe answered. "You don't have to take all of yours if you don't want it."

"What else is there to do?" she asked. "Beside, I always like to finish what I start. I suppose we'll be having dinner soon."

Jim Briscoe glanced at his wrist watch and saw that Miss Olmstead was looking at it too. It was a durable, practical time-piece, made of stainless steel and fastened on his wrist with an extra-heavy pigskin strap.

"Yes," he said, "they'll feed us before we get to Gander."

He was trying to estimate the amount of daylight there might be left at Gander. Being summer at that latitude, it would not be dusk till nearly ten o'clock, and he preferred daylight, under the circumstances.

"You must do a lot of hunting and fishing and things like that when you're not thinking about gargoyles."

In that moment's abstraction he had almost forgotten Miss Olmstead.

"Well, well," he said, "what makes you say that?"

"You've an outdoor type of watch with a Swiss movement," she said, "and I happen to know it's quite expensive, because my father has one like it."

He should have known far better than to have worn the watch, but then Miss Olmstead had given him an interesting piece of information. Watches like his seldom cropped up in real-estate-and-insurance circles.

A minute later the passengers were told that dinner was being served. In the second that he waited for Miss Olmstead to reach her chair by the window, Jim Briscoe was able to examine his brief case, which he had left so carelessly beneath his seat. It had not been touched. He could not tell whether he was glad or sorry—but then it was a very obvious business, monkeying with anyone's brief case.

Miss Olmstead had the gift of knowing when to talk and when to be quiet. As soon as dinner was over, she took from her overnight bag a pocket edition of *The Portrait of a Lady*, by Henry James, and put on a pair of horn-rimmed spectacles. She was a girl who was able to make glasses seem not so much like a necessary help to eyesight as an interesting accessory that adorned her personality.

Jim Briscoe, in turn, opened his overnight bag and took out a copy of Plato's *Republic*. If one's room were searched, it was hard to believe that there could be anything deeply sinister about anyone who read Plato; and almost the same, now that he came to think of it, might be said of Henry James.

With a trained observation it was impossible not to learn a good deal about the character of a stranger over a period of hours. Yet, in the end, the sum of all conclusions amounted only to something you might term personality, and personality often defied exact analysis.

The more he saw of Miss Olmstead, the more interested he became in her, in a purely professional way. He could detect no guile about her, none of that confidence in personal charm that marked many women he had encountered professionally. On the contrary, her naturalness was what appealed to him, and her lack of hesitation.

He could see that he and she were much alike, in that they both had an acute enjoyment of the present; but the motives for his enjoyment he was sure, were quite different from hers. Disillusion and suspicion had never touched her, and perhaps never would. She enjoyed the present primarily because she was happy and because she loved life.

She was happy when she put away her book and said that she was going to take a nap for a while, that she had been up quite late the previous night with farewell parties. There must have been several men who were in love with her and who must have been sorry to have her make the trip alone.

She looked happy when she was asleep, which was rare according to Jim Briscoe's experience, because one's guard dropped with sleep, and if anyone was as happy as Miss Olmstead, she had nothing to conceal. Her lips wore the trace of a half smile, and she only seemed to be waiting to be awake again. When they were a few minutes away from Gander, he touched her arm softly, and she passed immediately from sleep to wakefulness without the least confusion.

He was very glad that Miss Olmstead was not with him when someone took a shot at him at Gander, but then, perhaps, her presence would have averted it.

It was after the passengers had had coffee at Gander, he remembered, that he had grown tired of the large waiting room. In fact, the room had always made him nervous, since, like all other airport lounges, it was one of the most unstable places in the world. People who passed through it did so without interest and with no desire to remain, and most of them wished never to see the place again and possibly never would. Comfortable chairs with airfoam cushions, snack bars, real bars, and posters illustrating distant and exotic spots did little or nothing to alleviate this feeling of temporariness.

"Would you like to go outside?" he said to Miss Olmstead. "I think we could get permission, and it's the last chance we'll have to walk on the North American continent for a while."

"If it's all the same to you," she said, "I'd rather sit on the North American continent right here. I wish you'd put on an overcoat."

"Oh, no," he said, "it isn't as cold as that. Watch it for me, will you?" And he left his overcoat on the chair beside her.

"Come back soon," she said, "and tell me if you see an Eskimo or anything."

When they had arrived at Gander it had been windy; now the wind was dropping with the sun. The sun, he remembered, was setting behind a massive bank of gray and purple clouds, and in spite of the activity of that huge airport the cold remoteness of northern North America closed around the area, and nothing had changed the wilderness around it.

He knew the place rather well, and consequently he strolled rather aimlessly past some of the hangars, trying to remember how Gander had looked when he had seen it first, in wartime.

Of course he should have remembered his old lesson of never being too confident of anything, but then perhaps he had not entirely forgotten. Some planes were warming up in front of the hangars, and there would be no need for a silencer, he was thinking, on any gun at Gander. Living as he had, it was only natural that he should have developed an acute sense of apprehension. He had just come to the corner of a Nissen hut behind one of the hangars when he was aware that someone was behind him.

266

He was so certain of what was going to happen that he reached instinctively beneath his tweed jacket before he recalled that he had put his gun in his val-pack because he did not believe in being armed aboard a plane. His right hand was still beneath his jacket as he turned to see a man behind him, dressed in a mechanic's coveralls.

The light was too dim to reveal much of his features. What was important was that he held a gun and obviously had been bracing himself to shoot, at the very instant that Jim Briscoe's reaching for a weapon must have been disturbing.

At any rate, even a good shot is apt to snatch at the trigger when started. It was a miss, and Jim Briscoe's mind was working by that time. First, he let his right hand drop to his side, and then he let his knees buckle until he was on all fours and still sinking toward the ground.

He doubted there would be a second shot if he gave the impression of being hit, and his line of thinking was right. The man stood for a second, watching him, and then he pocketed his pistol and ran.

Jim Briscoe was on his feet the same instant, sprinting in the opposite direction. It had been highly foolish of him to have left the waiting room, and he returned as rapidly as possible. Miss Olmstead must have been watching the door, because she waved at him as he entered.

"I'm awfully glad you're back," she said.

"So am I," Jim Briscoe told her. "Delighted."

"There wasn't much to see out there anyway, was there?" she asked.

The plane, with its transatlantic load of fuel, was so sluggish on the take-off that he sighed with relief when they were over the water. He was thinking that Miss Olmstead was fortunate not to know the difficulties of leaving the ground.

"It must be nice to have friends in a place like Gander," she said. "I mean, people who let you in and out of the waiting room. It must help to break the journey."

Jim Briscoe laughed easily.

"I saw a good deal of the Air Transport Command in the war," he said. "A few of the old crowd are still around at Gander."

"Was the man you were talking with at the door one of the old crowd?" she asked. "I mean when you came back from your walk?"

Jim Briscoe turned toward her slowly. "Oh, yes," he said, "I met him out in the Pacific. It's funny, if you keep running all over the place, the way you do in a war, how many people you get to know rather well for a day or two, and then you forget all about them."

"He seemed very interested in what you were saying," Miss Olmstead said.

"Well," Jim Briscoe told her, "you can't help being interested when you catch up with someone, and now I'm going to make a suggestion."

He took a small vial from his vest pocket and shook two yellow capsules from it.

"I always find on these trips that you feel better in the morning if you take some sort of sedative. They won't do you any harm; would you like one?"

"Oh, dear," she said, "I wanted to find out more about you, and now you want to make me go to sleep."

"It's for your own good," Jim Briscoe said, "and besides, I hope you'll let me see you in London."

"You never can tell what people are like when they stop traveling," she said. "I don't know what you'll be like in London." She hesitated for a second and then took one of the capsules. "But I suppose it is a good idea."

It was a good idea, because there were several problems that he wanted to think through before he reached London. Nevertheless, he talked to her for another forty minutes, until she said she was really feeling sleepy. Then he called the stewardess, who gave her a pillow and a blanket. The bright lights had been turned down, and most of the passengers were asleep already, but a few were still reading. Mrs. Barnwelder was asleep, but Dr. Barnwelder was reading.

When Jim Briscoe rose and walked down the aisle to the washroom, he stumbled, and steadied himself by putting his hand on Dr. Barnwelder's shoulder. There was no doubt that Dr. Barnwelder was not high-strung. There was no galvanic tensing of the muscles, no guilty start, no irascibility or annoyance. Dr. Barnwelder simply looked up from his book, amiably, through his rimless spectacles.

"I beg your pardon, sir," Jim Briscoe said.

"It is quite all right," Dr. Barnwelder answered, "quite all right."

His voice was low and Midwestern, and it sounded more agreeable than it had on the recordings to which Jim Briscoe had listened.

"I never can seem to get my air legs," Jim Briscoe said.

A few minutes later Jim Briscoe walked to the bar compartment, and Jameson, the steward, smiled at him.

"Nightcap, sir?" he asked.

"Yes, thanks," Jim Briscoe said. "I'd appreciate it."

They were alone, and their voices did not rise above the drumming of the motors. There was no reason why he should not be seen exchanging a few words with the bar steward.

"No news from Gander, sir," Jameson said.

"All right," Jim Briscoe answered. "I'm glad he was a nervous shot."

Miss Olmstead, he was glad to observe, was sound asleep. He wished he could be as far removed as she from the problems with which he was coping. There had been a time when he had been delighted with the life he was now leading. As his former wife was no doubt glad to tell anyone, he had not been the sort of person who liked to settle down, and excitements of various kinds had added to his restlessness—but in the end, perhaps enough is always too much.

As of the present, at least, he had had enough of uncertainty, enough of danger, and enough of intellectual puzzles. This did not mean that his nerves were on edge. He was only weary of not being like other people. If there was only some way of taking a few months off, everything might have balanced with everything else, but now he was too much of a professional ever to be an amateur again.

The synchronized sound of the motors formed a reassuring background for Miss Olmstead's sleep. There would never be a better opportunity to go through her handbag and overnight case. He liked to think that what stopped him was not his conscience but his reason. In reviewing everything he had learned about Miss Olmstead, he could find nothing sinister and no quality of doubt that could counterbalance the trouble that would arise if some passenger should see him going through her purse—a remote contingency but still a possibility.

He adjusted his seat to a more comfortable angle and closed his eyes. His idea of lurching against Dr. Barnwelder, though obvious, had not been a bad one. Dr. Barnwelder's heavy build had proved that he was certainly the Barnwelder who had played left guard for Leland Stanford in the years just following World War I.

It was strange how an idea could sometimes start almost out of nothing. The whole Barnwelder investigation had actually sprung from nothing more than a nickname, and then only because Jim Briscoe had developed a long memory. On one dull afternoon about a year before, he had been going through transcripts of tapped telephone conversations, on an errand that had nothing to do with Barnwelder or espionage. There was nothing duller than accurately transcribed human conversation and, because of its prolixity and constant repetition, nothing harder on which to concentrate attention. Yet it was repetition that first aroused his attention.

Just when he was wishing that wire tapping could be prohibited, not only as legal evidence but as an investigating device, a word obtruded itself on his attention. The word was "Jumbo," and there was nothing surprising about it when taken by itself. In any sort of underground apparatus, active individuals immediately took the precaution of losing their identities under cover names, and the name Jumbo made as much sense as any of them.

The many references to the thoughts and desires of Jumbo in these tapped conversations indicated that Jumbo was a person of some importance, if Jumbo was the code word for an individual and not a group. It was not Jim Briscoe's task that particular afternoon to break any code. It was only when he was back in his apartment off Dupont Circle, standing under his shower, that he remembered another fact. A year ago he had glanced over the album of a college senior class and under a photograph of a thick-set young man he now recalled that he had read the nickname Jumbo.

It was strange how eccentrically one's mind could travel. It was not until the next morning that he finally remembered the real name of the subject in the class album. It was Dr. Barnwelder, then at Los Alamos, who had been referred to the organization for a routine security check. Of course, there was no reason why Jumbo Barnwelder should be the Jumbo in those tapped wire messages. It was all a shot in the dark, which had taken some time to prove. In fact, even now, the returns were not all in. Five seats and to the left, Jumbo Barnwelder was sound asleep. There was nothing so unpredictable as a scientist. You could never tell what sort of body would produce a magic brain. To look at him, Jumbo Barnwelder looked very stupid, and in some ways perhaps he was.

Jim Briscoe wished that circumstances permitted him to tap Dr. Barnwelder on the shoulder and to offer him a friendly drink. There were a number of things he would have liked to tell Dr. Barnwelder, and Dr. Barnwelder might have been grateful if he could have heard them.

He would like to have told Dr. Barnwelder, for instance, that nothing was going to happen to him, because he was very valuable in many different ways. There was no such thing, he would like to have told Dr. Barnwelder, as complete security in the realms of science and invention. The theory of nuclear fission and the general principles of electronics could not be veiled in secrecy. When any new device was made for peace or war and was distributed in many hands, in a short while it became public. All one could do was establish a certain amount of delay, and this delay was best gained by guarding as few secrets as possible, and these mostly in the category of future plans. There was no secret Dr. Barnwelder knew that was immediately vital. If Dr. Barnwelder could only be apprised of this, how much easier everything would have been for everybody.

If Jim Briscoe could only have said, in a friendly way, "Listen, Jumbo, we don't care a bit about any of the things you are going to tell. If we did, you wouldn't be crossing the Atlantic now. We don't care very much about your loyalty check-up. We've got your number, Jumbo, but we want you back safe and sound and comfortable. All we want to know is with whom you are going to get into communication when you get to London. Is it a Russian named Bjor, who goes under the cover name Max Blenheim? Is Jumbo going to meet Max? That's all we want to know, and if you would only tell, it would save a lot of trouble. We'll be delighted to have you tell anything you want to Bjor. All we want to know is, Do you and Bjor link together?"

It was too bad that the thing should be difficult. The main problem at the present time was to disturb absolutely nothing. Instead of breaking up a spy ring, it was far more valuable to know all about it and let it be. Things had gone so far that the Barnwelder meeting would bring everything into focus, because the Barnwelder meeting would confirm a whole chain of theories.

There was nothing, as Jim Briscoe's old chief used to say, so useful as a well-established, confident spy ring, every link of which one knew. You could feed and deceive a spy ring if you knew the links. If Jumbo met Bjor, this one led into very high echelons. At home it touched the executive personnel of at least two government departments, and in England it extended to the Foreign Office.

It was exasperating to think how delicate the balance was and how quickly a single wrong move would destoy the whole machine. On the one hand, those involved could not have known how far the investigation had gone—or Dr. Barnwelder would never have been flying the ocean. On the other hand, they knew that something was stirring or a .32 caliber bullet would not have whizzed by Jim Briscoe's ear at Gander. It was a safe guess, from the sound, that it was a .32 and not a .45.

271

They must have understood the risks they had taken with that shot at Gander. In one way Jim was deeply sorry for this, and in another way relieved. The shot meant recognition, and if one became too widely known, one's usefulness in the field was very nearly over. The present problem, however, was what he would do when he reached London. Obviously, he could show no interest whatever in Dr. Barnwelder.

Fortunately, this contingency had been reviewed in Washington on the grounds one had to be prepared for all contingencies. Fortunately too, there was another cover for Jim Briscoe. If he was suspected, as he obviously had been, he had another mission, with the papers all prepared. It was amazing how efficient some people were in Washington—sometimes.

Jim Briscoe lifted his brief case from beneath his feet and opened it with cautious fussiness. Then he looked around him suspiciously, to alert anyone who might be watching him. Finally he produced a razor blade, split the heavy leather cover of the brief case, and pulled out two sheets of folded flimsy paper, which he thrust self-consciously into his breast pocket.

He replaced the brief case beneath his seat and after a few minutes pulled the papers from his coat. They were headed *Most Secret* and contained suggestions for a revised liaison between certain British and American intelligence divisions.

Jim Briscoe read the papers for half an hour and then returned them to their place in the slip side of the brief case and fussed with the edge of the leather to conceal the opening. Feeling that he had done all he could under the circumstances, he then took a sleeping pill.

The stewardess awakened him when the plane was letting down for Shannon. He shook his head, yawned, and reached for his brief case. Someone had been at the edge of it. Someone had read the *Most Secret* papers.

Jim Briscoe was very much relieved.

A great weight was lifted from Jim Briscoe when the plane taxied to a stop at London Airport. He felt as he remembered feeling as a boy, at home in the attic on a rainy day, standing dry and safe and listening to the rain beat on the roof.

It was wonderful to know that the papers had been read; it was unfortunate, of course, that he had not spotted who had read them, but one could not do everything. Already he had a feeling of being safer than he had been for many hours. The pressure was gone, and he no longer had the sensation of being watched. From now on his British opposite numbers would take over the problem of Dr. Barnwelder.

As he waited with his fellow travelers while the passenger list was examined, he found himself guessing who had been at the brief case. Sometimes one had a hunch about such things, but his reappraisal of the passengers told him nothing. Everyone was glad to be off the plane, and conversation had the cheerful quality of a farewell dinner on shipboard. Miss Olmstead was like an old friend now that the flight was over. She seemed to have accepted him completely during the last few hours.

"I've never met many Princeton men," she told him. "Princetonians never seemed to be much interested in girls from Bucknell."

It was wonderful not to have to listen with strained attention any longer. The British were taking over. He could see his opposite number, Mark Cheltman, at the passport control. Good old Mark, he was thinking. Though Mark looked thin and almost anemic, he was an almost perfect street fighter, as Jim Briscoe had once learned in New Delhi.

"I was crazy to go to Bryn Mawr after school in Switzerland," Miss Olmstead was saying, "but father said Bryn Mawr was based on unreal values."

"Doctor and Mrs. Barnwelder, please," they called from passport control.

He watched Dr. Barnwelder move toward the counter. He thought his step was brisker and more youthful than it had been at Idlewild, and Dr. Barnwelder did not seem to be having as much trouble with his brief case and his overnight satchel. Jim Briscoe had a thought that the relief he experienced was being shared by Dr. Barnwelder.

Jim Briscoe turned to Miss Olmstead. It occurred to him, as things had developed, that he would have much more time on his hands than he had expected. In fact, except for a daily call at a building in the vicinity of Piccadilly, there would be nothing for him to do except be the amiable playboy he represented. He could only wait on the side lines now until the Barnwelder matter resolved itself. The British were carrying the ball.

"I don't know how well you know London," he said to the girl, "but if I can be of any help to you, please let me know. I've been around here a good deal myself, and you can always find me at Claridges. If you have nothing better to do, I could take you out to dinner, and we might do a little night clubbing."

"I'd love to," Miss Olmstead said. "It's awfully kind of you. I've only been in London for a day or two with father on the way to Switzerland. What about tonight? I'm staying at the Savoy."

"Good," Jim Briscoe said. "We might dine at the Caprice. Suppose I call for you at eight."

They called his name, and he held out his hand. Her handclasp was firm and strong. Their eyes met for a minute, and they both smiled. He wondered who in Bryn Mawr had told her about the Savoy, or if it was where she had stayed on her way to school in Switzerland. The clip with the small diamonds did not wholly check with the Savoy.

In the last ten years Jim Briscoe, like nearly everyone in his organization, had worked very closely with the British. On the whole the *rapprochement* had been rewarding. Yet he was never quite sure that he understood his opposite numbers, because there was a difference of approach and cleavages of viewpoint that became apparent when you least expected them.

There was a complacency about the British that was exasperating sometimes. They knew that they had the best intelligence service in the world. They might not have all the newfangled gadgets of the Americans—the cameras, the business-machine filing systems, the electronic devices, and all that sort of thing—but they had the best intelligence service in the world.

Jim Briscoe had always found them kind, cordial, and patient. He was enormously pleased on the few occasions when he found that he was right and they were wrong. He was secretly highly gratified when Sir Godfrey himself, who was the head of the division and who was sometimes facetiously called Sir God by the younger men, once told him that he had promise and ability.

"Of course, my dear boy," Sir Godfrey had said, "like all your countrymen you are lacking in sound training and discipline, and you have that cocksure conceit of all you Americans. Still, you are willing to learn. In fact, had you been born British, you might very well have been one of us—given time."

In the last few years Jim Briscoe had developed a warm affection for Sir Godfrey's book-lined offices off Piccadilly. The rugs were worn, but the furniture was solid, indestructible Victorian. Except for broken glass and a few fallen ceilings, the place had carried on well through the blitz. The elevator, as usual, was out of order.

"It's been out of order for the last eight months," Mark Cheltman said. "No spare parts, you know, because of its antiquity. Besides, Sir God says that stair climbing is good for wind and limb. I say, you *are* in good condition, aren't you?"

"I can still run just as fast as we did up those stairs in Damascus," Jim Briscoe said, "and that was really running."

"Yes," Mark said, "that was a good show, but one needn't run so fast right now, need one?"

Sir Godfrey was in his office, and the whole thing closely resembled Agatha Christie, but then Agatha Christie had doubtless seen many places like Sir Godfrey's office. Sir Godfrey was wearing striped trousers and a brown tweed jacket. A bowler hat and a lead-headed cane hung on the hatrack behind his desk. He was thin like Mark Cheltman; his close-clipped mustache was gray, and so was his carefully combed hair. He still had the posture of a former Sandhurst man. He had been hit in the leg at Vimy Ridge in World War I, but his limp was hardly noticeable as he walked around the desk and shook hands with Jim Briscoe.

"What is it you are carrying wrapped up in paper?" Sir Godfrey asked.

"It's my brief case, sir," Jim Briscoe said. "I think it ought to be tested for fingerprints."

"Indeed," Sir Godfrey said. "Mark, give it to Hawkins. You've no fellow in Washington as good as our Hawkins, Briscoe. That's a well-cut suit of yours, by the way, but arrogantly American."

"I'm glad you noticed it, sir," Jim Briscoe said. "It's meant to be that way. You see, for this trip I'm playboy Briscoe, spending my dollars at Claridges."

"Scarcely any disguise needed for that, eh?" Sir Godfrey said. "Gad, if I could only be fifty again and be there with you at Claridges. Did you have a pleasant crossing?"

"It wasn't so bad, sir," Jim Briscoe said, "but there was what you would call a bit of a flap at Gander. I was telling Mark about it, and he thought we'd better take it up with you."

"Well, sit down," Sir Godfrey said, "and let me fill my pipe." Unlike Mr. Henry back in Washington, Sir Godfrey believed in pipe smoking.

Jim Briscoe was so familiar with the technique of making a concise but accurate verbal report that he was able, while he was speaking, to admire the care with which Sir Godfrey followed every word. You could see everything in his mind come together as he listened. He smoked for fully half a minute after Jim Briscoe had finished, but his silence was not embarrassing.

"A pity, isn't it, that they spotted you," Sir Godfrey said, "but they do have some rather clever chaps. I gather, don't you, that you were fingered, as you Americans love to put it, by someone on the plane and not by telephone from the States or anything of that sort?"

"Yes, sir," Jim Briscoe answered. "I believe that's the way it was."

275

"Yet you were not aware of anything out of line?" Sir Godfrey said.

"Not until the last few seconds," Jim Briscoe said, "and then it was instinctive."

"Instinct does save lives," Sir Godfrey said. "That bit about the brief case was rather good, but it was a pity that you were asleep when the play for it was made."

"I was afraid it wouldn't be touched," Jim Briscoe said, "if I hadn't been honestly asleep. There's nothing easier to spot than someone faking sleep."

Sir Godfrey looked slightly annoyed.

"I know," he said, "I know. I only say it is a pity. But whoever the chap was, he managed things very neatly."

"Yes, sir," Jim Briscoe said.

Sir Godfrey nodded and their eyes met.

"A very artistic job, what? I know of only one school, aside from a little place of our own, where such work is taught so carefully."

"You mean Moscow, sir?" Jim Briscoe said.

Sir Godfrey smiled and nodded.

"That Slavic mind—whoever did it was not a one-term student. But you didn't see anyone Slavic on the plane?"

"No, sir," Jim Briscoe said, "and the passengers were screened before we left. But we'd better ask them to check in Washington."

"Yes," Sir Godfrey said, "send word will you Cheltman? Well, here comes Hawkins again."

All the fingerprint experts whom Jim Briscoe had ever known developed similar mannerisms as they rose to the top of their profession. They were all neat, fussy, and studious, and when they talked, they often made small gestures as though they were running through a card index. The light from the dusty windows behind Sir Godfrey's desk shone on the heavy lenses of Mr. Hawkins' spectacles. He was holding Jim Briscoe's brief case deferentially, and when he spoke he had a slight difficulty with his h's.

"No prints on the case, Sir Godfrey," he said, "except where Mr. Briscoe held it by the handle."

"Could you advance the opinion, Hawkins," he asked, "whether or not gloves were worn?"

"Not gloves, I think, Sir Godfrey," Hawkins answered. "In my opinion the brief case was wiped with a cotton hand towel. I came across several cotton fibers."

"What I thought," Sir Godfrey said, "the washroom. Mark, spring to action, please, and find out from Jameson and the rest which passenger, if any, entered the washroom with a brief case during the flight from Gander."

"Mr. Briscoe inquired while he was still air-borne," Mark Cheltman said. "No one was seen carrying a brief case into the washroom, but I'm afraid the concentration was on Barnwelder and not the washroom, Sir Godfrey."

"Oh, dear me," Sir Godfrey said. "Let me give a word of advice to you young men. Never, never, neglect a washroom. It is always a key position. Think of the material that has been flushed down toilets!"

Jim Briscoe and Mark Cheltman both nodded gravely, and Jim Briscoe blamed himself for not having cautioned Jameson. But then Jameson had not been entirely under his orders.

"The papers inside the cover," Sir Godfrey said. "I trust they were properly prepared, Briscoe?"

For the first time in the interview Jim Briscoe felt a twinge of annoyance.

"When they were inserted, Sir Godfrey," he said, "the papers had only my prints of course."

"There was another print on the papers besides Mr. Briscoe's," Hawkins said, "In very bad condition, and partially effaced."

Sir Godfrey picked up his pipe and relighted it.

"You see," he said, "no gloves. I have always maintained that gloves are clumsy. Well, who was it, Hawkins? Barnwelder?"

"No, sir," Hawkins answered, "it's nowhere in our files."

"Dear me," Sir Godfrey said. "Would you care to venture a guess whether it was a man's or a woman's?"

"There's too little left for any conclusion, Sir Godfrey," Hawkins said.

"I suppose so," Sir Godfrey answered. "Well, thank you, and send a wirephoto to Washington at once, won't you Hawkins?"

After Hawkins was gone and the door was closed, Sir Godfrey drummed his fingers softly on the desk.

"I think on the whole it was a good show, Briscoe," he said. "Where do you suggest we go from here?"

"Well, sir," Jim Briscoe said, "it looks as though they might be reassured, but your people will have to carry the ball from now on in, Sir Godfrey."

There was another silence, and Sir Godfrey looked worried.

"Barnwelder's being covered, of course," he said, "but this chap he may get in contact with, that's the difficulty."

"I'm afraid I don't quite follow you, sir," Jim Briscoe said.

Sir Godfrey sighed.

"I gather the reason we are all here," he said, "is because you people in Washington have a feeling that the man traveling under the name Max Blenheim is a Russian scientist named Bjor."

"Yes," Jim Briscoe said, "and I'm sure you follow our line of reasoning, sir. If Barnwelder is delivering information, obviously the only person capable of understanding it would be Bjor."

Sir Godfrey nodded and sighed again. "Naturally, we have quite a bit in the files about the fellow," he said. "He seems to be most retiring. They never put him into the game except at a big moment, do they? I understand that Bjor has been pointed out to you and that you can recognize him."

"Yes, sir," Jim Briscoe said. "I have seen him and I admit he is rather inconspicuous. He was pointed out to me at Dumbarton Oaks when there was more sweetness and light than at present."

"Dear me, Dumbarton Oaks," Sir Godfrey said. "And you think you could recognize him still?"

"I don't forget people like Bjor," Jim Briscoe told him.

"Oh, dear me," Sir Godfrey said. "I wish he hadn't been so retiring, because you're the only one who can spot him as far as I know."

"Why, there's Hall right in your office, Sir Godfrey," Jim Briscoe said. "Hall knows him better than I do. Hall saw Bjor when he was at Geneva two years ago."

"Yes," Sir Godfrey said, "that's just it."

He paused, seemingly waiting for Jim Briscoe to ask his meaning, but Jim Briscoe had gathered what the difficulty was from watching Sir Godfrey's expression.

"You see, Hall, poor chap, isn't here now," Sir Godfrey said. "He disappeared last week. He was going to meet me here for tea. He never came—no word, no sign."

"They got him, did they?" Jim Briscoe said.

"I fear so," Sir Godfrey answered. "Alive too, I suspect. Frankly, I've been somewhat worried about Hall's time reactions. They were too slow for a man his age. I'm very much afraid they will make him talk."

Jim Briscoe nodded. It was ridiculous to think anyone could remain silent under certain circumstances.

"Poor Hall," Sir Godfrey said. "There's only one consolation; I'm almost certain that he never knew you knew Bjor, and Dumbarton Oaks lies in another era. I suppose we ought to face the future. We'll cover Barnwelder, but when he comes in contact with someone we think is Bjor, you'll have to be with us to make the identification."

"You'd better save me until the last moment, then," Jim Briscoe said. "The chief wanted me to say especially that we are counting on not upsetting their apparatus."

"Oh, quite," Sir Godfrey said. "And now, since poor Hall isn't with us, how about a spot of tea?"

It was Jim Briscoe's old chief, Mr. Henry, who had pointed out Bjor at Dumbarton Oaks, and Jim Briscoe remembered the occasion very clearly. Mr. Henry had handed him a note, and he had glanced at it carelessly in the way Mr. Henry had taught him, folded it, and put it in his pocket.

Never leave any paper of any sort around, Mr. Henry had always said, and never doodle on scratch pads. Keep papers in your pockets, and after anything like the Dumbarton show, go to the office and burn them personally. Jim Briscoe could still remember Mr. Henry's note.

"Observe carefully man three from right of military attaché," Mr. Henry had written. "Features may be useful future reference."

That was how Jim Briscoe first saw the man called Bjor, who, intercepts showed, worked under the cover name Max Blenheim. He had seldom seen Mr. Henry evince as much interest, and later when they were safe in the office, Mr. Henry had been unusually loquacious.

"Frankly, I was surprised to see him there," Mr. Henry had said. "He's the best man they have in the NKVD. There's a rumor he's the one who got our proximity fuse, and it might very well be so. You'd better read his dossier; he plays around with all the physicists."

"How did you happen to recognize him, sir?" Jim Briscoe asked.

"Oh," Mr. Henry said, "I saw him once when I was in Moscow with the Dean party. We didn't speak, of course. He was just in the background at one of those receptions, but I remembered him because he had been pointed out to me previously."

"When was that, sir?" Jim Briscoe asked.

"Oh," Mr. Henry said, "that was before the war. He was in the Reading Room of the British Museum. He has a handsome academic face, you know. I don't know how the devil he got there, except that it was about the time the British were trying to negotiate that defense pact. Yes, he was right there in the Reading Room."

It always paid to remember everything Mr. Henry said. Few people were as familiar as he with the contemporary intelligence picture or with its general theory and practice. Although it was not required reading, Jim Briscoe had made a study of Bjor. It was important to know as much as possible of personalities across the fence. He still remembered the appearance and something of the personality of the man Bjor . . .

Sir Godfrey was sipping a second cup of tea.

"Can you describe the fellow for us, just in case—"

Sir Godfrey did not finish the sentence. It was not necessary. He meant, of course, in case something happened to Jim Briscoe.

"Yes, sir," Jim Briscoe said. ""I can tell you how he looked ten years ago, and I don't believe he's changed much."

"Splendid," Sir Godfrey said. "Get out your notebook, Mark."

"His age is now forty-seven," Jim Briscoe said. "Height, five feet eleven; weight about one seventy, and I don't believe he's put on weight—there are not many fat men in the NKVD—black hair like Uncle Joe's as a young man, slightly wavy and not close-cropped, the kind of hair that wouldn't have much gray in it at forty-seven; eyes, gray-blue and a trifle Mongoloid, but not the face. His face doesn't look as much like a potato as many Russian faces. It's on the intellectual side—the type similar to your own, Sir Godfrey.

"Forehead high, marked concavity at temples, eye sockets deep, cheekbones high, jaw long. I can give you approximate figures on a facial diagram. Left incisor gold, but that doesn't mean much for a Russian; complexion pale; cleft in chin; nose long; nostrils small; ears about type A; hands delicate; nails well kept; unusually well dressed for a Russian, but that could change. Have an idea he likes good clothes. You see, he came from an academic family."

"Yes, yes," Sir Godfrey said, "we know his background. And now may I suggest you go to Claridges? Enjoy yourself while you may, Briscoe. It's what I always tell my boys."

Jim Briscoe rose and picked up his raincoat. "There's one thing I've been thinking of," he said.

Sir Godfrey frowned, because he always liked to do the thinking.

"It's occurred to me," Jim Briscoe said, "that Barnwelder may never have met Bjor himself. It may be complicated for them to get together. I have a hunch, sir, where they may meet. It might be well to watch the Reading Room of the British Museum."

"Good gracious, why that?" Sir Godfrey said. It showed how much it paid to remember everything.

"He was seen there once before the war," Jim Briscoe said. "It's a sort of shrine, you know, for Communists. If you remember, Marx and then Lenin used to work in the Reading Room of the British Museum."

It was amusing to remember that his hunch about the British Museum had been correct. You could often guess what an individual might do if you had made a study of his personality, and in the last few months Jim Briscoe had been giving Bjor and Dr. Barnwelder his full attention. It even paid to recall anecdotes like the one about the man in charge of the Reading Room in the British Museum, who had said that a man named Lenin used to come there every day for several years, carrying his luncheon in a paper bag—a quiet, studious man.

"I wonder," the Reading Room director was purported to have said, "whatever finally became of him."

Whenever he came to London, Jim Briscoe, like all Americans had a sense of homecoming. He had seen London under the grim auspices of the blackout, about a year previous to the cross-channel invasion, when he had been flown from Washington on one of his early missions, involving a delicate piece of sabotage that included a parachute drop into France. Though people were briefed for this sort of thing almost daily in the third floor of a Georgian house not far from Berkeley Square, it was all a new experience to Jim Briscoe at the time.

Now, whenever he was in the vicinity of New Bond Street, the memories of that first visit began to crowd back. He could feel the old tensions and old excitements and, he could admit, an undercurrent of fear. Actually, there had been many things deserving of this fear, and he was glad he had not lost the faculty of being afraid.

He had stayed at Claridges for the few days before his party had moved out to an airstrip. Under the circumstances there had been no reason to save money, and because of association, Claridges had always seemed warm and friendly ever since. Whenever he returned, it seemed to him that Claridges welcomed him back with pleasure and surprise.

Things were very different now from the way they had been in the grim days of air alerts. There was no brick wall on the sidewalk protecting the front door, no blackout curtains for the windows, no crowds of uniformed officers, and no restricted menu. Claridges had undergone all the phases of austerity, and now it was itself again.

Nevertheless, the doorman and the interior made him feel as though he were starting out again on a career with which he was now very familiar. The young man in tails who greeted him when he signed his registration card must have received some sort of briefing.

"I'll show you your rooms, Mr. Briscoe," the young man said. "We are going to do our best to make you comfortable."

He had not asked for a suite, because there was always too much to watch in a suite at Claridges, but it was very kind of whoever made the arrangements. His baggage was there already, and a bottle of Scotch, with the compliments of the management. He immediately poured out a drink for Mark Cheltman, who had accompanied him.

"And now we'll ring and get some ice for me and soda from the room waiter," Jim Briscoe said.

Mark Cheltman began to laugh, which surprised Jim Briscoe, because in his opinion Mark had a rudimentary sense of humor.

"You're always leery of waiters, aren't you, since that time in Rio?" Mark said. "Jove, you really hit that chap, didn't you?"? And the knife went right across the room. It jolly near lodged in my thigh, in fact. Don't bother about the waiters or anything, old boy. They're all of them good young chaps who travel with our more important delegations, and don't start poking your nose in the closets. It's all clear, even the air shaft, old boy."

Jim Briscoe had to laugh too. England was always like getting home and at the same time a little different.

"Thanks, Mark," he said, "but I've always looked through my digs, to quote one of your British expressions, myself. It's routine, like brushing one's teeth. You'll excuse me, won't you?"

When the room waiter arrived with ice and soda, Jim Briscoe was still looking at the wiring and turning back the pictures on the wall. Mark Cheltman was amused, but then you never could tell, not even at Claridges.

When Mark Cheltman left an hour later, Jim Briscoe again felt that a weight was lifted from him. There was nothing for him to do until tomorrow forenoon, when he must call again at the offices off Piccadilly. Except for one final moment, the British would be carrying the ball. Jim Briscoe felt almost lonely, until he picked up the foreign-looking telephone from the rosewood writing desk in his sitting room and asked for Miss Edith Olmstead at the Hotel Savoy.

He felt, when he asked, almost the way he had felt when he made a date with a Wren the first time he visited London.

"Hello," Miss Olmstead said. "I was hoping you were going to call me. I've got the loveliest suite. The Savoy is just as fabulous as ever."

You never could tell what someone you met on a boat or a plane would be like upon land, and he wished she had not said "fabulous." Miss Olmstead, like himself, had a suite and this seemed a little fabulous, to use that word again, for the daughter of a real-estate-and-insurance man in Bryn Mawr, Pennsylvania. For just a moment he wondered whether Miss Olmstead too could have been given a suite with the compliments of the management, but he immediately dismissed the thought.

"I hope you can come to dinner tonight and dance afterwards," he said.

"Oh, I'd love to," she told him. "Do please come over as soon as you can. I'm feeling rather lonely. It's always like getting home when you get to London, isn't it? But at the same time it's different."

"Yes," he said, "it's different."

"I always love it," she said, "but at the same time I aways repeat my past here. I feel shy and a little bit afraid."

"Afraid?" he repeated.

He heard her draw in her breath quickly before she laughed.

"Oh, I only mean I was terribly nervous and excited the first time I was in London," she said, "about going to boarding school in Switzerland."

He thought that there was a slight pause before she mentioned boarding school in Switzerland.

"I know the way you feel," he said. "London is a lonely town, even at the Savoy."

Jim Briscoe, like others in his profession, had made his special list of rules for survival, one of which sounded like the advice doctors so often offered to harassed businessmen: Never take your worries home with you from the office.

It was, of course, impossible for him to apply this rule in its entirety, because some part of one's mind was always on watch; but Jim Briscoe had learned to make the best of every opportunity for partial relaxation, and that evening with Miss Omstead was a classic example.

He observed her long enough to be reasonably sure that she had no integral part in the picture with which he was dealing. By the time they were half through dinner at the Caprice, he was almost positive that the girl was exactly what she said she was—the daughter of parents, comfortably well off, in Bryn Mawr, Pennsylvania, a graduate of Bucknell, with honors in the fine arts, who was traveling for a while in Europe and about to visit friends in Rome before she sought a position as a fine-arts instructor in some girls' college.

He was reasonably sure that she would not hold such a position long. If there was not some man who wanted to marry her, someone would come along. His subconscious, which he had learned to trust implicitly, told him that he was no longer in danger. That indescribable feeling of something behind him had disappeared at the exact moment someone had tampered with his brief case.

There was no cause for worry about Miss Olmstead. He could look at her almost in the way he had once looked at other girls when he was young, before the war and before he had ever thought of stepping on a perilous, lonely path.

"You look well in a black tie," she said, "and you would look just as well in tails. I was terribly afraid you wouldn't."

Her remark was unexpected, but he was pleased by her approval. Considerable thought had been given by several people to the exact cut of his evening clothes. Their lines, to keep him in character, were slightly unconventional, but they still displayed basic good taste.

"Some men who look perfectly all right in a business suit look like night-club bouncers when you see them with studs in their shirts," she said.

"Well," Jim Briscoe answered, "some men I know give me that impression no matter what they're wearing."

"You look as though you could throw anyone out of here," she said "but you don't look like a bouncer."

Jim Briscoe laughed. It was the first time in a long while that he had been able to laugh with genuine amusement or that he had been genuinely happy with any girl. She had made him forget, almost, the imponderables that surrounded him.

"I don't want to throw anyone out of anywhere," he said. "I hate people who pick fights."

"Oh," she said, "of course you wouldn't, but I'm sure you'd do all right if someone else did."

"I'd try," Jim Briscoe said.

He was impressed again with the wideness of her eyes. She looked very pretty and young and pleased with life.

"I have the most inquisitive mind," she said. "It always acts up when I'm with someone I especially like. Oh, I'm glad we're having champagne."

"You can be as inquisitive as you want so long as you like me," Jim Briscoe said.

"Of course I like you. All women do, don't they?" she answered.

He had a moment's uneasy memory of his ex-wife and her dentist on the West Coast, and then he thought of his son, safe in a Colorado boarding school.

"Well, no," he said, "not always."

"You're married, of course," she said. "Whenever I begin to like a man, it always turns out he's married."

"I'm not at the moment," he said.

It occurred to him that he had not thought of marrying anyone for a long while, for obvious reasons. But now he had a momentary idea, not serious yet not wholly frivolous, that there could be worse things than being married to someone like the girl across the table.

He thought of a house in the country with dogs and horses, preferably somewhere in Carolina where there was quail shooting. For the first time in a long while he had a sharp feeling of regret that he could not settle down. He knew he would never see much more of Miss Olmstead. There could be no letters, no calls at her house in Bryn Mawr, no following her to Rome, and he was very sorry.

"You're awfully formal, aren't you?" she said. "Do you mind if I call you Jim?"

"Of course," he said. "I can't get over the idea that first names are valuable."

"I think so too. And don't call me Edith," she said. "Just call me E—plain alphabetical E, like something in a code message."

"All right," Jim Briscoe said. "And now if you'd like to dance, we might go to Les Ambassadeurs. It is only a street or two away."

They were just outside the doorway on the Caprice when she put her hand on his arm so insistently that he stood still, although he never liked to be silhouetted against lights.

"Look across the street," she said. "There go Doctor and Mrs. Barnwelder."

She was right about the Barnwelders. They were walking ponderously in the direction of the Ritz. He knew they were being followed, but the job was so professional he could not immediately see who was doing the tailing, and then he remembered that they were not his business any longer.

"Oh," he said, "you mean that atomic scientist? I don't see why you take such an interest in him."

"Why, darling," she said, and he was startled when she called him darling, although he knew the word meant almost nothing in her age group. "You must know by now that I'm interested everything. Don't look so worried. I'm not going to speak to them."

"That's swell," he said. "I flunked physics at Princeton."

"Let's pretend we've always known each other," she said. "I'm getting tired of being curious about you."

The thing to do, Jim Briscoe told himself several times that evening, was to live entirely in the present. The terrace at Les Ambassadeurs had never seemed so pleasant to him. When they arrived, there was still a trace of dusk left in the evening sky. She said she had never been to Less Ambassadeurs, but she seemed perfectly at home in that late Victorian mansion, and she danced beautifully. He had always been fond of dancing. He was glad that he had discarded the idea of carrying a gun, because he could not have done the more complicated steps.

Before midnight she said she would like to see St. Paul's at night. The street lights picked out the devastation of the old city, and he thought of the Temple and the old streets as he had seen them as a boy. They would never be that way again. His caution told him that it was not wise to linger in the vicinity of seed-grown cellar holes, but he still had no premonition of danger. He was sure that he was in the clear that night.

"Oh, dear, it's lovely, and I suppose I should be getting home," Edith Olmstead said.

The lights of the Savoy, after St. Paul's, were unnaturally bright and garish.

"Well," he said, and he held out his hand. "It's been a wonderful evening, E. You've saved me from being very lonely."

"Oh, don't go away just yet," she said. "Wouldn't you like to come up and talk a while—at least long enough to help me stop thinking about Saint Paul's?"

It was curious to find that his inclinations could struggle so intensely with his common sense. Mr. Henry would have said that it was not the thing to do at all, to go upstairs at the Savoy to a strange suite with a girl you had picked up on a transatlantic plane but suddenly he did not care in the least what Mr. Henry might have thought.

"Why, thanks," he said. "I'd like to very much, E."

He had guessed correctly that she would have one of the small river suites. He followed her through the narrow foyer into the sitting-room with only a single sharp glance at the closed bedroom door. Instead of switching on the lights, she stood beside him in front of the broad window that faced the Embankment.

The darkness of the room made him momentarily tense until she put her hand on his arm. They leaned out to look over London, and he thought again how pretty she was.

"Let's sit in the dark for a while and look out at the river," she said.

Professionally, he wished he could examine the room first, and then he felt ashamed of the thought. He put his hand over hers, and the faint light from the foyer and the lights from the Embankment showed her face turned up toward him.

"Yes," he said, "it's nice here in the dark." And he was thinking of what she had said about knowing each other for a long while.

There had only been a few times since his childhood that Jim Briscoe could call wholly happy. Happiness, he had found, was much more difficult to define than melancholy. It was a capricious mood, which one encountered when one least expected it, and he had found it advisable not to explore its sources.

For example, there were few valid reasons for being happy those few days in London. The whole Barnwelder theory had started as his idea, and he could not avoid believing that his reputation depended upon the accuracy of his guessing. Yet now and then, after that evening at the Savoy, he found himself forgetting the problem.

At first this deeply disturbed him, because he had learned the importance of never forgetting if one wished to stay alive. Also, it made him uneasy that any person could have such an effect on him. He knew, of course, that an immunity to women was vital in his business. It was easy to tell himself that he could take the charm of Edith Olmstead or leave it alone, as easily as he could decline a drink; but still there had been several times in those days when he had entirely forgotten that women were the most dangerous elements in Intelligence. Until the case broke, he had been happier in London than he had been for a long while, but it all became a memory when he learned that he had been right about the British Museum.

Sir Godfrey had told him the news three days after that evening at the Savoy.

"Well," he said, "our Doctor Barnwelder, has formed a pattern. Odd, isn't it, how human beings form routines, even if they stay in one place for only a day or so? Barnwelder has taken out a card to the Reading Room of the Museum. He was there yesterday morning, and he is there again this minute. It was intelligent of you to have made that suggestion, Briscoe."

Of course there was nothing more natural than for a man of Dr. Barnwelder's caliber to use the British Museum Reading Room during his stay in London. Still, Jim Briscoe was pleased with his guessing. For a second he had the angler's elation at having a fish strike at exactly the spot in the pool where he had guessed it would. Barnwelder was running with the line. It was only necessary now to be patient and careful.

"Does he act nervous or anxious, Sir Godfrey?" Briscoe asked. "Does he seem to be looking for anyone?"

Sir Godfrey pointed the stem of his brier pipe at Mark Cheltman.

"Since you have the matter in hand, I suggest you answer him," he said.

Mark Cheltman spoke respectfully. There were times when the atmosphere of Sir Godfrey's office was exactly like a headmaster's study.

"Everything is as merry as a wedding bell," Mark Cheltman said, "if that is the correct expression."

"Good heavens," Sir Godfrey said. "Have some respect for wedding bells."

"I only mean, sir," Mark said, "that Barnwelder does not seem disturbed by anything at all. Placid old chap, isn't he, Jim? Typical absent-minded professor. Yesterday and today he comes in at nine forty-five sharp. Never looks at anything except his book, never speaks to anyone except to thank the book boy."

Jim Briscoe felt completely satisfied. Dr. Barnwelder was acting exactly as he should have.

"What about the book boy, as you call him?" he asked.

"No fear," Mark Cheltman said. "He's one of our chaps—very keen."

Jim Briscoe knew it was not good form to make suggestions to one's opposite numbers, especially to Sir Godfrey. He waited and did not speak until it was obvious that Sir Godfrey expected him to do so.

"Of course you're checking all the card holders?" he said. "And they have my Bjor description in the Reading Room?"

"Naturally," Sir Godfrey said. "And every book that Barnwelder takes is examined. I think we've covered everything, Briscoe."

Dr. Barnwelder moved slowly, but Jim Briscoe had learned that deliberation was a facet of the Barnwelder character. It was ten days after that conversation with Sir Godfrey that the case broke. Jim Briscoe remembered the exact hour. His telephone on the rosewood desk in his suite at Claridges rang at half-past eight.

"Your suit will be ready this morning," a voice said. "May I suggest a preliminary fitting in about half an hour?"

Jim Briscoe remembered, when he set down the telephone, hearing the sound of horses' hoofs on Brook Street, more of a London than a New York sound. London was old-fashioned in many ways, but never backward. He was at Sir Godfrey's office fifteen minutes later, and for once the office had a festive air.

"I think we have him, my dear boy," Sir Godfrey said, and if Sir Godfrey called you "my dear boy," it meant that he was more than pleased.

There seemed very little doubt that they had run down Bjor at last. A man with the name of Max Blenheim had applied for a card only the day before. He had appeared in the Reading Room in the latter part of the afternoon. He had ordered four books, and had piled them eccentrically in front of him, but Dr. Barnwelder had not been in the Reading Room that afternoon.

"But he'll be there at quarter to ten this morning," Mark Cheltman said. "He's as regular as a clock. We'd better be starting now."

"We'll put you up in the gallery among the bookstacks, my dear boy," Sir Godfrey said. "All we need is your identification. I do really feel most happy this morning."

You could take Westminster, if you wanted, or the Tower, or Buckingham Palace, or Whitehall, but none of these buildings, in Jim Briscoe's opinion, were as representative of the spirit of Britain and of the Commonwealth as that sprawling Victorian monstrosity, the British Museum. Its sooty bulk as you approached it from Bedford Square had the imperial arrogance of an older day, and its size the same time had the generosity and calm of *Pax Britannica*.

In Jim Briscoe's younger days, when he had made summer tours to Europe with his parents, his father had often left him in the museum of a morning, and he had wandered for many hours, half lost in its corridors. The strange black lava heads from Easter Island, the feather cloaks from Polynesia, the bas-reliefs from India, still stood out in his recollections, but the achievement of accumulation was what he remembered best. He doubted whether as many diverse objects would ever be gathered into one place again.

Mark Cheltman went ahead of him that morning because there was every reason to be careful, and Jim Briscoe picked up a taxi in the Strand. When it stopped at Bloomsbury Street, the memory of his father was very strong.

"There you are, Jim," he remembered his father saying. "You have it all ahead of you. I'll call for you at the main entrance at twelve."

His father had gone, and a war had come and gone since then, but the entrance hall of the Museum still had the austerity of a conservative, old-line banking house. He did not need to look at the lighted floor plan. The Reading Room, he knew, was straight ahead, but he did not obey his impulse to stride purposefully in that direction. He had learned long ago that any unusual action on the part of anyone was always remembered in some quarter.

It was half-past nine exactly, and so he would be well ahead of Dr. Barnwelder if the doctor kept to his schedule, but he could not tell who else might be there, including some of the sharpest minds in the business. There must be no trace of haste, nor too great an emphasis on purpose. He was the rich young American named Briscoe, knowledgeable and interested in the fine arts. He was wearing his dark flannel suit and his crepe-sole sport shoes, which had been carefully tested for noise, were slightly garish and incongruous.

On entering the museum he had taken off his gray fedora hat, and his face glowed with respectful interest. He paused for an instant and gazed up at the capitals of the stone columns, because strangers entering a building often gaze upward as though afraid the roof might fall.

Well, well, he said to himself, you're here again, Briscoe.

When he thought he had gaped long enough, he walked slowly toward the Reading Room, like a tourist testing old recollections and reluctant to ask the way of an attendant.

There were only a few people in the entrance hall, all of whom, in his respectful enthusiasm at being there, he appeared not to notice. His ability to spot people off the beat was naturally above the average. Except for two men, obviously planted by Sir Godfrey, both dressed in attendant's uniforms, Jim Briscoe could observe nothing out of line.

He walked straight across the marble floor of the foyer and coughed gently so that the silence of his footsteps would not be too conspicuous. A frail elderly man in a black alpaca coat was waiting for him, too obviously, Jim Briscoe thought, but then the arrangements were Sir Godfrey's and not his.

As Jim Briscoe approached the Reading Room, the old man moved arthritically along a corridor to the right, and a minute later Jim Briscoe found himself among the stacks behind the Reading Room. He was pleased to observe that the elderly man also wore crepe soles. They both moved noiselessly into position behind one of the doors fronted by false backs of books that opened onto the first gallery. Sir Godfrey's office could not have chosen a better observation point. A small opening had been cut in the door; it gave Jim Briscoe a good view of the readers' tables in the room below.

Although the sight was peaceful, Jim Briscoe felt a surge of excitement. He remembered the huge rotunda and the starlike arrangement of the reading desks, which spread from the catalogue and reference desks in the center. The whole place had the appearance of studious concentration that one associated with any reading room. The day was cloudy, like most London mornings, and the reading lights above the occupied tables shone.

He could even hear the sound of turning leaves and the more decisive thumping of the heavy folio volumes that contained the catalogues of the Museum's more than six million volumes. The place, he noticed, because he was trained to examine exits and obstacles before turning to people, had been spruced up since prewar days. Though the oak woodwork still gave an impression of the great days of Queen Victoria, the dome, arching above the rotunda and one foot wider than the dome of St. Paul's, if Jim Briscoe's memory served him right, had been painted a pleasing blue, and fresh leather tops of the same general shade now covered the reading tables. The room where Marx and Lenin and Charles Dickens had once sat was half filled already with readers, who would have been fascinating to study if Jim Briscoe had only had the time.

He was looking for a single man in the Reading Room, and once he saw him all the other faces blurred to insignificance. There was no possible doubt as to the identification.

Bjor was seated at a table across the rotunda. All the physical details came immediately into focus. He looked older, but not much older. There was not much gray in his hair. It was thinner at the temples. There was the same concavity, the same high cheekbones and narrow jaw. There was no mistaking the nose and the delicate hands. It was a long way from Dumbarton Oaks, but there was Bjor again.

Jim Briscoe was annoyed that his heart was beating faster. He looked at his watch. There was still five minutes to go before Dr. Barnwelder was due to appear. As a matter of fact, Barnwelder was three minutes late, and Jim Briscoe, standing frozen, hardly daring to blink, remembered thinking that he would have done the same if he had been Barnwelder. There was nothing more suspicious than completely clocklike precision.

Dr. Barnwelder seated himself opposite Bjor, but as far as Jim Briscoe could see, neither of the men displayed the slightest sign of recognition. Dr. Barnwelder was obviously waiting for the books he had ordered, and the wait, before the attendant finally appeared with four volumes, seemed to Jim Briscoe interminable.

"Thank you," Dr. Barnwelder said, so distinctly and loudly that his voice carried to Jim Briscoe in the gallery.

Jim Briscoe remembered thinking again that Dr. Barnwelder had a pleasant voice. It seemed to him that the voice was unnecessarily loud, but Bjor did not look up. Dr. Barnwelder placed the four books in front of him, piled rather eccentrically—the exact code was unimportant.

They were both excellent at what they were doing down there in the Reading Room. It was so well done that Jim Briscoe could believe that Barnwelder's glance met Bjor's by accident—but of course it was not accident.

The two men had made contact.

The ring was closed, and every detail of the Barnwelder theory was proved in that one second. Jim Briscoe had done what he had crossed the ocean for, and it was time for him to leave the place as casually and unhurriedly as he had come.

The old man was still standing in the bookstacks just behind him. Jim Briscoe nodded to him slowly, and the old man nodded back. It wasn't every day that one could get the details of a perfect spy ring. Jim Briscoe felt a moment's letdown now that it was over.

It could not have been a minute later that he was in the entrance hall. He was halfway toward the doors when he saw a girl in a tailored gabardine suit standing close to one of the pillars. It was Edith Olmstead, and she had recognized him before he could move a muscle.

"Why, Jim darling," she said. "I thought you said that you always slept late in the morning. Whatever are you doing here?"

Jim Briscoe did not need to ask her the same question, because he had seen the astonished half opening of her lips and the momentary dilation of her eyes. He hoped that his face showed nothing, and that his smile was natural. Actually, his surprise was very deep indeed, the deeper because he had discounted her. This made him so surprised and so ashamed of himself that for a second or so his thoughts confused themselves with emotion, because it had been a long time since he had been so completely deceived in estimating a personality or a situation.

Now he saw that right from the beginning she had been detailed to keep watch over Barnwelder. She was on guard this minute to be sure that no one had observed the meeting in the Reading Room, and now she had seen him.

He could not avoid a moment's deep respect for her, of the sort that one skilled professional always accords to another. She had been caught off guard herself, he was thinking, because she had been deceived too by the planted paper in his brief case. That explained her surprise. Until the chips were down, they had both been mistaken.

All these thoughts ran through Jim Briscoe's mind as he walked toward her. The main thing, he was thinking, was to show no surprise or nervousness, because logic told him that she had no cause to believe that he had finally found her out. Why should she have, when she had deceived him so long? This was the card he held, but still it was a very delicate situation.

"Why, E," he said, "fancy seeing you here! But now you are here, I only have to make one guess what you're going to do."

His mind was moving more smoothly now that he was beginning to plan his immediate course of action. He could feel amused by the half-puzzled, half-watchful look behind her eyes. He even remembered thinking how very unspoiled she looked. In spite of what he now knew, she still looked like a graduate of old Bucknell.

"You always know all the answers, don't you?" she said. "Just in case I've forgotten, why don't you tell me what I'm going to do?"

Her voice and manner still showed what good friends they had become.

"You're a very unkind girl, I think," he said. "You've been planning to sneak up here and look at the Elgin marbles without me, or else you'd have told me last night."

"It's an old bad habit of mine. I've always loved this place," he answered. "Let's go and see the Elgins."

The situation was very delicate. The British ought to be informed, he knew, but there was no way to do it. The two men from the office had disappeared. The whole net had obviously been lifted at almost the same instant he had left the Reading Room gallery, since there was no use stirring up the smallest trace of suspicion. Then he saw that she was laughing, and she seemed honestly amused.

"What's so funny?" he asked.

Before she answered, she linked her arm with his and pressed it possessively against her, and Jim Briscoe could read the thought behind that gesture. As far as she knew, he was the only one who had observed that meeting in the Reading Room. Obviously she was not going to let him go until something could be done about him.

He hoped she did not know that he felt nearly the same way about her. If she gave a single word of warning, the whole combination would be spoiled. He deliberately dismissed from his mind the deep political implications of what had been discovered, and the gains that could accrue if everything could be kept quiet as long as possible.

He knew their minds were as one about that. They were like a happily adjusted married couple as they stepped into the finely lighted room where the Parthenon frieze was exhibited.

"I suppose these were all put in some safe place during the war?" she said.

The horsemen of Phidias had never seemed to him to be so full of life as they were that morning. He wished for one mad moment that he could be a professor of fine arts.

"Oh, yes," he said, "they were in caves in Wales."

"Why, how did you ever know that?" she asked. "Oh, I'm sorry. I didn't mean to be inquisitive."

"Don't be sorry," he said. "Everybody knows."

Her arm was still linked with his. He was doing his best, of course, to think what he would do if he were she. There was only one main fact. She would be planning to get him out of the way eventually, and in the meanwhile he was reasonably sure that she did not suspect what he knew about her. He knew that she had been shocked when she saw him, because she had been deceived by the brief case, but he was reasonably sure that she still thought of him as a gullible person.

They went over the Elgin marbles carefully and intelligently, because neither of them wished to reveal absent-mindedness or desire for haste. Her enthusiasm for those reliefs did not seem in the least artificial. He was sure that she had a genuine love for line and shadow, and he found himself speaking to her about archaic sculpture, mentioning some of his old favorites.

As he heard his own words, he was able to admire their validity. He wished to heaven that he had a gun now that he was aware again of clear and present danger, but he was reassured by something Mr. Henry had said in his early days at the Bureau.

"Unless you are dealing with underworld triggermen," Mr. Henry had said, "I'm against rod carrying as a general rule. When it comes to shooting, everything is usually too far along for it to help, and it's amazing what interesting results one can achieve without a rod, given education and correct coordination."

Jim Briscoe was glad to recall that quickness of hand and eye had been very helpful to him on a number of occasions, now that there was little doubt that he would have to avail himself of his skill in the very near future. After all, you could not go on looking at something indefinitely, even the Elgin marbles.

He noticed that people were beginning to glance at them with friendly amusement. They did not make a bad looking couple, and a casual observer might easily have thought that they were in love. He could not help thinking of a lacy valentine he had once received when he was in the seventh grade in grammar school.

"Two minds with but a single thought," the valentine had read. "Two hearts that beat as one."

Jim Briscoe sighed. "I wish we could stay here all day," he said, "but I don't suppose we can."

"If we did," she said, "we'd get museum fatigue, and I want to remember the marbles nicely, always. Darling, it's been wonderful."

"Yes," he said. "It's meant a lot to me, seeing them with you, my dear."

"Darling," she said, "why don't you take me somewhere to lunch if you're not busy?"

Jim Briscoe heard his voice ring with hearty, bright enthusiasm.

"I don't know why I didn't think of that myself," he said. "There couldn't be a better idea, but it's rather early, isn't it, for tiffin?"

The word "tiffin" sounded rather effective to him, because in his experience only fools referred to lunch as tiffin. He looked at his wrist watch.

"I suppose it *is* early," she said. "What time is it?"

He thought her voice sounded sharper when she asked the time. It was a quarter past eleven. They had spent much longer than he had thought with the marbles.

"We could go to the Savoy," she said, "and have a drink upstairs, and look at the river, and talk until we're hungry." She stopped and smiled at him shyly. "Or have you seen too much of the Savoy lately?"

"I'll never see too much of the Savoy, dear. Never," he said.

It was cloudy when they walked out of the museum and stood on the curb of Bloomsbury Street. A cruising taxi rolled past them, but Jim Briscoe gave no signal.

"Why, Jim," she said and her voice was as sharp as though they really were a married couple, "didn't you see that taxi?"

She would have done better not to have made the remark. Dumb as she may have considered him, she could hardly blame him for being discriminating about taxi-cabs.

"I was going to take one from the rank," he said. "It seems fairer, don't you think?"

"Of course it does," she said. "I don't know why it didn't cross my mind."

She undoubtedly had a number of things to think about, and so did he. She reached for his hand and held it tight as their taxi moved down Great Russell Street and threaded through the traffic of Charing Cross Road past Trafalgar Square to the Strand.

"Darling," she said, "I've never had such a good time in London as I've had for the last few days. Do you think you can guess why?"

"It's funny," Jim Griscoe said, "how great minds think alike. No one could have had a better time than I've been having."

He was trying, as he spoke, to get the layout of the Savoy suite clearly in his mind. She was so obviously relieved to be going there with him that there could not be much doubt that she had help available.

Someone standing at the bedroom window, he remembered, could see a considerable distance into the rest of the suite. Someone might risk a shot at him from the bedroom, but no one could very well be there when they arrived and on the whole he discounted the idea of shooting. Whatever was going to occur would necessarily be quiet. It might be a knife, except that knifing was messy in a place like the Savoy.

It was strange to be weighing possibilities while he was holding E. Olmstead's hand. It was strange that he could feel a genuine affection for her and a true admiration—but then, he could understand better than anyone else the difficulties under which she was laboring. He was aware more keenly than he had ever been before of her buoyant love of life. Vitality was useful in Intelligence, if you could keep it in control.

When they reached the lift at the Savoy, he was sure that she had given no signal to anyone.

"We could either have luncheon served upstairs," she said, "or go to the Connaught or Claridges."

"Oh, no," he said. "Upstairs by all means."

Inadvertently she had given him a useful piece of information. She had as good as told him that whatever the show might be, it would occur before lunch, not after.

He was still turning this over in his mind while she searched for her key in her handbag. His nerves must have been more on edge than thoughts, because she startled him when the suite door closed behind them. They were still in the narrow foyer when she turned and faced him.

"Darling," she said, "how about a kiss? I've been dying for one all morning."

Once again his mind returned to Mr. Henry. There were many dangerous things one necessarily had to face. Mr. Henry had said in one of his first talks when Jim had joined the Bureau. Believe it or not, Mr. Henry had said, getting out of a bathtub in a strange hotel was a very dangerous procedure and kissing a woman was almost its equal.

Jim Briscoe could remember the hearty laughter of the young men when Mr. Henry had been serious. You were vulnerable when a woman had her arms around you. She could be holding a knife, a small firearm, or a hypodermic. If she was strong and knew jujitsu, she could always knock you over.

Nevertheless, Jim Briscoe spoke promptly.

"Two minds, dear, but a single thought. E, dear, let me take your purse. You've never looked so beautiful."

She made no objection when he placed her purse carefully on the console table. As it turned out, there was no guile in her embrace. It was a moment of generosity and defenselessness for both of them.

"Darling," she whispered, "I've loved you so."

If Jim Briscoe noticed the past tense, still he was sure she meant what she was saying. She was sorry, and he was sorry too—much sorrier than he thought he would be that things had turned out this way for them.

He had another fleeting memory of Helen, married to her dentist. It had been a long while since he had even thought of caring for anyone. What was that dreadful joke Mr. Henry had made on the evening before he left Washington? That the dentist's life was more boring than his—and as always Mr. Henry was quite right.

"Dear," he said, and he meant what he was saying, "it's not only been, but it still is, wonderful."

She stirred gently in his arms.

"You've always made me feel so natural, so completely at home," she said. "Shall we have a drink? The Elgins have made me thirsty."

Mr. Henry had never needed to detail the problems involved with liquor, the pill and the vial—but, then, as Jim Briscoe had learned, E. Olmstead kept no bottle in the suite. In suggesting a drink she had as good as told him that it would be a room waiter who would do the work. It would be a fractured skull or a Mickey Finn, and he was inclined to believe in the fracture, because it would be quicker.

"Now that you mention it," he said, and he hoped his glance was as friendly as hers, "I could do with a drink myself. I'd love a Scotch and a splash."

He hoped that the mention of a splash made him sound stupid, and he was almost sure it did.

"I'll have one too," she said. "Sit down, darling, and I'll give you a cigarette while I ring."

Her judgment about the chair she gave him was highly academic. It was one of those low, deeply upholstered armchairs from which only a contortionist could rise rapidly. He gathered his feet beneath him and sat as near to the edge as possible, hoping she did not notice. He heard her move behind him.

297

He hoped she was ringing the bell near the entrance to the foyer, and not searching for some blunt instrument with which to do the job herself, but he could not disturb her by looking. He was relieved when she returned and sat on a small chair opposite him, holding out a pack of American cigarettes. He took one, and his attention relaxed for a moment.

"We've had good times up here, haven't we?" she said.

She was good—professionally at the top—he admitted, but not quite perfect or she would not have used the past tense again. He was glad his hand was steady when he leaned forward to light her cigarette.

"I'm having a swell time right this minute," he told her. "Every moment with you has been wonderful." He drew his breath in slowly and told the truth. "It couldn't help but be, because you're wonderful."

He was surprised to see her lips grow thin and the fresh color leave her cheeks.

"You really mean that, Jim?" she asked.

"From the bottom of my heart," he said.

It was an easy speech to make because it was absolutely true. She did not have time to answer before they heard the click of a passkey in the lock, and then he heard steps behind him, moving through the foyer. They were deliberate footsteps, which indicated that the waiter was a big man.

Her glance had left his. It was concentrated on a point above his head, which told him the height of the waiter's face.

Just as he thought, the room waiter was a big man. After all, great physical strength was desirable if you wanted to get through with one of those jobs quickly.

Jim Briscoe let his hands rest gently on the arms of his chair. He sat relaxed. Everything inside him was tempted, but he did not follow Edith Olmstead's glance.

"Oh, Robert," she said, and her voice sounded husky, "thank you for coming so soon. The gentleman would like a Scotch and a splash."

"Thank you, miss," Jim Briscoe heard the waiter say, and the voice, which sounded like that of a rubber in a Turkish bath, indicated that the man was just behind him. "And what will you have, if you please, miss?"

Without turning, Jim Briscoe could tell what was happening, because every noiseless move the man behind him made was reflected in Edith Olmstead's face. Her lips had compressed, and her eyes had narrowed. It would not be a gun or a knife; it would either be garroting or a blackjack. He was willing to bet on the blackjack, because the technique was simpler, considering the yielding upholstery of his low chair.

"Oh don't!" she screamed suddenly. "Look out, Jim!"

Actually he had timed the thing correctly in his own mind. He had jerked his body sideways and over the arm of the chair just as the blow came down. He was off his knees and in a crouch before the man recovered.

Jim Briscoe had always prided himself on being good at close work, and if he did say so, his coordination was excellent. There must be no noise and no mess, he told himself, because the situation was very delicate.

As he thought, the waiter was a big man holding a blackjack. Jim had a glimpse of his dress suit and a red, contorted face. The blackjack was half raised for a second try when Jim Briscoe struck the man in the groin.

When the man's body bent forward, Jim Briscoe had the opportunity to draw himself erect and whirl accurately on the ball of his left foot. The heavy neck just above the white collar presented exactly the target he wanted. With all his weight behind the blow, he hit with the edge of his right palm. It was a simple blow, but most effective when delivered correctly, and his timing had been right. Jim Briscoe had struck the man's spinal column just below the point where it joined the skull, and Jim Briscoe knew that the neck was broken. He could tell by the man's short stertorous breathing as he lowered the body softly to the floor.

The girl had not moved. She had not risen from her chair, and he remembered thinking that she had missed a chance. He found himself dusting his hands together gently, an absurd, instinctive gesture. Her handbag was on a small table beside her. He swept it to the floor, beyond her reach.

"That's right," he said. "Sit quiet. Believe me, moving around won't do you a bit of good."

He was glad she understood him. After all, they were both professionals, and they did not need to explain much to each other now that the chips were down.

"I had to scream," she said. "I couldn't bear to have you killed."

When you came to think about it, her speech proved that Mr. Henry's thoughts on women were correct. They could be loyal to a person and an idea simultaneously.

"Don't let it worry you, my dear," he said. "The warning was unnecessary, but believe me, I am very grateful."

"Oh, Jim," she whispered. Her face was very white. "It had to be you or me, didn't it? I never dreamed it would be you until I saw you there this morning."

Jim Briscoe nodded slowly, and then he found the package of cigarettes, offered her one, and lighted it.

"I'm afraid it has to be you now," he said. "In a mild way, I hope. You understand that, don't you?"

"Yes," she said. "I know—but if it is all the same, I'd much rather you didn't do it, Jim."

He had never liked her so much as when she made that request.

"You didn't mind so much, did you," he said, "when you fingered me at Gander?" He mentioned the whole thing lightly. She was frightened, and he did not blame her, but she fell in with his mood at once. She was a very high-class operator.

"No," she said, "but that was before I knew you." Her voice dropped almost to a whisper. "Please don't make the arrangements yourself, darling. Get someone else to do it."

"All right," he said, "then I'll use your telephone, my dear." His words were still soft but very cool. "Just smoke your cigarette quietly, and don't do one other thing or I'll chop you down like that goon of yours."

He felt awkward with the English telephone when he gave the number of the office and asked for Mark Cheltman.

"Hello, Mark," he said. "I'm in a bit of trouble at the Savoy," and he gave the number of the suite. "I'm right as rain personally but you'd better drop over right away with one or two chaps. It might interest Sir Godfrey to come too, if he isn't busy."

Jim Briscoe put down the telephone and prodded the body with his toe.

"I don't know what Sir Godfrey will have in mind," he said, "but you'll find he's a reasonable man."

"As long as you're not the one who does it," she said.

For the first time that reiteration of hers annoyed him.

"Listen," he told her. "You've upset the apple cart and all we can possibly do is buy a day or two now. No matter what is done about you, your people will be bound to get the wind up—but a day or two is something. You ought to tell yourself you've done quite well."

"Yes," she said. "Let's change the subject, shall we?"

But it was no time to change the subject.

"Just take that look off your face," he said. "This isn't Prague or Warsaw. You're going to live, my dear."

"More fools you," she said.

"Yes," he said, "perhaps you're right. You might tell me, because we'll be bound to find out. Where is Miss Edith Olmstead?"

The girl smiled at him, and she looked less tense.

"In Rome," she said. "I kept telling you I was going to visit friends in Rome, didn't I? She left the same day we did, but she left from Baltimore. All she had to do with this was to be leaving the country when I needed a cover."

Jim Briscoe sighed, because one could not think of everything.

"You people certainly know how to fake passports," he said.

"Yes," she said, "indeed we do."

He looked at her for a while without speaking. Her face looked harder, and the illusion of innocence was gone.

"I take it," he said, "you were born somewhere near Vienna?"

"Yes," she said, "Vienna"

"Well," he said, "I've never been able to blame the Viennese for anything they do. I suppose you're Moscow-trained."

"Yes," she answered.

"I ought to have known," he said.

She did not answer, and he had a feeling that there was nothing much left to say.

"Well," he said, "you certainly mixed things up for me, Miss Moscow. The boss always tells us to keep away from gals."

"Jim," she said. "I want to tell you something."

"What?" he asked.

"I've never yelled a warning to anyone before—only you, Jim."

Jim Briscoe smiled faintly, because after all there was no use being bitter.

"I told you it wasn't necessary," he said, "but thanks just the same, Miss Moscow."

"I know," she answered. "But please don't forget, I did it just the same. And Jim?"

"Yes," he said.

"Please don't hate me altogether. Please."

He did not have time to answer. There was a knock at the door of the suite and he remembered that the door was locked.

"Get up," he told her. "Walk ahead of me and open that door, and please do it without any postgraduate tricks, Miss Moscow."

Sir Godfrey lighted his pipe as soon as he seated himself to receive Jim Briscoe's report. When crumbs of tobacco cascaded onto the carpet, Jim Briscoe remembered what Mr. Henry had said about smoking.

"Dear me," Sir Godfrey said. "I don't see what else you could

301

have done under the circumstances, Briscoe. So he came in when she rang?"

"They work in pairs quite often, sir," Mark Cheltman said.

"Dear me," Sir Godfrey said again.

"It was my fault, sir," Jim Briscoe said, "not to have spotted her long before."

Sir Godfrey shook his head slowly.

"No, no," he said. "I was not thinking of that point. One always thinks of what one should have done, doesn't one? Of course, I should have given orders for you to stay back in the museum bookstacks until the place closed down at night. Stupid of me, really."

"I wish I'd thought of that myself, sir," Jim Briscoe said. "I suppose I should have."

"Well well," Sir Godfrey said, "things aren't wholly spoiled for us. We'll be able to give them a bloody nose, I think, if she didn't communicate with anyone. We'll have some hours—a day or two perhaps. Start making things secure, Mark."

"Yes, sir," Mark Cheltman said. "We've already begun."

There was no doubt that the British had taken over, and Jim Briscoe was relieved, because reaction was setting in, making him feel drained and tired.

"Briscoe," Sir Godfrey said, "I assume your chief knows what to do under these circumstances."

"Yes, sir," Jim Briscoe said. "All you need do is signal 'Second Situation.'"

"Then I think we have all the facts," Sir Godfrey said, "unless something further occurs to you."

"No, sir," Jim Briscoe said. "I think you have the fill-in. I'm sorry things didn't work out better."

"On the whole I think you did very well indeed," Sir Godfrey said. "But now I think the less you are seen about here the better, Briscoe. I'd leave at once. We'll take care of the young lady and handle the corpse, of course. Big chap, wasn't he? Must have been a good show, Briscoe."

Mark Cheltman laughed gently. "Jim's good with waiters," he said. "Always."

"Mark," Sir Godfrey said, "get him on the Ambassador flight tonight. Well, goodbye. It's a pleasure to have seen you again—pleasure indeed—Briscoe."

Jim Briscoe shook hands with Sir Godfrey and Mark Cheltman. He was wondering, while he did so exactly what they would do with Miss Moscow and how long they would keep her out of circulation.

It would depend, of course, on what might turn up now that important arrests were certain to be made.

It might be a long while before she took a plane to anywhere again. But that was not his problem. The worst of it was that he could say nothing to her—not a word of encouragement or regret—in front of the men who watched them. The strange part about it was that he found himself regretting a good deal, without exactly knowing what. Still, the main thing was to live in the present.

"Chin up," he said. "Goodbye, Miss Moscow. Believe me, I won't forget you. Ever."

"Nor I you," she said, and she smiled at him.

He wanted to shake hands with her, but that would have been absurd with the two men watching. When he turned on his heel and picked up his hat, he was reasonably sure that he would neither forget her nor see her again. He was even more sure when he closed the door of the suite behind him.

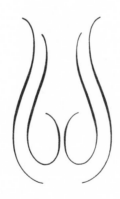

ONLY ON RAINY NIGHTS

BY MARK VAN DOREN

Mark Van Doren, the poet, critic, novelist, short-story writer and editor, was the younger brother of Pulitzer Prize winner Carl Van Doren. He was graduated from the University of Illinois in 1914 and received his Ph.D. from Columbia in 1920. He subsequently taught at Columbia, lectured, and served as literary editor and film critic for *The Nation*. His wife, writer Dorothy Graffe, was also on *The Nation*'s staff. In 1940 Van Doren won a Pulitzer Prize for his *Collected Poems*. His autobiography, *The Way to the Present*, was published in 1958.

THE NEXT RAINY NIGHT," SAID the Inspector, "I'll take you over there."

His friend, Professor Eldred, reached for the tall glass he had nearly forgotten. "All right, I'd like to go. But you musn't expect me to see more in him than you see. Your theory about us, I seem to remember, gives us credit for very little shrewdness when it comes—as in the present case it does—to looking at particulars. I'll go for the trip—a pleasure, always."

"No," said the Inspector, "I really want your expert opinion. And it may not be a pleasure to look at this particular face. I'd hate to think he was my son."

"Could he be?"

"That's academic humor." The professor nodded, confessing that it was. "No, he couldn't."

"Whose son is he?"

"His mother's, of course. The father I know nothing about except that he died when Root was a small boy. She is the proverbial poor widow—works hard cleaning other people's houses to sustain herself and him. He doesn't work, except for odd jobs now and then."

"Neither, I suppose, did the young man who was murdered. Were they friends?"

The Inspector reached for his own glass and considered its contents a while. He was a small, neat, reddish man, capable of intense and interesting silences. "A good question. Thanks, I'll keep it in mind. At least they were old acquaintances. They went to school together. Halfway through high school, when Root quit. Herrold went on, naturally, since his parents *aren't* poor. This summer was his second vacation from college. He came home on the tenth of June; by the fourth of July he had his sports car, muffler cutout and all; and on the twelfth of August we dug him up—down there in the woods. No, Herrold never worked at all, and I'll keep the fact in mind. Thanks, John."

Professor Eldred flourished his free hand—generously, but with the suggestion that he didn't know what he had been thanked for. "Why are you so certain he was killed for his sports car? It was found in the river, you tell me, not more than a hundred yards away. Couldn't he have merely lost control of it, run off the road and down the bank—been badly hurt—drowned—"

"And shot?"

"Oh! That's right."

"And then," said the Inspector, "you were probably about to say he buried himself. Incidentally, there was no water in his lungs."

"Of course not. Forget everything I have said. I was about to propose, though—and now I won't—that he was buried by some-one else, for a reason as strange as you say this boy's face is when he walks in out of the rain. The whole point, I assume, is that some-thing in the case strikes you as strange. So I was going to try to locate it in the motive for a burial—the motive, if you are right, of Archie Root. Whatever he did or didn't do, isn't that why you are taking me to Hadfield? You think I can read the history behind his eyes and ears. By the way, does he have big ears?"

"They do stick out a little."

"Did Herrold's?"

"No, from the pictures. Nice and flat—a smooth, well-cared-for head. What are you driving at?"

"Nothing. But now I must go."

It was midnight, and the Professor never stayed later than that. Mrs. Eldred preferred to have him home. He went almost every Thursday evening to the Inspector's apartment—where there was no wife, no child—and had better conversation there than he was able to have with most of his colleagues. Though not with his wife, who always stayed up, or sat reading in bed, until he came and told her what the two of them—the Professor and the Inspector—had said to each other over their drinks.

Tonight Mrs. Eldred was more wakeful than usual; William, their older boy, was still running a temperature and had kept her busy as well as anxious. But the boy was asleep at last, and she called down from the top of the stairs: "Hello, dear. What did the old man have up his sleeve this time?" The Inspector was only 55, but she chose to speak of him as if he were ancient beyond compute.

"Wait till I come up. Is Bill all right?"

"Better." Then while Eldred undressed in their room she glanced at him curiously, although she yawned a little, and pursued her inquiry. "He *did* have something up his sleeve. I can tell by your faraway look. You're still thinking about what he said—or what you said."

"What *he* said." Eldred smiled—reflectively, so that she knew only half of him was home. "He developed an odd theory about us who teach—or more accurately, us who learn and teach. He said he was struck by it last Sunday in the bus station. He was there, looking for he didn't say what reprehensible person, and suddenly he saw the difference between our faces and those of other people."

"*Our* faces? You can't mean yours and mine."

"I could, but he didn't. He hasn't the luck to know you. He meant university people in general."

"Oh, yes, I forgot. I'm sleepier than I thought." But she sat up in her bed while he got into his.

"I told him he took too narrow a view of the matter. The kind of face he meant—why, anybody can have it. It is a question, I said, of how life is lived. I even promised to show him a couple of colleagues who don't live it in such a way as to have the kind of face he supposes we all have. It was his good fortune to see Osborne and Kramer waiting for a bus; they do look like that because they live like that."

"Like what, dear? I'm afraid I don't follow you."

"Like me—the faraway look you just noticed. Osborne and Kramer are thinking men, and their faces show it."

"Absent-minded, you mean?"

"The popular construction. Or—excuse me, darling—the vulgar one. And it is quite adequate unless it refers, as it often does— and then it *is* vulgar—merely to the act of substituting some absent image for one that is present: last night's steak for tonight's hamburger, or Lucy for Mildred."

"I see."

"Not yet you don't. I mean it *isn't* that. The thing substituted is not to be understood as a thing at all; it isn't, that is to say, an image of anything. It is an *idea*. It is every idea. It is, in a manner of speaking, the whole truth and nothing but the truth—I am now quoting the Inspector. It is what a good teacher is staring at while he talks to a good student, or while the good student, more likely, talks to him. It is present for neither of them except insofar as their conversation has put it between them. But when it is most present it is most invisible—and therefore most difficult for others to see. But these two do see it—it is the only real presence for them. And if they form the habit of living with such presences—such abstractions—their faces tell the tale wherever they go."

"Even in a bus station."

"Yes."

"Or in this room."

"Certainly. The best place."

"Thank you, dear. But what did the Inspector say next? This

must have been a prelude to something more specific. A double murder, maybe."

"Not necessarily. He has a mind, and it pleases him to use it."

"I'm jealous because he never comes here."

"He will yet. His hair is the same color as yours—what there is of it." Hers, thought Eldred, was beautiful in bed: a sunflower on the pillow.

"No, he never will. He despises women. But anyway, who did the double murder? Did he do it with both hands?"

"A single murder, sweetheart, and the Inspector doesn't know who did it. But there is a boy whom he is watching—in Hadfield, where another boy was killed—"

"I know. Tracy Herrold. They say it was for his bright red sports car."

"You read everything in the paper, don't you? Yes, so they say. But nobody got the car."

"I know. It was in the river."

"That's right. But as I was saying, a certain boy in Hadfield interests the Inspector very much. He goes there on rainy nights and sits in a hot dog wagon and watches him. The boy thinks he is watching the Inspector, but it's the other way around. At least, the boy has no conception of the Inspector's singular interest in his face—which he says is one of ours."

"Murder, Incorporated."

"Sh-h-h. The law has ears."

"Well, you mean the boy in Hadfield is an intellectual child. But if so, what has that to do with—"

"Ah, the very point. The Inspector, who has been brooding over the academic countenance, wants to know whether this boy—when his mind wanders as he says it does, when he sits there with a frankfurter in front of him and forgets that it exists—the Inspector wants my opinions as to whether he is seeing a bright red sports car, and perhaps a bright red stain on Herrold's shirt, or simply the whole truth and nothing but the truth about the universe and its component parts. A criminal would be seeing the car—or some hideout he was headed for—but about this boy the Inspector isn't sure. He doesn't hide out; he stays in Hadfield, and on rainy nights—"

"Oh, yes. Those. And his name—what is his name?"

"Now, now, Sally. But as to the rain—yes. I don't blame you for goggling over that. I did, and I still do. You see the Inspector first noticed the boy on such a night. Having business in Hadfield, he stopped in at the wagon for a sandwich and a cup of coffee, and was sitting there when the boy came in, wet to the skin, and the proprietor remarked: 'The usual? One hot dog for one cold gut?' Something nice like that, something subtle and understanding. It seems the proprietor had become aware—slowly, over six or seven weeks—of a correlation between bad weather and the appearance of someone who for the time being shall be nameless. He even spoke of it to the Inspector. He said, 'Sure as hell, sir, soon as it rains in he comes. Yet he don't eat it, either, when I put it down. Funny thing!' He said this so that the boy could hear. And yet the boy didn't seem to hear—or even to care."

There was a silence that made the Professor wonder if she had fallen sleep. But she hadn't turned off her light, and pretty soon she said, "The Inspector must have other reasons for watching him this way. Does the boy have a gun?"

"Herrold had one, in a red-leather pocket under the dashboard. He had large ideas—highwaymen, you know, and he the prince, or at least the rich merchant's son. One shot had been fired from it, and the gun put back in the car. They are sure it was the murder weapon—possibly grabbed out of its owner's hand and turned against him."

"Fingerprints?"

"Well, no."

"How was the grave dug? I understand it was short and shallow, and poor Tracy had to be jabbed into it with a shovel or something. Has that been followed up? Is *that* the reason?"

"Herrold had everything—a little folding spade, for instance. It was found in the trunk compartment, but it had dug the grave. Some of the clay hadn't washed off in the river."

"Fingerprints on the spade?"

"No."

There was another silence, and this one was the last. Eldred, straining over, turned out her light, and then his own. She might only be pretending to sleep, but he had no answers beyond the ones he had given. She asked good questions. All three of them really should go to Hadfield, but of course she wouldn't be invited. He wondered drowsily if the Inspector could ever be convinced that she was the one woman in ten thousand who might help him . . .

Saturday, the last day of September, was unusually hot and bright. But the late afternoon sky had clouded over; by five it was raining and blowing, and by seven it was merely raining—a monotonous, lukewarm drizzle that promised to keep on all night.

Professor Eldred, looking out of his study window, saw the many fine drops as they pattered among the linden leaves and dripped to the lawn. How did the Inspector, he asked himself, spend Saturday nights?

The doorbell was the answer. He went at once, but his wife was there before him, welcoming the Old Man—she somehow treated him as such—who nevertheless refused to step over the threshold. He was too wet, he was saying when he saw Eldred over her shoulder, and even then he wouldn't change his mind. He looked smaller now, thought Eldred, than he ever had in his own home.

"I'll wait out here," he said, "till you're ready."

"Ready?" Mrs. Elred made an excellent show of not understanding.

The Inspector's eyes, shrewd under their sandy brows, expressed a polite indifference as to whether she understood or not. Perhaps, thought Eldred, watching them both, he knew she did. But he only said, "Your husband is going with me to Hadfield. I won't keep him long."

He hadn't telephoned in advance. It was queer, his certainty that the professor would be free on a Saturday night. As a matter of fact, Eldred hadn't yet eaten dinner; and the Kramers were coming over to spend the evening.

When these things were explained to the Inspector he said, "But I'll feed you out of the public moneys. And you'll be back in time to entertain your friends."

"Feed him?" Mrs. Eldred shook her head. "In a hot dog wagon?"

She had been deliberate, of course, in saying that. She now wanted the Inspector to know she had been told.

But he seemed not to have heard her. "Coming, John?"

And John went, the two of them so picturesquely different as they disappeared down the wet walk at whose other end the Inspector's car, invisible, revealed its presence as she listened sharply. He hadn't turned the motor off—he had been that sure.

Eldred said nothing until they were on the Outer Drive; the turn for Hadfield would be coming next. "I thought you would telephone first. This looks like an emergency. Is it? Has something happened?"

"Not a thing." The Inspector made the turn; Hadfield was now nine miles away. "But it's the kind of night I meant, and suddenly I decided—I hope your wife didn't think me too high-handed. I like her, by the way."

"You didn't even look at her."

"Didn't I?"

310

"No. Especially when she let you know I had talked to her about Archie Root."

"Well, of course not then."

"I didn't tell her his name."

The Inspector hesitated. "Good. But the general outline—you discussed that with her?"

"I always do. She doesn't miss a thing."

"Or *say* a thing? I mean, to others?"

"Oh, no. I'm sure she doesn't. Not that I give orders. But she wouldn't."

"Good. In a sense, of course, there *is* an emergency. He took a shovel with him down there this evening."

"What?" Eldred started; and perhaps unconsciously the Inspector slowed up a little. "Down where?"

"You know—or did you know?—we watch him. That is, we watch the place. People were coming there—they always do—and we thought we might pick up something from the way they acted. They stopped coming, of course, a month ago—except for Archie. Tonight the rain brought him out with one of those long-handled shovels. He wasn't trying to hide it—he simply had it, over his shoulder, all the time he stood and looked at the hole where Herrold was buried. I say he didn't try to hide the shovel. Of course he didn't know our man was there. He never does. But I think he would come anyway. A queer business, Professor."

Eldred pondered what he had heard. Perhaps a mile went by before he said, "It *is* queer. Nothing but a hole in the ground and yet he—"

"Nothing but. Yet for six days and nights before we found Herrold in it, mind you, it was not a hole. And somebody didn't want it to look as if it ever had been. Twice that week it rained—the first time, very hard—and the question is whether somebody was afraid then that the freshly turned earth would be washed away."

"*Some*body." Eldred contemplated the darkness flowing by them on both sides. "Possibly. And probably, you seem to be saying, Root. But then why *now*? What difference would a rain make *now*? Or at any time since—when was it? August twelfth?"

"Precisely. It's been a question with me from the start. But since I heard about the shovel, less than an hour ago, it has seemed—yet I don't want to exaggerate—an emergency. So here we are."

Eldred turned in his seat. "And where is that? What do you mean, an emergency?"

"I mean," said the Inspector, "there's no telling what a kid like that will do. I say kid—he's nineteen, but you will see how young he

311

really is. You know, of course, that I think he did the job. The truth is, I'm *sure* of it, though I have no evidence beyond the way he acts. If that's evidence. So that's why you're here. I need your judgment."

"I see," said Eldred. "We should have brought my wife. Her judgment—"

"That could be, could be." But the Inspector didn't stop and turn the car about; nor did he speak again until they were at Duke's Diner, whose orange sign blinked cheerfully through the fine rain that still was falling.

"If you are hungry," said the Inspector as he got out on his side, "you will enjoy Duke's cooking. I often have—but then I'm no epicure."

"Neither am I," said Eldred, "but I do happen to be hungry. I may impoverish the State. Will *he* be there?"

"Should be." The Inspector looked up at Eldred. "Don't think you have to act any special way. He'll do that. He'll assume, as I told you the other night, that *we* are the exhibit. He'll figure us out, the two of us. So take your time, and eat all you like. Last time I looked, the public coffers were full."

Duke waved them welcome into a long, narrow room that smelled of T-bone steaks and fried onions. That's what I'll have, said Eldred to himself, following the Inspector to a white-topped table at the farther end. The stools at the counter were mostly unoccupied; three customers there, evidently good friends, had finished their meal and were hunched comfortably over coffee cups whose contents they stirred as they talked. And only one other table had anybody sitting at it. Archie, of course, said Eldred. There he is, at the end opposite us. There he is, already studying us, and probably more curious about me than about the Inspector.

The two of them sat down with the entire length of the diner between them and the boy whom Eldred had been brought to see. If that was who it was.

It was, he learned almost at once; for the Inspector's hands, flat on the table top, lay quiet except for one finger that lifted a little, pointing.

"Well, gentlemen," said Duke—he had come suddenly to tower over them, his bald head shining like the largest light in all the place—"what'll it be?"

It was hard for Eldred to remember what he had told himself he would order, so aware he was of those black eyes upon him. Those eyes, and those pathetic ears—yes, they did stick out, as in a way the eyes did. Eldred thought of animals in danger—imminent danger,

312

so that nothing moved except their eyes, and they only by intensifying, moment upon moment, the burden of their concentrated terror.

"A T-bone steak," he finally said.

"A big one," added the Inspector. "But not for me. I've had my dinner. Coffee with him later."

"Fried onions? French fries?" Duke gazed down at the two benevolently; he was proud because the Inspector had come again.

"Both," said Eldred, smiling; and as he looked down he again sent a quick glance over the empty tables. Root's eyes, intent upon nothing else than his, made no effort to conceal the fact. Perhaps they were unable to, he said, as an animal's are when it is cornered; it thinks only of the enemy that will not go away.

And yet there was a glimmer in them—although he believed the Inspector had overstated this—of some delusion as to their own visibility; some suggestion that their owner supposed they saw without being seen. The boy, that is to say, was thinking his own thoughts, and it could be, as the Inspector had said, that the nature of those thoughts was nothing as practical as would be the case if he were a criminal. It wasn't quite as if he were cornered, or even pursued at all; it wasn't simple fear that made the eyes so prominent, so painful. For all the strains upon it, and the streaks of dampness that had not been rubbed away, it was a distinguished face: a naked, thinking face. The Inspector had been justified in letting Archie's face fascinate him.

"You see," said the Inspector, "he hasn't touched his sandwich. He could have the same one every night and he wouldn't know the difference. I wonder if Duke has thought of that." But Duke was off behind the counter now, diving out of sight for mustard.

"You're right about him," said Eldred. "He's not afraid of you—or me, naturally. He's not aware of any person in the world—not really."

"Herrold?"

"But he's not in the world."

"So you agree."

"Only to this extent. He's staring at something that isn't here for us to see."

"The place where Herrold was buried?"

"We *could* see that—I almost can, without having been there. You have only to remember."

"Sure," said the Inspector, closing his eyes. "I see it."

"But his eyes are *open*. The question, then, is what do they see. I wish my wife were here."

313

"For him to look at?"

"No. To look at *him*."

"Oh."

"But I think I know," said Eldred, "what she would advise us to do. If she were here, she'd do it herself. It is her way and it is a good way. She'd go over and speak to him. She would go right now. She would know he wanted her to do it."

The Inspector's hands slipped down into his lap. "You mean *you* know this? It's your idea?"

"I suppose so." Eldred didn't seem quite certain. "But it would be hers—I'm positive of it. She wouldn't wait a minute—assuming, of course, that you gave your permission."

The Inspector dropped his voice a little, though there was no necessity for this, what with the noises Duke was making at the counter, and the drone of three hump-shouldered men still idling over coffee. "What are you waiting for? I give it. Go ahead."

Eldred looked down at him. "Not without you." It was almost an order.

The Inspector shrugged his shoulders, squinting up at his tall friend. "No. This is out of my line. Beyond my depth."

"Nonsense! Come on." And Eldred stood up just as Duke arrived with an enormous platter, steaming and sizzling as if it still were on the stove. The Inspector rose too.

"What's the matter?" Duke was dumfounded. "Here it is and you—"

But the two of them walked past him as he set the platter down, and he watched them all the way to where the boy sat watching them while they came closer and closer. Then Duke returned quietly to his post, took up a rag, started wiping the coffee urn, and didn't look at them again.

To Eldred it seemed that Archie must have been waiting a long time for this to happen; the fear in his eyes, perhaps, was lest it never would. But the Inspector, whatever he may have thought, had to speak first.

"You're Archie Root," he said.

The boy blushed, as if his name had been a secret until now. But he continued to look straight into the officer's eyes.

"Do you know who I am?"

The boy nodded, then looked down at his hot dog, cold on its paper plate. He is starved, thought Eldred, starved in front of his own food.

"Do you have any idea why I'm here?"

The boy looked up swiftly—in relief, thought Eldred—and

314

nodded again. His torn shirt was still wet from the rain—at least, around the shoulders. His hands were working in his lap—Eldred wished he could see them, or that Sally could. One of her deepest convictions was that hands reveal a great deal about people.

"Where is the shovel you had tonight?" The question came hard, in a new key, as if it had been shot forth.

Archie, visibly struck by it, started. But then he seemed to be glad the question had been asked. "Out there," he said. It was a thin voice, yet it surprised Eldred by its depth. "Out there by the door."

The Inspector went to the door, looked outside of it, reached to feel something, and returned at once. "Not very bright of me," he said to his friend. "It was leaning there when we came in."

But Eldred was saying to himself: he *wanted* it to be discovered. And then Archie immediately confirmed this much—and more.

"You saw me down there. I know," the boy said quietly.

"*I* didn't." The Inspector watched him closely.

"One of you did. I always know."

"Hm-m-m." The Inspector was somewhat off his balance. "Well, then, what can you tell us? This is Professor Eldred—from the University."

He makes me sound, thought Eldred, like a criminologist or something. What if Archie knew I taught English?

But Archie wasn't caring what he taught. "What can I tell you?" he said. He seemed to have no idea what the Inspector wanted.

"For example, why do you go there only on rainy nights?"

The boy hesitated longer than usual. Then: "He was my friend," he said; and now his hands came up to wipe his face clear of—Of what? Eldred wondered. Imaginary things? They were fine hands, if weak. "He was my friend," the boy said again. "I wanted his grave to look nice."

"His grave!" The Inspector almost shouted it. "But he's not there!"

"No?" It was said slowly. "That's right. But he was once. It was his grave once, and I wanted it to keep looking nice. He was my friend, and everything he had was nice. So his grave, too—I was afraid the rain would spoil it."

The Inspector stepped nearer the table. "You mean spoil it for *you*. Before we found him. You were afraid the rain would *uncover* him. You didn't put him deep enough. That other shovel, the little one—"

The boy sighed tremendously. His hands disappeared again beneath the table, his shoulders drooped, his whole body seemed drained of breath. He looked away and down.

"That's right, isn't it?" The Inspector pressed him. "You killed him. You killed your friend."

It was as if the boy himself had suddenly died. Right there in front of them. His head sank to the table, a heavy weight which all the rest of him could barely lift.

"Why?" The Inspector didn't spare him. This was the time to strike. "Listen to me—*why?*" He looked at Eldred, half in apology, then shook the boy's damp shoulders—gently at first, but after a while with greater firmness.

The firmness brought results. Archie, without raising his head, started to speak. Both men had to bend down to hear him. "I wanted his car—just for one minute I did. Never before, you understand. And even the next minute I said to myself: What would I do with a *car*? His, anyway. Just for that minute, though, I did think of all the nice places I had never been to. I could drive there, I could be there; *nice*, I said. So I told him I was taking it. He thought this was funny till I went for him. We weren't in the car then. He had stopped it to see about some noise under the hood. He picked me up after supper, and nobody saw us—nobody knew. There was that noise under the hood, and so he stopped, and we were just standing there. I went for him, and he ran to get the gun out of the pocket in the car. He never had a chance even to point it at me. I grabbed his hand, and—well, you know."

"What do I know?" The Inspector, bent over him, speaking very softly.

"You found him. You know. And that was when I knew I never wanted any car. Not his, anyway. But I didn't know what to do. The best thing would have been to go and tell."

"Why didn't you?"

The boy's shoulders heaved with another tremendous sigh. "I killed my friend. And it wasn't an accident. Or maybe it wasn't—I didn't know. I don't know now. But I did kill him, and I had that to think about. I couldn't think much then, but I knew I could after I got him buried in the ground. So I put him in the other seat"—the shoulders quivered a little—"and drove him down by the river. Yes, I used his shovel. They say I jabbed him in, but I didn't mean to. That was the worst of all—I didn't even know about it till I read it in the paper . . . Then I started the car, jumped out, and let it ramble. I knew you'd find it in the river. I knew you'd find *him*. I knew you'd find *me*. But I thought it would be long before now."

The Inspector waited, then he said, "It didn't need to be so long. You could have come any time."

"I know. But what could I tell you? I never got done thinking

about it—never enough to understand, or to make you understand. There was a lot to think about, I tell you. My mother—she
won't *ever* understand."

The Inspector coughed. "What is there to understand?"

Archie, sitting up suddenly, searched the Inspector's face. "Why,
nothing, I guess. That was what I finally decided. Nothing—except
that I killed my friend. If I can't understand it, nobody can. And so
it makes no difference what anybody says. I did it, that's all. I mean,
you have to know—the *law*."

"I'm not the law." The Inspector touched the boy again, but on
the other shoulder. "I'm only this end of it. You have to come with
me, you know. We'll go now, and you can eat—Professor! What
about that steak?"

Eldred waved it out of existence. He was thinking: Sally ought to
have been here; it went as she would have had it go; at least, I think
so; I must see what she says; if I can only describe this boy—this
child.

Duke was busy as they passed him, and the customers at the
counter never glanced around. Later, they would buzz and buzz;
but now their silence was what the prisoner had to walk through.
He did so, stumbling more than once.

In the car, when it was headed back to the city, the Inspector had
one more subject to discuss.

"You saw me all the other times I was watching you there in the
diner?"

"Yes, sir, I saw you."

"What were you thinking about those times?"

Archie was silent.

"What were you looking at? What were you seeing?" The Inspector glanced at Eldred to make sure he was listening.

"You," said Archie.

"Yes, but what else? Who else?"

Archie was silent again.

"Tracy Herrold?"

"Of course," said Archie. "Him."

"After you had—"

"No! Oh, no! Before! I saw him as he always was, with all his nice
things. He was nice to me, too, you understand. I saw him that way,
just as if I never—I never—"

But he had.

That was the incomprehensible part.

CLERICAL ERROR

BY JAMES GOULD COZZENS

James Gould Cozzens was a sophmore at Harvard when his first book, *Confusion*, was published. He took a year off to write a second, but instead of returning to college afterward he went to teach children of American engineers at a sugar mill in Cuba. His keen interest in various aspects of life is illustrated in the subject matter of his novels: the sea in *S. S. San Pedro*, medicine in *The Last Adam*, the ministry in *The Just and the Unjust*, and war in his Pulitzer-winning *Guard of Honor*.

THERE WERE THREE steps down from the street door. Then the store extended, narrow and low between the book-packed walls, sixty or seventy feet to a little cubbyhole of an office where a large sallow man worked under a shaded desk-lamp. He had heard the street door open, and he looked that way a moment, peering intently through his spectacles. Seeing only a thin, stiffly erect gentleman with a small cropped white mustache, standing hesitant before the table with the sign *Any Book 50 Cents*, he returned to the folded copy of a religious weekly on the desk in front of him. He looked at the obituary column again, pulled a pad toward him and made a note. When he had finished, he saw, upon looking up again, that the gentleman with the white mustache had come all the way down the store.

"Yes, sir?" he said, pushing the papers aside. "What can I do for you?"

The gentleman with the white mustache stared at him keenly. "I am addressing the proprietor, Mr. Joreth?" he said.

"Yes, sir. You are."

"Quite so. My name is Ingalls—Colonel Ingalls."

"I'm glad to know you, Colonel. What can I—"

"I see that the name does not mean anything to you."

Mr. Joreth took off his spectacles, looked searchingly. "Why, no, sir. I am afraid not. Ingalls. No. I don't know anyone by that name."

Colonel Ingalls thrust his stick under his arm and drew an envelope from his inner pocket. He took a sheet of paper from it, unfolded the sheet, scowled at it a moment, and tossed it onto the desk. "Perhaps," he said, "this will refresh your memory."

Mr. Joreth pulled his nose a moment, looked harder at Colonel Ingalls, replaced his spectacles. "Oh," he said, "a bill. Yes. You must excuse me. I do much of my business by mail with people I've never met personally. 'The Reverend Doctor Godfrey Ingalls, Saint John's Rectory.' Ah, yes, yes—".

"The late Doctor Ingalls was my brother. This bill is obviously an error. He would never have ordered, received, or wished to read any of these works. Naturally, no such volumes were found among his effects."

"Hm," said Mr. Joreth. "Yes, I see." He read down the itemized list, coughed, as though in embarrassment. "I see. Now, let me check my records a moment." He dragged down a vast battered folio from the shelf before him. "*G, H, I*—" he muttered. "*Ingalls. Ah, now*—"

"There is no necessity for that," said Colonel Ingalls. "It is, of course, a mistake. A strange one, it seems to me. I advise you strongly to be more careful. If you choose to debase yourself by surreptitiously selling works of the sort, that is your business. But—"

Mr. Joreth nodded several times, leaned back. "Well, Colonel," he said, "you're entitled to your opinion. I don't sit in judgment on the tastes of my customers. Now, in this case, there seems unquestionably to have been an order for the books noted from the source indicated. On the fifteenth of last May I filled the order. Presumably they arrived. What became of them, then, is no affair of mine; but in view of your imputation, I might point out that such literature is likely to be kept in a private place and read privately. For eight successive months I sent a statement. I have never received payment. Of course, I was unaware that the customer was, didn't you say, deceased. Hence my reference to legal action on this last. I'm very sorry to have—"

"You unmitigated scoundrel!" roared Colonel Ingalls. "Do you really mean definitely to maintain that Doctor Ingalls purchased such books? Let me tell you—"

Mr. Joreth said: "My dear sir, one moment, if you please! Are you in a position to be so positive? I imply nothing about the purchaser. I mean to maintain nothing, except that I furnished goods, for which I am entitled to payment. I am a poor man. When people do not pay me, what can I do but—"

"Why, you infamous—"

Mr. Joreth held up his hand. "Please, please!" he protested. "I think you are taking a most unjust and unjustified attitude, Colonel. This account has run a long while. I've taken no action. I am well aware of the unpleasantness which would be caused for many customers if a bill for books of this sort was made public. The circumstances aren't by any means unique, my dear sir; a list of my confidential customers would no doubt surprise you."

Colonel Ingalls said carefully: "Be good enough to show me my brother's original order."

"Ah," said Mr. Joreth. He pursed his lips. "That's unfair of you, Colonel. You are quite able to see that I wouldn't have it. It would be the utmost imprudence for me to keep on file anything which could cause so much trouble. I have the carbon of an invoice, which is legally sufficient, under the circumstances, I think. You see my position."

"Clearly," said Colonel Ingalls. "It is the position of a dirty knave and a blackguard, and I shall give myself the satisfaction of thrashing you." He whipped the stick from under his arm. Mr. Joreth slid agilely from his seat, caught the telephone off the desk, kicking a chair into the Colonel's path.

"Operator," he said, "I want a policeman." Then he jerked open a drawer, plucked a revolver from it. "Now, my good sir," he said, his back against the wall, "we shall soon see. I have put up with a great deal of abuse from you, but there are limits. To a degree I understand your provocation, though it doesn't excuse your conduct. If you choose to take yourself out of here at once and send me a check for the amount due me, we will say no more."

Colonel Ingalls held the stick tight in his hand. "I think I will wait for the officer," he said with surprising composure. "I was too hasty. In view of your list of so-called customers, which you think would surprise me, there are doubtless other people to be considered—"

The stick in his hand leaped, sudden and slashing, catching Mr. Joreth over the wrist. The revolver flew free, clattered along the floor, and Colonel Ingalls kicked it behind him. "It isn't the sort of thing the relatives of a clergyman would like to have made public is it? When you read of the death of one, what is to keep you from sending a bill? Very often they must pay and shut up. A most ingenious scheme, sir."

Mr. Joreth clasped his wrist, wincing. "I am at loss to understand this nonsense," he said. "How dare you—"

"Indeed?" said Colonel Ingalls. "Ordinarily, I might be at loss myself, sir; but in this case I think you put your foot in it, sir! I happen to be certain that my late brother ordered no books from you, that he did not keep them in private or read them in private. It was doubtless not mentioned in the obituary, but for fifteen years previous to his death Doctor Ingalls had the misfortune to be totally blind. . . . There, sir, is the policeman you sent for."

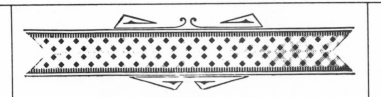

THE HUNTING
OF HEMINGWAY

BY MACKINLAY KANTOR

MacKinlay Kantor was born of divorced parents in Webster City, Iowa, on February 4, 1904. For a while he acted
as apprentice to his mother, who edited a daily newspaper in Webster City. As a young man he became a
reporter and free-lance writer before publishing *Diversey*,
a novel about Chicago gangsters, in 1928. Some of his
most notable writing has been about the Civil War and
America just after World War II. He is an expert fifer
and an honorary member of the National Association of
Civil War Musicians.

INSPECTOR BOURSE LOOKED VERY tired. He had been awake all night, and he was not as young as he had been in the days when he wore a gray helmet and sported a walrus-mustache.

The two young men and the two blowsy, over-dressed women crowded close around him as he sat crouched in the deep, gaudily upholstered chair.

Bourse asked, "How's your watch, Ricardi? And yours, Nick Glennan?"

Coonskin cuffs slid back from two husky wrists, and for a moment there was silence.

"Eight-eight, sir."

"That's me, Inspector. Eight-eight."

"You ladies"—he slurred the word—"got your guns in your pocketbooks?"

"Yes, sir."

"Then," said old Inspector Bourse, "I'd like to know what's keeping you. Go to it. Don't give 'em a break. They never gave a break in their lives, least of all Hemingway. And remember them vests. Shoot 'em in the kisser."

Said one of the women, whose name was Cohen, "That reminds me—"

"Shoot him in the pants," nodded the old chief, "the coat and vest is mine. All right, gentlemen."

They went out through the kitchen, and a uniformed patrolman opened the rear door. They went down two flights of bleak stairway and crowded into a red and black taxicab which had been waiting at the alley entrance with idling motor. Nobody said anything. The driver seemed very husky for a taxi driver—he should have been able to command an occupation more fitting to one who scaled two hundred and eight pounds and whose shoulders were all steel and wire.

At the Balmoral Street end of the alley, the taxicab turned left, and left a second time at Dorchester Avenue; now it was heading east and parallel to the alley where it had stood waiting a moment before. This block was lined almost solidly with apartment buildings of the less-than-first-class variety, though here and there an old residence stood out solidly, resisting the cheap encroachment of red and yellow brick walls.

"Right here," said the youngest, handsomest man, and the cab slowed to the curb in front of Number 1441.

The street looked innocent enough. It was then about eight-thirteen of an ordinary week-day morning, and Dorchester Avenue was an ordinary week-day street if ever there was one. A milk truck was parked ahead of the taxicab, and an express delivery van across the street. Protruding from a nearby delivery lane was the rear end of an Eclipse Laundry truck, and its driver was nowhere in sight. Apparently he had taken his little collapsible car and vanished within the nearest building, where no doubt he was gathering loads of soiled linen or distributing the unsoiled variety. From behind the flimsy, opaque curtains of an opposite apartment, Inspector Bourse looked down at all these things and called them good.

He knew, as well, that behind 1441 Dorchester Avenue a junkman was driving through the main alley and was just about to have an altercation with a city garbage truck which blocked his way. He knew that not all the tenants of 1441 were still asleep or sitting over early breakfasts. No, at least a dozen of those tenants had taken occupancy during the previous day and night—slyly, carefully, silently—and just now they would have firearms ready to hand.

In the stupid four-and-a-half story building which was numbered 1441, a young man sat in the tiny sun parlor of Apartment 327. He would have been exceedingly interested had he known that Inspector Bourse was watching his windows. He was not a nice young man. His face was the color of the paper in which your butcher wraps meat, and his mouth had come down directly from a remote ancestor who served as a torturer for Louis.

He was twenty-seven years old; he had killed men in Chicago, Dallas, Saginaw, Fort Wayne, Kansas City, Tulsa and in the town where he now sat. Mail trucks and banks had been levied upon, women had been forced to bestow their caresses upon him, and strangely enough some of them didn't have to be forced. The man's name was Chester Hemingway, and he had a personal, cash estate of three hundred and fifteen thousand dollars.

The young man was chewing something. His thin jaws worked knowingly, cruelly, and not with the comfortable carelessness of the habitual gum-chewer. They went crunching up and down, pulverizing some mysterious food between their gleaming white teeth. It was horrible but forever fascinating, to watch Chet Hemingway chew. He was always chewing.

"Chet," came a voice from the next room.

Without turning his head, Hemingway said, "Yea?" There was a scowl upon his face whenever he spoke.

"What's down there?"

"Cab. Couple of broads with two college boys in coon coats."

"They was making a lot of noise. I just wondered—"

Chet Hemingway told his companion, "Well, I'll do all the wondering that's done around here. Sure they're making a lot of noise. Anybody's making a lot of noise that's fried. These folks are fried—especially the two broads." He leaned an inch closer to the window and his icy green eyes stared down at the gay party advancing toward the court entrance directly below. "And broad is the word," he muttered to himself. "I like mine thinner than that."

He thought of Lily.

"Tomsk," he called, "where's Lil?"

"Still asleep, I guess."

"I wish to hell she'd get up and get us some breakfast. Tell her to get up."

He heard Tomsk mutter to Heras, and Heras went padding down the short hall to knock at a bedroom door. "Hey, Lil. Get up. Chet says for you to get up." Lil's fretful voice came back after a moment: "Oh, for God's sake!" She yawned. "Oh, all right," she said, "I'm comin', tell him."

Hemingway smiled. If one of those monkeys ever made a pass at Lily, he'd shoot his teeth out of his ears. Really, he must be getting fond of Lil—fonder than he'd ever been of anybody. That wouldn't do, to get fond of her. One of these days he'd have to get rid of her, one way or another. But for the present—

He heard the party of four—coon-skin college boys and fat, painted women, come lumbering up the stairway. His hand went to his belly-gun, then away from it. Drunks. Hell-raising punks with a couple of alley-cats they'd picked up during a night of revelry. Nobody to be alarmed about . . . Two Railway Express deliverymen came across the street, carrying a heavy box between them. Far down the hallway, a milkman clinked his bottles. There was the mutter of rubber tires close at hand—that laundryman was coming down the hall, knocking on doors as he came.

The radio mourned: "Laaaast Round-Up . . ."

Chet chewed and swallowed, swallowed and chewed. To the next room he called, "Hey, Tomsk. I hear the laundry guy coming. Tell Lil to get ready to go to the door. You scram, you and Heras." With sullen boredom, he lifted his eyes to the ceiling above his head.

325

How long, how long would they have to stay in this damn building, this damn town? But it was too hot to try for South America, yet. Maybe another month—

At that moment, he had the first notion that it might be a good idea to take Lil along with him when he went. He had meant to ditch her in New Orleans—give her a roll, if he felt she was safe, but ditch her. If he felt she wasn't safe, he could always put a hole through her and drop her off a bridge with an old steam radiator wired to her neck and legs. That had happened before, too. But not to Lil. That was Jenny. Jenny had never turned up again, either— the quicksands down deep in the river took care of that. It was one rap they'd never have against him.

Actually, Chet Hemingway was falling in love with Lil, and didn't realize it. It was funny: after all these weeks, and on this day when she was to be killed, that he should fall in love with her.

"Git along, little dogies, git along, little dogies—"

In the short stairway between the second and third floors, Detective Nick Glennan said to Detective Pete Ricardi, "Okay. Dave will be opposite that little service door in the side hall. Horn will go down there as soon as we pick up the Tom-gun."

One of the women, whose name was Cohen, gave a shrill and alcoholic laugh. He shone in the annual police vaudeville, did Benny Cohen. The other woman, whose name was Detective Barney Flynn, laughed even louder. But it was a coarse bellow; Flynn didn't make as good a woman as Cohen.

"You'll be bringing them out here, armed to the teeth," muttered Nick Glennan. "You sound like a hippopotamus, Barney. Okay," he said again, as they reached the third floor. Nick wasn't a sergeant yet, but he was commanding this squad, and if nothing went wrong he might very soon be a sergeant.

Detective Horn came trundling his laundry cart down the hall-way. He bestowed one solemn wink on the inebriated college boys and their blowsy companions; his face was rather pale. Ricardi leaned forward and lifted a Thompson submachine gun from under the pile of soft blue bags in the little cart. His coonskin coat slid from his shoulders; his slim hands moved capably from drum to trigger and back again; Ricardi was the best machine gunner in the entire police department.

The women were doing things to themselves. Their coats and henna wigs vanished—the dresses were brief and sketchy and wouldn't bother them much, though they lost their rhinestone-buckled shoes in a hurry. They emerged from their disguises

326

looking like nothing on land or sea, but they had .38's in their hands.

All this conversation, whispered as it was, and all this hasty disrobing and assembling of armature, took about three jerks. Horn ambled ahead, laundry cart and all, and vanished around the turn into the side hall where Sergeant Dave Glennan, Nick's fat brother, would be waiting inside the door of the opposite kitchen.

It didn't look like Hemingway and Tomsk and Scummy Heras had much of a chance. Across the street, Inspector Bourse and Chief of Detectives Moore were having a severe case of the jitters. Another minute, another two minutes—

The two Railway Express men dumped their box inside the vestibule on the opposite side of the court, and turning, drew their guns. In the alley at the rear, three detectives on an odoriferous garbage truck and two more detectives on a junkman's wagon, all became embroiled in a vituperative argument, which made it necessary for them to descend and gather opposite the back stairways.

A milkman came along the hall. He wore white and had an account-book, but his name was Detective Kerry. Silently the four other officers crept down the hall beside him. Kerry jangled bottles in the little wire basket he carried. *"Git along, little dogies,"* said Chet Hemingway's radio, *"git along—"*

They were on each side of the door of apartment 327. Nick Glennan pressed the little pearly button; Ricardi motioned for Kerry to jangle his bottles again, and under cover of the musical tinkle he made ready with his machine gun.

They heard a distant blatting of the kitchen buzzer; that was Horn.

"Milkman," chanted Detective Kerry.

"Laun-dry . . ." droned Detective Horn, far around the corner.

"Laaaast Round-Up . . . git along, little dogies . . ." Somewhere inside there was a woman's voice, and a man replied.

"Who's there?"

"Milk-mannn . . ."

The door opened a crack. Cohen reached up with his foot and shoved it back; the man inside was Two-faced Tomsk, and if indeed he had possessed two faces he couldn't have looked any more surprised.

"Stick 'em up, Tomsk," whispered Glennan. "You haven't got a chance."

They heard Sergeant Dave Glennan's voice from the kitchen door: "Look out, Horn!" and they heard the sharp report of a small automatic. Lil wasn't taking any chances, either—she must have carried a gun with her when she went to the door.

Two-faced Tomsk threw himself forward in a dive, wrenching out his revolver as he came. Scummy Heras had been lying flat on the high-backed davenport, out of sight, but he came up with a .45 in each hand.

Tomsk had fired once and his bullet went between Kerry's arm and the side of his body, and then Tomsk continued forward to the floor with two of young Nick Glennan's Police Positive souvenirs in his head.

Scummy Heras was more of a problem. The stool pigeon hadn't lied when he talked about bullet-proof vests. Ricardi's machine gun dusted the davenport in a quick staccato, but all it did was bruise Heras' ribs. One of the gangster's guns was empty by that time; he had put a bullet through Barney Flynn's chest, and a lot more too close for anybody's comfort.

Through the kitchenette and little hallway, Sergeant Dave Glennan and Laundryman Horn came roaring in a flank attack. "Drop it, Scummy," they were yelling, but Scummy didn't mind worth a cent. He was backed against the French windows, and he kept going as long as he could. A fistful of slugs from Dave's sawed-off mashed him back against the yielding windows—the panes went cracking to bits, and Heras' body dropped, turning and twisting, to the paved court three stories below.

But where was Mr. Chester Hemingway, who had slain men in Chicago, Kansas City and points east and west? When the screaming roar of exploded cartridges died down, the little radio was still mourning about the lonesome prairies, but Chet Hemingway wasn't around. Nick Glennan tripped over an upset chair and raced on into the sun parlor; his brother and Horn were diving into bedrooms, and from every stairway came a thunder of feet as the squads converged on apartment 327. But Chet Hemingway was not at home to receive them.

Nick flashed one baffled glance around the sun parlor. There was the radio, and there was Chet's half-burned cigarette already scorching the carpet, and there was—Nick swore, heartily. He climbed up on the table and stepped from there on top of the radiator. A square hole had been sawed in the ceiling, and through that hole it was evident that Chet Hemingway had gone soaring.

"Two apartments," Nick sobbed to himself. "Two! And nobody had an idea about it—327—427, right upstairs—to hell with that stool pigeon—"

He thrust his hands through the ragged opening and found solid wood still warm and slippery from the clutch of Chet Hemingway's hands. He hauled himself up into apartment 427. A scraping sound, somewhere—and, sure, he might have had a bullet through his head if Chet Hemingway had lingered to give it to him . . .

The apartment was furnished, like the one below, but it was evident at a glance that no one lived here. They had rented it for only one purpose—the very purpose which it had served. With a little more warning, the whole gang would have climbed through that square hole and disappeared.

The door into the hallway was wide open—Nick ground his teeth. A ladder stood against the wall at the end of the hall, and a trap in the roof was opened. To think that those devils would have anticipated the whole thing—ladder and all! He paused only to bellow at the men below him, and then swarmed up the ladder.

He came out into a glare of cold sunlight, and a bullet screeched beside the trap door. Nick Glennan growled, and raised his gun. On the next roof but one, a slim figure in white shirt and black pants was vaulting over a three-foot barrier. Nick had one un-exploded shell left in his cylinder. He spread his feet wide apart and took careful aim; the gun banged. The distant figure fell forward, recovered its balance, and sprinted ahead with torn shirt fluttering.

"Those *vests*," sighed Nick, "those inventions of the devil . . . and to think he wore it under his shirt . . . ." All this time he was racing across the gravel and jumping narrow chasms and leaping low walls, like a runaway maniac. He came to the last building of the row, and looked over the edge to see that mocking figure dropping from the last rung of the fire escape. Nick whistled; he yelled and beckoned to the other cops who were swarming out of the distant trap door; he threw a perfectly good gun which smashed on the pavement, missing Chet Hemingway's head by only six inches.

But it was all too late, now. Hemingway went up on one side of a taxicab; he thrust his gun against the driver . . . The detectives started after him one minute later, but that minute made about a mile's difference. And in crowded city streets, a mile is a mile. Still chewing and swallowing, Hemingway rode out of the detectives' lives. Temporarily. . . .

For all the secrecy with which this coup was planned, there had been a leak somewhere in the department. The press had been tipped off, and for once the press had not gummed things up. Men from the *News-Detail* and *Tribune* came swarming eagerly into the building from Dorchester Avenue; already flashlight bulbs were

329

flashing in the dim courts and alleyways, and reporters were clamoring.

Inspector Bourse and Chief of Detectives Moore fought their way through the crowd and up to apartment 327. With grim satisfaction they contemplated the prone body of Two-faced Tomsk and the shattered window where Scummy Heras had taken his last tumble. But when they looked around, hopefully, for another corpse—and found it—they were not so pleased. Miss Lily Denardo was the other corpse.

"Well," said the old Inspector. He looked down at the pretty, white face and the ridiculous folds of stained crêpe-de-chine which swatched the slim figure. "How'd this happen?"

Sergeant Dave Glennan's jowls trembled slightly. "I don't know. I'm afraid it was me."

"Had a gun, eh?" Bourse's foot touched the little automatic. "I don't think we'll be blaming you for this, Dave me boy."

The sergeant said, "That wasn't it. She did take a crack at Horn and me, but her gun jammed or something. Just one shot, and no more. She started in here—Scummy was shooting at the whole world, and I ups with my shotgun—"

Bourse looked at him. "And kills the girl with a .45 caliber bullet?" he asked, calmly.

Glennan blinked. "Thank Heaven for that! I never realized, sir. Yes, that hole does look like a .45. I—thought—"

"Never mind what you thought. Let's find the bullet."

"Here it is, sir," said Horn.

The bullet had driven through Miss Lily Denardo's heart, with the sad artistry of which that caliber is capable at close range and had lodged in the wall. They dug it out.

"Who was shooting .45's?" barked the Inspector.

Kerry scratched his torn sleeve. "Nobody except the Tom-gun—Ricardi. We all had regulation guns. And Ricardi's bullets would have had to ricky-shay to hit her where she was a-standing. No, sir—take a look at Scummy's guns. There's one on the floor, and I guess he took the other with him when he went through the window."

The ballistics expert established it later in the day; Scummy Heras had shot Lily, by design or accident. They never knew just how or why. It didn't matter. All the detectives were glad that none of them had killed her. She was too pretty.

"And so," Inspector Bourse grunted, at three o'clock that afternoon, "you let him get away. The meanest devil this side of hell, and you let him slide through your fingers."

330

Every man who had taken part in the Dorchester Avenue raid—except Flynn, who lay in the hospital—was in Inspector Bourse's office.

"Mind," he said, "I'm blaming not a mother's son of you—individually. You all worked hard and had your nerve with you. Young Nick Glennan especial. I'll say that. When he went kiting through that hole in the ceiling, he took a mighty chance."

Nick sat there and looked at his shoes. He felt his cheeks burning.

"But nevertheless, there you are. We had the best shots of the Bureau up there this morning, and we had the edge on that gang. And we let Hemingway get away. Sure, we didn't know about that apartment upstairs. Nobody did. The stool pigeon didn't. But our job was to get Chet Hemingway, more than any of the rest. We didn't get him. *Your* job was to get Chet Hemingway. *You* didn't get him. There it is. Eat it up; may it make you sick at the stomach."

His desk telephone jangled. Slowly, Bourse reached down and lifted the bracket. "I told you not to bother me," he growled at the operator. "I—What? . . . All right," he said, "connect me."

He looked at the rows of faces across his desk. "A man," he said. "Claims he has something important about this morning."

A new voice came on the wire. The eyes of Inspector Bourse froze bitterly as he listened.

"This," said the voice, "is Chet Hemingway—"

"Yes," said Bourse. His voice crackled. His hand slid across the transmitter as he snapped at Ricardi, who sat directly in front of him, "Get on a phone. Trace this call! . . ."

"You didn't get me this morning," came Hemingway's voice, "and I'm still in town. Listen, you dirty flatfoot—you had to kill that little frail—she was a peach of a kid—she—"

Bourse said, "We didn't kill her, Hemingway. Scummy did it."

"Yeah?" snarled Chet. "Listen—I'm not going to stay here long enough for you to trace this call. But I read the papers. Every damn sheet in town was shouting the praises of the noble detectives you had up there—and by *name*—get that? By name. I'm going to stay in town until I get every last guy who was in on that job. And you, too! I'll get you all."

There was a click.

Bourse leaped to his feet. "Did you get it?" he roared through the open door where Ricardi had gone.

No, no. There hadn't been enough time . . .

Briefly and pointedly, Bourse told the men what Hemingway had said. They weren't much impressed; most of them had heard that story before. "Go out and get Hemingway," said the old man in dismissal. And they went, hopefully.

But it wasn't so funny an hour later. Chief of Detectives Moore came in, with no ceremony. "Ricardi's dead," he cried. "He was crossing the street at Comanche and Main, and a car came past and hit him. Head on. Dragged him three hundred feet."

Bourse kneaded the cigar-stub in his fingers. "Must have been an accident. He turned around and looked at the window.

"Hit-and-run?" he asked, over his shoulder.

"Yes," said Moore, "Hit-and-run. They got the car ten minutes later. It was a hot car. But the driver was gone."

The Inspector sat in silence for a time, drumming on the desk with his fingers. "We traced Hemingway how far?"

"Well, he took the taxi driver's coat and cap, and made him get out of the cab at Fourth and Mississippi. They found the cab about eleven o'clock on Mulberry Street. It had only been run nine miles in all, according to a check. We can't say definitely that we traced him to Mulberry Street, as we don't know what happened in between—"

Bourse nodded. "I'm thinking I'd better talk to my stool pigeon."

"It may mean his life, now," said the chief of detectives.

"So it may. His name is Adamic. Know him?"

"No. Who is he?"

"A pawnbroker and loan-shark down in the Delta. On Sage Street, to be exact.

Moore wagged his head. "I remember, now. George Adamic. A small, gray fellow with black eyes."

"Yes. It seems that he knew Two-faced Tomsk from 'way back, and had disposed of some bonds for him after that Western Savings stick-up. Adamic is as close as the tomb. We could never have sweat nothing out of him; he came to me voluntarily, and made me swear—" Bourse made a wry face. "We both belong to the same lodge, and it's one to which you belong as well. He made me swear I wouldn't turn him in."

Moore asked, "Why was he singing about Hemingway?"

"He knew they was in apartment 327 at 1441 Dorchester Avenue, and that was all he knew, except that they had a young arsenal and wore vests. Moore, it seems that Hemingway pushed over a man named Kolchak in Chicago last month. And Kolchak was George Adamic's brother-in-law. Family ties—nothing less. That's the only reason he talked."

"You'd best talk to Adamic now," nodded Moore.

Bourse took up his phone.

"If he's still alive," added Moore, softly.

And when George Adamic didn't answer the telephone which rang so long and stridently in his narrow little shop, Inspector Bourse sent Squad Sixteen whistling in that direction. Sergeant Dave Glennan and Detectives Horn and Kerry found the store unlocked, and it was a wonder that folks in that scrubby neighborhood hadn't looted the place of every last thing. Only their inherited terror of George Adamic and the power he wielded over their sad little lives, had kept them from raiding his shop, unguarded and defenseless as it was.

Detective Horn it was who found George Adamic in a dark washroom behind the rows of secondhand overcoats. Adamic was shot through the heart and the medical examiner estimated that he had been dead since about nine o'clock that morning.

Nick Glennan's handsome face was a bit drawn. Inspector Bourse's harsh accusation was still ringing in his ears; he felt that he had failed, miserably enough, when circumstances demanded the most of him. And now, to be sent for—private and special—Maybe old Bourse was going to ask him to turn in his gun and badge. And after being promoted to plainclothes only last fall! Well, heaven knew that he must have deserved it.

"Sit down, Nick," said the old inspector.

"Begging your pardon," murmured Nick, "I'll take it standing up."

There was a sudden, misty twinkle in the older man's eyes. He saw that his door was locked and the heavy shade drawn over the window, and then he sat down behind his desk and looked at Nick. Distantly a chiming clock announced that it was five-thirty.

"Glennan," asked Bourse, "do you know why I sent for you?"

"I'm afraid I do. But I hope I don't."

Bourse grinned wearily. "Pshaw, why are you a-worrying? That was a bad break." He smoked in silence for a moment. "Nick, you're young—"

"Yes, sir. I'll be getting over it as rapidly as possible."

"You've got nerve."

"I hope so, sir."

"And brains."

"Well," said Nick.

"Every man in my department has nerve, and most of them have got a brain or two. But you have something else. You showed it when you was a rookie cop and helped clean out that gang on Acola Street; and you showed it when you ran down those Kentucky

333

gorillas that had us all stumped, in the fall. That's the reason you're wearing plainclothes. You have that strange and fortunate thing which you have through no fault of your own: instinct, my boy. A nose for it."

Bourse wrinkled his own pug nose in demonstration. "Your big brother Dave is a good sergeant; I wouldn't be asking for none better. But he ain't got the hunch that you have—the kind of natural, hound-dog notion of being a good detective—smelling things out. Nick, did any of your ancestors, rest their souls, have second sight?"

Nick wriggled. "I've heard that my father was the seventh son of a seventh son, sir. But I'm only the second son of a seventh son."

"However that may be, what would you do about Hemingway?"

"I'd like to get him, sir."

"I want you to tell me, me boy."

Nicholas Glennan stood looking at the carpet for awhile. "We haven't much to go on, sir."

"Mulberry Street is right near Adamic's place. You know about Adamic? Very good. Hemingway must have ditched his cab, walked in there, shot Adamic, and walked out again."

"Yes, sir. But not in taxi clothes."

"What would he have done?"

"At least he would have put on a good suit and hat, and maybe taken a suitcase or traveling bag. The store was full of 'em, and some not half bad. Hemingway's always been one to take life easy and comfortable, sir, or so his record shows. Probably he had money on him. Maybe a belt, under that bullet-proof vest."

Bourse nodded slightly. "I'm 'way ahead of you, boy. But he wouldn't show that face around town—not with the papers full of it, and a million people gasping for the reward."

"But he wouldn't have had time for much disguise, sir. Not a hair-bleach or nothing like that. It would have to be quick and simple."

"The usual? Glasses? Mustache?"

"That's my notion, Inspector. This loan-broker had whole cases full of bankrupt notions—glasses of various kinds, even false whiskers, perhaps."

Bourse sighed. "Blue goggles and green whiskers! I thought better of your perspicacity, me boy."

"It's doing fine, sir. My per—what you said."

Bourse played with a pen-holder. "And then?"

"The witness to the killing of Ricardi said that a young man with glasses drove the car, sir."

Bourse hunched his shoulders, as if expecting a bullet to come through the window behind him. "Do you think he'll make good his boast, and stay around town long enough to get every one of us, as he promised?"

"No," said Nick, promptly, "when he's cooled off he'll see that the average is ag'inst him. But he might try to get another one or two."

"You feel certain of it?"

"He's a mad dog, they say. What the stories call a Lone Wolf. A red-hot killer, and always has been. And like all of them, he is what you call an ee-gow-ist. He'll want to write his name in large letters before he leaves town."

Bourse slammed up out of his chair. "I'm afraid we're getting nowhere. What do you think is the best bet? What would you do if you had your choice and was playing a free hand? I've got men all over town, a-raiding here and a-raiding there, and every cop on every corner is on the lookout. But what would you like to do?"

"Begging your pardon," whispered Nick, "but I'd like to stick beside the man he's most like to come after, next."

"And that's—"

"Yourself, sir."

Chet Hemingway looked very dignified and circumspect. He did not look at all like a mad dog, although he might have answered up to Nick Glennan's characterization as an egoist.

"Drive me," he told the taxicab driver, "to 561 Alamo Street."

"Yes, sir." They started away from the curb.

The minutes passed to the feeble ticking of the meter. Dusk was here, and the low-lit auto lights swished past on every side. Alamo Street was a narrow, quiet court a bare mile from the heart of town; it was here, at 558, that Inspector Bourse lived with his plump wife and his plump, old-maid daughter.

The driver set Hemingway down promptly enough in front of the old apartment building numbered 561, and Hemingway paid the bill. He tipped, not extravagantly or penuriously, but in an ordinary fashion; it was not well for the taxi driver to have a too clear memory of his passenger. Then Hemingway stepped into the lobby of the building and examined mail boxes until the cab drove away.

He walked back out to the curb and glanced to the east and west. Couldn't be better. There were only two cars parked in the entire block, and between Number 561 and the next building ra~ a narrow sluice which led to a rear alley—he could see the lights back there glistening on the lids of garbage cans. Inspector Bourse lived

335

straight across the street. If he had come home before this, he would be going out again. Hemingway's mouth slid back in a bitter smile, his killing grin, as he reasoned how stupid the motive which had prompted Inspector Bourse to have his address and telephone number listed in the directory.

Chet Hemingway leaned among the shadows near the opening of the area way and waited. He could wait without jumping nerves or too eager mind; he had spent a good share of his life waiting for men to come, waiting for mail trucks, and bank watchmen. Once he had even waited eighteen months in a penitentiary before his chance came. But whenever the opportunity appeared, the opportunity for which Chet happened to be waiting, no one could grasp it any quicker than he. That was how he happened to have more than three hundred thousand dollars stowed in various corners of the country, and a good fifteen thousand dollars fastened next to his skin, under his expensive silk undershirt.

Two girls passed; an old man; a plump woman; solitary young men. Homegoing folks, bound for dinner and quiet evenings in their apartments. Only one person entered the building at 558, and that was a young girl—stenographer, probably. Idly, Hemingway wondered whether she knew Bourse. He put his hand into his coat pocket, took out his usual food, and began to crack it between his teeth.

He thought of Lily. Sentimental and superstitious, like most of his kind, he began to think of Lily as a swell dame—a kind of saint—now that she was dead. "I'll get the dirty louse, kid," he told her. This would look good in the tabloids. *Lone Wolf Killer Avenges Murder of Sweetheart Slain by Cops.* It was pretty good stuff.

He stiffened. Here was a cop, a big, stupid patrolman, lumbering down the street with idly-swinging club. He might flash a light into the narrow path between the two buildings, and it wouldn't be safe to hide there. Chet didn't want to bump off a cop. He wanted to bump off Inspector Bourse.

So he bent forward and peered into the gloom. "Kitty," he began to call, softly, "here, kitty-kitty." The cop came closer. Hemingway still called to his cat. The heavy feet ambled past.

"Oh, officer," Chet said.

The man stopped. "Yeh?"

"If you see a black kitten down the block anywhere, would you mind sticking it in the vestibule here at 561? My kid's cat. Run away . . . Here, kitty-kitty-kitty."

"Sure." The cop lumbered away. Chet stared after him with narrowed eyes. Like to let him have it. Now he hoped that Bourse wouldn't appear on the doorstep until the cop was around the next corner.

The patrolman had just disappeared when a big car hummed into Alamo Street from the Avenue. Its brakes crunched; it stopped in front of 558 . . . A department car; yes, Hemingway could see a gong above the running-board. Bourse got out.

Chet swallowed the last tiny morsel in his mouth. He brought out his gun; the belly-gun from inside his trousers—he had two, now—and one had been taken from Adamic's shop that morning. Wait until the car was at least half a block up the street. The old devil would still be fooling with his door key, or at least standing in the vestibule, plainly visible from outside. The men in the car would either have to turn it, or else jump out and run back; that was all the start Hemingway would need.

"Nine o'clock."

"You bet, sir."

A cab was coming from the direction of the avenue, coming slowly, as if hunting for an address. The big department car moved away from the curb—screeched into second gear—went purring away down the block. Chet's left hand went to the automatic, Adamic's gun, and brought it out. He would have to stop that cab before it interfered, though experience had taught him to fear nothing from the terrorized bystanders at such a scene.

Inspector Bourse's portly body was sharply outlined against the vestibule lights. Oh, you old Mick, thought the bandit, I've seen you more than once before this . . . His belly-gun began to stutter. Bourse fell against the door. Those were soft-nosed bullets, and they would play hell with any man's ribs. With his left hand, Hemingway turned his automatic toward the advancing taxicab. One shot in the radiator or windshield—he wasn't particular—

A long, bright smear came from the side of the cab, and something tore at the skirt of Chet Hemingway's coat. He snarled, and stepped back into the narrow court between the buildings. He had fixed old Bourse, but he wasn't expecting this. Bullets squirted all around him, flattening among the bricks. He let his whole clip speed toward the taxicab, then he turned and ran. In his heart he was cursing savagely. Those damn fly-cops—they were half a block or more away, and out of the picture. But this cab—Who in—

A bullet screamed from the concrete beside him, and still he could feel that wrenching blow which had torn his coat. Just that close . . . He sprinted twenty yards down the alley, dodged between a line of garages, and sped out into the street beyond. It was a through street, and there were plenty of cars, parked or moving. In

337

the distance behind him he heard yells and pounding feet. At the first entrance he found, he dodged inside. Luck. Plenty of it. He needed it.

It was an office building with an L-shaped vestibule opening on the side street and on the avenue as well. Over here the humming traffic had drowned all the affray on Alamo Street. Chet strolled around the corner of the corridor, trying to still the hammering heart inside his body. The one elevator man on duty nodded at him.

Hemingway glanced at the directory on the wall. The little white lines of names were swimming. He picked one out . . . Jacobson, Rudolph. 420. He turned to the elevator man.

"Is Mr. Jacobson gone?" His gasping lungs pushed up against his throat, but he fought them back.

"Yes, sir. It's after six. Most everybody's gone."

"Okay."

He went out to the avenue. A row of waiting taxicabs blurred before his eyes, and distantly he could hear a siren whining. These folks would think it was a fire truck. Well, it wasn't any fire truck.

He stepped into the first cab. "Let's go downtown," he said.

"Yes, sir."

They went toward the bridge, through the evening crush of cars, and Chet Hemingway had the pleasure of watching traffic cops clear the northbound lanes to make passage for a rocketing squad car which hooted its way toward Alamo Street. He fumbled for a cigarette, and found a torn paper of matches ground into the hole in his coat pocket. The bullet of the would-be avenger had come just that close. He swore. But there was his food—a little of it, still left to him. Chet began to crack it between his jaws.

He'd better get out of town as soon as possible. One way or another. They'd have picked men at every station, and the highways wouldn't be very safe. He'd have to think.

He arrived at his hotel safely enough and went without further incident to his room. But during the next hour, when he sat munching, enjoying a cigarette or two and coldly reenacting the finish of Inspector Bourse, his leaping brain would have turned to jelly had it visualized the steel net which was closing in on him.

Bourse drew a long breath. "Glennan," he said to Nick, "what was that about your being the seventh son of a seventh son?"

"It wasn't me. It was the old man."

"Nevertheless—"

"Heras will be hotter than ever in hell, sir, when he realizes that you was wearing his bullet-proof vest."

The old inspector rubbed his sore body and examined the shreds in his clothing. "It's a wonderful vest, boy. I don't see why hoods always have these things better than the cops, but they do. At least nobody could ever blame you for not dropping Hemingway, up there on the roof."

"I should have drilled him through the head, sir."

Bourse fingered a tiny scrap of limp, gilded cardboard which he held in his hands. "At least you drilled this out of his pocket."

"Yes, but it's twice in one day that I had him under my gun and let him get away."

They stood there together in front of a gleaming spotlight while officers swarmed through every nook and cranny along Alamo Street. Bourse turned to Sergeant Dave Glennan. "No use, Dave. He's gone. But he left his calling card."

The fat sergeant waddled over to the shaft of light. "I'll take you on, sparrow cop," he told his younger brother, "at any shooting gallery in the Palace Amusement Park, when it opens in warm weather."

"You go to hell," whispered Nick.

"Shut up your big gab, Dave," added the inspector, kindly. "Nick was shooting from a moving taxicab, into the dark—shooting at gun-flashes—and anyway, if it hadn't been for him you'd be getting your shoes shined for an inspector's funeral."

He offered the torn scrap of cardboard. "This was over there across the street where he stood, when we looked for bloodstains."

Dave turned the fragment between his big fingers. He spelled aloud, "Diamond Match Com . . . E . . . L. And what's this that looks like the west end of a spider?"

"It's a coat-of-arms, Owl Eyes." snarled his brother, "and that is by way of being his stopping place. You don't recognize the souvenir matches of high-priced hotels, but the inspector does. He says that is part of a fold of matches from the Aberdeen Hotel."

"Just because you found it over there—"

"If you look close, Owl Eyes, you can see the fuzz of lead along one side. The luck of Nicholas Glennan was working; I ripped open his pocket, and half the torn paper of matches comes out."

"But," cried Dave, "that's no sign he's there!"

"He took a suit from Adamic's store, or I don't know where else. And do them secondhand guys leave matches lying around in the pockets of their suits? No, Macushla. He gathered that up today since he's been on the loose. And not in no one-arm restaurant, but likely enough in a hotel room."

The inspector said, "Get your squad together, Dave. Tell Rhineheimer to get his."

"Yes, sir. But—God—you can't raid the whole hotel. It's got twenty-two hundred rooms!"

"We cannot. But we can soon get a list of the folks who registered today, and their room numbers. And after that, in case we run up against a snag, your kid brother that once was a sparrow cop in a park—well, he's got an idea. And I've observed that his ideas are apt to be good."

"What is this idea that he has, inspector?"

For reply, Nick displayed some very small, silvery fragments in the palm of his big hand. They were egg-shaped bits, crusted with a strange and frosty deposit, and none of them was longer than three-quarters of an inch. "Over there on the sidewalk, beside that alley," his polite voice announced.

"*Them!*" snorted Dave Glennan. "*Them!* What the hell! What's the worth of those? Nicholas, why don't you turn in your badge and gun, and become a member of the white wings? You scavenger, you."

"Well," said Nick, "I've seen them before. And many of them." He dropped the fragments into his vest pocket.

"We're a-wasting time," Inspector Bourse announced to the listening world.

The chambermaid—Number Seventy-two, she was, of the Aberdeen Hotel—had plenty of nerve. Really she didn't need a lot of nerve, since she wasn't compelled to place herself within the range of direct gunfire. When Nicholas Glennan tapped softly upon the door of Room 1661, and an answering bark came from inside, the woman controlled her quivering throat adequately.

She crouched close beside the thick wall and said, "Chambermaid."

The man inside the room seemed waiting for something. Finally he spoke in a voice full of annoyance. "I don't need you, girlie. Trot along."

For a fatal moment there was silence in the hall, and inside the room.

"Just to clean up your room, sir."

There had been people outside the door, up there in Dorchester Avenue—milkman, laundryman—the door had been opened, and then the law had come. Chet Hemingway wasn't taking a chance in the world.

He snarled, "Run along and peddle yourself some place else!"

Gently, Nick Glennan drew the frightened chambermaid around the corner, past the house detectives and the group of hard-faced officers from headquarters. "What he says is good advice, lady," he murmured. "You'd better go." There was a tense shuffling of feet on the thick rug.

Glennan looked coolly into the eyes of a brother detective. "It's him?"

"Sure. His voice. I was a witness in K. C. when they had him up for trial. Know it anywhere."

"Okay," breathed Nick Glennan.

He said, "Hemingway. Are you going to come out, or do you want to be carried? Last fall we said that to some hoods, and they decided to stay. We carried them out and embalmed them. What do you say?"

In 1661, Chet Hemingway took out his two guns and turned toward the door. He fancied how it would look, in the headlines. "I say come and get me, if you're man enough!" He put a heavy slug through the door.

"I am," responded Nick, "and here—I—come."

A machine gun was lifted, but Nick's gesture stayed the ready finger. "No," he muttered, "I missed him—twice. This time it's me or him."

He took care of the lock with his first three bullets, and heavy pebbles of lead gouged whole strips out of the veneer as he kicked against the wrecked door . . . Inside, there was the distant slam of the bathroom door, so Glennan braced his whole body against the big slice of wood which blocked his way. He crashed to the floor, the sundered hinges flying wide. The bathroom door opened a crack, and in that crack was a jet of dancing flame . . . turned out the lights . . . well, one or the other of them, there in the dark.

Flat on the floor, with the air splitting beside his ears, he took steady aim at a point above the flashes, and scattered his three remaining bullets there. There was sudden silence—a cough, and then the sound of a body falling into a bathtub.

They switched on the lights, and sniffed in the doorway.

"He got Glennan."

Bourse groaned from the hall, "Oh, the black-hearted—"

"The hell he got Glennan," said Nick. He climbed to his feet and pushed the bathroom door wide. For one in Hemingway's messy

341

condition, the bathtub was a very good place for him to be sprawled.

Inspector Bourse looked at the corpse. "You must have second sight," he muttered.

"No indeed, sir. It was the shells."

He found them in his vest pocket, and juggled them in his hands.

"Pistachio nuts," somebody said.

Nick Glennan nodded, soberly. After all, Hemingway had been a man and now he wasn't anything. Rest his soul if possible . . . "The nut shells was all over the sun parlor, up on Dorchester Avenue," he said. "They was also scattered on the sidewalk tonight when he waited for the inspector. He was a pig for them, it would seem. When the bellboy said that the man in Room 1661 of this hotel had sent twice for pistachio nuts during the day, it had to be Hemingway and no other. Probably he's feeding on them this minute, wherever he's gone."

"I'll answer that," remarked his brother, grimly. "If Hemingway is eating pistachio nuts this minute, he's eating roasted ones."

THE BOTTLE MINE

BY KENNETH L. ROBERTS

Kenneth Roberts (b. Kennebunk, Maine, December 8, 1885) was a newspaperman, an editor, a translator and a voluminous writer. Poet Robert P. T. Coffin called him "a quicksilver mind among the leaden historians, a running almanac and encyclopedia of Maine, from cooking to colonial wars." Some of the best American historical novels are his *Arundel, Rabble in Arms, Northwest Passage* and *Lydia Bailey*. He and his wife published an excellent translation of Morceau de St. Méry's *Voyage aux Etats-Unis d'Amerique*. Mr. Roberts died in 1957.

ANTIQUE COLLECTORS DEVELOP strange and sometimes unpleasant traits. Certain forms of antique collecting, furthermore, seem to bring out these traits with unusual virulence. The collecting of curly maple frequently makes a collector wholly unreasonable and irresponsible. The collecting of Currier & Ives prints occasionally brings out his stubbornness and miserly traits. The collecting of pewter is apt to accentuate his indecision and vacillation. The collecting of early pine is likely to develop his intolerance and conceit; while the collecting of fine Chippendale furniture is more apt to bring out his boastfulness and arrogance.

Worst of all, however, in the development of hidden and unsuspected traits, is the collecting of early American glass and bottles. Such collecting, in many cases, works as insidiously on the character of the collector as did the hellish liquors that were so often contained in the bottles.

Why it should be so, I do not know. The fact remains that one can never tell about the bottle specialist. He may be normal as any other collector; and then again, beneath an impassive and seemingly harmless exterior, there may lurk a relentlessness of purpose and a cruelty that would shock and horrify a Chicago detective sergeant.

Whitney Leet was one of America's greatest bottle specialists. His knowledge of glass was so extensive that he refused to purchase any of the glass known as Stiegel unless he could get at five-and-ten-cent store prices, inasmuch as he knew there are nineteen glass factories in existence able to make a grade of glass that Baron Stiegel could not have told from his own products.

In the matter of bottles, however, Leet made no effort to control himself at any time. He frequently traveled halfway across the continent to look at an amethyst or blue whiskey flask of unknown origin or unusual design; and from the prices that he occasionally paid for such flasks, one might have thought that they were going to yield a return of 25 per cent a year for the remainder of his days.

In his home life he was gentle and kindly; but when he embarked on the trail of a rare flask, he became as hard-boiled and cunning as a gunman under the influence of opiates.

If a friend or an acquaintance attempted to vie with him in the purchase of a desirable flask, Leet became almost ferocious in his attitude. He never resorted to kicking or biting at such moments, so far as was known; but he had no hesitation in treading heavily on the tender portion of a foot, or of thrusting himself rudely in front of other people.

I would, however, have suspected him of no greater infraction against good taste and decency if Leet himself had not called me to him early in the spring and told me the harrowing tale of Bill Swiggert and the Bottle Mine.

It seems that the late autumn had found Leet nervously exhausted from the intensive hunt for early American flasks in which he had indulged during the preceding summer and spring. Instead of hunting leisurely through the countryside, as he had been accustomed to do in his early days of flask hunting, he had been obliged to compete with such energetic newcomers in the field of bottle collecting as Joseph Hergesheimer and Edwin Le Fevre, whose squirrel-like activities had forced him to use high-pressure methods of the most exhausting nature in order to keep abreast of them, to say nothing of occasionally putting himself a jump or two in advance of them.

Haggard and worn by his strenuous toil, Leet determined to banish all thoughts of flasks and bottles from his mind for several months, and to travel to California through the soft warmth of the great Southwest, where the burning rays of the seldom-obscured sun scorch the poisons of fatigue from Eastern bones and brains; and where antiques, in the true sense of the word, are unknown.

Occasionally, in the West and Southwest, Leet knew, one encountered a so-called antique shop. Its stock, Leet had further learned, invariably consisted of the least desirable types of Empire furniture; while post-empire black walnut chairs and sofas, with bunches of grapes carved promiscuously on their frames, were assiduously sought by the so-called antique collectors who lived in those sections.

Consequently, he embarked on his trip secure in the knowledge that he would be tempted to indulge in none of the exhausting hunts for antiques that had made life in more effete sections of America so strenuous and debilitating. As a matter of precaution, however, he carried with him an amethyst Corn For The World flask, so that it could be exhibited as a sample in any section where the need of investigating the flask situation should arise.

Leet traveled by roadster, driving himself and without companions. From Chicago he drove southwest to San Antonio, Texas. He made a perfunctory inquiry for flasks in San Antonio, but found only one repulsive-looking Masonic flask in the most offensive brown glass.

He struck the Mexican border at Laredo, and then turned westward into the face of the setting sun, constantly acquiring new strength and vigor from the warm, dry air that blew across the endless seas of mesquite, and resting his shattered nerves on the flawless and—to Eastern eyes—untraveled roads that carried him ever westward through Eagle Pass, Del Rio, the Big Bend country, and past the barren hills and the towering smelters of El Paso into New Mexico and the purple mountains of southern Arizona.

It was late on a hot December night that his car coasted down the hill slopes of the mining town of Douglas. Parched by his dusty ride, Leet forbore even to stop at the hotel to secure a room, but pressed on another half mile and crossed the border into Agua Prieta to revel in the dry Martinis and the brimming beakers of beer that, for Americans, surround even the most tawdry and dirty of the Mexican border towns with an atmosphere of romance and old-world quaintness.

The Boston Bar and Café, which Leet entered, was entertaining a group of Douglas businessmen, who had laid down their bridge hands in the Elks Club for a moment, according to their usual after-dinner custom, and hastened over to Agua Prieta for their second drink of the evening. Shortly after Leet's entrance they hastened back to their bridge games in the Elks Club; and Leet found himself alone before the bar, except for a single morose individual in flannel shirt and overalls, who gazed gloomily at a bottle of Mexican rye whiskey and occasionally helped himself to a drink from it.

In· the course of time Leet struck up a conversation with the morose individual by asking his opinion of the Mexican whiskey that he was absorbing. It was, the overalled man said, neither good nor bad; merely drinkable. Leet, though slightly repelled by his gloominess, invited him to dine with him, and the two of them wrestled with a beefsteak that for thickness and toughness—like most of the beefsteaks in the great southwestern cow country— rivaled a sheet of crêpe rubber.

It developed, during the dinner, that the gloomy person's name was Bill Swiggert and that he was a prospector. He had, he revealed, combed through the Hauchuca Mountains and the Continental Divide in search of metals of a more or less precious nature until his interior had taken on the character of the country. He came out of the mountains after a prospecting trip, he said, like the Copper Queen of Bisbee—like a big blue hole in the ground: a copper-lined hole.

That was why, he explained, he always purchased a bottle of

346

Mexican rye whiskey when he entered a Mexican bar for drinking purposes. Anything less would be as devoid of chemical action as spraying a cupful of beef tea into a copper boiler with a perfumery atomizer.

Leet ventured the statement that his road to California led him through the ancient mining section of Arizona—through, in particular, Tombstone. Tombstone, Leet opined, must be a strange and wonderful sight, deserted and redolent of vanished glories.

Bill Swiggert remarked that Leet would be surprised. Tombstone, he said, was just like any other place except that the old front of the Birdcage Theatre was still standing. Outside of that, there were just as many people hanging around doing nothing as there were anywhere else in southern California or the Southwest. Everybody had a Chevrolet or a Buick or a Ford; and the high-school girls wore silk stockings and skirts just as short as anywhere else, and gave passing tourists the eye without meaning anything, the way they do in Ohio and Iowa, and so on.

For real spooky sights, Swiggert said, you had to go back into the mountains and look at some of the real deserted camps through which he had traveled and in which he had frequently resided, alone except for his pack mule, for weeks at a time—such camps, for example, as Canned Tomato, Full of Hell, Soak Hollow, Sinful, and Parboil. In some of these camps, declared Swiggert, they must have devoted themselves almost exclusively to drinking, if such remaining signs of human habitation as whiskey bottles could be trusted.

At this point Leet excused himself and went to his automobile. From one of the side pockets he took his amethyst Corn For The World flask, wrapped carefully in sheets of cotton batting, and returned with it to Swiggert.

Had Swiggert, asked Leet, unwrapping the bottle as though it were a star sapphire, ever seen anything like that in his wanderings among the deserted mining camps?

Swiggert examined the flask with some care, helped himself to another drink of Mexican rye whiskey, and asked Leet what sort of bottle it was. Leet explained that it was one of the early type of American bottles which had been made in great numbers around the time of the Mexican War and the Civil War, as well as earlier in the century. Through breakage, however, they had become scarcer and scarcer, he said; so that good flasks, especially colored flasks, had become somewhat valuable.

Swiggert essayed the opinion that if they were valuable, he supposed a bottle like Leet's would be worth as much as two or three dollars. Leet, somewhat distressed at having one of his finest flasks undervalued in this way, laughed unpleasantly and said that if Swiggert could buy one for a hundred dollars, he might consider himself lucky.

The flask seemed to hold a strong fascination for Swiggert. He studied it from every side. He wished to know whether a bottle had to have that color in order to be valuable. A blue bottle or a green bottle, for example—would these colors be valuable? he asked.

Leet told him that a blue bottle was nearly as valuable as an amethyst bottle, but that a green bottle or a brown bottle was not one fifth as valuable as the other colors. A golden yellow color, however, was moderately valuable, and an aquamarine, or colorless bottle was worth more than a green or a brown one.

Swiggert then wanted to know about the design on the bottle. Leet's for example, had a likeness of an ear of corn in the glass, and the words "Corn For The World." For a bottle to be valuable, he wanted to know, did it have to have this design.

It was around this time that Leet awakened to the possibilities of the situation. He knew from long experience that to the average human being a bottle is only a bottle; just as furniture is merely furniture to the person who has never been educated in antiques. The person who knows nothing about antiques can enter a room furnished with the finest Chippendale, Heppelwhite, and Sheraton and see no distinguishing marks about any of the pieces.

In the same way, the person whose attention has never before been directed to bottles is unable to distinguish any design that may be blown in the glass, or the color of the bottle. Frequently he is even blind to its shape, unbelievable as this may seem to the average bottle collector. Consequently, Leet realized that Swiggert had somewhere encountered other whiskey flasks, and that he wished to keep his discovery to himself until he knew all about the bottles.

Leet therefore dissembled busily. He dropped his Corn For The World Flask into his pocket and said indifferently that for a bottle to be valuable it should have an ear of corn blown in its side. There were, he added with a seeming lack of interest, one or two other designs that gave a bottle a certain value, provided its color was right. At the moment, he added, he had forgotten what these other designs were.

Swiggert then confirmed Leet's suspicions by asking whether a bottle was any good if it had a train of cars on one side of it. Leet asked whether the bottle to which he referred was a green bottle or a brown bottle. Swiggert replied that it was a blue bottle.

Leet at once displayed the cruelty and relentlessness that had been developed in him by bottle collecting by replying that if this blue bottle merely had a train of cars on it, it was worth two dollars, but that if it had the words "Success To The Railroads" on it, as well, it was only worth seventy-five cents for one bottle or five dollars for a dozen.

After some meditation Swiggert wished to know whether a large, pot-bellied bottle with a picture of Jenny Lind on it was any good. Leet, who had bought at least forty Jenny Lind bottles at high prices, shook his head regretfully and said that the shape of these bottles prevented them from having any value. For such a bottle, with a picture of the glass works and a single star opposite the likeness of Jenny Lind, he admitted that he was willing to pay fifty cents, provided the color of the bottles was either blue or lavender. For any other color he wouldn't pay anything at all, though as a special favor he would be willing to carry away these bottles without charge, provided blue or lavender Corn For The World bottles could be found for him.

Having thus prepared the ground, he told Swiggert that he could see that somewhere in the surrounding country there existed bottles that Swiggert had seen. Unless these bottles could be viewed by a bottle expert like himself, they could not be valued, either singly or in the mass. Descriptions by mail or word of mouth, or hearsay evidence, where flasks were concerned, were valueless. If, therefore, Swiggert wished to lead him to the bottles, he would be glad to estimate their value and even to purchase the rights to them at a fair price. If Swiggert did not wish to do this, the bottles would be valueless to him as they were at the present moment.

At these words Swiggert drained the dregs from his bottle of Mexican rye and hurled it to the floor with a morose curse. He would, he said, be at the front door of the hotel at six o'clock on the following morning, and would lead Leet to the biggest damned mess of bottles that he had ever seen.

Promptly at six o'clock on the following morning Leet was sitting at the wheel of his roadster in front of the hotel in Douglas; and five minutes later, with Swiggert sitting gloomily beside him, they were speeding over the long straight road toward the Continental Divide.

They twisted through the tortuous mountain roads leading up to Bisbee, past the mountains that man had removed from their beds of copper and hurled into valleys, and through the rugged and barren canyons of the Divide.

Beyond the Divide they turned toward the jagged peaks of the Hauchuca Mountains; and in the course of time, high up among the hills, they came to the gray frame cabins and the deserted false-fronted saloons and gambling halls of the forgotten mining camp of Soak Hollow. Gophers, erect on their tails, watched their progress through the dead town with inquisitive noses held high; and angry marmots hurled themselves beneath the decaying cabins with shrill and outraged whistles.

Swiggert gloomily directed Leet to a small cabin at the far end of Soak Hollow's single street—beyond the warped board front of the Grand Opera House, beyond the Freedom Dance Hall, beyond even the Feed Bag Café, The Hot Breath Saloon, and the Full Up Drink Parlour.

The small cabin straddled a depression in the hillside. When Leet, preceded by Swiggert, poked his head between the door posts, from which the door hung crazily askew, he saw that there was barely room within for a single wooden bunk, a chair made from a nail keg, and a few bricks on which a small stove had once rested.

Beneath the bunk was a small square hole. Swiggert pointed solemnly to the hole and observed without emotion that the cabin must have once belonged to the town drunkard.

Leet advanced to the hole and peered into it. The owner of the cabin, apparently, had reclined dreamily in his bunk and finished bottle after bottle of early American liquor; and as he had done so, he had dropped early American bottle after early American bottle into the small square hole immediately beneath his numb and careless hand.

Leet could see an aquamarine Pike's Peak bottle reposing on the top of the heap. Several glints of amethyst caught his eye. Deep in the center of the heap he caught a flash of blue on an unidentified flask.

Swiggert left the cabin and climbed into the depression which the cabin straddled. He reached into the pile of bottles, drew an amber sunburst flask, and held it up to Leet.

"What," asked Swiggert, "is this bottle wuth?"

"That bottle is worthless," replied Leet, who had paid through the nose for an amber sunburst flask only three weeks before.

With a low curse Swiggert flipped the bottle away from him, using an underhand flip which carried it far down the gulch and against a large protuberant rock, where it disintegrated with a musical tinkle.

Swiggert pawed over the pile of bottles once more and drew out an amethyst eagle and Washington flask with the motto "Remember The Cherry Tree."

"My God!" said Leet, who had heard of the existence of this flask but had considered it a rumor on a par with other old wives' tales.

"How's that?" asked Swiggert avariciously.

"I said 'My God,'" replied Leet, "because I thought you were going to take me to some really valuable bottles. Instead of that, you show me flasks like that one!"

"Ain't it a valuable one?" asked Swiggert ferociously. "It's the same color as yourn!"

"True," admitted Leet, "but the eagle on it spoils it. If it weren't for the eagle, I would be willing to pay ten dollars for it."

Again emitting a foul oath, Swiggert dashed the flask into the gulch before Leet could stop him; and a shower of amethyst glass splintered from the rock against which it landed. Leet, turning the color of oak ashes, beckoned Swiggert to reenter the cabin.

"Look here, Swiggert," said Leet, when this gloomy guide again stood beside him, "I don't believe I could do much with these bottles, but I'm willing to gamble on them. If you'll give me all the rights to them, and promise to keep your mouth shut about them, I'll give you two hundred dollars for the lot."

"Two hundred dollars ain't enough!" declared Swiggert malevolently. "I've been around in my time, and I know a thing or two. Oh, I seen your face turn pale when I busted that last bottle. Them bottles are wuth a thousand dollars if they're wuth a cent!"

"All right, Swiggert," said Leet desperately. "I'll give you a thousand dollars for them."

"You bet you will," said Swiggert offensively, "and you'll take me East with you while you sell 'em, and you'll give me twenty-five per cent of all the money over a thousand dollars that you make when you sell 'em."

"My heavens, Swiggert, I can't do that!" protested Leet. "If I sold those bottles all at one time, I'd break the bottle market all to pieces. Why, if I sold those all at once, you'll be able to buy amethyst flasks for ten dollars!"

"Oh, is that so!" said Swiggert with a malevolent laugh. "I guess those bottles ain't so wuthless after all. That being the case, I ain't agoing to sell 'em. No, sir! I'm a-going to take 'em East myself and sell 'em!"

At these words, said Leet, he became very cold and calm. "Are those your final words, Swiggert?" he asked deliberately.

"I'll say so!" ejaculated Swiggert coarsely.

In the twinkling of an eye, said Leet, all his long, happy antiquing expeditions swept across his brain. Should he, he asked himself, permit all his past pleasures to be set at naught by this ignorant man? Should he permit the pride of bottle collectors all over America to be dashed into the dust through the headstrong act of an unschooled and reckless prospector?

He thought of his eighteen Pitkin flasks. He thought of his amethyst Dr. Dyott and cross-eyed bartender amethyst flask. He thought of Joe Hergesheimer's twenty-four best bottles in America. All the bottle lore of a lifetime flashed through his mind.

Without another word Leet reached into the side pocket of his well-worn tweed jacket, drew out an automatic pistol, and shot Swiggert through the heart. With a deft movement he caught the body as it fell and guided it so that it fell through the hole in the floor and slipped, with a musical tinkle of breaking glass, to the bottom of the pile of bottles.

A moment later he was kneeling beside the body. Having assured himself that life was extinct, he hastily selected a few of the finer flasks from the pile—five amethysts, six blues, two golds, and a jade green. Then, with deft hands, he concealed the body beneath the bottles; and fifteen minutes later he was on his way to California with his newly acquired bottles safely tucked in his automobile, and with a song of thanksgiving deep in his heart.

Leet felt, he said, that he must tell somebody about the whole affair; and so he told me. What, he asked, should he do about it?

I thought of my dark blue Pike's Peak or Bust bottle. I thought of my amethyst A Little More Grape Captain Bragg. I thought of my twelve-dollar jade-green Pitkin flask. I thought of my aquamarine Jenny Lind with star and glass works. How, in view of these, could I give him an unbiased opinion?

Finally, with a deep sigh, I advised him to forget the whole affair; and so far as I know he has done so.